STAR CROSSED

D. K. MARLEY

HISTORIUM PRESS

Star Crossed

A Fractured Shakespeare Novel

Book Three in the Series

ISBN Paperback 978-0578288031

ISBN Ebook 978-0578288048

Follow the author:

www.dk-marley.com

Published by Historium Press

Macon Georgia

www.historiumpress.com

2022

To my my poet cousin, Alicia

Thank you to my ARC readers whose
invaluable comments helped bring
this story to life.

Celia Martin

Juliane Weber

Caroline Anderson

Renee Yancy

Angela Moody

Two households, both alike in dignity,
in fair Berlin, where we lay our scene,
from ancient grudge break to new mutiny,
where civil blood makes civil hands unclean.
From forth the fatal loins of these two foes
a pair of star-crossed lovers lives doth end;
whose misadventured piteous overthrows
with their love, buried with their country's strife.
The fearful passage of their death-mark'd love,
and the continuance of their countries' rage, which,
but these children's end, nought could remove,
is now the seven years' traffic of our prose;
the which if you with patient minds attend,
what here shall miss, our toil shall strive to mend.

1

Julia

October 1944

The day I turned sixteen is the day I fell in love with a Nazi. Tragic circumstances for such an emotion to blossom but it did, nonetheless. I knew him before, or at least, I knew of him. We did not run in the same circles, me being a Mischling, a half-breed according to the new Nuremberg laws with a Jewish mother and German father, and he, Rhen, a full-blooded, blonde-haired, blue-eyed poster boy for the Wehrmacht. We both lived in the east end of Berlin, at least for a while, until his parents moved to the more affluent neighborhood near Zehlendorf; since we both were about the same age, me being two years younger, inevitably we knew some of the same people.

His cousin, Olga, and my sister, Kitty were friends, for a time at least, until it was outlawed for Germans to associate with the Juden. When that law passed, even my own father abandoned us and joined the Nazi party. Seems odd to think about now, how just years ago we all used greet each other in the street, and now they won't even look in our direction. I never even gave Rhen a thought before the night of my sixteenth birthday party when I snuck out of the house afterwards and followed Thomas and Kitty to the masked ball at the Moka Efti nightclub. My mother made other plans for me, inundating my mind with thoughts of Aaron Schwartz, my intended, the one my aunt, my mother's sister and our family shadchanit, matched me with when we were not yet thirteen. She often praised her ability to have foreseen it the day of my bat mitzvah. *But how was I to know what was to come?*

That night, the dance hall... no, I will not recall that beautiful memory just yet. That is for another day. Other thoughts now loom before me as I stare up at the rusted metal sign arcing above me, the frightening entrance emblazoned with dreaded words.

Albeit Macht Frie

I shivered with fear and cold. Soft angelic snowflakes drifted from the clouds mingling with the rancid grey ashes billowing from the tall chimney stacks silhouetted against the sky. I wonder about the rumors I've heard... surely, they can't be true. In my innocent days, my tongue delighted in tasting the snow. Now, I clenched my lips shut, afraid that the remnants of my friends rained down on my face.

All of the women and some of the men are crying now. In single file they push by me as I stand here fixated on the sign, the snow, and the ash. Never in my silly wandering imaginations, my day to day dreaming of becoming a famous writer while clutching my favorite Shakespeare book, *Romeo and Juliet*, did I imagine standing at the gates to Auschwitz. *Who would imagine such a thing?* Hitler, of course, and his henchmen.

Did Rhen imagine such a thing when he first became a part of the Youth squad? No, I know he did not. He saved me in more ways than one, at least for a time... a glorious time, and he promised to save me again. *Will he?*

The doors to the boxcars slammed shut behind me, and as the steam from the train engine pulsated behind me, a remembrance stirred in my mind of when everything changed ten years ago. *Only ten years?*

It all seems a lifetime away, but even at twelve years old I knew (we all knew) of the tension rising in the city. Each night, father paced the floor, mother cried into her pillow, and Berlin morphed into a city of fear. My childhood vanished, even as we attempted to lead a relatively normal life as we peered around corners just walking to the market or to the Synagogue. I remember two days of pure hell raging in my house, but in reality, the previous two years of my father's indecisiveness reigned as he vacillated between loyalty to my mother or loyalty to the party. But when Hitler unleashed his power against SA leader Röhm the summer of 1934, my father made a stand... choosing the party over us. Not to mention, the party gave him no choice, either he divorce his Jewish wife or face the end of his military career.

For two days our house mimicked the "Night of Long Knives" as my parents fought without letup, their muffled words indistinguishable to me as I curled beneath the bed covers with a pillow over my head; but then, curiosity tugged on my heart and I crept down the hallway to gaze into the living room while Kitty and Thomas hid away in their rooms. Father stood there like a dark raven in his pressed black uniform, his words spraying in spittle over my mother's face. She cowered on her knees in front of him, pleading, tears streaming, with the imprint mark of his fingers splayed purple on her cheek.

I heard the words and shivered. He accused her of the most horrid things, foremost of bewitching him with her Juden magic, and because of his military career, rising in the ranks due to his friendship with a man named Göebbels, his loyalty finally affixed to Hitler's rising star and he announced their divorce as final. He was done living with a

Judenschwein and her half-breed piglets. He left that day, absolving himself from any filial attachment to us, and bound himself to the SS. The rage he left behind in Thomas spurred him to later join the resistance... and the emptiness in Kitty sent her trying to fill her heart with liquor and music. *And me?* I escaped into my books.

During those two days, in a brief moment of reprieve in our house, my cousins Samuel and Gregory leaned against a lamppost outside my window, discussing the boiling pressure in the city and their newfound hatred of their former friends who were cousins to Rhen and Olga. Their words ached my stomach. Even now, the memory is as clear as the rust on the sign above me. I can hear their voices in my head.

+++++

Samuel tossed his glowing cigarette to the ground, crushing it with the toe of his patent-leather oxfords.

"If I see them today, I will crush their heads like this. They are dogs, every one of them."

Gregory chuckled and folded his arms over his chest. "You are so full of yourself, Sam. I know full well that you will run with your tail tucked in your skinny ass the minute you see those brown shirts coming around the corner."

Sam pursed his lips and scowled. "I will make a stand... as we all need to do. Their attacks on the Jews are increasing and the atmosphere around here is thick with hatred. Like for like, is what I say. I hate them all."

Gregory stood up straight, looking over his shoulder as if to gauge if any of the group approached before he spoke. "Again, you do not hate them so much so as to bed a few of those blonde-haired, blue-eyed girls we've danced with at the Resi."

Sam winked. "Well, you are right about that, Gregory... I will fight the men and bed the women, both with ease."

"I wish you would stay away from the politics and the mingling, Samuel. Keep to our girls... besides, with all the upheaval tingeing the air, I'm not sure how safe it is to tangle with either, even if the fight is with the higher-ups."

"Yes, the higher-ups and with us, for we need to show ourselves ready to stand. Why do we need to be ashamed to be Jews? Besides, with everything happening with the SA, I'm not sure they will even show their faces in the streets for fear of their own deaths."

Gregory cleared his throat and nodded his head towards a group rounding the corner. "Hush, I see some of them coming down the street."

I eased back from the window into the shadows, yet still attuned to their words.

Sam gritted his teeth and patted his right front pant's pocket. "Just let them try anything... I will cut them open."

Gregory nudged him with his elbow. "I must admit, I hate them, as well. Stand back and let's see if they will take the bait from my frown."

"Frown?" Samuel chuckled. "No, let's do one better, let's see how they like this salutation."

He brushed his hand across his jaw, folding his fingers until his solitary raised middle finger brushed alongside his nose as the group of three brown shirt clad young men passed by. I knew immediately there would be trouble; the Sturmabteilung with their distinctive muddy-brown uniforms and red armbands regularly engaged in street fights with their political enemies... and they took great risk since the start of Hitler's *Röhm Putsch*. I was about to run to find my mother and tell her when the brownshirts took notice of Samuel's gesture.

The one nearest him, a tall lanky golden boy, set his hands on his hips and glared at Samuel. "Look at this, boys, we have ourselves a bold *Untermensch*, a dirty Juden flicking his dirty finger. I think he wants to fight; what do you think?"

The one next to him chuckled and crossed his arms. "I actually believe he does. Look at him. He thinks he will win. What say you," he yelled to Samuel, "do you wish to fight us?"

Samuel brandished the kitchen knife from his pocket, and the sunlight glinted on the blade. I caught my breath and covered my opened mouth with my fingers. Gregory balled up his fists, and the leader of the brownshirts waved his fingers in the air, beckoning them forward.

"Draw your blades, *if* you are men!" Samuel shouted.

They rounded each other, corralling in a circle, each eyeing the other and making threatening thrusts to taunt and entice. My heart pounded in my chest. No one dare challenge the Sturmabteilung, for it was well known of many who simply just disappeared without a trace, as well as others whose bloody bodies lay mangled to a beaten pulp in some dark alleyway. This could not go well, and the tears started burning my eyes. Still, I remained silent and unsure for fear the group might bang on our door after they finished with my cousins. Images of them dragging my brother, Thomas, out to join the melee flashed in my mind.

Unfortunately, the flash turned reality as the boys taunts and yells brought onlookers to the street, including the very one whom I prayed did not hear. Right below my window, the front door of the apartment building opened and my brother rushed out to add his voice and anger to the fray. From across the street, another German boy in regular civilian clothes ran between the groups and held up his hands. I recognized him as Rhen and Olga's cousin, Bernie.

"No," I yelled, leaning forward on the window frame.

Thomas looked up and winked. "Get back inside, Julia. All will be well."

"Do you promise?"

"I promise if you promise to close the window and shut your ears."

He tossed a smile, that endearing smile that always brought warmth to my heart. I nodded and backed away, pulling the lace curtain across but not shutting the window. Still, I watched, unable to resist knowing the outcome, their raised voices echoed from below and into my waiting ears.

Bernie flattened his palms, opened to the sky as an offering, and pleaded with them all.

"Put up your weapons and your hatred. Please," he urged.

Thomas pulled up his pant's leg and snatched a blade from the leather sheath strapped to his shin; Bernie did the same, even as he protested the fighting.

All the boys were now armed and salivating for blood.

"Look at you," Thomas sneered, "calling for peace with a blade in your hand. What a bunch of hard-boiled eggs, you are! I will slice you all to pieces for I hate the taste of you."

The leader of the brownshirts stretched his mouth into a grin and cracked his knuckles. "Come on, you *Judenschiesse*, I will take you on."

Thomas laughed out loud, pointing his blade at the boy. "Your days are numbered anyway, might as well get it over with."

The boy's brow wrinkled. "I think not. It is your kind that are numbered."

Bernie took Thomas' cue and rushed to the boy's side, placing his hand against his chest to keep him from lunging. "What he says is true. You know of Hitler's warning that no one is allowed to bear arms except for the Reichswehr... besides, have you not heard? Röhm is dead, along with all of our commanders. If the SS sees you brawling in the streets, they will arrest or kill you as sure as they will kill these Jews. We should put away our knives and clear the street."

But Bernie's words failed. I clutched my stomach as the sounds of metal against metal filled the air, along with the shouts of anger and bursts of painful cries as the blades met flesh. Even through the lacy curtain, the unmistakable splattering of blood on the gray stone pavement shown clear and unmistakable. I gasped and closed my eyes.

My mother tried to shield me after father left, no longer allowing newspapers in the house, keeping our only radio tuned to Berlin's *Funk-Stunde* only when the approved music played, and demanding that Thomas not discuss politics during dinner. But, as I said, my childhood was over. Even at twelve years old, I knew more about the Wehrmacht and the Reich than I did about paper dolls and piano lessons. Bernie's warning proved true; Röhm and his faction disagreed with Hitler on too many things and Hitler settled scores with old enemies, purging any opposition to his regime. Even though the brownshirts played a part in the rise of the little man with the severe mustache, everyone sensed Hitler would not tolerate any dissension within his flock.

In the midst of the fighting, car doors slamming shut opened my eyes and I snatched the curtains back from the window. Below me, a conglomeration of foes met face to face, taking sides and spouting rage. My father and another SS officer stood next to their shiny black Mercedes Benz with fists balled, flanked by the Gestapo with their guns raised at all the boys; my mother stood on the sidewalk clutching Thomas' arm, and Rabbi Hersch stood near her tapping his cane against the pavement as if he called all to attention. All of their words cascaded in a wild cacophony of fear and nonsense.

"You are all under arrest," shouted my father while the verbal insults continued to fly from the boy's mouths.

"*Judenschiesse!*"

"*Du hurensohn!*"

Until the Rabbi stepped forward in an act of bravery (or foolishness), raised his cane and hand, and silenced them all with his words.

"Stop, this! What is this fire in your blood, and this blood tainting the streets of Berlin? Throw down your blades and your rage, this ignorant and vile upheaval that pains God's ears and heart. Everyday I walk the streets, I see this violence, and your actions are causing all the citizens to war one against the other. Are we not all Berliners? Are we not all Germans?"

My father came up to him, face-to-face, and pushed him backwards. My mother caught the Rabbi as he crumpled to the sidewalk; still, the old man gazed up, straightening the black fedora on his head, and stared up at him.

"You were ever kind to me once... when Rachel was your wife. Those days before Hitler filled your ears with cankerous words. You even ate at my table."

My father leaned forward with his hands on his knees and hocked a gob of spit on the man's woolen coat.

"A mistake I will never make again. You think to rule us with these words, old man? You are mistaken. I will clear the streets of these brash boys, but not with words."

In a swift movement of his hand, like lightning striking, my father pulled a Luger from his waistband, aimed at the Rabbi's head, and fired. In a flurry of stunned gasps and running feet, all those fighting fled, even the brownshirts who feared for their own lives.

When the smoke cleared and the fluttering wings of the unsettled pigeons calmed, I clutched my chest and took a breath. Mother's wails billowed up the stairwell to the apartment building, along with Thomas' pleas for quiet. Outside, two of the Rabbi's friends dragged his body away, his blood smearing in a trail behind him. My eyes fixated on my father's face as he smiled and sat back against the seat in his car, polishing his Luger as the car sped away. I knew then, I'd never see him again, and my heart teetered between sheer sickening hatred and nauseating sorrow. Still, I did not cry. I only felt a measure of relief for my mother, for she would never again feel the back of his hand across her face. The images and the sounds of the morning branded my soul – the fiery words... the gunshot... Mutter's cries... Rabbi Hersch's brains spilling out across the sidewalk... replacing my innocence with anger, confusion, and fear.

Samuel looked up to the window, his worried eyes realizing I saw everything. He called out to me and waved as I slammed the window shut.

"Julia! Julia!"

A forceful jab in my back from the matron's stick and the sound of Hannah's voice echoing my name released me from the trance. Before I realized it, in the dizzying memory, I fell to my knees. Aaron's mother and the guard struggled with each of my arms like two children fighting for a rag doll.

"Get up," the matron screamed. "Schnell, get up, you stupid Jew."

"Please," Hannah pleaded. "I will take her. She is just in shock. Come, Julia, come along with me...."

In the chaos, my book tumbled to the ground, caught beneath the shuffling feet of the women herded through the barbed wire fencing. I darted for it, oblivious to the barking dogs pulling against their leashes at my sudden bolt. By the time I slid onto my knees, bruising and bloodying them against the frigid ground, and snatched the book from destruction, they were on me, snarling and biting, whilst the guards pulled me to my feet. The matron eyed me up and down, her icy blue eyes sending shivers more harrowing than the cold winter air burning my skin. With one swift blow, she struck me across the cheek. My head jerked to the side, my dark curling hair cascading across my face and hiding the disgust in my own brown eyes; yet I could see her scowl, as well as the smiles on two of the Strumtruppen clutching Hannah by the arms in between them.

"Please, Julia, hold your tongue..." she cried out. She did well to advise me to silence, for I had long given her grief with my sass and defiance, starting with my opposition against marrying her son, Aaron; although my reasons remained hidden from her, even to this day.

The matron eased close to me, snatching the book from my grip, and gritting her teeth until her pale lips narrowed into a thin line.

"She speaks well, you filthy Jew. You had best not say anything back to me else I will let the dogs finish with you." She held the book up, brushing the dirt from the cover and revealing the title.

"Ah," she continued, "we have a romantic pig here. Romeo and Juliet?" She narrowed her eyes. "You know the Gaulieter of Berlin, Herr Göebbels, is an avid Shakespearean. He would be pleased to see you reading this instead of that rancid Torah. Perhaps, I will take this little treasure for my own, a nice little decoration to my desk to remind me of the first pig I killed with my baton."

"No," Hannah shouted, but I remained stoic, my eyes never wavering from the matron's face. Her stern lips curved into a sadistic smile and she raised the club high into the air. Still, even with my lips trembling and legs weakening, I did not look away. I wanted her to remember my face, my conviction, my unflinching bravery in the face of death... I wanted her to remember me in her dreams. Swallowing hard as the baton came down in a sudden swirl, the woman turned, finding the target for her full-on assault. The crack of the baton meeting bone struck like a bolt of lightning, and a spray of blood showered my face.

2

Rhen

October 1944

The night I rode the escalator at the Moka Efti cafe is the day I fell in love with a Jewess. One day before hell broke loose, as I recall. I didn't mean for it to happen, and although she responded in kind, the innocent yielding in her look spoke the truth.

I knew of her; after all, her father, Herr Cappell, was the Kommandant of the unit I was assigned to after I signed up with the Youth squad, the young nationalists in our brown shirts spouting the Wehrmacht's propaganda. In truth, I'm not sure I even believed the things I said or if it was just an attempt to fit in. My cousin, Bernie, and my best friend, Max, who were ever by my side, said I was too much of a romantic to be involved with the movement but when they signed up, so did I.

Now, those romantic musings seem a lifetime away with all that has happened over the past six years, especially since my time on this earth is nearing an end... or, at least, I feel the breath of death so close on my neck as I look across at my captors – the Polish resistance. I fell victim to them after traveling with Hauptsturmführer Horn to Lublin to inspect his "wares" at the warehouse there, his essential workers coming from Lodz Ghetto. A roadside car bomb ensured my quick capture as Horn sped away into the night, leaving me behind to try and coerce my survival, which I've done successfully for over a year now. But the same question rises in my mind each sunrise – *will this day be my last?*

And as always, the girl, Julia the Jewess, haunts me with those perfect pink lips and dark eyes. There was a time when I saw her sister from time to time at the Resi dance hall, and after my friends and I followed her home one evening, I got a shadowy glimpse of her younger sister staring through the lobby glass door of their apartment building in east Berlin. Just a ghost-like illusion as she darted away after my cousin, Bernie, ran into the street and blew her a kiss. *But how was I to know what was to come?* My head was too full of Rosamund Thoss, the woman of my dreams, the woman of the moment, and the perfect reflection of Renate Müller, Germany's ideal Aryan screen actress. I felt sure I was going to marry her.

That is... until the day I saw Julia at the dance hall six years ago.

+++++

Rhen
November 8, 1938

"Rhen! Where are you, Rhen?"

I heard Bernie calling before I even saw him coming through the oak trees in Tiergarten. I rolled to my side from my lounging position on the top step ledge of Wagner's imposing granite statue and shielded my eyes from the sun. The clear delft blue sky peeked through the rustling autumn colors, and my cousin bounded towards me through the drifts of fallen leaves.

Bernie knelt next to me, his radiant and hopeful smile urging me from my dark mood.

"Rhen, your mother is looking for you," he said. My sour disposition returned and I closed my eyes.

"She is always looking for me. What does she want now?"

He sat on the step near my head, tossing acorns into the fountain.

"Well, for one, she wanted to make sure you were far away from the fray of this morning."

I sat up, curious. "Fray? What fray?"

Bernie propped his arm across my shoulders. "Not to fear, my friend and cousin, for I told her I saw you last wandering near the waters of the Spree with your head in the clouds. Your father went on and on about how you spend too much time meandering through the woods instead of putting your mind into the meatier matters of today. He called you his *launischer welpe*, a moody puppy with sad eyes whimpering at the moon and begging for a pat on the head."

Bernie mussed my hair, elbowing me with, "... a pat somewhere else, is more like it, eh, cousin?"

"No such stuff in my thoughts, Bernie. Here I lie in dead Siegfried's lap, gazing up in Brunhild's mournful eyes and wonder where such love resides. Surely not with any Fraulein I know."

"Ah," Bernie acknowledged with a nod. "Lost love is a powerful reason to mope about, as is found hate."

Puzzled, I caught his gaze with mine. "What means you? The fray you spoke of?"

"Yes, the fray. It was a good thing you spent your days pining for love here in the park than meeting the blade and the SS wrath this morning. Nothing much to say... just another common skirmish between the Gestapo and some of the Jews. You know there is a resistance group building here in Berlin?"

I grabbed hold of his arm. "Yes, I've heard. So, what happened?"

"The same as usual. You know Gunther and his brash ways since he left his "brownshirt" days and joined the Gestapo after what happened four years ago during the purge. He still stalks around Berlin in search of blood, and he found a pocket of resistance fighters near the apartment building of Herr Cappell; or at least, his former residence, I should say."

"Herr Cappell? His wife was a Jew, was she not? And the children are Mischlings?"

"Yes," Bernie replied. "And now they are left to fend for themselves, for Herr Cappell divorced his wife and is now a lieutenant in the SS Guards, nuzzling up to Göebbels, himself, like a dog begging for treats. You remember the sister, Kitty?"

We both chuckled and nudged each other. I reared back, pawed the sky, and released a loud 'meow', adding, "She had quite the purr while dancing cheek-to-cheek to some of that American Jazz. Quite the Cabaret girl before..."

"Before we learned of her pig roots," Bernie chortled, slapping me on the back.

I frowned. "I wasn't going to say *that*. I meant before the command came down from headquarters forbidding association with the Juden anymore. I think all the propaganda is going to your head, Bernie, and you need to be careful. We are dancing on a volcano, indeed; a world of oxymorons - brawling love and loving hate; weighty lightness and serious vanity; misshapen chaos of well-seeming forms; feather of lead, bright smoke, cold fire, sick health, and still-waking sleep. The feelings buried deep inside me recognizes no love in any of the world surrounding us. Love for Germany? Love for our race? I think love resides not in these hard words."

"Even if you are being told to believe from our youth up, your nature will not have it so, Rhen, and this is what your father fears. You have too gentle a heart for Hitler's fist to pound such an ideal into the tender chords. And yet, your weepy words astound me." Bernie rubbed his eyes with his knuckles and let our a mournful moan, yet mocking me with a smile.

"Are you laughing at me?"

Bernie widened his eyes. "Not at all, cuz. I truly weep for your good heart. As you say, we live at the precipice of a lava bed, and souls like you..."

"Will be the first to fall," I finished. Bernie raised his hand to object, but I shrugged away his gesture. "It's true, and you know it; so, I will be away as much as I can. I am tired of the Youth Group, the incessant boring meetings of the Jugend." Running my fingers along the smooth white granite stone jaw of Bernhild, I sighed. "I long for a world of love."

Bernie lowered his voice and pulled me close. "You say you fear for me and my willingness to listen to the talk but, cousin, I fear for you and your words. You best keep them to yourself or you will find yourself sent to a labor camp for sedition."

I stood up to leave him, taking two steps down to the sidewalk, when he grabbed my sleeve, spinning me around.

"Are you leaving me here without an answer to my words?"

I shrugged and looked back up into the glorious sky. "What can I say, Bernie? I am not myself these days, and these days are not themselves. I know I am not the best of company right now. Forgive me."

He stood and came next to me, again wrapping his arm across my shoulder.

"Tell me what's eating you, Rhen? Is it this volcano, or is there more in your heart that you are not speaking of?"

I swallowed hard, for the words bubbling up tore through my chest like a knife. "It is a very rough time to be so in love."

Bernie smacked me on the back. "In love? So, that is what all of this is about? Who is she? Tell me, and I will make a pact with you to win her to your bed."

His eager support made me smile. "No, she will not be won like that, I assure you. For if flattering words, or winking eyes, or gifts will not woo her from her chaste ways, then you will lose out in your jovial persuasion, for sure."

Bernie scrubbed his fingers over his whiskery jaw. "So, she is one of those girls; one who stands much too close during a public dance and feigns innocence in private. I say, forget *die hündin*, and find a more willing lady."

I shrugged and wrinkled my brow. "Tell me how to do that? How do I forget Rosamund? Her beauty fills my heart's eye, and I can see none other but her."

Bernie snatched up my hand in a firm grip. "I will take that wager, dear cousin. You will set your eyes on a fair Fraulein before this night is over, and all this turmoil in your mind and heart will be overthrown. Come along, the moon now beckons us to find a girl and find a bed."

Walking through the streets of Berlin as night blanketed the sky brought a measure of uneasiness. Shadows of darkness hung in alleyways, and passing black cars easing past us sent shivers speeding down my legs. The tension in the city was palatable; thick in the air, bitter to the tongue, and stinging the eyes with visions of flapping red swastika banners popping in the chilly winter wind, and the viable taste of hate lingered like bitter absinthe in the back of the throat. Even though I still carried my Jugend card, I had long abandoned the attire, donning the frowned-upon checked sports jacket, baggy pants, and crepe-soled shoes. Hip, Hollywood, and easy clothes for the Lindy Hop.

Since Hitler's appointment as Chancellor by President Hindenburg just five years ago, many viewed the succession of laws and control as the enlightening advancement of a brilliant man and a nation of Aryans. I did not share the view even though, as Bernie so aptly pointed out to me, we were all indoctrinated from a young age, from six years old when I first joined (or was forced to join) the Young Folk group and was sent on my merry way to so-called "adventure" camps to learn to be a good little Nazi. Later on, we all transferred into the Jugend to continue on the path of our Chancellor's vision.

My vision, however, was quite the opposite, and I knew I was a continued disappointment to my family; my father, especially - Herr Herman Montabauer, a WW1 veteran and assistant to Herr Höss. While others wiled away their days goosestepping and repeating laws in rote, my feet preferred the dance floor at one of the swing clubs, enrapturing my ears with a little Benny Goodman. In secret, of course, or in disguise; and sometimes I longed to wear a mask to hide away my face from the narrowing eyes. Each time I crossed the threshold of the Resi nightclub, or slipped away for a day trip to the Hot Club in

Frankfurt, I kept my eyes alert to possible informants. Jazz, especially American Jazz, was a no-no for German citizens, said our propaganda minister. But I adored the finger-snapping tunes, the wild arm-snatching dances, and even got a kick out of being called a schlurf. Everything in our life was controlled, and I had had enough. But, of course, all these thoughts I kept to myself as I wandered the woods of Tiergarten, and I did everything I could to distance myself from the Jugend, but as was the case, Hitler's infiltrating laws clenched their death-like grip around all of our throats. *What could we do but submit, or face our mortality at such a young age?* I was a schlurf in secret, while a good Nazi in public.

Bernie snapped his fingers in front of my face and pointed to a group of girls filing into the entrance of the Moka, all of them tossing lash-fluttering glances in our direction and giggling. My heart did not stir, for all I could see was Rosamund in each of their pink-cheeked faces.

Bernie clapped his hands together, and cocked the fedora on his head. "Now, you can't tell me that there is not one among them that catches your attention. I mean, look at them! Berlin is overrun with Aryan beauties."

Another voice drifted over my shoulder, flavored with negativity. "Take your pick, boys, for the way this dream is moving, our manhood will be ground into the dust on the front lines in a matter of months."

I spun around, and my friend, Max, grabbed my arms.

"Max," Bernie shouted and shook his hand. "I thought you were on some assignment with your division."

Max lit a cigarette, sucked deep, and blasted a puff of smoke into the air. "Assignment? Nothing of the kind." He nudged me with his elbow. "Rhen knows my mind, don't you? The fellows in Hamburg send their regards and want to know when you will be back their way for some new moves."

"Not anytime soon.," I replied, leaning against the outside wall to the club. Max frowned and propped himself, shoulder to wall, next to me.

"What is your problem?"

Bernie chuckled, still eyeing another flurry of girls going inside. "Ah, Max, Rhen is in love, a sick love."

Max joined in the laughter. "A sick love? Oh, *schiesse*, then we will have to push you to the dance floor tonight to bring you out of this misery."

I adjusted my hat and slid one of Max's cigarettes from his jacket pocket. "No, I am not in the mood for dancing tonight. Here, give me a light..." Sucking deep, the smoke wafted around us and the lights from the neon sign pulsed in the air. "My heart is too heavy for dancing."

Bernie leaned over my shoulder, whispering a jeer. "Rosamund has rejected him, feigning chasteness after a tease. You know the type."

Max arched his eyebrow. "Indeed, we have all suffered from such a woman. But, come, my friend, for I will not let you pine away tonight, for as I said, tomorrow we may suffer from the Führer's sufferings, and I fear a lot of blood will fill his cup before he is revived." He slapped me on the back and urged me to the door, giving me no option but to go with them.

"Wait," I shouted, with my hand against Max's chest. "I don't think either of you understand the depth of my mind. This is not just about Rosamund, this stretches into avenues of what is happening to Germany. I feel lost and my dreams are filled with the most frightful things. You both can act the fool and let your feathery minds float away from these weighty things, but I cannot."

Max shoved my hand away and gritted his teeth. "Dreams? Are you serious? You think my feathery brain does not dream or see the lead black star fixed in that dream? You are wrong, for my dreams are as dark as yours and full of unrequited love, and a future of gray nothingness."

"Tell me," I urged. "I want to know. I want to know that there is another soul who feels like I do. What haunts your dreams?"

Max's face fell into the shadow beneath the dance hall sign, and the end of his cigarette glowed orange in the dark pools of his eyes. "Dreamers lie, Rhen. What does it matter?"

"You cannot tell me that I lie, for you know as well as anyone that dreams speak the truth."

Max chuckled as Bernie disappeared through the club doors to follow a flirty blonde with a tight skirt. "If they speak the truth, then tell me about Queen Mab, for I think she has been with you."

I shook my head and rolled my eyes. "This is stupid, Max, and how dare you mock my love for poetry when I am deadly serious. Have you been drinking already?"

"I do not mock you, Rhen. You know I understand. All the drink in the world cannot make me unsee what is happening around us. These ideals permeating the air, pounded into our brain, saturating our hearts, originate from less high-minded desires than anyone cares to admit. And Queen Mab is a fitting goddess for this madness, for she comes at night and pricks our thoughts, this victorious golden-haired, blue-eyed fairy who rides this dark vision of humanity in her pea-sized chariot. Can you see her? Each dream she brings sends us deeper into depravity and brutality, and I can imagine her nightly thrusts began with Herr Hitler, himself. Now, we all dream his dream, and she brings his vision into our minds. Lovers, like you, dream of love, lost and won; solicitors dream of the Führer's law; the SA and SS dream of slicing the throats of supposed enemies of the state; the Judenschwien dream of money; and these women," he points towards two young girls walking by us, "dream of propagating a new nation of blonde-haired babies, sacrificing their former virtue to the cause. There is not a soul in Germany who will not imagine their own dream in the midst of Hitler's dream; all delusions, a single prick of her fingertip which sets our course." He threw down his cigarette and crushed it with his patents. "And I can tell by the wrinkle on your brow that you think I talk of nothing."

"Air," I said. "And I wish you peace, Max, for I did not mean for my mood to set your mind on fire."

"Ah," he replied, "it is not fire that stirs my dreams but an idleness that heralds some approaching doom. I fear Germany is doomed, yet she gallops forward into this mad dream of our Chancellor. You know I can only speak these things to you."

I nodded, understanding him completely for Max and I shared some of the same ideals, except while mine leaned more towards peace, his tilted towards violence. The wind picked up, shifting the hat on my head, and I looked up at the storm clouds tumbling by the moon. Bernie rushed back out, wrapping his coat around his body.

"Come on, this wind is blowing you both off course. There are some heavenly bodies inside to draw your eyes from the sky, and get this, it's a maskenbälle. Now we can stalk the girls behind our masks, but unfortunately, we've arrived too late to hear the Wagner selections from the orchestra."

Max rolled his eyes. "Who cares? I've heard enough Wagner to last a lifetime."

"And I fear we've arrived too early, for my gut is telling me to get as far away from here as possible. Death hangs in the stars..." I glanced to Bernie who sneered at my poetry. I smiled back and shrugged, letting go of the misgivings and gesturing to the door. "Wherever the wind blows, I will go. Lead me on, my lusty friends, and show me the girls."

"Woo hoo!" Bernie shouted, as he reached in his coat pocket and pulled out three black masks. He handed us one each, and opened the door for me and Max to enter.

We wove through the dapper crowds bedecked in all manner of attire – black SS uniformed officers, women adorned in shimmering silk draped gowns, a few other young men dressed like us, and others in tuxedo and black tie. Of course, I knew the interior of the Moka intimately, having spent so much time lounging on the velvet couches beneath the Moorish arches of the Turkish salon while listening to the haunting melodies of James Kok's violin waft through the smoke-filled air. A different time... the time before Kok's swing music was banned and he fled to Switzerland. As we squeezed through the crowds, Bernie stopped to chat with the group of girls we saw entering the club earlier, and Max tugged on my sleeve, pulling me towards the famous escalator, the feature of the Moka Efti.

"Come on," he shouted. I smiled up at him. Like some floating angel full of wisdom, words, and struggle, he rose up the ascending staircase with his arms outstretched to each side as if he drew all to his attention and prepared to deliver some wild speech. I waited for the words, even as I stepped on the first step that morphed out from the floor. Bernie followed close behind and we gazed up at Max as we, too, rose into the heights leading to the second floor.

And then, it happened. A perfect pure angel appeared at the top rail of the escalator, following close behind another group of young ladies coming down the opposite side. In the midst of the giggling girls, her beauty sparkled beneath the golden chandeliers – black wavy hair cascading to one side over her shoulder, lips kissed with the softest shade of pink, and luminescent creamy velvet skin revealed at the draping neckline of her white satin gown and pearl choker. Like Aphrodite reborn, she floated from heaven. She kept her eyes lowered, her gloved hand touching lightly on the moving rail... and we passed by each other, she descending, me ascending. She raised her eyes to meet mine as she passed. Her cheeks flushed pink and my heart leapt in my chest. *Can love take hold so suddenly? Did I see my destiny in her dark eyes?*

When I, at last, arrived at the top floor, and she at the bottom, I grabbed hold of Bernie's arm. I pointed to her, drawing my cousin's attention to her as she mingled into the crowd.

"Look, there, who is she?"

Bernie shrugged. "Who? The little one with the big eyes behind her white feathered mask?"

"Yes, the one with the starlight in her eyes."

He shrugged, once more, and added a laugh. "I don't know who she is... but come on, Rhen, you can't be serious? I thought you might set your sights on some worthier dame who might rest her head on your pillow tonight. That one looks too tame to be of any temptation."

But my heart spoke different, and my words echoed the lustrous flame sparking in my heart. "Oh no, you are wrong, Bernie. Look at her again, for I swear that she teaches the stars to twinkle. Like a rare jewel hanging in the night sky, she is indeed too beautiful for such fleshly pursuits as a one-night-stand."

Bernie rubbed his brow and scowled. "Are we looking at the same girl, for she appears nothing next to the golden goddesses next to her. Look at the ones I spoke to before we came up the escalator; now there is a bouquet of Aryan beauties if ever I saw any. And what about Rosamund? Just an hour ago you were sick over her."

He waved to them, and they all waved back, batting their eyelashes and propping their hands on their hips to parenthesize their assets.

"No," I added, "this one is a dove among ravens. I'm not sure I knew what love was before seeing her face. Wait, where did she go? Can you see her from this perch? I swear if I find where she goes, I am going to say something to her."

But Bernie's eyes were too full of the girls, especially as they, one by one, made their way up the escalator. He slapped me on the back and chuckled. "My dance card is filled tonight, cuz, and if you look for me I will be out there." He pointed towards the crowd of waltzing couples, swirling around the floor to Mozart, another of Göebbel's approved musicians.

I narrowed my eyes, wondering what happened to Max, but soon turned my attention back to the beauty on the first floor. Within a few minutes, I saw her as she skirted through the crowds and entered the corridor leading to the pastry shop.

Perfect, I thought, hustling back down the escalator, two steps at a time, not waiting on the mechanical descent, and pushed my way through the crowds. The corridor to the pastry shop was a well-known attraction, long and shadowy, styled to look like a sleeper car from the

Orient Express, all fitted with dark green velvet drapes, rich wood paneling, and hidden niches for private tête-à-têtes. As I entered the doorway, I saw her engaged in conversation with a couple of other dark-haired companions, both of whom I recognized behind their masks... the "Kitty" I purred about earlier, and Thomas, the mischling son of Herr Cappell. I smirked, knowing that they obviously stalked around in secret, keeping their Juden affiliation quiet so as to have a good time among the purists in the crowds. All it would take is one word from me to the mingling Gestapo and they'd all meet their end... but... this girl... *who is she? A friend to Kitty and Thomas? Surely, she is not a Jew?*

Easing past them, I tucked myself into one of the vacant nooks, peering at her through the slit in the curtain and waiting for a moment to speak with her. Kitty and Thomas left her, melding back into the lobby throng. She ambled along lost in thought, her face falling in and out of the shadows, a succession of lights above her head illuminating her radiant eyes each time she took two steps down the corridor. She approached, near enough for me to slide my hand between the slit, ease my fingers around her wrist, and edge her to the other side of the curtain separating us.

She gasped, frightened by my touch, and tried to pull away. I softened my words, and noted her worried brow ironing out as she listened.

"Wait, don't go. And don't take my boldness for rudeness, I beg of you. If my sudden seizure frightens you, let my words ease your mind as to my intent, and I will kiss your hand to soothe the sudden grip."

I raised her hand, and let my lips linger across her fingers. Her right eye, peering through the narrow gap, met my right eye, transforming from worry to wonder in a split second.

"You do wrong your hand, sir, by such boldness. I, for my part, shall keep mine folded in prayer."

I smiled and urged her through the curtain till we stood face-to-face. "Prayer only, dear lady? Prayer is good, but it is not the only thing God gave us hands for..." I kissed her fingers again. "Nor did he give us lips for only uttering words to him. There are other kinds of blessings, such as a single kiss which sweeps away sins."

She blushed and lowered her eyes. "Is there such a kiss? I would not know."

I touched my forefinger to her chin, lifting her face till she opened her eyes to gaze in mine. Moving near her, I parted my lips and she sighed, hesitant but surrendering as she tilted her head back and closed her eyes. Our lips met, and time stilled. The murmur of laughter, glasses clinking, and Beethovan's no. 2 op. 50 lilted through the air, enveloping the moment like Shakespearean poetry.

I eased away from her, cupping her jaw with my hand to gaze into her goddess face, but she seized me around the neck and pulled me to her again, her words breathing across my lips.

"Sweep away my sin again..." Her fervent innocence morphed into a hungry need, a delightful satiating of every sense coursing from her soul to mine; and our hearts thrummed against each other through our clothes.

"Julia! Julia, are you here?" Kitty's voice rang down the corridor, and the girl pulled away from me, her hand covering her bruised lips and her eyes startled.

"Oh, dear God," she whispered.

I peered through the curtain slit. "It's Kitty Cappell. Is she looking for you?"

The girl, this beauty, patted down her hair and stood straight, pushed me onto the cushioned bench seat against the wall, and whispered.

"Stay here; I will find out what she wants."

I remained where she sat me, my skin tingling with wonder at the unexpected fervent kiss. Still, through the gap I could see their exchange of heated words accompanied by a flurry of gestures and frowns, ending with my beauty storming off towards the corridor entrance. Kitty looked over her shoulder to my hiding place. I adjusted my crumpled shirt and strode out into the hallway, removed my mask and faced her narrowing eyes.

'Hello, Kitty... it is nice to see you again. You are taking a great risk being here tonight, even with the mask. I could report you very easily."

She shrugged. "So, go ahead... but if I remember right from our past friendship, you cared very little for the politics of Germany. I think I remember you loving swing dancing a little too much."

Her words made me grin. I couldn't deny the truth in them. She glanced over her shoulder in the direction of the girl's departure. "What were you doing with Julia?"

"Julia, that's her name? Where did she go?"

"I told her she was too young to be here, so Thomas put her in a taxi and sent her home."

"Who is she? A friend of yours?"

"She's my sister, or did you forget I have a sister?"

My heart sank and I looked to the doorway, the line of her departure. "Your sister? Oh, dear God..."

"What did you do?" Kitty growled, as she tried to hold onto my jacket sleeve but I snatched away from her grip and ran into the crowd just as Bernie appeared near the entrance to the club.

"Bernie!"

"Cousin, where have you been?"

I grabbed his arm and pulled him out onto the sidewalk, looking side to side to see if I might discover Julia's taxi. No such luck. She was gone. Max wrapped his arms over both mine and Bernie's shoulders, and laughed into my ear. His breath reeked of schnapps, coffee, and cigarette smoke.

"Come on, boys, the night is young and so are we. Let's get back inside and dance away our dreams."

I followed, but I knew my mind. Before this night was out, I would kiss Julia again.

3

Julia

November 8, 1938

I knew the moment that the taxi dropped me back in front of my apartment building and I sauntered up to my room, that my life had changed. *Or had it?*

I had no idea who the mysterious young man was behind the mask; and, I supposed, he didn't know who I was, either. Which made the clandestine encounter even more heart-racing than I could have ever imagined. *My first kiss! And by a complete dashing stranger!*

Sleep eluded me, so I slipped into my favorite white cotton gown, tiptoed across the room and opened the window. This, by far, was my favorite room in the house, the only one with a window facing the courtyard behind the apartment building, and after much pleading, my mother relented and let me put my bed in here even though we used the small space for storage. Now I was surrounded by our family treasures – an old oak wardrobe packed full of my mother's flapper dresses and my grandmother's Victorian gowns, a rocking horse, trunks of blankets, and a stack of paintings my grandfather collected during his days in France; and tucked near the window was my special writing desk, another relic from my grandfather's antiquarian bookshop on Kurfürstendamm street. He had long since closed his shop and fled to Switzerland, begging all of us to follow him, but my mother remained loyal to her German husband despite the warning signs. Loyalty, an affection my father did not share when he was "encouraged" to file for a speedy divorce from his Juden wife. Well, I should say his loyalty leaned more towards the Führer than my mother and it turns out, they made better bedfellows. And now, hate raged in my stomach towards my father, I suppose just as much as he hated us in return.

Tracing my fingers across the desk, I stared out the window to the night sky. A dark blanket of twinkling stars filled my eyes, even with the lights of the city muting them. I opened the narrow drawer and removed a single sheet of paper and my writing pen, intent on retracing the feelings the stranger's kiss ignited in my heart. I wanted to be a writer, that was my fervent desire – to follow in the footsteps of my grandfather (who wrote books as well as sold them) and publish my first novel before I turned twenty. I still had four years to go. And now, with this new experience, the words gushed from my brain and my hand sped across the page. Still, a moment of trepidation surged and I paused, balled up the paper, and threw it in the trash basket beneath the desk. *What if my mother discovered the confession of the kiss?* The thought raised my eyebrow and I set the pen aside, intent on burning the crumpled paper before retiring to bed for the night.

Instead of writing, I decided dreaming might be best, for dreams are the sole possession of the dreamer. I sat on the windowsill, pulling my legs to my chest and resting my cheek on my knees. The city sounds murmured through the soft night air – a distant radio playing at someone's window swirled Wagner into the clouds, a couple of cats added their own disagreeable arias to the refrains, and the occasional laughter and honking horns trickled across the air, muted by the building between me and the street.

As much as I wanted to think about the young man at the Moka Efti, my mind reeled back to my own parents. *Were they ever in love?* I think they were once upon a time. When I was small, smiles and bright eyes filled out house; at least, that is what I remember about my mother. Thirteen or fourteen years ago I was just a toddler but even a child knows when love or hate fills a house.

They met and married in 1920, when Berlin and the whole world surged alive with music and dancing. Glancing over to the door to the wardrobe, which stood open and revealed my mother's dresses, I wondered about the woman she was back then. From the cut of some of them and the sequin fringe, she had to have been a wild thing – just the sort to draw in a war-weary German soldier still recovering from the first world war. And, after all, my mother counted herself among the majority of Jews her age who were Jews in name only. Even I knew (from my sister's whispers) that the ratio of her attendance at the synagogue back then to burning up the dance floor at the Resi was ten to one in favor of the new Charleston rave from America.

My father was a different kettle of kippers. His disillusionment with the Kaiser's war morphed into an outrage that Germany yielded to the terms of the Versailles treaty. Like most patriots, he wanted absolution, so when Hitler emerged from that war's rubble like a enraged phoenix, others followed right behind him.

Yet, in the picture on the mantel, my parents looked happy. Mother's eyes gleamed even as she tried to conceal the slight stomach bump behind her wedding flowers. Thomas was born six months after their wedding, and Kitty was born the next year, just as the first tinge of hate flavored the speeches of the boisterous little man from Austria who became leader of the National Socialist German Workers' Party – the Nazi's – that same year. *And me?* I came along in 1923, the month Hitler tried to seize control of the government in Bavaria and was sentenced to prison for his role in the scheme. *I wonder if things had turned out different if he had served his entire five years, and if they had not given him paper and ink for him to write about his inner struggles?*

My eyes drifted from the wardrobe back to my pen and paper on the writing desk. *What of my own inner struggles? If Hitler can write a book, so can I... one day... perhaps.*

The moon shone high and bright when the front door shut and Kitty's footfalls echoed through the house. I knew she would find me, coming with her overbearing sisterly advice and reprimand about my venture out to the club hours ago. *And why should I not want to dance the night away? I turned sixteen today and felt quite old enough to join the dancing crowds at the Moka.*

As expected, the door swung open and Kitty tiptoed near me with her arms crossed and a frown creasing her brow.

"I thought I'd find you here," she said.

I turned my head away from her, and she sat down on the opposite side of the wide window ledge. Taking my hand in hers, she eased her reprimanding words.

"Sister, dearest, I know you think you are old enough... that you are ready for this wide crazy world, but trust me, you are not. You know Thomas and I are just trying to look out after you. There are beasts in that club who would devour someone innocent like you."

I met her pleading stare, narrowing my eyes. "What about you? Why is it all right for you to go, then? You're only a year older than me."

She squeezed my hand. "True, but even I cannot take the chance anymore. Things are changing rapidly; besides, Mother has put so much responsibility on my shoulders to care for you since Father left. She has her own worries, and she is trying to do the best she can under the circumstances, such as talking to Aunt Gerta about your engagement to Aaron Schwartz. You know the Schwartz's don't approve of the Berlin nightlife. They want a good Jewish girl for their son."

I rolled my eyes and snatched my hand away. "But what if I'm not a good little Jewish girl?" Walking over to the wardrobe, I took out one of my mother's fringed flapper dresses and held the pink silk against my body. "What if I'm like Mother?"

Kitty snorted a laugh. "I'm like Mother, dearest. You know it and I know it, and I'm not ashamed of the lifestyle I've chosen. That being said, it is not the lifestyle I want for you." She stood next to me, hung the dress back on the rod, and curled her fingers around my jaw. "Julia, you have such a sweetness to your manner, an innocence that we all want to protect. Can't you just let us? Which brings me around to the encounter I interrupted at the Moka. What happened between you and Rhen?"

"Rhen? Was that his name?"

Kitty arched her eyebrow. "You didn't even know who it was?"

I frowned. "Well, no... we all had masks... I mean, you know this..."

"What happened?" She pressed.

Dare I tell her? No, the sweet secret is mine alone, and she will only rail against me.

"Nothing happened," I replied, walking back to the window and gazing back up at the moon.

Kitty walked up behind me and wrapped her arms around my shoulders, clasping her hands tight against my upper chest and squeezing.

"Good, I am glad to hear it. Rhen is part of the Nazi Party, Julia, just like Father is, and their hatred for all things Jewish is becoming ever more apparent. We are all being corralled into whatever future Hitler is devising. You know this; you know what was announced yesterday - no more schooling for any of us, no more of our cultural activities, and no more Juden newspapers. Rhen is charming, to be sure, for even I loved meeting him at the swing clubs years ago, but these are dangerous times. I don't want you to be hurt by him or by anyone, really."

I wrapped my hands over hers. "I know you care, sister, but I am growing up. I will be careful, I promise."

She kissed the side of my head and squeezed me, again. "I love you, little sister. I'm sure Thomas will have his say before this night is over, as well, so you best get to bed so you won't get another earful."

"I will. I just want to do a little reading."

She removed her high-heel patent leather pumps from her feet, dangling them on her fingertips, and sauntered out of the room, blowing me one last kiss as she shut the door. I know she cared, she always had since we were little. For a long time, we were two peas-in-a-pod in our matching print dresses sewn by Mother, and our giggling Kosher tea parties. Those were the days when Father still allowed a measure of freedom for Mother to practice her religion and read to us from the Torah, even if she did it sporadically for she never claimed any orthodoxy. But as time went by, we drifted from each other in personality and desires. Kitty leaned more to our German side, cutting her hair in a bob and smoking like a smokestack. But something about our Jewish heritage intrigued me, even if a curiosity about Kitty's nightly crawls to the cabarets and dance clubs lingered in my mind. I was a doll tugged by the arms, stretched by persistent children – a struggle between my heart and my mind, between religion and politics, and my own search for a place in this world.

Thomas found his place as a resister to all things standing for the Nazi party, even joining a group headed by a fiery young man named Herbert Baum; Kitty discovered her place amid the neon sparkling world of cabaret, wine, and who knows what else; and both of them displaying a fierce selfishness reminiscent of our father.

Where was my place? I couldn't help but think my newly discovered place was in the arms of this German boy... Rhen. *But what if he found out I was a Jew?* That might change everything... and as Kitty so aptly pointed out, she didn't want me to get hurt. I sucked in my breath, trying to steady my thrumming heart. *How can I know for sure? Or was this just a passing and meaningless encounter brought on by the excitement of the club, and too much wine?*

Opening the drawer once more to the desk, I clutched my favorite book and ran my fingers across the title.

"Romeo and Juliet," I whispered, then fanned the pages open to Act One, Scene Five as I eased out of the window and walked across the small flat rooftop that covered an outdoor patio to the gardens. Our apartment was the only one with access, and the trailing ivy and cascading arms of the oak trees offered a special private haven to me.

"Go, ask his name," I recited. "His name is Romeo, and a Montague, the only son of your great enemy... My only love sprung from my only hate! Too early seen unknown, and known too late! Prodigious birth of love it is to me, that I must love a loathed enemy."

I closed the book and held it against my heart, sat down and curled myself into a corner with my cheek resting on my opened palm, and my elbow wedged in between the iron spokes of the terrace railing. I looked up at the moon gleaming through the dark leaves of the tree and sighed.

+++++

I heard Bernie and Max's echoing voices before I even saw them as I tucked myself in the shadows of the alleyway. They were *"betrunken wie eine gekochte eule"*, drunk as a boiled owl, and I knew there would be no talking sense to them.

"Rheee.... eeeen? Where are you, Rhen?"

"Come on," Max wailed, "you, arschloch... where are you?"

I peered around the edge of the building, watching as Bernie shrugged and Max propped himself up against a dimly lit streetlight.

"Perhaps he went home," Bernie slurred.

Max nodded, his head heavy with his gesture. "Yes... you are prob... prob... probably, correct, sir. Off to bed..."

Bernie motioned in my direction and I eased back in the shadows, still with my gaze fixed on them.

"I saw him run this way, but then he just... disappeared... vanished," Bernie said with his mouth gaping and his eyes wide as if I had performed some astounding magic trick.

Max stumbled forward, narrowing his eyes as he tried to focus on the street in front of him. He raised his arms high. "Shall I conjure him for you, Bernie? Rhen," he shouted to the sky. A light from an upper window across from me switched on. "Rhen, you mad, passionate lover and fool, come forth and appear before us! I command you! Come on, just say one word to let us know where you are and I will be satisfied…"

A shadow appeared at the illuminated window and the figure slid open the frame. A burly bare-chested man in pajama pants scowled from his perch.

"How about "get lost"," he shouted.

Max looked up at him and bowed, sweeping his arm across his chest in a deep flourish. "Ah, I behold the fair bald-headed Cupid from the window… tell me, sir, have you seen a young man of my height and more sunny disposition come this way? He is searching for his fair Rosamund, a pretty blonde-haired Fraulein with knockers out to here." He blasted a laugh and cupped his hands out in front of his chest.

The man pressed his lips together and his cheeks flared red. "I said, get lost. Can't you see there are people trying to sleep here? Give me one reason why I should not call the Ordnungspolizei right now and have you both arrested?"

Bernie ran up next to Max and tugged on his arm. "Come away, Max. Rhen has left us, probably already asleep in some girl's bed, and we don't want to rouse the SS or the Gestapo."

He pulled him along down the street, and the man closed the window. As for me, other thoughts held their grip on my mind and my heart. I waited until they disappeared around the corner, and looked right and left to ascertain my location. Herr Cappell's former apartment building was just two streets over, a Mietskarsernce rising six floors. I had no way of knowing which apartment window along the vast rows of windows belonged to the Cappell's but I decided to wander through the main entrance to the courtyard just to see if I might catch a glimpse of Julia looking out her bedroom window. Just being here, wandering through the sparse trees and bushes of the disgruntled green space made me happy.

As I rounded one of the oak trees, gazing ever upward in hopes of seeing her, a soft voice floated down on the gentle breeze, mingling with the slight rustle of the leaves.

"Who's there?" I whispered, waiting for an answer, but no one responded. Stepping forward, my hand brushing against the tree trunk, my eyes glimpsed a shadow tucked in the corner of the roof, and two bare feet dangling through the pickets. I caught my breath.

"Is this her?" I questioned and hoped to myself. "I pray it is. Oh, dear Julia, come out and shine across this shoddy garden, and let the moon hide itself in shame at your brilliance. You have so struck my heart with wonder that I cannot breath. Please, let this shadowy figure be the girl of my dreams."

The moon crept out from behind a cloud, casting beams across Julia's face. She appeared like an angelic ghost, her white gown glowing, and her face pale in the moonlight.

"Oh, dear God, it is her... and now, what shall I do? How can I tell her what she has done to my heart? Can love truly take hold so suddenly? Wait... she speaks, and yet I hear nothing."

My eyes followed the path of her intent gaze which fixed upon the stars above us. "She speaks to the stars. Maybe she is praying... for me... or for some other fellow... or maybe just conversing with her Juden god. I'll wait to show myself until I know more, else I might scare her to death."

"Oh my, what am I to do?" She said, aloud.

My heart thudded in my chest, her tender voice filling my soul like air. "Speak again, please, else I shall die right here below your feet, gazing at you as if looking into heaven itself and seeing the brightest angel."

She opened a book clutched to her chest, licking her forefinger and pushing each page open till she arrived at the one she wanted. Holding the book in front of her, she rose from her hidden place and walked along the railing, her voice full of passion and wonder.

"O, Romeo, Romeo... wherefore art thou, Romeo!" She giggled and gazed out towards the garden, her eyes brushing over my hiding spot. "O, Rhen, Rhen, wherefore art thou, Rhen?"

My heartbeat surged into my throat and her words fired my soul. *She called for me!* Still, I kept silent until I heard more.

She shook her head and touched her fingertips to the edges of her eyes. "A Nazi? How can Rhen be a Nazi? What does any of that matter now that my heart is his. Jew? Nazi? Love does not see such names... and I swear, if he knew I loved him, perhaps we might run away from all this chaos; after all, what does any of this have to do with me or with him? I don't know the Führer or his reasons for what he does... and I bet neither does Rhen. All I know is this sudden love beating in my heart. If there was no Nazi nor Jew, we would just be ourselves, would we not?" She pinched her forearm. "I mean, I am just Julia... and he is just Rhen... a boy and a girl... no, a man and a woman who shared the most perfect kiss. If he asked me, I swear I would forsake everything I know for another one of his kisses."

"And I will ask you, dear lady," I replied with boldness, revealing myself from the shadows.

She startled and backed away, her eyes searching the shadows of the garden. "Who's there?"

I walked into the moonlight. "It's me, Rhen, but call me something different if my name offends you, for as you said, are we not just a man and woman, not Jew and Nazi?"

She leaned forward, with a hint of a hesitant smile and her eyes twinkling like distant stars. "I am an enemy to you."

"No," I replied, "you are not."

"But the Nuremberg laws... you will be captured and imprisoned if anyone finds you here associating with me, especially at this hour of the night."

"And yet, you sought out the company of the good German boys at the Moka Efti. Were you not afraid of being caught?"

"No," she said, "for the red arm bands reveal those to avoid and I thought it was a good night for secrets since it was a masked ball. Seems you thought the same with your face hidden for how did you know that you were not kissing a Jewish girl?"

"Jews don't come to the dance hall anymore, at least I thought they didn't until I saw your sister Kitty. You all took a great risk in coming. I didn't know who you were until she told me."

"I thought that would make a difference to you and that if you knew, I would never see you again. Isn't it odd? Only ten years ago, when we were children, you and your sister, Olga, would play with us in Tiergarten. Your parents and my parents were great friends at one time... until the law. How is it that you are here now... does none of Hitler's speeches matter to you?"

"No," I stated, firmly.

"But you are a Nazi. I know you are a part of the Jugend, even if you choose not to wear the swastika."

"And you are a Jew without a golden star hanging from the chain around your neck."

"And yet, are we not both simply Germans? I was born here, the same as you. I was born a Jew, as well; I did not choose it. You, however, choose to be a Nazi."

"No," I answered back, "you are a Mischling, and thus you have different privileges than a full-blooded Jew... I know your father is German and now part of the SS. As far as me choosing to be a Nazi, do you know what they are doing to young men who refuse?"

"So, it seems we both are cornered into our fates. The state demands something of us according to our birth, so how can we talk of anything else, especially love?"

"But, as you said, love does not see such labels."

Her fingers touched her lips and she squeezed the book to her chest. "Love? You speak to me of love? You don't even know me." She questioned, her breathy words escalating.

No holding back any longer. The very mention of the word emboldened me and I climbed one of the latticed, vine-woven columns holding up the roof. She gasped as I jumped onto the roof beside her. Reaching out I took her by the hand and led her back beneath the shadowy arm of the oak tree. One by one, I kissed the tips of her trembling fingers and cupped her jaw with my hand.

"And you do not know me... yet, I heard you declare yourself just moments ago."

Her cheek flushed pink and she turned away. "And now I chide myself for such foolishness, for what must you think of me? A silly girl speaking to the moon about her fanciful notions of love. I feel I've been spending too much time in books and dreaming about a world far away from Berlin." She held up the book in her hand and I took it from her.

"Romeo and Juliet," I read aloud and smiled. "You are fortunate that your favorite book is an approved one by the Reich. Herr Göebbels favors Shakespeare, did you know?"

She shrugged, still facing away from me. "And is that something I should thank him for? All these regulations control our life, even yours, and I saw what the generous Reichsleiter did to all the books in my grandfather's shop. They were all burned in the square of the State Opera when I was eleven, and Göebbel's words burned our ears spouting that the era of extreme Jewish intellectualism was at an end. Every day that passes chips away at my Jewish heart, and now, here you are offering your German hand with a bit it back. How can I believe you? Were you there that night, right among them, burning my grandfather's books?"

"Yes," I confessed, embarrassment warming my neck and face. I fanned through the pages of her book, reaching the balcony scene and the exchange between the two young lovers. "And how I wish we were in a different world and time, Julia. These two lovesick Veronian children are not you and I. Our world has aged us overnight, and we have seen things they never saw... and, I fear, more things to come that we cannot imagine. You have reason not to believe me. We've spoken less than a hundred words between us in a world where trust teeters on the edge of a vast volcano. I've seen it again and again... a Jew trusting a helpful German only to be dashed against a wall. Perhaps you think that of me."

She glanced over her shoulder, and the moon glinted in her soft look. "I want to believe you and yet, I don't know why. My sister says I need to stay far away from you, and if my brother Thomas ever found out, I hate to think what he would do to you."

Secretly, I did not worry about Thomas. He was full of fight and chose to use his passion against those of the elite Schutzstaffel. We had never exchanged words and I, for my part, chose to avoid any street scenes which ended in meaningless scuffles. I could not imagine he would even care about his sister's love life in the midst of trying to support a resistance group against Hitler. Yes, the Nazis knew of the Baum group... but again, I withdrew to the back of such heated talk at the rallies or Jugend meetings, relegating myself to dark corners as they vowed to crush their skulls.

Flattening out the page with my hand, I cleared my throat and read. "With love's light wings did I o'er-perch these walls, for stony limits cannot hold love out, and what can love do that dares love attempt; therefore thy kinsmen are no let to me. Alack, there lies more peril in thine eye than twenty of their swords; look thou but sweet, and I am proof against their enmity."

I closed the book, handing it back to her as I eased close behind her, laying each hand on her upper arms and resting her against my chest. My words whisper through her hair and into her ear. "I have night's cloak to hide me from their eyes; And but thou love me, let them find me here. My life were better ended by their hate than death prolonged, wanting of thy love."

And she closed her eyes and continued. "Dost thou love me? I know thou wilt say ay, and I will take thy word. Yet, if thou swear'st, thou mayst prove false; at lover's perjuries, they say Jove laughs. O gentle Rhen, if thou dost love, pronounce it faithfully, or if thou think'st I am too quickly won, I'll frown and be perverse and say thee nay, so thou wilt woo, but else not for the world. In truth, fair Nazi, I am too fond, and therefore thy may think my haviour too light; but trust me, gentleman, I'll prove more true than those who have more cunning to be strange. I should have been more strange, I must confess, but that thou overheard'st me, ere I was ware, my true love's passion; therefore pardon me, and not impute this yielding to light love, which the dark night hath so discovered."

She turned to me then, her gentle arms spreading like angel wings encircling me, tilting her head back and parting her perfect pink lips to wait for the seal of a kiss. I caressed her face with my eyes, etching every detail in my mind – the delicate arch of her soft eyebrows, her dark eyelashes lying against her creamy skin, the way her cheek dimpled when she smiled, and the constellation of muted freckles over her elegant nose. This was no inferior being, a Judenschwein, to abhor – this was a found treasure to hide away and protect. I touched my finger to her lip, pressing the pillowy softness as I moved across, then leaned forward and followed the line of my fingertip with my own lips. A kiss and a vow in one breath and heartbeat shared between us.

The calm night air shivered with the sound of Kitty's voice breaking the perfect moment, and Julia reared back, pushing me deeper into the shadow of the oak tree.

"I am here," Julia shouted.

"Come inside," Kitty urged. "Why are you still outside at this time of night?"

Julia cut her fearful eyes at me, and put her forefinger to her lips to silence me. She peeked through the branches and smiled at her sister. "I will come in soon. I cannot sleep and thought to read a bit in the moonlight."

"No," she chided, "you must come inside now. You know Mother hates for you to come out here at night... it's not safe under the circumstances."

Julia giggled. "Afraid some brown shirt will carry me off? Not to fear, Kitty, for remember we are detestable to them."

Kitty huffed. "Detestable only according to their law.. they are still men, Julia, and give little care to what is on paper when spurred by lust. You know what happened to Leah Goldman six months ago, and she is still suffering from the attack."

I saw Julia shiver and she ran her hands along her arms. "Yes, yes... I remember. Just let me finish this one page and I promise I will come in. Go fix me some hot tea, I feel chilled."

She turned back to me, her eyes filled with the former uncertainty. I took her hand in mine.

"What happened to Leah Goldman?" I asked, even though I was almost sure what her answer would be.

Tears pooled in the corner of Julia's eyes. "She was raped by a group of drunk SS officers... the very ones who spout their nonsense about the nasty Jews and keeping their Aryan race clean and pure. Your people did that."

I sighed. "Not my people, Julia... I am not one of them, I promise you. I am yours from this night forward."

"Prove it," she declared, her jaw firm as a single tear raced down her cheek.

"How?"

"Take me away from Berlin... somewhere in the world where we can just be a man and woman in love. No Jew, no Nazi... just you and me. We could marry and defy them all."

My heart pounded against my chest. "Marry you?"

"Yes, and in Juliet's words - 'if thy bent of love be honorable, thy purpose marriage, send me word tomorrow by one that I'll procure to come to thee, where and what time thou wilt perform the rite; and all my fortunes at thy foot I'll lay, and follow thee, my lord, throughout the world.' At what time shall I send for you?"

I tapped my finger on the cover of the book still clutched in her grip. "If we follow the story, then it shall be at nine o'clock."

We kissed again, deeper and with urgency, and she whispered in my ear. "Good night, good night, parting is such sweet sorrow that I shall say good night till it be morrow"

I held her face between my hands and kissed her closed eyes. "And sleep dwell upon thine eyes, peace in thy breast. Would I were sleep and peace, so sweet to rest."

As a promise, I took the silver ring from my right finger, held her hand in mine, and slid the ring onto her third finger. Her brow wrinkled as she gazed at the skull emblem shimmering in the moonlight.

"Forgive me," I said. "It is the only thing I have to offer as a seal of my word."

"This is a totenkopfring, a symbol of death... and only given to members of the SS by Himmler. How did you get this?"

I swallowed hard. "Alas, dear angel, I must confess to you. Yes, I abhor the ideals of the Nazi party but with my father's own ascension in the ranks rippled down over me. What could I do but be an obedient son? Tomorrow morning I am to be sworn in to the elite guard with treason hanging over my head like an ax if I speak against it."

She started taking the ring off but I held my hand against her fingers. "I cannot wear this," she said, "... you know I cannot. If anyone saw it, what would they think? And now, knowing this... about you... and the meaning of the ring." She whimpered and turned away from me. "I am a fool," she whispered.

Taking her hand in mine again, I turned her to me, and pointed at the symbols on the ring. "Julia, let us anoint the ring with your tears, and baptize these symbols of hate in love. Look here," I said, touching the skull face, "my love is stronger than death." Twisting the ring around, I pointed to the next symbol. "And this, the Sig Rune, a symbol of the sun and the powerful energy, so my love is powerful and constant as the rising sun. And here, the next one, the Hagal Rune means to enclose the universe in you and you control the universe, thus you are my universe and I am yours. Our destiny is our own. And next, the double rune is God, a holy vow between you and I..."

Her eyes flashed up to mine. "And the last one, the swastika, whatever can that mean between you and I but a fated division?"

In truth, I did not know what to say. She was right, and yet I pulled from Shakespeare to soften the hated symbol of not only this Nazi star but of her Juden one, as well.

"Look here, both the hagal and the swastika look like stars" I replied, noting the opposite sides of the ring, one side with the swastika and the other with the hagal – two star-like symbols linked together in silver. "We are star-crossed lovers, Julia, with death in our future. But this ring, when given to me, included a note that read: "A reminder at all times to be willing to risk the life of ourselves for the life of the whole." Now, this ring bespeaks my heart and what I am willing to do to risk my love for you."

Still, she removed the ring and gripped it tight in her palm. With a worried smile, she gazed into my eyes. "Then, I shall treasure it with my own life and wear it on a chain close to my heart, and I vow the same to you. Yes, we are star-crossed but I swear our story will be different. We shall defy the world, Rhen, and prove love conquers hate even in a world gone mad."

With one last lingering taste of her lips, she pulled away and disappeared into the dark as the moon slipped behind a dark storm cloud. I pulled my jacket tight about me and the sky grumbled with thunder. Just as I exited the alleyway to the street in front of her apartment building, the pouring rain gushed from the clouds.

4

Julia

November 9, 1938

Morning approached quick, the night fading away as I dreamed of Rhen. The blissful moment, the taste of his lips still lingering like honey in my mouth, filled my soul with a passion I never experienced before. And yet, the warmth surging through my veins pumped real enough, and I gazed about me as I raised up on my elbows. I was naked, my cotton gown cast to the floor, my legs tangled in the downy blanket, and my extra pillow lay alongside my body like an imaginary lover tucked and curved against my breast. As my eyes peeked open and I pushed back the loose hair from my brow, I took a deep breath and wondered for a moment if all was a dream, too unsubstantial to be believed.

The door to my room creaked open and I snatched the covers to my bare chest as my mother peeked through the doorway.

"You're up," she said with a sleepy smile.

"Yes," I replied, yawning.

"Good, because I wanted to talk to you this morning."

I frowned, noting an agenda flavoring her words as she closed the door behind her and sat next to me on the bed.

"Oh, Mutter, can we please wait until after breakfast? My head is swimming this morning."

She arched her perfectly plucked eyebrow. "No, this cannot wait as I suspect your dizzyness is from lack of sleep and too much wine. Kitty told me what you did last night and you are just fortunate that she and Thomas found you when they did. I am very disappointed in you, Julia."

I pulled my knees to my chest and rolled my eyes. "Disappointed? But Kitty has gone to the dance hall so many times! Why is it all right for her to go but not for me? I'm sixteen now."

She cocked her head and narrowed her amber eyes. "Kitty knows things are different now than when she used to go. Yes, times were different even just a year ago. Now, we must be careful in everything we do, and I say this out of love, dearest. You cannot go out dancing and imagine things are like they used to be; even your brother and sister are changing their former ways. It is a necessary thing to protect us, not one any of us wishes. You are young, Julia, and have seen so little of the world and I want to keep that innocence in your eyes for as long as possible."

I reached down and scooped up my nightgown, sliding it over my head and resting my feet on the floor. I could not look at her so I let my hair dangling loose around my face as I fixed my gaze upon her fluffy bedroom slippers next to my bare feet.

She reached up and pushed my hair behind my ear, revealing the tears trailing down my cheek.

"I know this is hard," she said. "As I said, you are young and I know all you want is to enjoy your youth. I remember those days... of course, back when I was your age our life here in Berlin was filled with champagne and cabarets. 1920 was a year filled with hope and excess after those horrible years of the war." She wiped the tear and pinched my cheek. "But I was hoping since things are so different for all of us now, that maybe I might give you a glimmer of something different than dancing at a club, but just as exciting."

I raised my eyes to meet hers. "What is it?"

Her eyes beamed and she bit her bottom lip as she looped her arm with mine. "A wedding!"

"A wedding? Whose? Is Kitty getting married?"

She shook her head, and her eyes twinkled with the secret. "No, not Kitty... but someone close to us."

"Who? Tell me," I urged, the excitement racing my heart.

"Well," she said, standing up and walking to the window, "I will tell you. You remember that your Aunt Gerta is our shadchanit, our matchmaker endowed with an incredible gift that she has used for decades now?"

"Yes, I remember her making some kind of prediction about me and Aaron Schwartz, which is simply ludicrous for there is no way I would ever marry such a pasty-faced unambitious droll. I adore his sister, Elena, but something is so lacking in him."

She jerked around to face me. "How can you say that? That is quite unbecoming and extremely unfair. Aaron is a good boy, and a devout Jew... actually very Orthodox, and I think he is a good match for you."

I scowled and cut my eyes to the nightstand next to my bed. The ring Rhen gave me rested below the lip of the brass menorah stand and I reached across, took it in my palm, and tucked my hands in the folds of my gown.

Aaron Schwartz... how can she even think I would go through with my Aunt's silly matchmaking... especially now that I have vowed my heart to Rhen? They are like night and day. I closed my eyes, imagining my fingers running through Rhen's golden silky hair... and then, the image transforming into Aaron's dark course curls. I shivered and shook my head, knowing I could not give away anything about my attachment to my beloved.

"Julia, are you listening?" She touched her hand to my shoulder. "I said, I think he is a good match for you. What do you think about getting married? After all, with Thomas gone most of the time and furrowing out a life for himself, and Kitty toying with the same idea of marrying Benjamin Hoffman, well, I think it is time for you to consider your future, as well. I cannot provide for you the same way as when your father was here, and the meager income I make from tending your uncle's jewelry store has really fallen off since those brownshirts plastered that nasty sign in the window. But, what can we do? If we take it down, another will replace it and they will beat us for making a stand. It is better to live our life quietly and submissively. Aaron will make you a good husband and he will be able to protect you in a way I cannot." She pushed the other side of my messy bed hair back behind my ear. "What do you think of marrying, Julia?"

I shrugged, thinking of Juliet's mother encouraging her to marrying Paris. "Mutter, is is an honor I dream not of."

She giggled and kissed my cheek. "Well, I give you full permission to dream of it, dearest, for Aaron is eager to make you his wife. And he is not as milky as you make him out to be; he is a respectable young man with great prospects as a doctor."

I huffed. "A doctor? Mutter, he was forced to leave the university two years ago after Hitler imposed the law forbidding the higher education of Jews; how in the world do you suppose he has a future as a doctor?"

She waved her hands in the air. "Well, you know, this can't go on much longer. The German people will tire of Hitler's rage and things will go back to normal, so I am wanting you to think about life after all of this. Tell me, Julia, do you think you can love him?"

Nausea crept up into my throat. *Love him? The very notion turned my stomach. And how can my own mother talk to me about love?* Her own experience of failed love and marriage left her quite unqualified to encourage any match of anyone, much less her own daughters; however, I knew she was doing her best in raising me and keeping me tied to our faith, despite the oppression she must feel from my father's blatant rejection of her. And, honestly, thoughts of him lingered in the back of my mind and tainted the love I felt for Rhen.

What if it ended the same as my mother and father? They were in love at one time, as well, until choices were made that altered both their lives forever. A chill raced up my arm. Choices, a powerful word directing our hearts and our heads – free will given to us by God. Now, with my vow to Rhen tucked in secrecy, my choice went against everything our world taught, even from the Jewish side. Yes, the government enforced the laws of the State, our minds, but religion effectuated laws of God on our hearts. Our love and declaration broke everything. *Can a love like that shatter a steel ceiling?*

I rubbed my hands up and down my arms, and mother wrapped her arms around me, kissing me on the top of my head.

"All I ask is that you think long and hard about your decision, but I must say that you will make me a most happy mother if I can go to the Schwartz's and give them an answer. I think we all feel that this must happen sooner than later with all the tension in the air."

I laid my head against her shoulder. "I promise to think about it,

Mutter, but only if you are intent on giving your approval."

She took my face in her hands, her steady and firm gaze giving her answer. "My answer is yes. You will marry Aaron Schwartz before the start of Hanukkah. Make plans, dearest, for in less than a month you will be a happy bride."

+++++

Rhen
November 9, 1938

How to marry Julia?
In truth, I had no way of knowing how to arrange a marriage between a German Protestant and a German Jew, especially with everyone, even the priests and rabbis looking over their shoulders for fear of severe repercussions. Hitler held a knife against the artery of Christianity, sensing the heartbeat and threatening to slice any dissension against the Reich, which meant while God's love was preached from the pulpit in Germany, it was haloed in the staunch support of his agenda – Aryan superiority and bringing the inferior Jews to heel. *After all, they were responsible for the murder of Christ, so how could any of this be wrong?*

Most Germans knew nothing of his true agenda, that of wiping Christianity off the map and reinstating the old paganism of the early Germanic gods and the new paganism of Nazi extremism. Hitler, our new German God... our Emperor, offering a world where science would destroy the last vestiges of superstitious nonsense. Nazism and Christianity could not exist together in the world, and Germany would no longer tolerate the 'black bugs' and 'abortionists in black cassocks'. All Christian values were enemies to Nazism, not just the Jews. And Hitler surrounded himself with vehement supporters. Himmler hated Christian sexual morality and the idea of mercy. Obstacles, he called them with a wink and a laugh, spouting his amoral goal of making the entire nation into a cult of the Teutons. And here I was a signed-on member of that arrogant party. The thought chilled my skin, still I said nothing.

After the swearing-in ceremony to the SS elite, I stood on the corner of Oranienburger Straße taking in the scene before me – a street filled with shuffling feet, lowered faces, passing cars, and the ever-present red flags popping in the wind. I adjusted the collar of my black leather trench coat around my neck, tucking the ends of my woolen scarf inside, feeling quite uncomfortable in the new SS uniform but knowing the appearance allowed more freedom to come and go and speak with whomever I wished. Honestly, the cloth against my skin seemed to burn, and I wished nothing more than to rush home and crumple the entire costume in a heap beneath my bed.

Earlier, while fixed in proud rows in front of Feldherrenhalle, my father was so proud when I pronounced my obligatory 'Heil Hitler' and accepted the position as an Unterscharführer, even if I held no real authority and performed only menial tasks under my father at the Sicherheitsdienst as he obtained special intelligence on Hitler's "enemies". The uniform protected me in a sense, and I knew, for a time, would protect Julia... if I could help it. I determined to use my position to our advantage in advancing our love, if possible.

The speeches during the induction mimicked Hitler's own passionate pronouncements, words spraying across lips and the spittle falling across the eager faces as if a God showered us all with holy water, but I was not among those who truly believed. Silence was my ally, at least for a while. Now, I had to find a way to marry my Julia, the Jewish girl of my dreams, and the only way to do that was to trust my secret and my words to another soul. *Who do I tell? A priest? A Rabbi?* At this point, I didn't care who God used to unite us, as long as the deed was done and I could move forward with my next plan, which was to find a way for Julia and I to leave Germany.

Two options lay within my view. First, the towering work of art of the Neue Synagogue, with its stunning glass domes and arches, large enough to seat 3000 worshipers. I was among a group of the SA brownshirts just two years ago, shoving and taunting the attendees as they left a Sabbath Eve liturgy... well, my companions did most of the shoving and taunting, I stayed in the shadows. The second option, the Englische Kirche zu St. George, a smaller (seating only 300) but equally impressive Anglican church with a slate roof and stained-glass windows, sat near the Synagogue and Monbijou Park.

Who would keep my secret? I folded down my collar and marched with resolve in the direction of St. George, hoping to find a sympathetic priest as my father had entail that the pastor, Heinrich Grüber, had already been warned several times of helping non-Aryans to emigrate via illegal documentation. Perhaps he might be the key to not only our marriage, but to our escape.

The crowds parted as I walked down the sidewalk. I saw their look, some with admiration (very few) and some with fear; some raising their arm in our national salute, and some hurriedly rushing into a department store whether they needed something from there or not. The uniform opposed my nature in every possible way, for as my cousin pointed out to me that day beneath Wagner's statue, I saw Berlin through rose-colored glasses. He called me an unrealistic positivist blanketed over by the black and reds of the Reich. He was so very right in his assessment, and I directed my gaze to the concrete sidewalk in front of me to avoid any more eyes.

Within a few blocks, the sunlight breaking over the rooftops and flooding my face made me adjust my hat to shield the rays. I lowered the brim and rushed along the sidewalk, colliding with another person coming in the opposite direction. We both toppled to the ground, just outside the doors to the Neue Synagogue, and when I regained my composure and stood, the woman's fearful voice filled my ears. I brushed off the front of my coat and offered her my hand, but she cowered on the ground, surrounded by a flurry of books and scattering papers. I knelt down and stacked the books near her as she scurried to tame the flying pages.

"Forgive me, Fraulein, I was not looking where I was going," I said. "The sun, you see, blinded me."

She said nothing, still grabbing at her papers, and I noticed her knee scuffed and bleeding. Again, I stood and offered her my hand.

"Come, let me help you, Fraulein; you're bleeding."

She gathered up the books in her arms and stood by herself, raising her eyes to mine in proud resistance.

"Thank you, sir... I am all right."

I knew from the shiver of her chin that she feared me, and I looked to the left noting we were at the doors to the Synagogue. This stout little woman with her dark eyes and round body raised her chin to me, waiting for me to insult her, perhaps even for a slap across the jaw.

"What is your name, Fraulein?" I asked.

"I am Regine... Regine Jonas, Herr Unterscharführer."

"Ah," I said, raising my eyebrow. "You've had dealings with officers before, I take it, since you know the proper greeting."

"It is a thing I have learned so as to not provoke," she answered.

I smiled, trying to put her at ease. "I suppose that is a good thing to learn nowadays, is it not?"

She did not return the smile nor another answer.

I pointed to the doors. "Are you arriving here or just leaving? This is not a day for services, Fraulein Jonas." I knelt down and picked up one of the loose pages still flapping in the breeze beneath my boot. Smoothing out the paper, I read aloud. "Can a woman be a rabbi according to hallachic sources?"

Looking back up into her face, her skin ashened and a single tear eked from the corner of her stern eyes.

"Well, can she?" I asked.

Still, she did not answer. I handed her back the page, which she tucked inside one of the books, and eased my hand around her elbow, directing her back towards the doors of the Synagogue. She hesitated and I urged her with a gentle nudge.

"I've never seen inside," I said. "Could you show me?"

Her eyes flashed up. "Inside?"

"Yes, inside... if you please. Go along; I will follow."

As we entered the main lobby area, she looked left and right as if ascertaining anyone's presence. Beads of sweat along her hairline shimmered in the amber candelabra light.

"Is there somewhere private we can talk?" I urged.

Her eyes flashed again a different sort of fear, and I thought immediately of Leah Goldman. Again, I tried a reassuring smile as she led me to a small staircase leading to a set of private rooms.

"These are study rooms," she said, her voice quivering.

I closed the door. "Perfect." I pointed to one of the chairs. "Sit with me."

As she lowered herself onto one of the leather swivel chairs and released the books onto the tabletop, her tears gave way and she buried her face in her hands.

"Herr Unterscharfuhrer, please, I've done nothing wrong... I am a good German citizen... born here in Berlin. These books, here, take them if you wish... forgive me. I only wish... I mean, I wished..." Her words gurgled out with the flood.

I reached across and eased my fingers over her arm. "Hush, now, do you wish for everyone to hear you in here crying? I mean you no harm, Fraulein. Please, believe me."

Her sobs softened. "Believe you? But you are.. you are..."

"One of the schutzstaffel?"

"Yes."

"And you fear the schutzstaffel?"

"Of course... we do."

"Because you are a Juden?"

She nodded.

"And you wish to become a Rabbi? A woman Rabbi?"

She bit her lip and hesitated.

I leaned forward, lowering my voice. "Your desire to become the first woman Rabbi in Germany goes against more than Hitler's beliefs. I imagine you have a mountain to climb to overcome your own people's ideals about women leading your holy services."

She wiped her eyes and looked up. My caring smile finally

engendered a slight crook at the corner of her lip.

"You are right, Herr Unterscharfuhrer."

I patted her on the arm. "Please, call me Rhen."

Her brow creased and she darted her eyes to the door.

"Sir," she managed, "do you wish to see inside the synagogue?"

I took a deep breath, knowing my next words might put me in a more fearful position than what she was feeling.

"No," I said, the word catching in my throat. "I am in need of a Rabbi."

A moment of silence passed between us, and another look filled her eyes, one of confusion mingling with the fear.

"You, sir? Why?"

I closed my eyes and took another breath. I had never prayed to God before since my mother was a non-practicing Anglican, and my father an atheist, but for a moment, a silent prayer whispered through my mind; not so much for myself, but for Julia if this woman risked what I was about to ask her. The risk for all of us was immense.

"I know you sit here and look at me in this uniform," I began, "but if you could see my heart you would see something quite different. This room... it is quite private, is it not?"

"Yes, it is. As I said, it is for study... and to be honest, no one uses it anymore for fear of the laws against Jewish education."

"You are afraid the SS might barge in at anytime and arrest you?"

She nodded and I patted her hand again.

"Do not fear that today, Fraulein, for if anyone comes into the synagogue today I will simply tell them I am interrogating you for information for my father."

Her brow crinkled. "Why would you do that?"

I took off my hat and clutched the black patent visor in my grip. "Because, Fraulein, I need your help."

Our eyes connected and I willed the desperation in my heart from my gaze to hers. Her voice eked out, soft and unsure.

"What can I do for one of the Fuhrer's guards? I am no one."

I had to find a way to reassure her that this was not a trap. Honesty was the only way I knew to bring this about... full disclosure and let things fall where they may.

"Do you know of Herr Cappell?" She nodded. "Then you know he is one of Goebbel's assistants, but did you also know that he divorced his wife on grounds that she is a Jew? He married her right after the first world war and they had three children who are now nearly grown."

"Yes," she replied, "I know of them. Rebekah Cappell, I think... and her children, Thomas, Katherine, and Julia. I've seen them before here at the Synagogue but only rarely. Rebekah is friends with my sister, Lydia."

I held her stare and spoke the next words in a whisper.

"I am in love with Julia, and we want to marry as soon as possible. I've got to get her out of Germany."

I noticed her chest rise as she sucked in a surprised gasp.

"In love? You... you are in love with a Jewish girl? But... it is... it is..."

"Forbidden," I finished. "Yes, quite forbidden." I smiled and shrugged. "But what can I do? Love does not see these things," I said, fiddling with the eagle emblem on the front of my cap.

"You are sending her to her death, sir, if you are discovered."

I shrugged, again. "And my own, for I made a vow to the Fuhrer to uphold the purity of the Aryan race. My own father thinks I am besotted with a beautiful blonde vixen named Rosamund who I spent much of the summer wooing. But that is long gone, a vaporous infatuation in comparison to what I feel for Julia Cappell. You know I speak the truth now for confession of such love might send me to prison, and you only need to speak to her to corroborate what I say. You are Jewish, she is Jewish, thus she will trust you, and you will trust her. I thought to inquire of Herr Grüber for help, but..."

Regine's eyes darted back and forth, and she put her finger to her lips contemplating the situation.

"No, you were right to come to me for the Gestapo keep their eyes on the Bureau Grüber. Tell me everything," she said, her eyes now bright with possibility.

And I did. Everything; even our intimate words spoke between us during the night... our vows, our kisses... and my promise to help her escape the nightmare darkening Berlin.

She reached across and took my hand in hers. "Rhen," she said, finally using my name, "I'm not sure why I believe you, but I do. There is something different in your eyes... and perhaps my foolishness will send me to prison after you leave here and expose me to the Gestapo, but something in my heart is telling me you speak the truth. I'm not an expert in love... I mean, I've never experienced what you've told me, but if a person can truly transform so quickly, and if love can take hold with such speed, then there is hope in this world after all. I will help you, Rhen. I received my semicha three years ago and was ordained as a Rabbi, so I can marry you and Julia."

My mouth fell open. "Really? You can? Here in the synagogue?"

She chuckled. "No, not here. You were right when you said I have an uphill battle for even the Jewish community here in Berlin frowns on me. I applied for employment here at the Synagogue but they turned me down, so now I just use the study rooms, and work as a chaplain in private ways. You give me a perfect opportunity to bring a glimmer of light into a dark world, I think."

"And it does not matter that I am not Jewish?"

She shrugged and lifted her hands to each side as if to say 'who knows', adding "I'm not sure God will care one way or the other under the circumstances. Being a woman Rabbi in a man's world puts me in quite a liberal position, so I am not opposed to your interfaith alliance. I'm sure I can simplify things since you know nothing of the traditions, and besides, we will need to do it in haste lest someone discovers us. What of Julia, when will you speak to her?"

I bit my lip. "Well, I told her I would send word to her at nine o'clock this morning. Do you think you can send someone to her, perhaps requesting she come to you at a time and a place that won't cause suspicion with her family? I mean, after all, if I was to show up at her home, especially dressed like this and ask to see her, well, you see how that will not work at all. But I am anxious to get this done quickly."

"Yes," she said, tapping her finger to lips again, "of course." She looked at her wristwatch. "It's nearly eight o'clock now, so we have one hour before she is expecting word from you. Here is what we shall do, and we must do this wisely and slowly, for fear of stumbling in too much haste. I will visit with my sister and ask her if she knows a young girl who might can assist me at the Jewish hospital. I might even casually suggest if her friend, Rebekah, has a daughter she might can ring up. You go home, put on something less conspicuous, and call me at this number in an hour." She tore off the corner of one of the pages and scribbled a number, then tucked it into my hand. "How does this sound?"

With sudden joy, I rushed across and threw my arms around her. She gasped, throwing her hands up in the air, and we nearly toppled to the floor. Finally, she patted my back and chuckled.

"Sir," she said, "all will be well... you will see. Your example will prove that love can conquer hate."

I sped away to my father's house in the borough of Zehlendorf, thankful the 'Banker trains' would get me there and back before anyone at the SS offices knew I was missing. And as for the secret meeting at noon... well, I knew I had to come up with a good reason for my father to allow my absence. But for now, all I could think of was Julia. Just a matter of hours and she will be my wife, and perhaps in a few weeks we will find ourselves on the other side of the world; and if I could arrange it, Fraulein Jonas will escape, as well.

As I walked down the sidewalk in front of my house, a familiar singing voice broke my concentration. I looked up to find my cousin, Bernie, and friend, Max, lounging on the front steps surrounded in a cloud of cigarette smoke.

Max took a long draw and blew out with his words. "Well, well, if it isn't the long lost and lovelorn Rhen creeping in after a night in some lady's bed."

I crossed my arms and frowned. "No such luck, my friend."

Max narrowed his eyes and frowned back. "You, sir, are an arsch to leave us bellowing for you in the streets last night. Don't tell me you had no such luck, for why else would you abandon us?"

I held out my hand for him to shake but he refused. "Please, Max," I entreated, "forgive me, but my business was a serious matter and one I could not share with either of you. You know just two weeks ago my father arranged for my appointment as a Unterscharfuhrer at the intelligence bureau, so some of my assignments are classified." I smiled a crooked half-smile trying to coax their forgiveness. "Forgive me?"

"Yes, we see you all flowered out in your finery. You have nothing to do with us now... the lowly Mann. Just call me MaxSchütze."

Bernie laughed and slapped Max on the back.

"There is nothing lowly about you, my friend," I said. "You are the soul of wit and my dearest friend. I will not leave you behind ever."

"A soulless wit these days, for I am spent and I have no more words for you. I forgive you, but your absence left me sour."

"Sour? Did something else happen after I left?"

Bernie stomped on his cigarette, crushing it beneath the toe of his boot. "Happen? Oh yes, more fray is all, for that headstrong Jewish son of Herr Cappell challenged Max to a fist fight after lunch today. So we will eat and then stomp the little mistweib in the ground."

My heart leapt into my throat. "You must leave Thomas Cappell alone, Max."

Both Bernie and Max crinkled their brows.

"What?" Max asked, confused. "He is a Judenschwein, Rhen... what does it matter if I crush his skull against a wall. I might even get a promotion if I do it."

"No," I stated, emphatically. "You cannot meet him."

Bernie chuckled. "What's wrong with you, Rhen? What do you care about the Jew?"

I adjusted the cap on my head and ran my fingers through my hair, trying to regain my composure and find the right words in my brain.

"I don't care," I replied, "but... but..."

Max slapped his knee and bellowed a laugh. "Listen at you! But... but... You sound like a honking goose. Too much wine last night, or too much weibstück has left his brain mushy."

I ignored them and headed to the front door, anxious for the call to Regine. To my dismay, they both followed right behind me up to my room. Max collapsed on my bed and Bernie turned on the radio while lighting another cigarette. Bach lilted into the room along with the smoke as I scrambled to find some clean clothes.

I jumped as a knock reverberated through the room, and the door creaked open revealing my mother standing there in her silk nightgown and a glass of brandy in her right hand. She fingered the loose golden curls about her face, trying to hide a cut above her left eye.

"Rhen," she said, surprised, "what are you doing here? Your father is expecting you at the office. He has already called here looking for you."

The blood rushed to my face and my heartbeat escalated. "Yes," I replied, "I know. I'm sorry... and I will call him straightaway."

"He had a rough night, Frau Montabauer," Bernie added with a chuckle.

She fixed her blue eyes on me and pinched her lips in a line. I knew that look since childhood; her reprimand was imminent.

"You promised your father no more following that schlurf crowd, no more American Jazz, no more swing dancing; you know it is forbidden. What am I going to do with you? It is an honor you received an appointment into the SS... think of your future, son."

Her words were as hollow as the vacant look in her eyes. I wanted to reach out and comfort her as she held back the tears pooling along her lower lashes. She spouted the words but they came from an empty heart coerced to say them for fear of another bruise on her face. I saw my father's anger splashed across her jaw too many times to count, and now she walked around the house most days like a ghost, with a drink in her hand, staring out windows while Wagner played in the background on the Victrola. For a moment, I saw myself in her eyes – a lost romantic on the verge of forced conversion or doing something insane... like suicide. Not a day passed in my house when I did not awake to wonder if we might find her floating in the tub with her wrists slit. And yet, here she still stood, alive and breathing. *Why?*

I took her hand and kissed her on the cheek. "I know, Mutter, you are right. It is an honor and I promise to call father right now. No more swing dancing, I promise."

She brushed her fingers through my hair and smiled. "And you will be home at a decent hour tonight?"

Now was my chance to concoct a perfect lie, not only for her but for Max and Bernie.

"Well," I said, "I may be on an assignment but its secret so don't tell father that I mentioned it. I may be gone for a week or so," I said, looking over my shoulder. "So, I may need some clothes and a suitcase."

"How exciting," she drolled. "The suitcase in is the hall closet, and the housemaid folded your clothes and left them on your bed."

I turned to see Max lounging across them.

He laughed and shuffled his butt into the pile. "Oops, sorry!"

I shook my head and looked back at my mother. "Will you be all right while I am away?"

She took a sip of her drink and offered me a wide insincere smile.

"Of course, my darling, why wouldn't I be?"

She kissed me again and drifted away down the stairs. I wondered if I would ever see her again, and for a moment, imagined she might be better off if she died. The sadness of such a thought about my own mother tore my heart and her acquiescence to everything happening in her life steeled me even more for my plans with Julia. I would not end up like her, molded by the battering hands of my father, nor the iron grip of Hitler and his laws.

I took the suitcase out of the closet and shoved Max out of the way as I scooped the clothes inside.

"So, you are really going away for a while?" Bernie asked, turning down the volume on the radio.

"Yes," I stated.

"So, you are not going to join us in the brawl with Thomas Cappell?" Max asked.

I stopped and looked at him. "Didn't I say to leave him alone? Besides, what does one Jew's taunts matter to any of us? The SS and Gestapo will take care of all of them in due course, you have to see that."

Max crooked his arms behind his head as a pillow. "Then, if they are all to be dealt with eventually, what does it matter if I bash his brains?"

There was no getting through to him, but I knew I had to find a way to protect Julia's brother; after all, just a few more hours and he will be my brother-in-law, my new family.

"Where are you meeting him?" I asked.

Bernie came up behind me and laid his arm across my shoulder. "That's more like it, Rhen! We need you there, and come dressed in your uniform to scare the shite out of them all."

Max sat up and shook my hand. "We are meeting at the Venusbassin in Tiergarten around two o'clock. You will come?"

"I promise I will try if I can sneak away from the bureau; but for now, I must make some phone calls. Stay here if you like and we will ride the train back into Berlin and grab a bite to eat before I meet up with my father."

Bernie turned the music back up as I headed downstairs to the one telephone in our house on the front table in the hallway. Looking over my shoulder, mother was nowhere to be seen and I kept my eyes on the upper staircase in case Max or Bernie showed their face. I slipped the torn piece of paper from my pocket and picked up the receiver. One click and a woman's curt voice answered.

"Exchange here, how may I help you?"

"Berlin, 407888, please."

"Thank you. Please, hold."

The burring ring hummed in my ear, once, twice, and the third time, and my heart thrummed against my ribs.

"Hello?"

"Go ahead, please," the switchboard operator said.

"Fraulein, this is Herr Montabauer. We met this morning if you recall and you said you might know more about my friend in the hospital."

"Yes, of course. Your friend's condition is stable and if you wish to visit, you can come to the front desk and I will leave a note there of what room your friend is in. I can tell you more in person if you are there around 1:00 if that works with your schedule."

"Yes, that is fine." And I hung up. I knew the switchboard operators were trained to listen in for the Reich, so I took no chances in saying more. The next call was more of a challenge and I took a deep breath to prepare to speak to my father.

"Exchange here, how may I help you?"

"Berlin, Sicherheitsdienst, 1011, please."

"Thank you. Please, hold."

"Yes," my father barked.

"Go ahead, please," the woman said.

"Father, it's Rhen."

I closed my eyes, imagining his gritting teeth and balled fists. "Rhen? You dummkopf; where in the world are you?"

"I'm at home... I had a really bad night."

I heard him pound his desk. "Get yourself back here as soon as possible. We have work to do and I don't give a rat's arsch if you had a bad night or not. Do you think the Führer stops what he is doing if he had a bad night?"

I wanted to say something sarcastic, but I held my tongue.

"Yes, father, I know. I'm sorry and will be there as soon as I can. And just so you know, I have been working. I received information on Baum's group and I have a stop to make to follow up on the entail, if that is acceptable to you, sir."

"Baum?" He paused. "Yes, of course, we need all we can get on such resistance groups."

"I'm not sure how long it will take, sir, but as I vowed I will do all I can for the Reichstag. I will not fail you, sir."

"Get on with it," he barked, again, "and get back here later today. This will be a late night."

"Jawohl, Herr Haupsturmführer."

And I hung up, closed my eyes and held my palm against my heart.
No turning back.

5

Julia

I could barely think straight after breakfast. *Marry Aaron? How in the world could I ever do such a thing now that Rhen is in my life?* Comparing the two... well, there was no comparison. Rhen was the sun, my breaking dawn, while Aaron was a cloudy night.

As I sipped on the hot tea, my favorite blend of Darjeeling with a splash of milk, the phone in the hallway purred to life. Mother answered, her voice chatting away with the other person on the line, yet too low for me to pick up on the conversation. I looked up at the clock on the wall, watching and listening as the second hand clicked away... ten minutes till nine. Just ten more minutes until my life changed, at least, I hoped and prayed.

But what if he didn't call? I mean, after all, what do I even know of him? What if the entire romantic scene last night was an act, a ruse to lure a poor Jewish girl into a forbidden alliance with a Nazi, a SS officer no less, thus sending her to an early death? And not just me, but my entire family would be targeted... they would not care if it was just my weakness, for they viewed any weakness as a corruption of our genetic makeup. My foolishness last night may have just sent my entire family to a firing squad.

I set my cup down and rubbed my hands along my arms, still the chills remained. Kitty sauntered into the kitchen, rubbing her eyes and yawning. Her rattling pots in the kitchen sink, and banging cabinet doors open and closed pounded my brain.

"Please stop," I asked her.

She ignored me and filled up the tea kettle again.

"We never have clean cups," she barked. "Why can't you wash the dishes sometimes, Julia?"

"That is not my job." I replied, taking another sip of my tea.

She chuckled and looked over her shoulder as she lit the stove and set the kettle on the heat. "Not your job? That's quite funny, little sister. You'd better get used to it being your job. Mother told me that she gave consent for you to marry Aaron Schwartz before Hanukkah."

I shrugged. "What do you care? Besides, what about you? It's not like you are going to escape Mother's plans of marrying you off to Benjamin, so the way I see it is you need to wash your own dishes so you can practice, as well."

Kitty crossed her arms, leaned against the counter, facing me, and narrowed her eyes. "There is a big difference between you and I, Julia. I want to marry Benjamin. I mean, who wouldn't want to marry him, he is a dream with his dark eyes and secure in his father's jewelry business." She walked near to me and kissed me on the top of the head. "Poor little sister, having to marry that pasty-faced Schwartz boy. I suppose that's why you wanted to get in a few moments of fun with that blonde-haired Adonis last night."

My eyes flashed up at her as she rinsed out a mug in the sink. "You didn't say anything to Mutter, did you?"

She giggled. "Of course not. Why would I? I mean, after I spoke to him last night and he realized who you were... well, I cannot imagine him coming around to pay you a call. He is a SS officer, just like our own father who abandoned us upon Hitler's order." She leaned forward across the table, catching my eye. "But you are still thinking about him, aren't you?"

"No," I blurted. "He hates us."

She cocked her head, still peering into my face. "Yes," she replied, "he hates us. They all do, and I would think that would be enough for you to forget him. Aaron may be a dull boy, but thoughts of someone like Rhen will damage all of us; remember that."

The tea kettle whistled loud as my mother walked into the room, her eyes and mouth smiling.

"Well, well, here are my girls, soon to be wives... and hopefully will give me a grandchild to spoil before I get too much older." She lifted the cup in her hand and Kitty poured some of the hot water as she plopped a brewing basket filled with tea leaves into her cup. Sitting down across from me, Mother arched her eyebrow and clasped my hand.

"I had the most interesting phone call."

I looked down to my cup as I swirled the remaining liquid in a circle, watching the loose leaves spin round and round. My stomach knotted, sure she was about to tell me about her conversation with Aaron's mother.

Kitty sat down, as well, sipping on her tea.

"Who was it," she asked.

"Well, you are not going to believe it, but it was with my friend, Lydia Jonas."

I looked up, wrinkling my brow. "Lydia Jonas?"

"You mean the sister of that woman who is trying to become a

Rabbi?" Kitty scowled.

"Yes," Mother replied. "The very one. And her sister is not just trying, she is one, and she is attempting to practice services right here in Berlin. Can you imagine? A woman Rabbi? I think its just nonsense, as do most in the community... anyway, that is not what she called about although it does have to do with her sister. She said that Regine is looking for a young girl to assist her at the hospital; you know, just doing errands, taking notes... that sort of thing. My first inclination is that under no circumstances will I have either of my daughters involved with such a woman, and I told Lydia that very thing. But what she said is so curious... something about recommending one of my daughter's to meet her sister in the hospital chapel and help her on love's errand for some poor patient who is in need. To be honest, I cannot figure out what she is talking about, but Lydia assured me that Regine's intentions are most honorable and it might do one of you good to assist her." Mother rubbed her brow. "I'm not sure, and yet, what could it hurt, this one day." She reached across and took Kitty's hand. "Perhaps you might go."

"No, I will go," I announced, suddenly recognizing the allusion to the "Nurse" in Romeo and Juliet.

Mother shook her head. "Not you, Julia. I need you here today to help me clean up. Your aunt is coming over tonight with Aaron's mother, and Thomas asked us to have some of his clothes packed since he is insisting on moving to Hamburg." She sighed and propped her jaw with her hand. "All of my children will be gone..."

"No," I interrupted. "I want to go, Mutter. You always let Kitty do everything and I always have to stay here. Let me do this, please, and I promise to dote on Aaron's mother tonight and give you no problems about my wedding day. Please, let me do this... this last wish as your youngest child?"

Kitty rolled her eyes. "Oh, let her go, Mutter, if it means that much to her; after all, I had plans to go with Sarah to her sister's house and look at patterns for a wedding dress. If Julia goes to the hospital, then you can go with me and help me find the perfect one."

"Please," I added.

Mother smiled and nodded. "Oh, all right, you can go, but she said you need to be there at noon. Just remember, the announcement yesterday from Herr Himmler has all of us jumpy; just leave soon since you can't use your bicycle or public transportation. Are you sure you will be all right?"

"Yes," I said, beaming and squeezing her hand. "Everything will be perfect."

+++++

Rhen

As much as I wanted to change into regular clothes and disappear into the crowds, luck was not on my side having my two friends shadowing me back to the city center. We stopped at the nearest beer garden, PraterGarten, and grabbed a few pints of stout, and some of the best bratwurst and kartoffelsalat I ever ate.

Max patted his bulging stomach and belched into his hand. "Even better than my Oma's recipe, I must say. I'm stuffed; now if I can find a shady spot and sleep out the rest of the afternoon; that is my plan."

I took a sip of the ale and breathed deep, hoping his stuffed stomach might keep him from his appointment with Thomas in Tiergarten.

"Well," I said, "I'm off. Sorry to have to leave you two rusticating louses, but I have some business to tend to with my father."

"We can tag along until we have to go to take care of our own business with that Judenschwein," Bernie replied, wiping his mouth on his sleeve.

My heart sank. They had not forgot. *But what could I do?* Julia waited for me, hopefully, and if all went as planned, I might could rush over and put an end to the fracas they intended to cause. If I brought them all to peace, I was sure Thomas might look on me with different eyes, which was my goal even if I could not tell him the real reason.

"No, you cannot go with me, Bernie."

Max stood up and bowed to me. "Yes, Bernie, we cannot follow in the footsteps of our elevated friend any longer. He floats above us now on some mighty Olympian cloud beneath the Führer's feet. Let him go... we have our own plans."

I pursed my lips into a narrow line, throwing darts at him with my eyes. With a laugh and a 'friendly' gesture of his middle finger, Max grabbed hold of Bernie's jacket and they disappeared into the sparse crowd.

I waited for a few minutes more, finishing my beer, to make sure they did not wait to follow me. After feeling relatively sure, I pulled my coat tight around me and headed towards the nearby Eberswalder U-Bahn Station, glancing at my wristwatch to gauge the time I needed to get across to the Juden hospital. At least my uniform allowed an ease of getting around Berlin without question, but showing up at the hospital might raise a few fearful eyebrows, to say the least. I knew I must take every precaution, even with the Jews, to ensure our safety and the utmost secrecy.

As I entered the subway car and the doors closed, I wasn't sure how I was going to protect Julia, but I knew I must. I held on to the wooden bar above my head, catching the stare of a man seated across from me. He was an Orthodox Jew, decked out in his dark black suit and long coat, and the curled locks of hair dangling on each side of his face beneath his wide-brimmed hat. His silver rimmed glasses sat on the end of a wide nose and the end of his beard shivered to the rumbling of the car across the tracks. Our eyes locked. We both knew he was breaking the rules – no filthy Jews on public transportation – and I knew he waited for me to do something, as did the other onlookers on the train.

What could I do? My heart and mind battled. Everyone expected me to approach him, to shout in his face, to pry open the doors and shove him from the train. I knew the routine... and the spying eyes trained on me. The Jews weren't the only ones who feared the laws. Everyone cringed with fear. No letter, no telephone conversation, word on the street, or whisper was safe any more. The person sitting next to you might be an informer. Since accepting my post, my father inundated me with the facts, beginning with the small number of Gestapo – 800 officers – in relation to the vast 4.5 million citizens residing in Berlin. So, as a result, a 'good Nazi' was encouraged to spy and turn in anyone who spoke against the State, and citizens were turned into block wardens who kept a close watch on forty to sixty households like a cat flicking its tail and stalking a mouse. Even the smallest perceived deviation might end up as a tip or denunciation. If I faltered in the slightest, especially as a member of the SS, I was ensuring my arrest, interrogation, and imprisonment as a traitor in one of Göring's "private prisons". And my father would have a field day on me if he discovered my secret, probably opting to be the one to break my jaw and kick his polished boot in my gut.

For just a moment, while I assessed the situation, and while we both fixed our stares, I noted the intensity behind the man's muddy brown eyes. I did not see fear, I saw a bravery teetering on foolishness... and perhaps, I saw a faith I did not understand. He looked into me but also past me, as if his eyes saw a promised future in heaven... or whatever they believed in. I pondered his eyes and those of Julia's, the similarities and the differences. The bravery was there in her eyes, as well, but when she looked into me, her gaze settled upon me as if knowing her future, her salvation, rested in my heart. This man's gaze, this Jew, held the realization that his death was imminent, and the sudden realization that I struck such fear seared my soul with a sharp lightning bolt of pain. I wanted nothing more than to reach my hand across and shake his hand, reassuring him with a smile and kind word. But I couldn't. I had to follow my vow. The pressure from the German eyes all around me pelted me and I wanted the train to stop so I might rush out onto the platform and disappear, but the train kept moving and the sweat beading below my hat brim rolled into my eyebrows.

As the train finally pulled into the next station, for show I removed my Luger from my holster and motioned to the old man.

"No Jews on the trains," I yelled, my teeth gritted.

The doors opened and the other passengers rushed out past me. Some on the platform, seeing my gun and the seated Jew, stepped back and hurried down the platform to another car.

Only seconds would pass before the doors closed. *What do I do?*

The man stood and without the slightest flinch in his eye, he walked past me and out onto the platform. I stood in the way of the door, fixing my boot so they could not close, raised my gun and clicked the barrel back. He paused, facing away from me.

"Turn around," I shouted.

He turned, facing me, and time stilled.

"Why are you so defiant?" I growled at him, again for show.

He placed his hand over his heart and answered in a soothing confident voice. "No matter what you do to me, what you do to any of us, you will never take away what is in here."

Without asking for permission, as if preparing for a bullet to puncture his body, he took a breath and walked away from me. I moved my foot, the doors closed, and I slumped down onto the seat where he sat, my entire body trembling. I looked left and right, realizing I was alone... and the tears burned my eyes.

The train traveled on to my destination, and in the steady clicking of the wheels over the rails, my thoughts drifted back to the words of the ghostly Father, the abbot who married Romeo and Juliet, and the ominous prophecy clouded over me, but not for me and Julia... for Germany.

These violent delights have violent ends
And in their triumph die, like fire and powder,
Which, as they kiss, consume. The sweetest honey
Is loathsome in its own deliciousness
And in the taste confounds the appetite.

Hitler's violent delights foretell violent ends, and even in his triumphs, they will die, consumed in a fiery kiss of death. His 'honey' patriotic words devoured by this country already confounds my appetite and, I predict, will leave Germany with a loathsome emptiness. As much as they believe, these Aryan gods, their fall will come, and I intend to not be among those whose wings melt in the sun.

+++++

Julia

My mother and Kitty left at eleven o'clock to meet up with Kitty's friend, Sarah, at the market down the street, giving me the perfect opportunity to get ready for my wedding day. I culled through my mother's old dresses and found the perfect one in a dusty rose shade with a dropped waist, delicate scooped neckline, a sheer flounced skirt, and a lovely cape-like ruffle cascading across the back from the shoulders. Pulling my hair back into a bun and gelling the sides in tiny finger waves around my face, I looked every bit as glamorous as Zelda Fitzgerald in those magazines my mother used to look at before they were banned. After sliding the ring Rhen gave me onto my right forefinger, I put on my black wool coat and matching hat, and took one last look at our apartment as I closed the door. *No, there was not a single thing I would miss when Rhen took me away from here... not even my own family.*

Within thirty minutes of walking through the streets of Berlin, I stopped in front of the hospital and leaned against the wall near the front steps to catch my breath. As I approached the front desk, a stern looking woman with piercing blue eyes raised her chin and looked at me.

"May I help you?" She asked.

My throat dried and I swallowed hard, trying to remember Rabbi Jonas' instructions.

"I'm here for an appointment with Rabbi Jonas. She said for me to meet her in the chapel."

The woman placed a pen on the counter and pointed to a paper with a list of names.

"Please, sign in and I will direct you where to go."

I scrawled my name on the line, my eyes scanning over the names above to see if I might see Rhen's name among the list. Nothing. My heart sped up in my chest and an uneasy fear knotted my stomach. *What if he didn't come? What if it was all a pretense? What if the Gestapo waited for me at the chapel and this stern woman with her blue eyes knew everything and was taking me to my doom?*

But, I followed her. The sounds of her high heel shoes clicking along the polished floor, and my eyes fixed on the dark line drawn on the back of her shins... something Kitty taught me to do to mimic wearing stockings since none of us were allowed (or could afford) such luxuries nowadays. Something about seeing the woman doing the same thing eased my nervousness. She opened the door to a staircase and pointed.

"Go down these stairs, two flights. When you get to those doors, go to your left and you will see the sign for the chapel."

"Thank you." I smiled but she just turned on her heel and marched back to the desk.

As I descended the staircase, the light dimmed and I took a moment to ponder the life we all led now. That woman with her stern, yet sad, eyes offered no return smile. She just meandered through the motions of her routine and unprofitable future. I wondered if she was a Jew, seeing as this was a Jewish hospital, but I doubted it since most Jews had to give up their positions to full-blooded Aryans. Some even had to give up their homes, and I wondered if my mother might face the same fate very soon. *Where would she go?* And I knew my father wouldn't even care or offer any kind of assistance now that he was married to a voluptuous blonde named Margot (or so I heard) who was already pregnant with their first golden child. We, his dark children, his piglets, were outcasts and I knew I would never hear or see him again.

I knocked on the door to the chapel and a small woman cracked open the door. She smiled when she saw me and grabbed hold of my wrist, pulling me inside as she looked left and right down the hallway.

"Julia!" She whispered with excitement. "Dear me, look how you have grown," she added as we crept through a row of benches to the back of the chapel. The woman's face alighted in the candlelight, and we sat down on the back pew.

"I know you don't remember me," she said, "but I remember when you were a little girl and your mother used to bring you to Shacharit with your grandfather. How is Isaac?"

"I suppose he is fine, Rabbi Jonas, but we have not seen him since he left in 1933. He left not long after the SA ransacked his bookshop and took most of his books to burn at the great Nazi bonfire. He tried to get my mother to go with him and bring all of us, but at the time, well, you know, my mother thought my father would protect her and his children. We never thought..."

She squeezed my hand. "Of course, you never thought such things would happen. How could any of us know, but hopefully this fire will burn out soon and we can return to our lives. Who knows, right? But now, we are here on a very special day, aren't we?"

The heat rushed to my cheek, noting the uncertainty tingeing her words. "Yes," I answered back.

She arched her eyebrow. "Are you sure of this, zeeskeit? While we are waiting on your gentleman you can confide your heart to me. I must admit, I am unsure of this. He is quite efficacious and believable, but is that not why men of that sort are recruited as SS officers? How can you be sure of this?"

I bit my lip and fought back the tears. "I'm not sure," I confessed. "You are right, we live in a world where deception and lies and propaganda is the norm, but there is something in Rhen's eyes, the connection we had, as if we had known each other from another lifetime. I truly don't feel that in his heart he is a true Nazi."

"And what of you? Are you not a true Jew, for it is not only the Nuremberg Laws that forbid marriage between an Aryan and a non-Aryan, but our Jewish laws forbid such interfaith alliances."

Again, I hesitated, and shrugged. "I know... and, in truth, I don't know who I am except who I am when I am with Rhen. How can a God of love not see beyond the labels of Jew or Nazi? How can love in the midst of all this hate be a bad thing?"

Rabbi Jonas touched my cheek with her fingers and brushed away the tear trail. She smiled an acquiescent smile but her eyes could not hide her doubt.

"You are such an innocent, zeeskeit, and I pray we are not all quite naive in this matter but my heart tells me to bring the two of you together in this, if not only for the sake of saving you and your family. If you bind yourself to this young man, and with his connections, you may find a way out of Germany for all of you. My intentions in this are honorable and I pray God blesses this union. So, tell me now, are you resolved in this?"

I raised my eyes and smiled wide. "Yes, Rabbi, I am resolved."

"Then, let me find my tallit, my prayer shawl, and something to cover you with for the Bedeken."

I reached in my coat pocket and removed a scarf of fine sheer silk, my mother's own veil that she wore during her wedding to my father. "I have something already," I replied. She led me to the center aisle, opened up the scarf and said a blessing while I removed my coat and hat.

Just as she finished, the door creaked open and we both turned with a gasp. My heart raced inside my chest as a tall man dressed in a full SS uniform strode through the doors. He removed his hat and the candlelight glowed against his golden hair.

"Rhen," I said aloud, rushing to him and crushing my face against his chest. He kissed me on the top of the head, and pulled me away to gaze in my face.

"Darling Julia, I wasn't sure you would come."

I giggled. "I thought the same about you."

He leaned me back with a kiss, then whispered in my ear. "Ah, dearest Julia, if the measure of thy joy be heaped like mine, and that thy skill be more to blazon it, then sweeten with thy breath this neighbor air, and let rich music's tongue unfold the imagined happiness that both receive in either by this dear encounter."

I closed my eyes and held him against me, ignoring the feel of his harsh Nazi uniform or the embossed gold buttons imprinting an eagle into my left cheek. I did not want to let him go, and I answered back Juliet's own words.

"Conceit, rich in matter than in words, brags of his substance, not of ornament. They are but beggars that can count their worth, but my true love has grown to such excess I cannot sum up sum of half my wealth."

He wrapped his hands around my face, smudging away the impression of the button, and kissed my eyelids, then resting his lips on mine in the softest and sweetest of kisses.

"Enough," interrupted Rabbi Jonas, "enough, or else you will waste away this time with poetry and passion leaving an opening for someone to find us here. Come along, we will get this done quickly and I will have to dispense with some of the traditions... most like, since this is quite nontraditional in every sense, but by my heart, standing here looking at the two of you together, you make me believe in love and that there is a future to be had for us all."

She held out the scarf to Rhen. "Here, take this and place over Julia's head. This is the Bedeken, which pictures the love you have for not only her outward beauty, but the beauty within."

Rhen draped the scarf over my head and we both giggled as the lace caught on his epaulet.

He took my hand and we stood in front of Rabbi Jonas. We said our vows, our gaze never departing from each other, and my heart fluttered watching the candlelight twinkle in his eyes like stars shimmering over blue water. I etched his face in my memory – his soft blonde lashes, the firm chiseled jaw, and the way his smile created two perfect parentheses around his full luscious mouth. No matter what happened from this day forth, this moment branded into my mind, and his honey vows filled my soul.

Rhen

After the vows, and after I slid a gold band over her finger, and she slid my own ring back onto my hand, I closed my eyes as she walked in a circle around me. I had no idea what the tradition meant, and Rabbi Jonas did not add any more words, but the feeling of her hand tracing across my chest, then my upper arm, over my back, over and over, seven times, impressed upon me our connection. The moon circling the earth, the earth circling the sun, always there, always continuous, forever bound in this fixed orbit, this dependent symbiotic dance. Each time she crossed in front of me, I etched her face in my mind – her soft black lashes, the yielding jaw, and the way her smile created two perfect dimples to each side of her full luscious mouth. I knew no matter what happened from this day forth, this moment branded into my mind, and her honey vows filled my soul.

Rhen and Julia

Rabbi Jonas spoke seven blessings, emphasizing the power of love, joy, companionship, and celebration. She apologized for not having a cup of wine during the ceremony but, in truth, neither of us cared. We were married. Man and wife. No longer just I, or he, or she... but us. At the end, the Rabbi wrapped a small glass in her prayer shawl and placed it on the floor in front of us.

Rabbi Jonas

Rhen crushed the cup with his boot, and we all stood there in silence. I'm not sure what ran through this young couple's minds but for me, as the woman who just married them, the sound of his leather boot breaking the glass sent a sickening jolt of nausea through my stomach. *What did I just do? Did I just seal all of our fates and is this splintered glass spilling to the floor a prophecy of the future?* In truth, I wanted to believe in love, in hope, but as I looked up into their faces, all I saw was a Jew and a Nazi standing face to face, with an uncertain shadow creeping into their eyes.

6

Rhen

We sat on the front pew of the chapel for a long while after Rabbi Jonas left us, kissing and letting our words of love breath across our lips. And we made plans.

I knew whatever I did I had to do with the utmost stealth, for to help a Jew in anyway was paramount to a quick bullet in the back of my head. Even as I lingered my mouth on hers, my hand caressing the curve of her delicate shoulder, the song of the Storm Columns and the pounding leather boots goosestepping down the streets of Berlin echoed in my brain.

Only when Jews bleed, are we liberated. No more negotiations, it's no help, not even slight. Beside our Adolf Hitler we're courageous in a fight.

I shook my head and scattered the words into a dark corner of my mind, and took her face in my hands.

"Tonight, then?"

She nodded, and her innocent cheek blushed as she lowered her eyes and smiled.

"Where shall I meet you?" I asked.

Her hopeful eyes flashed up. "The same as before, in the garden. Meet me on the roof. There is a ladder on the side of the balcony covered with vines. I will be waiting..." She giggled a soft, girlish laugh and blushed.

Goosebumps raced over her warm skin as I brushed my fingers down her arm.

"Then, my beautiful wife, I will see you at midnight."

With one last passionate kiss, we parted at the opened door to the chapel. Julia watched me around the edge of the door as I walked backwards to the stairs, our gaze clinging to each other until, at last, the closing of the chapel and stairwell doors broke the thread.

The day blazed unseasonably warm after I left the hospital, and a suffocating haze blanketed over Berlin. From the corner of the street across the way, I watched as Julia walked away in the opposite direction, lost in a daydream with a smile on her face. The image of her dress fluttering behind her beneath the dark coat filled my heart with hope. *Yes*, I thought, *there is ethereal beauty beneath this dark cloud hovering over the skies.* I smiled and turned towards Tiergarten, my heart full of love and assurance that I might win over my friends who ached for blood. I prayed I was not too late to stop the brawl between my dearest companions and my brother-in-law.

After another brief ride on the train, and a short sprint to the long rectangular garden pond, I saw Bernie and Max stretched out below the staring faces of the Musikerdenkmal. Beethovan, Haydn, and Mozart glared down over them with disapproval in their hollow marble eyes, but I was thankful no other fellows were about. I rounded the last of the chestnut trees which offered shade beneath the blazing sun, removed my coat and hat, and hollered a greeting, rousing them from their slumber.

"Lo ho, my good friends! What, is this the brawl?"

Bernie leapt to his feet and shook my hand, laughing. "What is this? I thought you had business to keep you away from such menial things as this. Look, Max, Rhen has come to back our fight with his uniform and pistol ready."

Max narrowed his eyes. "Is this true, Rhen? Are you lending your hand for the brightness of your eyes speaks a different purpose."

I tossed my hat and coat on the steps and slouched down next to him. "And you would be right in saying that, Max, for I was hoping to bring you both to peace."

"Peace? Are you kidding with us?" Bernie questioned as he stretched out next to me.

"No," I replied, "I am not kidding. Let this go, my friends, for we have much loftier things to concern ourselves with than falling to a mere fight in a park. You know how these things will go... let the State take care of those brash rebels like Thomas Cappell. He will bring his own ruin, I assure you, for I have it on the strictest confidence that he meddles in some of the resistance groups poised to oppose Hitler. Let the Gestapo handle this, for I fear what might happen to either of you if his hand turns violent."

Max blew out a cloud of cigarette smoke and Bernie leaned over towards him. "Maybe Rhen is right. Besides, I'm already pouring sweat and desperate for a glass of ice at the Moka. What say you, Max, shall we do as Rhen asks and cool our heels?"

"Ha!" Max barked. "You are one to talk, Bernie, for you are as ready to fight as any man I know."

Bernie pulled his hands to his chest and frowned. "Me? I have no idea what you mean?"

Max leaned over me, directing his cutting words at Bernie. "Yes, you. I've seen you pick a fight over the stupidest of things. When it comes to brawling, you are a dummkopf of the highest degree with scrambled brains before and after a beating. Don't you remember punching that Jewish grocer just because he passed by us on the street and coughed into his hand? I think you are not the one to teach me a thing or two about quarreling with Jews."

I laughed at their banter, which often led to the two of them wrestling on the floor, but this day, fate stepped in. I looked across, distracted by the sudden flight of a kit of pigeons rustling through the trees, and noticed Thomas, banked by four of his friends, coming towards us along the sidewalk.

"Well, there are here," I said, bringing them both to silence.

Max took another puff of his cigarette and slouched back against the monument. "It's too hot to fight. Let them go."

Thomas walked up, his arms outstretched to each side. "Well, well, I see you are all here, ready and able to settle this matter. But first, I will have my say with Rhen."

"Words?" Max snarled. "You will ruin the brawling with words?" He stood and pressed his chest against Thomas', their faces within inches of one another. "Come on, you Judenschwein, let's see what you are made of."

"Wait," I shouted as I pulled them apart. "I will speak to you, Thomas." I motioned towards the garden pond. "But in private, if you will."

The two of us walked to the water's edge while the vibrato of the others bounced back and forth between them like sword slashes from the lips. I eased my voice to a whisper, padding my words with genuineness.

"Thomas, please, this quarrel is not necessary. I fear for your life if someone reports this to the Gestapo. There is no need for anger."

He narrowed his doubt-filled eyes. "Fear for my life? When has an SS officer ever feared for the life of a lowly Jew? Are you mocking me?" His chest puffed out as he balled up his fists and took a step towards me. "You know why I'm angry at you. I want to know what happened between you and my sister, Julia, at the Moka."

My throat dried and I lowered my eyes and voice even more. "If you only knew..."

He grabbed hold of my uniform collar, crumpling it in his fist. "Knew what? What did you do to her, you filthy Nazi?"

I pushed him away, snatching my jacket from his grip, and gritted my teeth. "Thomas, for the reasons I have in my heart, I will overlook this brash gesture which defies our laws. Before too much else is said or done, I will take my leave of you, sir."

Turning away from him, I walked over and picked up my coat and hat, put them on and fingered the Luger in my pocket. As I turned, Thomas, once again, grabbed hold of my coat, his rage spitting out with his words.

"Oh no, we will have this matter settled between us. You, the poster boy of the Reich, will learn a lesson this day to not put your hands on our Jewish girls."

We glared at each other and my forefinger eased over the trigger. "Let go, Thomas, you don't know what you are doing or what you are saying. I have done nothing to injure you or your sister, but until I can speak more, be assured of the esteem I hold for your family."

"Ha!" He bellowed in my face. "Esteem? More sarcastic banter? They teach you well how to ease your brow when you are about to bash someone's brains, don't they?"

Max ran to me, grabbing hold of Thomas' arm as he pulled back to aim his fist into my jaw. The three of us struggled to the ground – a trio of flailing limbs, grunts, and shouts – and we rolled against the monument towering over us. Bernie and Thomas' friends circled us, shouting insults and encouragement in one breath.

"Let him go," Max spat into Thomas' ear. "You fight the wrong man, you schafskopf! I will take you on, Tom Cat, and all of your nine lives."

Max pushed me out of the way and pounded his fist into Thomas' face.

"Stop it," I shouted as I tried to pull Max away. Looking over my shoulder, I called to Bernie. "Come, help me! This is not the way to end this matter."

The seconds ticked away, slowing as the words fell from my lips. Another flutter of wings filled the sky over our heads, frightened by one single gunshot piercing the air. We all stopped, gazing around to discover the source, and I scanned the edges of the park, waiting to see the Gestapo approaching the chaos. Instead, my eyes filled with Max's form slumped forward over the knee-high fountain wall surrounding the composer's monument. He coughed and a spray of blood dappled the bright white marble.

"No!" I yelled, my voice sounding far away, somewhere in the clouds, muffled by the pounding of my heart in my ears. I spun around, looking at hands to find the smoking gun. Thomas took a step backwards, his hand trembling as he dropped the pistol to the ground, and our eyes locked. I took the Luger out of my pocket, aiming at him.

"You, stay right there," I ordered, kneeling next to Max. My friend crumpled into my arms, forcing me to take away my aim, and giving

Thomas and his friends the chance to run. I started to bolt after them but Max, with the last of his power, grabbed hold of my jacket and pulled me near to whisper in my ear, the metallic smell of blood and death creeping into my nostrils.

"Such irony, is it not, Rhen?" He eked out.

"Irony?"

"Yes, here you are the consummate romantic whose friend will die a quite Shakespearean death. Teach me to do it well, Rhen, my friend."

I chuckled and pulled him close. "Nonsense, Max, hold on and we will get you to the hospital."

"Shall I run for help?" Bernie asked, leaning over us.

"Yes," Max replied, "all will be well; go." Again, he strained upward to my ear. "What is the eloquent thing I can say? I know, here it is... ask for me tomorrow and you shall find me a grave man. A plague on both your houses, for a Jewish rogue makes me a dish for worms."

"No," I said, "you are all right, Max. I will not have you say such things. The wound cannot be so bad, after all, here you are being as sarcastic as ever."

I laid him in the grass and pulled back his jacket. His once white shirt ate up with the spreading blotch of red pumping from a wound in his chest. He coughed again, spraying his blood across my face. I closed the jacket and held him close.

"See," he said, gurgling out his words, "nothing but a scratch. If you had just let me fight him, man to man, fist to fist. Why did you come?"

"I thought only for the best... to bring you to peace."

"And now, I have it," Max whispered out, and closed his eyes.

Bernie ran back up behind me, gasping for breath. "They are coming, Rhen, the Ordnungspolizei. We can tell them what happened, and they will find Thomas and take him into custody straightaway."

"Max is dead," I said, wiping the burning tear from the corner of my eye and smearing the blood across my brow.

I stood up, and Bernie fell next to Max, sobbing. Looking down at Max's blood painted across my chest, a sudden cold wind chilled my mind, yet a fierce raged consumed me. The Luger in my pocket burned my skin, the metal pulsing revenge as my forefinger teased the trigger.

"Now," I whispered to myself, looking down at Max. "fate takes us all."

I looked over my shoulder as the city police, three of them, walked near and assessed the scene. There, clutched in the grip of two of the officers, Thomas stood with his hands tied behind him.

The head officer came up to me, throwing his arm up in a perfect salute. "Heil Hitler, Unterstrumführer!"

I gave a perfunctory return, a limp arm and scowled at Thomas. "You found him?" I asked the officer.

"Yes, well," he answered, scratching his head. "We saw him running down the street, guilty-like, and thought best to apprehend him from suspicion. And then, here... Herr Weber found us, telling us this Jew shot a German citizen." He motioned to Max. "And I see we were right to take him into custody."

"Yes," I said, calmly, my mind resolving in a matter of seconds. Walking up to Thomas, I put on my officer's hat, adjusted it, and glared at him.

"You good-for-nothing pig. Max was a good man, one of my dearest friends, and you will pay for what you have done to him."

Thomas reared back and hocked a wad of spit into my face. Without breaking my calmness, I wiped my sleeve across my mouth, turned and took one step away from him.

"You are the pig," he snarled. "A Nazi pig, and soon all of you will be dead."

I turned and in one elegant motion of my arm and hand, like a waltz beneath the music of the masters who peered down over the tragic scene, I aimed directly at his forehead and pulled the trigger.

"You first," I said.

I walked in a daze on the way back to the Sicherheitsdienst, still clutching the Luger in my fist as if the metal melted into my skin the moment the bullet left the chamber. People gawked at me as they passed, rushing away, gasping... as I, unaware, parted the crowds with the blood of two souls splattered on my coat and face. Max, my dearest friend, the one who offered me his hand the day I stumbled while marching the first day I joined the Youth Group – years ago, those innocent days when we stared bright eyed at our Kommandant with a golden Aryan future awaiting us; and now, Thomas, my brother for only one hour, who will never know the actual pain my heart felt nor will he ever know the secret I share with his sister. With each step along the sidewalk, my heart beat in time, accusing me with each pulse – over and over... why? Why? Why?

"Why did I pull the trigger?" I whispered to myself as I stopped and sucked in a deep breath. Gazing up to the sky, I realized I stood on the street near the entrance to the SS headquarters, the mighty columned portico stretching over me. A door to my right opened, the squeaking hinges awakening me from my nightmare, and I looked up into my father's face.

He glared at me, with what? Pride, or disgust? Sometimes I could not tell the difference but then, with a smile he distinguished the two and eased me inside with his arm over my shoulders.

"Herr Amsel, the head of the city police called me and told me what happened. Are you all right, my son?"

Still, I said nothing. Reaching up to steady the pounding in my head, my fingers swiped through the blood and I held my hand in front of my face as we walked up the stairs to his office. Two other young Unterstrumführer's passed by us, all shiny and bright, and patted me on the back, congratulating me on such an achievement.

Nausea crept up into my throat and a chill sped along my spine. I could not even shoot the Jew on the train, the man who meant nothing to me and whose blank name never etched a letter on my mind, but I never blinked once as the hammer released, ending Thomas' young life. I had known him my whole life. My cousin, Olga, used to flirt with him when our families met for picnics in Tiergarten, even as young as seven or eight years old. We were all innocent then, blank slates, unabashedly irresponsible and rushing headlong into the red, black, and white future flapping in the wind. And Julia... *oh dear God, Julia... what have I done?*

When father closed the door to his office, the nausea and searing pain bolted from my stomach, heaving regret, sorrow, and beer into the wastepaper basket at the end of his desk.

My father chuckled and slapped my back. "I underestimated you, my boy, and now for your bold actions it seems you have caught the attention of Herr Himmler, himself. To shoot a Jew without a thought, exacting justice for his blatant disobedience to the State laws for appearing in a public park and, not to mention, murdering a valuable member of the Nazi party... well, you are to be congratulated,

Unterscharführer Montabauer."

He unfolded a piece of paper on his desk and handed it to me. I read the typewritten words and stared blankly at the Fuhrer's own signature.

"I'm sorry, Father... I mean, sir, but I do not understand. This is a reassignment?"

"Yes," he replied. "It seems your abilities are needed in Dachau at the SS training camp and as an assistant to Kommandant Eiche."

"Dachau? The concentration camp?"

"The very one."

"But that is half a day away by train."

Father leaned back in his chair, narrowing his eyes. "And I suppose you have some pressing reason binding you to Berlin?"

I said nothing but Julia's face flashed in my mind.

"You knew when you accepted the rank of Unterscharführer that you might be asked to accept any assignment." He continued. "I think you might learn much in Dachau from Kommandant Eiche... besides, there are things at work here in Berlin, some changes beginning this very evening, and I need you here with me to help coordinate some of the activities which will lead to an increase of prisoners at the camp."

My stomach knotted again. "Activities? What is happening?"

He stood and patted me on the back. "I will have my secretary send up a new uniform. Change your clothes, get something to eat downstairs in the SS Mensa. Rest, that is what you need. You've had quite a day... your first kill but don't worry, my son, the stench of Juden blood washes clean. It was a strong, decisive, and just action in defense of our nation, never forget that." He urged me to the door. "Go on, but return as soon as you can and we will talk about the activities of which

I spoke. Today is a big day for Germany, for Hitler, and for the Reich...
you will see."

7

Julia

The shattering of glass...

I awoke with the sound and the image of Rhen stomping his black boot on the hidden glass wrapped in Rabbi Jonas' shawl. Glancing down at my side table, the second hand on the clock raced around and the hands showed seven o'clock. I walked to the window and pulled back the curtains. A soft fog hovered over the surface of the roof and an echo of lightening rippled across the sky. The darkness enveloping the air was thick and foreboding, the kind of inky hue which bespoke sheer evil lurking in the corners – the color well suited to the uniforms worn by the Schutzstaffel officers.

I brushed the palms of my hands up and down my arms, willing away the thoughts and shivers, and closed my eyes to dream of Rhen. Just five more hours and I will be his... he will be mine... we will be each other's, bound together in mind, body, and soul.

A knock echoed through the room and I looked over my shoulder as the door eased open. Kitty peeked around, her smile wide and eyes sparkling.

"Julia, Aaron and his mother are here." She crept into the room and kissed me on the cheek, glancing down at my dress and fingering the soft silk. "Isn't this mother's dress?"

"Yes," I replied. "I didn't think she would mind. After all, I want to look my best for Aaron."

Kitty giggled and shrugged. "I guess you know what you are doing but I wouldn't be caught dead in such an old-fashioned dress. Anyway, Thomas should be on his way, as well. I think we are all going to have a nice dinner together, and Thomas has promised to do a proper Ma'ariv for us all since he said that it is not a good idea for us to go out tonight."

"Why?"

She shrugged, again, and sat me in front of her at the vanity while she fiddled with my curls, bobby pinning them back from my face. "Who knows, but you know our brother; he has his fingers on the pulse of the city, more so that even Mutter knows, and I think he is suspecting some trouble. After all, didn't you hear the news from Paris today?"

"News? No, I didn't. What happened?"

She put her hands over my shoulders and held my eyes with her own in the mirror reflection. "A Jewish student killed a German diplomat... Grynszpan... I think."

Her brow wrinkled as my eyes widened. "Herschel Grynszpan?"

"Yes, now that I think of it... that is his name. Do you know him?"

"No, of course not... but I remember the name from Danka Schmidt. You know the family who came here from Poland five years ago? I think he had a crush on her for a while but she discovered he had quite the temper when she rejected his attention. I remember her saying that his parents sent him to Paris to live with his uncle, and she was so thankful to be rid of him. He really shot a German diplomat? I wonder what will happen to him."

Kitty nodded and patted down the last pin curl. She arched her eyebrow. "I think we all know what will happen to him if the Nazis ever get hold of him; I suppose he should be grateful that he only sits in a French prison at the moment. But, this is the reason that Thomas is worried for any of us being out of the house for tonight."

I nodded and my thoughts swarmed to Rhen. *Might something like this change his mind about Jews and Nazis... about me?*

Kitty kissed the top of my head and urged me to my feet. "Now, so much better. You will leave Aaron speechless, bubala."

She waited for me at the door yet my feet glued to where I stood, and I touched my fingers to my chest, pressing the cold silver ring to my skin hidden beneath my dress. I knew I had to act the part of an excited young girl enamored with her prospective chosen match.

Kitty motioned me forward. "Come along... and put those thoughts of Grynszpan out of your head. Aaron is waiting..."

I took a deep breath. "In a moment... can you give me one moment alone and I will meet you there."

She winked. "Of course... I will tell them."

She closed the door and my eyes darted to the suitcase tucked beneath my bed. When I returned from the hospital and before falling asleep, I packed a few things to ready myself for Rhen's plan to leave Berlin. All I needed now was a word from him and I would never see my family again... or, as I hoped, for now at least. The disappointment in my mother's eyes, the anger from Thomas, and the fear in Kitty's all flashed in succession in my mind. *Was I doing the right thing?*

I chuckled to myself. "What am I saying?" I whispered. "The deed is done... I am Rhen's wife. We have to leave Berlin, and as soon as possible."

I shook my head to release the negative thoughts and took another steeling breath, opened the door and marched down the hall to the kitchen, where all gathered around our small dining table. All eyes settled on me as I entered the room.

+++++

Rhen

The kartoffelsuppe and beer stuck in my throat and settled heavy in my gut as I sat at the table in the Mensa hall. The murmur of voices buzzed in my ears from the other young SS trainees and officers gathered there, all smiling, and words tinged with the news of the day. The assassination of the German diplomat, Ernst von Rath, by a Parisian Jew overshadowed my own killing of Thomas Cappell, at least in the mouths and interest of everyone else. For me, I thought of nothing else, especially since the image of Julia's tear-streaked face when she discovers her brother's death flickered over and over like the images in an old-time nickelodeon. She will hate me... my own wife for only four hours now, and my stomach flip-flopped wondering what her first words to me might be when I arrive in the garden at midnight.

I glanced at my wristwatch, noting the time, and sighed. Seven o'clock. Just five more hours until our planned meeting, and in my daze I had done nothing about our plan to leave Berlin. Holding another spoonful of potatoes to my mouth, the shiver in my hand quaked as I noticed Max's blood still caked beneath my fingernails. Yes, justice prevailed in my actions. Anyone could see that, after all if it had not been me who took Thomas's life in exchange for his own murderous hand against Max, someone with the Gestapo would have done the same. Even Julia had to see that a life paid for a life, and Thomas was not above the law.

I looked up and gazed around the room. Our black and grey uniforms set a mood of stark coldness, rigidity, and order. The Schutzstaffel were the law in Germany now, and any action taken to uphold those laws were correct. We are German citizens, Julia and I, irregardless of faith, and she is my wife, required to uphold my headship in all things. Even her Jewish faith teaches her that. I lifted my chin, accepted the acknowledging nods from a few of the other officers, and headed to my father's office.

As I exited the hall, I looked up and saw Bernie sitting on the last step of the staircase, his head in his hands. I walked up and extended my hand to him.

"Max would say, no tears."

"Max said a lot of things," he replied, his words shaking.

"Yes, he was a man of many words, for sure. I will miss him terribly... but none so much as you, I fear."

He nodded, but did not look up. "Yes, you were always the loner, but while you wiled away your hours by yourself, Max and I clapped together as brothers. I will never find another like him..."

"No," I answered back, "nor will I."

He finally looked up and stood next to me. "The execution was just, Rhen, you do know that, right?"

"Of course," I said, the words catching on my momentary doubt.

And he noticed, as I knew he would, since he, Max, and I had been inseparable since childhood and knew all the ins-and-outs of things not said; the truest of friends. I knew, too, that secrets between friends are a sacred bond.

"What is it, Rhen? I see it in your eyes, and hear it in your voice. There is more than grief there."

I pressed my lips together and motioned him outside to the far end of the front courtyard, weaving in between the rows of flagpoles and flapping flags, and pulled him into the shadows near an alcove.

Looking left and right, I tugged on his sleeve and lowered my mouth to his ear.

"I do have something more to say about this matter, Bernie, but you must swear to me that our friendship means more to you than our loyalty to the Fuhrer."

His eyes widened. "Wha... what?"

I grabbed hold of his coat, each hand holding a side of the lapel and looked him square in the eyes. "On Max's blood, and our friendship, swear to me, or I will not speak a word."

He held up his hands. "I swear... you know I swear, Rhen."

I let go and again, looked right and left as he straightened his jacket and chuckled.

"Krass, Rhen... you would think you've gone and turned traitor instead of putting a bullet in a Jew's head. What is wrong with you?"

I slouched against the column and confessed. "Perhaps, I have, Bernie."

He ran his hand through his hair and offered me a smile. "Sorry, what?"

"Did you know Thomas Cappell?"

He shrugged. "Sort of, I mean, I know his father, naturally... all of us know him from the Jugend."

"Did you know he has two sisters?"

He rubbed his chin and his eyes darted back and forth as he searched his mind for a remembrance. "Of course," he finally answered, "I know Kitty... but they have another sister?"

"Last night when we went to the Moka Efti, do you not remember the dark-haired beauty I pointed out coming down the escalator... or were you too enraptured by the golden German goddesses on each of your arms?"

He laughed and widened his eyes. "Oh, yes, I think I remember her... so, she was Thomas's younger sister? Krass, who would've thought that... she was a real schöne schwein, then."

I grabbed back hold of his jacket. "Watch what you say about her."

He held up his hands, again. "Sor... ry! What's all this about; are you going to tell me?"

"She's Jewish," I prologued my confession. "But... she is also... as of today... this morning, after the induction ceremony... and before I met you all in Tiergarten.... Well, I... I..."

He slapped me on the back and rolled his eyes. "Just spit it out, Rhen... you aren't the first Aryan to sully his race by bedding a Jewess. You think I'm going to turn you in for being a man?"

"It's more than that, I'm afraid."

He guffawed loudly and two Strumtruppen looked our way as they passed. I watched them until they were out of sight.

"More than that? What can be more than that?"

I leaned near to his ear and whispered the words. "I married her. She is my wife, and what is more... we plan to leave Berlin as soon as possible."

Bernie pulled away from me and walked a short distance, gazing up to the blue sky above us with his back to me. He glanced over his shoulder.

"You are serious?"

"Yes."

"Why are you telling me this, Rhen? You are putting me in a very awkward position."

"You swore to keep my secret... on our friendship."

"And I will," he said firmly. He neared to me and pulled me in close. "Does she know... of her brother's execution... and that you are the one who carried it out?"

I lowered my head. "I don't know... and is one of the reasons for my revealing this secret." I looked up into his face, hoping he might read the pleading in my eyes. "I need your help, Bernie. I love Julia more than my own life, and what happened today between me and Thomas was... well, when I saw Max lying there, his blood pooled around him, all I could hear was the Jugend song we used to sing - 'just let them romp and scream and brace themselves against us... we will be victorious' - and I pulled the trigger, without a thought. And now, she will hate me, but I have to know, Bernie... you have to help me know for sure because my father is sending me away to Dachau as an assistant to Eiche. If she hates me, if she never wants to see my face again, I will go and never look back; but if there is the slightest hope for forgiveness, that she might understand that her brother's death comes as a result of his own actions... then I will move heaven and earth to flee this volcano on the verge of eruption. Please, will you find out for me as quick as you can?"

He clapped his arms around me in a tight hug. "Of course, I will."

+++++

Mutter's eyes brimmed red with tears, and Kitty stood there with a hand over her opened mouth. Aaron and his mother, along with my aunt, lowered their eyes, and I glanced to the empty chair at the head of the table.

I giggled. "So, Thomas is late again?"

No one said a word as Mutter collapsed in her chair and buried her head into her crossed arms, sobbing. Kitty leaned over her and wrapped her arms over Mutter's shoulders, also giving way to tears. My stomach roiled and my heart leapt into my throat, wondering if they all had somehow discovered my secret.

My aunt finally walked near to me and offered me her hand. "Come, sheifale, sit here next to your mother."

I sat and scanned the tear-stained faces around me, waiting for someone to say a word, any word. After a few minutes of listening to the cuckoo clock pendulum click away the seconds, I took a breath and broke the silence.

"Will someone say something? Just spill the secret."

Aaron lifted his gaze from the table and fixed his eyes on me, softening his anxious look to one of deep concern and sympathy.

"I will tell you," he replied, firmly. I lifted my chin, preparing for the revelation of my marriage to Rhen.

"Thomas is dead," he whispered, his words sputtering out over his own shaking lips.

The words clouded my mind and I jerked my eyes back to his empty chair. Something crumbled inside my heart as the words I thought I would hear were replaced by others I did not expect, and a bubbling sadness erupted from my gut, spilling out in a sudden gush from the corners of my eyes.

"No," I said, determined to know more. "This cannot be. What happened?"

Kitty urged Mutter to her feet, and her intense sobs echoed along the hallway as Aunt Gerta led her out of the kitchen to her bedroom. When Kitty returned, she offered me a clean handkerchief and wrapped her hands around mine. Both Aaron and his mother sat down in chairs opposite us.

"Sister, dearest, we heard the news just now, just before you came in the room. While we waited on you, a man from the Ordnungspolizei came to the door and told us what happened."

I wiped away my tears and squeezed her hands. "And?"

"Perhaps it is better not to know," Aaron added.

My eyes flashed up. "No," I answered. "I want to know what happened to my brother. You know, do you not? Was it his association with that resistance group... the same one I know you are a part of? You all think your efforts will make a difference, that you can sacrifice your time and effort to destroying Hitler instead of finding a way to get your family out of Berlin, but the only difference now is that my brother is dead." The heat of my words spilled out and Aaron leaned back against the chair as his mother clutched his arm.

"No," Kitty replied, grabbing hold of my wrists and pulling me towards her. "Your anger is misdirected, Julia. Yes, Thomas was with a group of resistance fighters but his quarrel was more of a personal nature, nothing to do with politics... except for the politics of his little sister."

"You should not tell her," Aaron's mother whispered.

I bit my lip. "Tell me," I urged, my heart now wondering if Thomas's death connected with my marriage to Rhen. Perhaps he discovered us, followed us... and what if he confronted Rhen. *Oh, God... no!*

Kitty wiped her cheek with the back of her hand. "You remember when Rabbi Hersch was killed out in the street in front of our house years ago?"

"Yes," I answered, gritting my teeth.

"The boys who taunted Thomas back then, quarreled with him recently about his resistance entanglements. What we did not know is the extent of their quarrel, and when Thomas saw one of them with you at the Moka Efti... well, he went to meet them today in Tiergarten to settle the quarrel."

A spark of hope kindled in my heart. Rhen was with me at the hospital... so, the quarrel was not with him.

"You are saying that Thomas was going to defend my honor," I said.

She nodded.

"Go on," I urged.

"From what we have heard from the polizei is that only a handful met. Thomas and a few of his friends confronted a couple of Wehrmacht soldiers, some they had seen at the Moka Efti that night you showed up there. Thomas asked about the man he saw with you... Rhen Montabauer. Remember, I said something about this to you after that night, of how incensed Thomas was after I told him of seeing you speaking with Rhen."

Another stream of tears rolled down my cheeks. "So, Kitty, what you are trying to tell me is that it is because of me that Thomas is now dead, right? Is that the words you are trying to skirt around?"

Kitty tried to squeeze my hands again but I pulled them away. Still, she did not answer my question.

"Thomas is dead because of me," I repeated.

"No," Aaron interjected. "Thomas is dead because of his insistence on quarreling with Nazis. The resistance is fighting a losing battle; we cannot win against them. Even if Thomas was justified in his heart to uphold your honor, he is a Jew and we are nothing in their eyes. If he had remained silent, he would still be alive today."

I turned to him and glared. "What kind of courage is there in silence?"

"The alive kind... besides, what did his sacrifice gain?" he replied back.

"A sister's love and pride," I answered, raising my chin. Turning back to Kitty, I brushed her tears away with my fingertips. "So, the two soldiers he confronted killed him?"

To my surprise, she shook her head. "No... I mean, yes, there was a brawl, but Thomas shot one of the men, killing him; and then, he and his friends ran off."

I wrinkled my brow. "Ran off? Then, how..."

"They brought him back... I mean, two of the Ordnungspolizei caught him and brought him back to the scene, before witnesses who saw the whole conflict. The other soldier identified him... and the man that Thomas was looking for, he had arrived. Turns out, the man Thomas shot was Rhen's best friend."

My heart sped up and I swallowed hard. "Rhen *was* there?"

"Yes," Aaron spouted. "And the bastard put his gun to Thomas's head and executed him right there on the sidewalk."

A lightning bolt shot through my body and bile filled my throat. I rushed to the kitchen sink and heaved up nothing but sadness and pain as Kitty came up behind me and patted me on the back.

"Thomas loved you, zeeskeit, you know he did."

"Rhen executed him?" I spat as I watched the saliva, tears and snot streaming from my face swirl in a circle down the drain.

"Your pain and your tears speak of your love for Thomas... it is natural. Let us not speak that Nazi's name in our house ever again. Damn him and damn all those black ravens!"

I spun around, grabbing her by the arms. "Hold your tongue; how dare you speak such words!"

She narrowed her eyes. "How dare I? How dare I not! You would defend the demons?"

I glanced over to Aaron and his mother who eyed us curiously. Lowering my voice, I answered her.

"Not defend, Kitty, but warn you against your words, for we all know that we live in a dangerous world of eavesdroppers and informants, even some we might not have thought. You know the Gestapo have far-hearing ears and we know of many friends who have vanished for speaking less. Besides, how do we know for sure the story is true? The Ordnungspolizei would give no thought to speaking lies and sullying Thomas's name while putting Rhen on a pedestal. I can't see how he could have been there."

"How would you know that?" She asked, her eyes searching mine.

I wiped my face with the kerchief and shrugged. "I mean, I don't know but you know those officers have more to deal with than menial brawls in the streets."

Kitty bit her bottom lip and quelled the tears puddling in her lower lashes. "You are right, Sis, I am sorry. I know I should bury my feelings else my anger might provoke my own actions against them all. Aaron is right in this regard, I think. Silence is prudent... but I still say, I don't want you saying his name around Mutter, especially now. This is a blow to her already fragile mind. Now, you go, speak to Aaron and his mother. I'm going to go check on her, and perhaps the thought of your wedding day will give some hope to her."

Kitty left the room, but I didn't want to talk to Aaron, especially not now when my heart was breaking. And I couldn't say a word to anyone. My secret weighed upon me like a bag of stones tied around my heart.

Aaron stood as I walked back up to the table and crossed my arms.

"Our wedding plans..." he started.

"Are delayed, of course," I finished. His brow creased and his lips narrowed in a line, displaying his displeasure.

"You must understand, Aaron," I continued. "Now, of all times, is not a time to talk about a wedding when my mother has just lost her son and I, a beloved brother."

"How long?" He asked.

I shrugged.

"You know," he said, setting his hands on his hips and frowning, "I am overlooking much by agreeing to still marry you after the little episode at the Moka. Thomas told me that he tried to find out what happened between you and that Nazi, but you refused to answer him. I can only assume your silence on the matter speaks volumes about secrets you wish not to reveal." He leaned forward. "Do you know what kind of reputation you might have if it got out of you fraternizing with a Nazi? Our wedding would put all rumors to an end... unless, of course, there is something you haven't told anyone."

Aaron's reticent mother stood next to him, linking her arm with his and coddling him as I tightened my crossed arms.

"Believe what you will, Aaron, but I will not be induced to give credence to rumors, and I will not be forced into a wedding in the midst of mourning. Either you wait, or we can end any agreement right here and now."

I saw his mother squeeze her fingers into his arm.

He gathered up his coat and hat and motioned her to the door.

As he closed the door, he paused for a moment and fixed one last stubborn stare my way.

"We wait, then, but know this, Julia; after you are my wife you will learn the ways of a true balabusta, a good homemaker such as your mother taught you to be, and one who shows proper respect to her husband in all things." He touched his finger to his lip. "With no backtalk."

The door closed and I sped back to my room, throwing myself face down onto the bed, the tears raging from my soul and muffling into the downy pillow. I curled my fingers into a fist and cuffed the mattress.

"Why? Why? Why?" Each outburst with another punch.

"Oh, Thomas, my dear brother... and yet, my stupid brother; and my darling husband... and yet, now my mortal enemy. Oh God, my thoughts are mangled inside. Thomas would have killed Rhen, so Rhen killed Thomas. If Rhen had not killed Thomas, he would be dead. Happiness and sadness in one fell swoop, eternally combined and now I fear I will never see my husband again in this lifetime. How can he want to see me, the sister of the man he murdered? And how can I want to see him, the murderer of my brother? But there has to be something more to this story, something is missing, and I would know that before I fix the rest of my days in widowhood and sorrow. But how?"

A ping vibrated the window pane, again, and again. Pulling back the lace curtain from my window, another small pebble flew against the glass. My heart leapt and I threw open the sash, praying that when I ran to the edge of the balcony that I might see my husband's face.

Looking down, a man's face peered around the trunk of one of the oak trees in the garden. He waved to me and I shimmied down the lattice and vines overlooking the portico.

"Psst," he whispered from the shadows.

When his face came into view, I recognized him as one of the boys who taunted Rabbi Hersch in the street not so long ago.

"I'm Bernie," he said. "Rhen's cousin and friend."

I nodded but kept cautious and hidden from his view for fear of those suspicions I raised with Kitty in the kitchen about informants and spies. He noticed my apprehension and continued without me saying a word.

"He sent me here to check on you, and to offer his explanation of what happened today between him and your brother." Bernie cleared his throat. "I was there, Fraulein, and my cousin had no choice, you see. Your brother, Thomas, broke the law. He murdered a soldier of the Wehrmacht and there were many witnesses to the act. Rhen, your husband, had every right... but he knows that that cannot offer any consolation to you in your grief. He understands if you never want to see him again, and bid me tell you that he is being sent away on a special assignment."

I took a breath, my answering rattling across the tearful lump in my throat. "When?"

"Almost immediately. He said if you have any message for him that your former plans will continue, to send word through me but only if you wish it."

"And he trusted you with this secret? You, a vowed member of the Nazi party whose sworn allegiance is to Hitler only, and who has vowed to report any treasonous activity?"

He shrugged. "He is my cousin, Fraulein, and even if this party comes and goes, he will remain my cousin."

I smiled at his words, and the sincerity in his eyes offered a small bit of comfort and trust. Sliding the chain over my neck, I opened the clasp and slid my wedding ring onto my palm, and held it out to him.

"Then, tell my husband our plans still remain. Tell him I will wait for him on the roof where he can put this ring back on my finger."

8

Julia

November 9, 1938

The tension in our house was palatable, not just inside, but the chilled night air outside filled with premonition. Mutter went to bed early, and Kitty curled next to her as her muffled sobs into the pillow continued. I left them alone, peeking once inside and whispering a *"guten tag"* and *"eich liebe dicht"* to them both before closing the door. Just one more hour now and Rhen, hopefully, will meet me on the rooftop... and our life will begin, away from all the sadness and madness of the world around us. Touching my fingers to my pulsing heart and looking at Thomas's closed bedroom door, I wondered how our conversation might go. *How was I to forgive Rhen? How might I forgive Thomas?*

"Thomas put himself in harm's way," I whispered to myself. "Rhen had no choice..." *or did he?*

Swallowing hard, I eased down the hallway and removed a small mattress roll Mutter kept in the closet for guests. The dusty dank smell filled my nostrils, a familiar scent conjuring memories of the times Papa carried it over his shoulder when we picnicked in Tiergarten. He said the size was perfect for even a man his size, which was considerable, and the down-filled contents provided a most comfortable and convenient bed for a good nap beneath the golden

German sun. Mutter always shook her head and protested, saying he might help with the food, but Papa always prevailed. Those were happy times... Kitty splashing her feet in the fountain, Thomas floating a paper boat, the splotchy shadows playing along the sidewalk as families laughed, dogs barked, and the image of Papa resting his head on Mutter's lap while he lounged on the unfurled mattress; all brought a smile to my face.

Slipping back into my room, I changed into my cotton nightgown and slippers, put on my wool coat, and tied the bedroll with a thick blanket over my back with the belt of my robe, and eased out of the window. The ascent to the building's roof from the portico balcony was easy enough, at least, to me; after all, I had done it so many times I probably could have climbed in my sleep. Plus, being tucked in an unused corner between our building and the next, the tangling vines hid the ladder from view. I felt sure no one even knew of its existence any more. Once I reached the top, six stories above Berlin, I caught my breath and dropped the mattress onto the roof. From this height, silence reigned over the city, except for the muted hum of distant cars passing along the street and a vast velvet canopy of stars along with a spying crescent moon.

I dragged the mattress to a dark corner, unrolled the roll, tucked myself beneath the blanket, and scanned the mesmerizing sky.

"This night, my life begins with the moon as my faithful witness," I whispered and my heart raced, anticipating Rhen's arrival.

"Yes." I heard a voice speak from the shadows.

My heart leapt and I gasped. "Rhen?"

He showed himself in the moonlight, hands tucked inside his trench coat and tears filling his eyes. I held my hands out to him, but he looked away.

"How can you even look at me now?"

"I love you, my husband," I answered back. He bit his lip and ripped off his coat and hat, tossing them aside as he fell down next to me and took my face in his hands. Our kisses devoured each other, and I tasted the salty tears on his cheeks.

'No more tears, my darling Rhen... you are alive, that is all there is at this moment. If not he, then you. Thomas made his own fate... as we will make ours. I forgive you."

He buried his face in the crook of my neck, his fingers tangling in my hair. "Dear God, take away this pain. I am so sorry, my love, so very sorry..."

I quieted him with more kisses and we laid back on the mattress, entwined in each other, and watched the moon peek from behind the clouds. Breathing deep the clean scent of Onalkali schaumpon in his blonde hair, and Kitty's lavender parfum that I spritzed behind my ears, I pulled him close.

"Rhen, tonight we are no longer those people. We can let it all go and begin anew. Yes, I will miss my brother terribly, but perhaps I might be sitting on my bed grieving your death instead, with no one to tell." I pulled his face to mine, looking him in the eyes. "Believe me when I say I forgive you. Germany has gone mad. I cannot fault you for mistakes made... if it was a mistake. It was, wasn't it, Rhen? I mean, you did not mean to kill him, right?"

"No," he replied back. "I did not mean to kill him... just, Max was dead... and the song in my head..."

"Shhhh," I whispered, closing his eyes with my kisses.

"Look," I said into his ear. "The moon is waning gibbous tonight. Do you know what that means?" He shook his head against my cheek. "My Aunt Gerta, she is an Hasidic Jew who studied Kabbalah, and the mazalot, or the study of the stars, means a great deal to her. She is, or was, my shadchanit, my matchmaker, and told me that on the night of a waning moon, I would find my true love."

I sat up next to him, easing the red Nazi armband down his arm, and slowly unbuttoning his black jacket as I spoke, all the while neither of us unlocked our gaze.

"You see," I continued. "Hasidics believe in the spiritual over the physical. This Nazi jacket, this armband, means nothing." I balled up the band and tossed it to the shadows. "When the two are unified, when you cannot tell where one begins and the other ends, the uniting reveals God's hidden power, the perfection desired by him." I lifted his hand to my breast, his palm over my throbbing heart, and I eased my hand inside his starched white unbuttoned shirt. My fingers warmed against his bare chest.

He sat up and released himself from the constraints of his SS uniform, while kissing my ear and following my lead. "You kiss by the book, then, my sweet Juliet. Thus, from my lips, by thine, my sin is purged."

He laid me back, brushing the hair back from my brow. "Then have from my lips the sin that they have took."

He smiled and held his mouth near mine, so close our breath mingled. "Sin from my lips?" He asked. "O trespass sweetly urged! Give me my sin again."

As the moon slid behind a cloud, darkness enveloped us, we succumbed... a man and woman... no labels... no hate... only love.

Deep in the night, our bodies still warm from passion, and Rhen fast asleep with his cheek pressed against my breast, a sudden chill raced down my spine.

A gun shot pierced the air. *And was that shattering glass?*

"Rhen," I whispered, trying to stir him with a nudge.

He wrapped his arms and legs around me, pulling me closer beneath the blanket.

"Rhen," I said, again. "I think I hear something from the streets."

A scream followed, along with more shattering glass.

"It is nothing," he mumbled. "Nothing for us to worry about. We are far away from it all... the pogroms do not mean anything to us."

"The pogroms?" I said, sitting up. "What do you mean, my love?"

He tried to pull me back down, but my thoughts flew to my mother and sister inside the apartment.

"Rhen, you have to tell me what is happening."

He sighed and brushed his fingers through his hair, his eyes now wide open as he tucked his hands behind his head as a pillow.

"My father received a telegram today, as did all of the SS officers, from Herr Heydrich. Summing it up, he said the following orders must be carried out without delay – all synagogues burned, stores and residences of Jews destroyed but not looted, taking care not to damage non-Jewish businesses or property. Polizei are not to intervene, only to supervise, and fire departments are not to put out any blazes unless Aryan properties are in danger; and all relics and documents from synagogues and offices are to be reprimanded to the offices of the SD. All healthy Jewish males from 18 to 65 are to be arrested and sent to Dachau, Sachsenhausen, or Auschwitz as soon as possible."

His words electrocuted my blood, sending fire through my veins, and yet, disbelief throbbed in my brain. "Wha... what do you mean?"

He sat up and wrapped his arms around my shoulders, caressing my back with his fingertips. "Do not worry, my love, you are in the safest place in all of Berlin at this moment. I will not let anything harm you, I promise."

Another scream. A cacophony of yelling. More glass.

I looked up at the once peaceful night sky, a night when my heart found a home, and realized Rhen and I were two lost souls in a small boat desperate not to capsize in this maelstrom. With the stars as our witness, the clouds gathered and wept over us... a soft misty rain.

+++++

Rhen

Fear reigned in Julia's eyes. Just an hour ago, they twinkled with ecstasy, with uninhibited passion drowning in our love. *Now, what do I do? What can I do?* Even as I declared my vow to protect her, I see the doubt lingering in her eyes.

She stood up, drawn by a orange glow lighting up the night sky, haloing over the tops of the buildings in the distance. *Perhaps it is the Fasanenstrasse synagogue... or even Neue, but what does it matter? What's done cannot be undone.*

She pulled away from me as I said those words out loud and walked to the edge of the apartment building, wrapped in her wool coat, her gaze fixed on the rising fire. Wrapping the blanket around my naked body, I came up behind her and encased us both with the blanket.

"What's done is done," she repeated, her words tinged with a tone that pained my heart.

"Do you regret marrying me now?" I whispered in her ear.

She turned towards me, resting her head against my chest. "Regret? No, I have no regrets. Only, I fear for my family, Rhen... and my friends. My cousins, Samuel and Gregory, what will happen to them if they are arrested? And *why* are they arrested? Is it now against the law to be a Jew? I knew Nazis hated us, but to go this far?"

My body tensed at her last question, still I remained silent. Her body reacted in kind, and she looked up into my face.

"Do you hate me, Rhen?"

"No."

"But I am a Jew."

"No," he replied. "You are my wife. Do you hate me?"

"No," she said. "You are my husband. But what are we to do? My mother and my sister... my cousins... am I to do nothing to protect them now that I am your wife?" She clung to me, seizing my arms, her eyes pleading. "You can help them, Rhen; I know you can."

"I can help *you*, Julia. I can help *us*. Remember, I said there is a way we can escape Berlin... or rather, you can escape and you must do it tonight. My father is sending me tomorrow morning to the SS Officer's training camp near Dachau, along with all the prisoners taken tonight."

Her body slackened and a tear rolled down her cheek. "But I thought... you cannot save them? And I must leave them here tonight?"

"You have to trust me, Julia. Once you are away from Berlin and you are safe, and I meet up with you, there is a better chance we can get them out."

She managed a small smile and I wiped away the tear with the tip of my forefinger.

"I do trust you, my love," she replied. "What do we do?"

Another pop of gunfire tatted through the air and Julia shivered. Our eyes followed the eerie silhouettes of a group of men running down the street, pausing at the corner and raising their hands towards Appelbaum's grocer. The bright discharge from their guns popped the darkness. We both jumped as the pane glass windows of the store exploded in shards, and the group rushed away, their laughter echoing up to our ears.

Julia ran back to the mattress and collapsed in a heap, her sobs muffled in her hands.

"Why?" she cried. "Why does Hitler hate us so? What did we do?"

I curled next to her and pulled her close. I had no answers, not for her... nor for me. Cupping my hands around her jaw, I lifted her face, wiping her tears with my thumbs.

"Listen to me, Julia. You must listen to what I am about to tell you. This must happen exactly as I tell you; do you understand?"

She nodded as I pulled her tight against me.

"You must go to the Englische Kirche zu St. George near Monbijou Park; do you know it?"

She nodded again as our pulsing heartbeats thrummed in unison.

"You must find the pastor, Heinrich Grüber, and tell him that you need help to immigrate to Switzerland."

"But why would he help me? There has to be hundreds who are desperate to escape."

I hesitated. "Tell him... tell him that if he does not, that Herr Montabauer will pay him a visit before the day is out." She flinched, but I held her tight. "Make sure to use your married name on the documents, but it must be a new name... our new name to begin our new life. What shall it be, Julia? You decide."

Her eyes lit up and she looked to the stars. "Montague... no, Montag. Rhen and Julia Montag."

As the dawn pinked the horizon and the smell of ash permeated the soft morning air, we succumbed again to the fear and passion surging through our hearts and bodies. Tears. Passion. Urgency. As if we might never see the next day bold, bright, and exposing our night's secrets; as if we might never see each other again... and the thought ripped our souls.

I collapsed next to Julia, both of us gasping for air as our hearts calmed. She caressed her fingers across my chest, sending goose flesh tingling across my stomach.

"Look, love," she whispered. "What envious streaks do lace the severing clouds in yonder east. Night's candles are burnt out, and jocund cay stands tiptoe on the misty mountain-tops. I must be gone and live, or stay and die."

"More light and light, more dark and dark our woes," I continued.

We both got up and dressed, somber and sad, wishing we might spend eternity on this rooftop, high above all the chaos in Berlin, in our own clouds, tucked near the stars.

I abhorred putting the SS black jacket back on, and the red armband, but Julia held it open for me with a smile and a nod.

"When you have your papers, I'll send word to you of where we are to meet with enough money for you to get to Switzerland, where we will meet up."

I kissed her hard, bruising my own lips, but I wanted the touch to linger as long as possible. "Please, promise me, Julia, that you will do exactly as I told you with no variations, and I will see you there."

She smiled and touched her fingers to her lips, her eyes watering. "I must hear from thee every day in the hour, for in a minute there are many days. O, by this count I shall be much in years ere I again behold my Rhen."

"I will omit no opportunity that may convey my greetings, love, to thee," I replied, echoing Romeo's words.

"Do you think we shall ever meet again?"

I narrowed my eyes. "Hush, Julia, don't ask that. We are the makers of our future and need not follow the fate of those star-crossed lovers."

"And y...yet," she stumbled, "I have an ill-divining soul for I fear Germany's Chancellor has other ideas for your wife. Methinks thou lookest pale, my love."

I swallowed the knot twisting in my throat. "And trust me, love, in my eyes so do you. Dry sorrow drinks our blood."

We kissed again, one last time before she climbed down the rusty ladder. With one last look up, one last blow of a kiss, she disappeared through her bedroom window.

9

Julia

November 10, 1938

Before Mutter and Kitty even rose, I was out the door, desperate to get to the church and plead my case to Herr Grúber. Rhen assured me that any mention of his father's name would send the man scrambling, so I used the time of walking from our apartment building to absorb the night's chaos lying in scattered pieces on the sidewalks. A muted fear permeated the air as feet shuffled quickly by, people's eyes darting away, pulling their coats tighter, afraid to gaze on the remains of the once bustling businesses. As I rounded the corner of Fredericksburg Strausse, the acrid smoky air burned the inside of my nostrils and I coughed into my hand as I gazed up to the once towering spire of Neue Synagogue. The smoke still billowed and gawkers stood with their hands on their hips, some wagging their heads, others applauding, while a teacher drove a gastle of school children past the smoldering ruins. I paused in the shadows to listen as she spouted the Nazi agenda into the innocent ears, inculcating the words into their brains. One of the beefier young boys, who looked no more than ten, picked up a rock and heaved it with all his might at one of the last remaining windows. Shouts of triumph along with 'tod für Juden' ensued from the gathering crowds, and my heart throbbed in confusion and disbelief.

Was this my Berlin shouting for Jewish death? The Berlin I adored?

The Berlin where I walked unafraid in the streets with my family only a few years ago? No, I fixed in my mind, *this is not my Berlin.*

While everyone kept their eyes on the fire, I turned towards the Englische Kirche zu St. George, eased open the door and tucked my hair beneath a scarf tied around my head. I walked to the center of the aisle, turning in a circle, my gaze following the patterns of light filtering through the stained glass window and over the rows of seats to the towering pained figure of Christ over the altar. I knew the church's history, as all in Berlin knew of her connection to the Crown Princess Victoria, the stained glass donated to the church by her British relatives, and the church built upon funds sent to Albert and Victoria upon their silver wedding anniversary. A sigh escaped my lips. *Now, there was a real romance, not one from storybooks,* my mind whispered. *A good omen that I stand here desperate for mine and Rhen's romance to survive and thrive.*

Yet, another thought taunted me. *Here I stand, a Jew in a Christian church, seeking escape;* a sudden fear enveloped me. *Wasn't Hitler a Christian? Doesn't Christ teach kindness and non-violence; or are the wrongs done in our history now visiting us as retribution?*

A shadow fell across the floor in front of me and a hand touched my sleeve.

"Miss? May I help you?"

I spun around to the kind eyes of a petite woman with mousy brown hair cinched in a bun, and dressed in a somber grey sheath dress; yet, if not for the strand of pearls looping twice around her pale neck, she might have blended into the very shadow she cast.

"Oh..." I stumbled, "I... well, I mean... I was wondering..."

She smiled and the genuineness in her face soothed my fears as she directed me towards a hallway.

"Come," she said, "perhaps you'd like to see Herr Grüber?"

I paused, the fear mounting again. "How... how did you know?"

She pointed to my necklace and my fingers enclosed the star of David hanging around my neck.

"Oh..." I said, wrinkling my brow. "I forgot I had it on."

She nodded and knocked on the door to the rectory. "And you might take care not to wear it out in public right now, dearest... I mean, for your own safety."

The door opened and a couple skirted past me, their arms linked and a small little girl clutching tight to her mother's skirts.

"Lilia?" I blurted.

The girl's mother looked over her shoulder, pressing the child closer as her husband grabbed hold of her arm.

"Julia?" Lilia's mother, Anna, replied, her eyes filling with questions. "You are leaving Berlin, as well? And your mother and sister?"

"Well," I hesitated, knowing any hint of my secret might ruin everything for Rhen and me. "Yes... I am here to see Herr Grüber, the same as you as it would seem. And you are set? You will be safe?" My eyes drifted down to Lilia's innocent smile.

Daniel, Anna's husband, patted the outside of his coat and the distinct sound of papers rustled beneath his touch.

"B'ezrat HaShem," I said with a smile, tussling Lilia's hair, praying in my heart that God would help us all on this journey. Anna leaned near to me, kissed me on the cheek, and they hurried through a side door.

"We have many who seek our help, and we are glad to offer our hand," the woman said, holding open the door.

I turned and peered into the dimly lit room, noting the small man leaning over a desk full of books and papers scattered in front of him.

The woman coughed into her hand and he raised his tired eyes, removed his wire-rimmed glasses and narrowed his eyes at me.

"Ah," he said in a hoarse voice, "I see you've met Laura. She is a godsend for the Bureau here. And you are?"

Laura directed me to sit, answering his question before I had a chance. "Another soul in need of our services, Herr Grüber."

"Just one?" He asked, scratching his forehead. "Most unusual. Do you not have any other family, Miss... Miss... sorry, it has been quite a morning already, especially after the events of last night. Did you tell me your name?"

"No, sir, I did not," I answered back, suddenly unsure if I was to give him my real or fake name. I took a breath and let the fake roll off my tongue.

"It is Julia Montag. I am needing a visa to Switzerland... Zurich; my cousin is ill, you see, and I need to..."

The man smiled, reached across and patted my hands that rested on the top of the desk. "Hush, now, no need for all that. We make no judgments about your reasons for leaving the city... we are here to lend a helping hand." He winked as he opened the drawer to his desk. "A Samaritan and a Jew, right? And I will show you the way to the Inn?"

The words fled from my mouth and I sat there, astounded, as he offered a package to Laura. She patted me on the back. "Be back in just a moment. Not to worry, Miss Montag; for a single person, the papers are a cinch. Do you have your identity papers with you? I will need those, as well."

I reached inside my coat and took out the small folder holding my identity papers, all branded with the official 'J' across the document. She took the packet and scurried out of the room.

Herr Grüber added as he wiped the glass of his spectacles with a dingy handkerchief, "She'll have that ready in no time at all; much harder for a family like the Sterns. That took a few days to arrange, but you... well, I think there is a train leaving for Zurich this evening from Anhalter Bahnhof, an overnight sleeping car for one Miss Julia Montag, German citizen, born in Hamburg, parents deceased, traveling to visit your cousin, Hilde; is this all correct?"

I nodded, yet the lie flushed my cheeks.

He patted my hands again. "Not to worry, my dear. Stick to your story; show your papers; keep your chin up. You will be there in no time at all."

A few minutes passed in silence as he shuffled through another stack of papers, humming some obscure little song in his throat, while my heart beat in time with the cuckoo clock on the wall. I jumped as the little bird sprang to life, tweeting nine times to announce the hour. Herr Grüber tapped his wristwatch and adjusted the pin on the side just as the door opened and Laura strode back in with a small packet.

"All done," she said and motioned me towards the door.

I stood and paused, my legs trembling as I glanced over my shoulder.

"Thank you, sir," I said.

"My pleasure," he replied, "and please let any others who might want to take a little trip this time of the year to come see me."

I must admit that as Laura led me to the side door to the alley, I was thankful I didn't have to use the threat that Rhen told me to use if he gave me any problems. The whole event was a 'cinch' as Laura said, and she gave me another wink as I exited through a narrow passageway which ran along the side of the rectory. The adjacent street buzzed with motorcars, bicyclists, and pedestrians all vying to maintain a facade of normality in the midst of chaos.

I emerged from the shadows, the sunlight peeking through the buildings, greeted by a array of red Nazi flags popping in the brisk foggy morning air, all cascading from each streetlight in a row down the sidewalk. I knew better than to stand still for long, for gawking always engendered suspicion, so I hurried along the avenues, taking as many back ways as possible to make it back home without raising any attention.

No luck. Just as I rounded the corner a block from my apartment building, a hand reached around my upper arm and snatched me into an dark alleyway.

I threatened to scream, but the stranger's fingers locked over my mouth, and his breath tickled through the hair over my ear.

"Hush, it's me; Bernie."

I relaxed and he let me go. "Bernie," I whispered as I tried to turn to face him. "You scared me near to death. I thought..."

"Yeah, well, you need to be scared. Don't turn around, and get back home as quick as possible. Rhen wants to know if you got what you needed."

I nodded, still hesitant about trusting him.

"And give me a clue so as I know you'll be getting on the train, something to recognize you in the crowd. He wants me to see you get on the train."

"A red suitcase," I replied. "I have a small red suitcase."

"Good, and before you get on the train, I'll slip a packet inside your coat pocket."

"All right. I will be there."

"Good luck," he answered back, and with that he hurried in the opposite direction, disappearing into the fog.

I took another breath and made haste to home. As I eased along the back alley of the building leading to the courtyard garden, two more figures morphed in front of me, blocking my way. A matchstick sparked in front of one of their faces, lighting up the eyes as the man lit a cigarette.

I pressed my hand to my heart and gasped.

"Samuel! Gregory! You're here... you're not..."

They both chuckled and looked around them, nervous as cats. "Arrested?" Gregory asked. "No, we slipped the noose, so to speak, and came to check on you, your mother, and sister."

Samuel leaned forward and narrowed his eyes at me. "But we never thought to catch you sneaking round out here. What are you doing out this early, especially after what happened last night?"

I shrugged, unable to come up with a quick reply, but they appeared not to notice my own nervousness, so I diverted the conversation.

"We are fine, but what of you two? You have to get out of the city."

They both chuckled again, and Samuel stomped his glowing cigarette into the dirt with the toe of his boot.

"No, we are staying right here, but we came to arrange for the three of you to get out. You see," he lowered his voice to a whisper, "Gregory and I joined up with Aaron as part of the resistance here in Berlin. We have connections, Julia, that can assist your escape from the city. What happened last night is only the beginning of the pogroms against the Jews, but we are determined to fight them all."

"Yeah," added Gregory, pounding a fist into his palm, "until they are dust."

My heart fluttered in fear for them both, for their words echoed my brother's sentiments, *and where did it get him? A quick grave.*

"I'm sure Mutter will listen to you both but I'm afraid getting her to leave her home is going to be near impossible."

"You must persuade her," another voice from the shadows added. Aaron came up from the side and slid his hand around my waist. "Besides," he said, "she will do anything once she knows we are married and all on our way to America."

"America?" I spouted as I pushed his arm off of me. "I'm not going to America... and especially not with you. Not now, not anytime."

"We can get you there," Gregory added. "There is a ship leaving from Frankfurt and Aaron has arranged passage for all four of you."

"Yes," he said with a smirk. "I'm leaving the resistance here in Berlin and I think it's time to protect my own family instead. Our whole family, Julia. Me, my wife, our mothers; documents and passage a gift from those working in the resistance in exchange for some my entail regarding movements here in the city. I still have a few connections to those in the party who view money as a greater reward over any loyalty to the little mustached man."

I rolled my eyes at his bravado, suspecting that his knees would quake if an SS officer appeared right now. He would most certainly fail at a match of swords betwixt he and Rhen. And then, his words dawned on me.

"But what about Kitty?"

"Kitty?"

"Yes, my sister. You didn't mention a ticket for her. Do you think I would leave my own sister?"

Aaron eyed my cousins and shrugged. "She doesn't know?"

"Know what?" I asked, the heat rising in my neck.

Samuel lit another cigarette. "Kitty is with us... she is part of the resistance. We have her working on some things here in Berlin, so we need her busy with other important things. She's proven to be incredibly skilled in her methods."

In truth, I wasn't shocked to learn of her involvement since she and Thomas often shared secrets which bound them in most things. I was always the younger third wheel who never fit into their carousing the dance halls till late in the morning. Still, the notion of leaving her... and then, I remembered the papers hidden inside my coat.

"No," I answered back. "I will not go. If Kitty stays, we all stay."

"But as my wife..." Aaron retorted.

I glared at him and moved toward the pergola lattice banked up against the side of the building. "I am not your wife, Aaron! Now, go, all of you, before someone sees you. I don't want any of you arrested."

Samuel grabbed hold of my ankle as I climbed, and I looked down. "Wait," he said, "one thing more, cousin. If you need us, leave us a note for us to find. If you need anything at all."

I nodded. "Where?"

He looked around and pointed to an abandoned bird house hanging from a tree limb in the garden. "There, but remember, it may take a few days for us to check so as to avoid suspicion."

"I understand," I replied as I climbed the lattice. With a last look down into the fog, the boys disappeared into the shadows.

Once I sat back down on my bed, the chill of the morning air tingled on my skin and I knew it was from more than the cold. Fear stuck to my soul and I wondered if I left tonight on the train, *what would happen to my mother and sister? Surely, Samuel and Gregory would still get them out, if need be. Yes, many were fleeing the city, but could things really get any worse? Worse enough for my mother to leave the only home she's known since Thomas was born?*

The aroma of coffee wafted into the air, Mutter watering down the little bit we still had, and the soft sound of her and Kitty's voice murmured from the other side of the door. Still, I sensed the tension in the indecipherable words. While they talked, I slid the small red suitcase from underneath my bed and stuffed a few necessities inside – just enough for a few days visit with my 'cousin' if I was searched along the way. I tucked the papers beneath my cotton nightgown, clicked the latches closed and set it next to my nightstand near the window. Quick and easy. All set.

A knock on the door broke my worried focus and I greeted Kitty with a smile as she peeked round the corner.

"Hey, sleepy head. Breakfast is ready. Mutter and I thought it best to let you sleep in since everything that has happened last night." She sat down beside me and wrapped her arm over my shoulder, pulling me to her. "How are you, sis?"

I shrugged, never looking into her face; the red suitcase within my sight filled my heart with more trepidation.

She kissed my cheek, the lavender perfume she wore emanating from her hair and reminding me of last night in Rhen's arms. My cheeks flushed with the memory.

"Are you all right?" She asked, trying to catch my gaze.

"It's all just too much, Kitty... you know? First, Thomas... and with Aaron's pressure to marry... I... I... just can't find the strength to move forward."

Kitty nodded and stood, walking to the window and pushing back the curtains to gaze out across the balcony.

"Yes, I know what you mean but things will be different soon. I am looking into some things. You will see. Once you and Aaron are married... and once I..."

"When were you going to tell me about your involvement in the resistance?" I interrupted.

Her shoulders tensed, still she kept looking forward. With a sigh, she answered. "I wondered if Samuel and Gregory spoke to you... or was it Aaron last night after I went to check on Mutter?"

"It was all three," I replied. "Kitty, Mutter will be devastated if she knows you are part of the same group as Thomas. His actions cost him his life... how do you think she will survive if the same thing happens to you?"

She shot a glance over her shoulder, her eyes cold and distant.

"No, his actions did not cost him his life. He died at the hands of a monster. They are all monsters, Julia, and deserve to be destroyed. And you are not too young to know what kind of world Germany is becoming. Just this morning, on the radio broadcast, it was announced that Jews can no longer leave our area without a permit, and our property is confiscated. All of it now belongs to the State to do with as they please. The world needs to be rid of Nazis."

I bit my lip, choosing my next words with care. "But, Kitty, aren't there ones who are working with you? Which means there are some good people inside who hate what is being done."

She tossed her head back with a laugh. "Sure, but if they are true Nazis with loyalties to that vile man, they will never waiver in their feelings. Those who help us do so without facing the consequences of their actions... they hide in plain sight instead of facing the bully with raised fists. Cowards... all of them."

"Maybe they are just afraid," I offered.

"Yes," she said, turning towards me and crossing her arms. "Afraid of losing their precious German citizenship."

"Or their life," I added. "What might you do to save your life, Kitty? To protect your family's life?"

The silence after my question thickened and she turned back to the window, the toe of her pointed pumps bumping the suitcase. Her eyes darted from it to my face.

"Going somewhere?" she asked.

I smiled, trying to appear unnerved by her question, stood and picked up the case, sliding it under my bed. She grabbed the handle and we tugged back and forth, her eyes narrowing as my own widened. In the struggle, the case burst open, scattering my clothes and the packet of papers falling at Kitty's feet. As I scrambled to grab them, she snatched them away and opened the folder, her mouth gaping open.

"Ah, so my little sister is not so innocent to the things happening, after all. Where did you get these?"

I gritted my teeth and snatched them back from her. "None of your business, besides if you are so well informed then you should know who is helping Jews get papers to leave Berlin."

She cocked her head, her eyes studying my face. "So, Aaron got you the papers? You've agreed to go with him? He didn't tell me that he already got the papers to you and, to be honest, I am surprised he chose to trust you with the documents. He is quite the sergeant when it comes to such matters but I know he will protect you." She paused and her eyes darted back and forth, a habit she had when thoughts swarmed her mind. She leaned back on a heel, examining me and I avoided her stare. "Ah, I see. I understand. These are not from Aaron, are they? My little sister has plans of her own. And you would leave us behind?"

Anger surged in my heart and I fixed my eyes on her face, clutching the suitcase as I sat back down on the bed. "Leave you behind? Aren't you the pot calling the kettle black? Aaron said you were staying behind to help with the resistance instead of coming with me and mother on the ship to America... so, it appears you have your own selfish agenda. I had plans to get you and mother out once I left. What about you? Are Mutter and I even part of your resistance activities?"

She chuckled and fiddled with the necklace around her slender neck. "Ah, you've caught me, I suppose. Samuel, Gregory, and Aaron assured me they would help you escape, so I never worried about it. Seems we are not so different, you and I; are we?" She looked down at the suitcase with an indistinct look I could not read. "Yes, we are very much alike, and I am just now realizing that about my dear little sister."

Her face lightened and she bounded near me, kissing the top of my head. "Mutter always said that, you know, that we were more alike than in just our looks."

She winked at me as she opened the bedroom door. "Don't do anything just yet, Sis, besides if you are anything like me, you'll want to do things at just the right moment without bringing too much attention to yourself. Now, come to breakfast; I am starving."

The door closed and my gaze glued to the floor. *What did she mean? Had she figured out everything? Was she thinking of my encounter with Rhen at the Moka? Did she link the clues now appearing so stark and revealing as the blue threads in the Persian carpet covering my floor?* Fear gripped my empty stomach, wondering if she might block me from leaving.

What do I do?

Breakfast was a somber event filled with forks scraping across our plates, shoving the eggs around and tearing the toast in bites to soak up the runny yellow. I spent more time sipping the watery coffee, peering over the rim to watch Mutter and Kitty's faces and trying to decipher my sister's words from earlier. Zarah Leander's song lilted on the air around us as Mutter mouthed the words in a quiet whisper.

"*Ich weiss, es wird einmal ein Wunder geschehen.*" She spat a huff. "One day a miracle will come? With all that is happening, that seems like a dream."

"The propaganda of fools," Kitty hissed.

Mutter rose from her chair, set her still full plate on the counter, clicked off the radio and turned to us.

"Neither of you are to go out today, do you understand? The restrictions on *usud* are mounting, and I will not lose another one of my children to these assaults." Tears flowed down her cheeks as she reached for a handkerchief in her apron pocket. Blowing her nose and dabbing the tears, she lifted her chin and spoke, her chin trembling.

"Your father abandoned us and I fear he is going to take further measures against all of us to ensure we are no longer connected to him in any way. I received a note, you see, this morning. He wants us permanently out of his life."

"But we are his blood," I replied, my fingers entwining in my skirt.

Kitty huffed. "And therein lies the problem. What does he want, for us to leave Berlin?"

"He doesn't say," Mutter replied. "But he indicated something is coming which will solve the problem." She paused, sipping her coffee, her fingers shivering. "I'm afraid for you, my daughters. Afraid for all of us."

Kitty stood up and wrapped her arms around Mutter's waist, squeezing her tight. "Trust me, Mutter, I will find a way to protect us. No matter what," she said firmly, glancing to me.

The rest of the day, the long fear-filled day, the three of us floated through the apartment like lost souls searching for answers to their quick demise. The radio clicked on and off with the passing of the hours, sometimes filling the room with sweet hope, and other times pounding our brains with patriotic vibrato. As the shadows crept across the living room floor, my night escapades weighed down my eyes with sleep and I lay across the living room sofa, dreaming of my 'Romeo' awaiting me in Switzerland.

10

Rhen
November 10, 1938

"She got on the train?"

"Yes."

"Tell me how it happened?"

Bernie sucked the last of his cigarette and flicked it onto the sidewalk, then gestured with his hands matching his words. "She came out of the ticket office and walked away from me down the platform. I slipped up behind her as she stepped up into the train car, whispered over her shoulder for her to have a safe trip, and slid the packet inside her pocket. Smooth as silk." He slapped me on the back and chuckled. "Not to worry, Rhen, my friend. All went just as we discussed. A couple of Gestapo guarding the platform gawked at her, nodding to me and smiled, saying what a looker she was with that red lipstick. I never got a good look at her face, but she carried the red suitcase in her hand as our signal."

A chill ran down my spine. "Red lipstick?" I couldn't imagine Julia wearing red lipstick and wondered how she even managed to get her hands on that shade nowadays... but, of course, her brother worked for the resistance who had their hands in the black market, as well. Shaking off the strange premonition, I reached out a hand to Bernie.

"Thank you, friend, for helping us."

"Sure. Anytime." He scrubbed his foot through the rocks as we stood outside the headquarters. "So, what will you do now, Rhen?"

I looked toward the doors, watching as a group of eager, back-slapping devotees dressed in their new black uniforms strode past us. "What can I do? I must leave for Dachau on my father's orders. I've already talked to him this morning. A transport of one hundred prisoners leaves in an hour and I have to make sure they arrive on time. What about you?"

Bernie's brow wrinkled and he hesitated. "I've joined the Waffen. They are sending me to Austria with a new pogrom against all Romi."

I had heard the whispers in the food hall. The purity of the Aryan race now extended further with the plebiscite in Austria, the referendum ratifying the Austrian Auschluss merging the country into a province of Ostmark, thus becoming part of Germany. With each passing day, Hitler's dream bloomed while the ordinary fellow's hopes, like mine and Bernie's, burned away like fog in sunlight. Still, knowing Julia was now bound for Switzerland filled my heart and strengthened me towards my goal of securing a way to get to her.

"Parting is such sweet sorrow," I whispered, remembering her face as she descended the ladder just last night.

Bernie laughed. "Verflix, Rhen, I didn't know how much you cared."

We both chuckled, but the underlying current of the unknown future tainted any true joviality.

Bernie shook my hand and smiled. "Take care, my friend, and viel Glück. We'll drink a beer together after all this craziness is over."

I shook his hand, squeezing and holding it for a moment. "Promise me."

"I promise," he replied, dropping my hand and seizing into a rigid, right-arm salute of 'Heil Hitler'.

The ride on the train reminded me again of Julia's own train perhaps nearing the border by now and crossing the Alps. While her journey led to life and hope, mine led to death and hopelessness, at least for the poor souls who huddled together in a shivering mass in the cattle cars attached to our posh officer's car. While we sipped brandy, they strained their necks like little birds towards the rain droplets dripping through the filthy cracks in the ceiling.

Before the doors closed I scanned their faces while standing their with a baton under my armpit. I had no intention of using it to crack some skulls but tapping the shaft against my palm produced the needed fear in their eyes. These were 'political prisoners' as they were labeled, extremists against the Wehrmacht, unworthy beings whose breath must not mingle with Aryans. And here I stood, overseeing this offensive ideal.

But what do I do? Shall I join them in the cattle car and give up any chance to be with my love? No, I shall do what I must to survive, and when all of this is over, Julia and I will forget all of this.

The midnight moon eased out from behind the clouds witnessing all of us barking our orders at the men spilling from the cars when we arrived at the gates of Dachau. Used as a camp since opening in 1933, the abandoned munitions factory was expanded and surrounded with barbed wire and guard towers to house all those deemed enemies of the Reich. The lattice iron gates of the Jourhaus opened wide like a starving succubus ready to suck dry the blood of these latest victims and we, her conspiratorial hellions, prodded them towards their doom. I flinched as I tried not to look in their eyes as they moved forward in the darkness, everyone one of them passing by her branded motto of 'Albeit Macht Frei', knowing what type freedom awaited them - death.

Others relished the job, one in particular, a fellow SS trainee named Hans, another SS-Unterstrumführer like me, who thrived upon torture... and not just physical torture, but the mental torture of slowly extracting hope from a brain. He nudged me in the side as the men shuffled past.

"Look at them... so confused about what lay beyond those gates. Schnell," he shouted. He chuckled and nudged me, again. "Watch this."

He grabbed hold of one of the prisoners and stood him in front of me. With a wide menacing smile, he leaned near to the prisoner's ear and hummed a tune, adding words to the melody.

"Lieber Herr Bott, mach mich stumm, Das ich nicht nach Dachau komm." He leaned forward holding his hands on his knees, the laughter erupting from his throat, then rising up to the man's ear again. "It did not work, did it, you pig?"

Two more officers joined him, their voices ringing out to the stars. "Dear God, make me dumb, that I may not to Dachau come." The men rolled with laughter, while I stood stoic, looking deep into the man's eyes. There in the black hollows, hope slipped away and his face paled as we both heard the slicing crack of a whip punctuating the ground behind his feet.

Pop; the first stroke of the whip in Hans' hands slashed across the man's back, and the coppery taste of blood spraying on my lips reminded me of the day I shot Thomas. Before anyone could see the film of water glazing over my eyes, I turned away from the 'welcome beating' and marched alongside the thousands pouring out of the trains into hell.

"You are late," seethed Eiche, as all of us new arrivals stood at attention before the formidable Kommandant. His reputation preceded him, and my father schooled me on his temper and his tactics, thinking I might learn to be more of a man under his tutelage. That was the purpose of the Dachau "school" - to educate us in violence and masculine indoctrination which reflected the ideal SS officer. This was another attempt by my father to rid me of any romantic weak leanings in my personality. So, as a means to an end, I knew how to play the game. I lifted my chin as Eiche strode past me, spouting his mantra which we had all heard through rumors and whispers told over a mug of beer.

"I will not tolerate any minor infractions," he continued. "You were sent here to rise to the level expected from our Führer and Dachau is the touchstone by which all other camps will look to for guidance and example. Gunter, step forward."

Another man took a stiff goosestep forward and stood at attention, his gelled blonde-hair falling forward over his emotionless eyes.

"This is Gunter; he is part of the Kommandantur, whom you will know by the K on the right shoulders of their uniforms, and you five will join the ranks with your new assignments in these folders. Gunter, if you please."

The man issued us each new uniforms and a packet informing us of our new position. All the others, especially Hans who gained the rank of block leader due to his notorious and much discussed thirst for brutality, buzzed with excitement and smiles. My packet remained closed as I chose to read my 'sentence' in private; however, Eiche had other plans.

He stood in front of me and scowled.

"Your father is Standartenführer Montabauer at the Sicherheitsdienst in Berlin, assistant to Herr Hess, is he not?"

"Yes, sir, he is."

"Hmmm," he said, scratching his chin. "And I suppose you think you deserve special treatment with such lofty connections?"

"No, sir, I do not."

Eiche smiled, which appeared as an infrequent visitor to his mouth, more so on the line of sinister instead of endearing. "Good... good... since we plan on keeping you under our watchful eye in our offices here at the headquarters. Montabauer told me to make sure you return to him a man worthy of wearing the black."

He walked back to the center of the room, clasping his hands behind his back, and finished his speech.

"Here you represent the Dachau spirit, the authority and the power of the Reich, and while I appreciate your boldness in administering the traditional 'welcome', Herr Jäger, we ask for a more discreet method of Prügelstrafe, a flogging administered for transgressions of camp rules. However," he said, raising a finger along with another snaky grin, "I might grant some latitude in terms of the degree of offense... after all," he chuckled, "these are not humans we are dealing with; are they?"

His derisive joke turned my stomach, but the rest in the room broke out in laughter and applause. After another twenty minutes of filling our heads with the height, breadth, length, and width of the rules and the camp layout, the pain in my head matched the nausea in my stomach. After he dismissed us, I sank down onto my cushy bed in my own private room, covered my eyes with my forearm and cursed myself. That bullet into Thomas's brain brought me here. I might still be wandering Tiergarten, oblivious to the Nazi cloud blackening the sky while my mother's pleading words to my father kept me from any real party involvement. My own actions brought me here, and now I must dance to the approved Nazi tune else I might not ever see Julia again.

11

Julia

November 11, 1938

My eyes fluttered open and I realized I was still on the couch in the living room. Sitting up, I shook the confusion in my brain and tried to gain a little clarity. The side table lamp was off, and since there was no window to the outside from the living room, I wasn't sure if it was morning or night. My heart leapt and my gaze flew to the mantel clock. Three o'clock. *Morning? Evening? Surely I had not slept long since I only fell asleep right after lunch. I have an hour till the train leaves... and I must check on Mutter and Kitty.*

I walked down the hallway, stopping at my mother's door and peeking through the opening. She was already dozing, taking an afternoon nap like me. These trying times and grief sapped all of our energy. Standing there for a moment, I thought to wake her and give her a hug goodbye, wondering if I would ever see her again.

Stop it, I whispered, *Samuel and Gregory will get her out, and if not, Rhen promised once we are in Zurich that he will arrange everything. And Kitty has means now, too. She has a better chance to get her out than I do... and we will all meet up... in America? I wonder what Rhen might think of going to America?*

I smiled at my mother and blew a kiss, easing the door shut, then turned to Kitty's door. Raising my hand to knock, I hesitated. *No,* I said, *blow her a kiss and be on your way, just as Rhen said.* Still, I tried her doorknob. Locked; which was typical for my sister to maintain her privacy.

Tiptoeing down the hall to my room, I pushed on my door which was curiously open. My gaze darted to the opened window and the moonlight filtering through the fluttering lace curtains. Realization struck hard and I gasped. 3:00 at night, not the afternoon.

"No," I blurted, my hand covering my mouth. From the window, my eyes traced down, across the carpet to the spot where I left my red suitcase. My heart pounded against my ribs as I fell to my knees, searching beneath my bed for it or the papers. Clarity hit me full force, and a scream erupted from my throat. I ran to the window, and bolted out onto the balcony, echoing Kitty's name over and over again. A few lights from nearby apartments burst to life, and the tears poured as I crumpled to the ground.

Within moments, Mutter's hands reached round my shoulders, urging me back inside. Numbness enveloped me as she kissed my forehead, wiping away the wet strands of my hair from my cheeks.

"Hush, zeeskeit, what is it? Kitty is in her room. You must have had a nightmare."

I bolted up and grabbed her by the arms. "No, Mutter, she is gone."

Mutter smiled and shook her head. "No, I tucked her in myself. She is sleeping and I am surprised you didn't wake her with all your shouting."

"But my suitcase..." I replied, glancing again to the floor, hopeful I just missed it the first time. Still, gone.

Mutter wrinkled her brow. "What about your suitcase?"

How do I tell her? If I say anything about the suitcase she will wonder about my own plans for leaving... and what did it matter now. I failed in the instructions, sleeping right through the train's departure. My forged papers, gone forever, stolen by my sister, I was sure, along with all hopes of ever seeing Rhen again.

I pulled a bobby pin from my hair and ran to Kitty's door, praying she was, indeed, sleeping and that she had hidden the case in her room, thus the locked door. With the pin, I unlocked the door, pushed it open and rushed to the bed with Mutter following close behind. Flinging back the covers, my tears flooded again as three pillows fell to the floor which served as a decoy while she planned her theft and escape. I spun round, meeting Mutter's watering eyes.

"Gone!" I yelled.

Mutter steeled her chin and wrapped her hands round mine. "Hush, zeeskiet, and listen to me. I know where she is. She thinks that she and Thomas hid things from me but I am not a dummkopf; I know what they were doing. I know, too, what Samuel and Gregory are doing. They are trying to get us out, and your Aaron, too. He is such a good man and will make you a fine husband when you are all out of the city."

I snatched my hands from her, the pain of not being able to tell her about Rhen ripping through my body. "I'm not marrying Aaron, Mutter. How can you even bring that up right now? And what do you mean, when we are out of the city? What about you?"

She slacked down onto the bed and sighed. "Oh, no, Julia, I'm not going anywhere. I must stay here, you see. This is my home; Berlin is my home... I am too old to start fresh. I will be all right, you will see. When all of this is over, perhaps your father will come home..."

I eased down next to her, realizing my mother's losses matched my own so I wrapped my arms around her and we sat there sobbing against each other's shoulders.

What more could I do? Rhen was far away at Dachau... perhaps on his way to Switzerland by now. Kitty was gone, Thomas was dead, my own father abhorred me, and we were caged into the assigned district of Berlin with our rights absconded at the word of our Chancellor. Adrift on the black Nazi sea.

Neither of us slept for the rest of the night. I wrestled with my covers while Mutter strode back and forth from her room to the kitchen, the sound of her flopping bedroom shoes echoing down the hollow hallway. When the sun finally announced a new day through my window, I curled up into a ball and released soft tears into my pillow. My mind haunted me with dangerous thoughts.

My life is over. I might as well be a widow. I might as well be dead.

12

Time sped away from us for the next two years, the same drudgery day after day of standing in ration lines and avoiding confrontations with the Gestapo, and our personal liberties snatched away. I watched my mother transform into a waifish ghost – pale with soulless eyes, her hope dissipating with each swing of the clock's pendulum. She even gave up the tradition of touching her fingers to the mezuzah as she entered the apartment.

As for me, the empty hollowness of life without Rhen ate into my very bones. I considered going back to the priest to get more fake documents but without knowing where to meet Rhen in Switzerland, the attempt was pointless... not to mention, I walked around our confined area in Berlin without any identity papers to speak of anymore, which I knew put me in a very dangerous position. With no way to send word to Rhen, with no word from Kitty, and hope fading that Samuel and Gregory were still alive, the days drifted by without meaning and I took to cloistering myself in the apartment for fear of the Gestapo stopping me and asking me for my papers. I had no idea why I never heard from Rhen, if he ever reached Switzerland and found me absent, and wondered if the folly of our marriage was now the joke he told among his fellow officers. Just like my father.

Sometimes in my dreams I saw him throwing back a mug of stout with a hearty laugh as he whispered to Hitler about his fling with a

Jewish witch who put a spell on him. Always, Hitler slapped him on the back and assured him that he would handle all the 'Judenschwien' by putting a bullet in their brain. Inevitably, the nightmare recurred over and over, of Rhen standing in front of Thomas with the gun to my brother's head, jarring me awake as the hammer released and the bullet tore into my heart instead.

Our lives changed in ways we never imagined, and I feared this was only the setting of the sun. More darkness awaited us all. After the night of broken glass - the night of passion I spent in Rhen's arms, and the night of unleashed Nazi passion against the Jews – my family ripped apart even further. We eventually received word that the Gestopo arrested Aaron, Samuel and Gregory during their attempt to fight the destruction of some of our neighborhood's Jewish businesses. Their meager blows melted like snowflakes in a squall, and they all three ended up at the Sauschenhausen Camp as enemies of the State. When the word came of their ultimate execution, I had already prepared my mind and heart. My mother, however, sank further into an unimaginable chasm of grief. One by one, our family disappeared, and she turned to clinging to me like a frightened kitten.

Even during our solitary moments of eating a couple of slices of hard toast as another day broke, she'd reach across and grip my hand as if I, too, might disappear in front of her eyes. I tried as best as I could to reassure her with a feigned smile, yet, in truth, I had no idea of either of us escaping this with our own lives intact.

And Aaron's mother wasn't any different. Without Aaron's strength at her side, she crumpled under the weight of the Nazi shadow.

With our finances dwindling to pittance since the Gestapo seized all of our property, and my mother too weak to work at one of the assigned factories, my own paycheck from the work at the Jewish hospital was barely enough to survive on. We agreed, then, for Aaron's mother, Hannah, his grandfather Moshe, his brother-in-law Reuben and sister Elena, along with their twin daughters, Danka and Gerta, to move in with us to alleviate the expenses. My mother gave her room up to Hannah and moved in with me. Moshe took Thomas's old room, and the rest huddled together in Kitty's room.

For a while, having other people around, those we knew and those whose hope still burned in their eyes despite the initial shocks of loss, was a blessing. Yet, the longer the oppression lasted and the tighter the grip squeezed around our necks, the sparkle in all of our eyes faded to a dull blank wide-eyed stare revealing the fear building in our hearts.

Any remaining flicker burned out when we heard the news that Germany invaded Poland, and the following whispers from some of our Jewish neighbors of the horrors many Polish Jews experienced in the camps at Auschwitz and Dachau.

Dachau. The very word sent shivers up my spine as I imagined Rhen at the forefront with his machine gun rat-a-tat-tatting against the Jews corralled there out of the cattle cars. Still, my mind lingered back to our vows, and his promises to never again raise his gun to take a life. *Yet, why had he not written to me? Did they send him to the front? Is he unable to write? Is he injured... or worse, is he dead?*

And in all my questions and fears, I could say nothing to no one, and with us basically imprisoned in our apartment building, I had no hopes of finding Bernie to send Rhen a message. More than likely he discovered I was not in Switzerland and concluded that I could not escape with the murderer of my brother, after all; when, in truth, I wanted to shout from the rooftops of my love for him, echoing all the way to Dachau that I trusted him and that I waited for him, still. My love grew stronger with each absent day, and the burden of not being able to speak about it singed my heart, burning my insides like hot ashes ready to erupt into an inferno.

Mutter's despair over Kitty's continued silence and Thomas's death consumed her every waking moment, and she and Hannah spent much time weeping and talking about their lost children. In all this grey misery, each night Moshe shuffled into the kitchen, washed his hands, and filled the apartment with the Meeriv; his voice soothing us as he sang the Siddur.

Always, when he spoke of the 'false deities being cut off from the earth', some of that fading hope sparked alive... if even for a moment.

In quick succession, the war around us progressed from bad to worse. From the invasion of Czechoslovakia and Poland, which thrust Britain and France into the fray in an attempt to protect this small country, one by one the dominoes fell. We heard the news spouted daily in our ears from the propaganda machine, the airways controlled by Goebbels, but always told from the point of view of the victories of Germany. To our ears, the Chancellor was winning with countries squashed under his shiny patent-leather boots. After his armies goose-stepped across Norway and Denmark, with Mussolini joining the march alongside Hitler, and ending up marching down the Champs d'Elysses in Paris, there was not a shred of hope left in any of us.

And with more and more reports, of which we could not verify, of the atrocities against our fellow Jews at the concentration camps, we wondered how much longer we would last in the capital city, the beating heart of Hitler's regime.

I woke to the sun shining through my window, a vivid blue sky peeking through the fluttering leaves in the courtyard, and I sat up with the sudden sad realization that it was my two-year wedding anniversary. For the most part, my heart was healing and I resigned myself to life without Rhen, even assigning myself as a widow who lost her husband somewhere in the Alsace countryside. I knew what Rhen would say, and he was right – my romantic notions bled even into the machine of war.

Shaking my head to scatter the thoughts, I slipped on my robe and wandered to the kitchen, wishing to smell the awakening aroma of coffee. Hannah looked up from her bowl of porridge and I sighed.

"I guess it was too much to hope for coffee this morning, or eggs?"

She attempted a smile and shrugged. "With the blockades, I'm afraid coffee is a distant memory, and even if Berlin had a supply, it would not be for the Jews." She lifted her bowl beneath her nose and took a deep breath, trying to lighten the mood.

"But the porridge smells divine," she said, her smile widening.

I spooned a bowlful from the pot on the stove and shrugged down into the chair across from her.

"I hate porridge," I replied. "Even when we had more to eat and Mutter would fix the most creamy, buttery porridge, I refused it. Now, I eat it only for survival, but I promise this, if ever this war ends and we return to our normal way of life, I will never eat it again."

I took a huge bite and we both chuckled as we chewed. Danka and Gerta skipped into the room, arms linked, in an adorable five and six-year-old way and stopped just short of the table, echoing a 'not again' as their mother came up behind them and popped their behinds.

"Not another word, you two." She spooned out their portion and motioned for them to sit like a commandant demanding obedience. "Now, eat, and wipe the frown from your faces. We are grateful for whatever God provides, the same as we did in the wilderness when he fed us the manna."

Danka's eyes widened. "You were in the wilderness, Ma-ma?"

We all started laughing and Sarah leaned against the kitchen sink, shaking her head. "No," she said through her giggles, "I'm not that old, zeeskeit."

"What about Grandpa Moshe?" asked Gerta. "He's old."

The question added to our laughter and before long we were wiping our eyes from the tears. The release of our built up nerves and the tension in the house flooding down our cheeks.

The front door to the apartment opened and closed just as Reuben poured himself a glass of water from the pitcher in the icebox, his deep guffaws adding to the sounds as his wife told him what was going on. From my seat at the table I saw my mother rush by from the door towards her bedroom without stopping at the kitchen.

Hannah caught my eye as the laughter died down, replaced with the sounds of spoons scraping the bottom of the bowls. I leaned towards her and whispered.

"Where has my mother been this morning?"

Hannah shrugged. "Today is for clothes rations. I did hear her say she needed some shoes. Maybe she went early to the line?"

I nodded, thinking the answer logical, yet a sudden knot formed in my stomach. Finishing my bowl of porridge, I kissed the girls on the tops of their heads and headed back to my room. Before I even opened the door, mother's unmistakable whimpers greeted my ears. I took a breath to prepare myself to comfort her, once again, and opened the door.

She lay prone on the bed, face down, with her face buried in the pillow and her shawl over her head. Sitting down next to her, I reached up and tried to pull it away from her face, but she pulled it tighter.

"No," she spat. "Go away, Julia."

The knot in my stomach tightened. "Mutter, what is it? Are you sick?"

She turned away from me and faced the wall. "Leave me be. Let me rest... I just want to sleep."

Wrestling between obedience and curiosity, the desire to know why she hid her face overwhelmed me, so I waited for a moment that her hands relaxed and I snatched the shawl away from her. Her shriek and intense tears unfurled at me as she sat up, her hands grabbing for the shawl. Within moments, Hannah knocked, her voice muffling through the paper-thin door.

"Is everything all right?"

But everything was not all right. I held my mother's wrists tight until she settled and our eyes locked. The widening black and blue mark beneath her right eye spoke all I needed to know.

"Yes," I answered back towards the door. "We are fine. Mutter just needs to rest."

I waited until her footsteps faded down the hallway before I released my mother's arms and slid my hands into her palms, instead.

"What happened?" I asked, softening my voice.

She tried to pull away and the tears flowed, again. I reached up and brushed a strand of hair away from the battered side of her face.

"Please, Mutter, tell me what happened."

She turned her gaze out the window, staring at that brilliant blue sky, the golden sun sparkling in her sad eyes.

"I... I only... wanted some shoes... you see."

I reached in the side drawer of the nightstand and retrieved her lace handkerchief, an heirloom from her grandmother, and she dabbed her cheeks.

"Yes," I prodded. "Hannah said you might be there. And did you find some?"

She shook her head. "No... there was... no time... you see. The Gestapo..." She took a deep breath and sobbed into the handkerchief.

I closed my eyes, knowing where this was leading. "The Gestapo did this to you?"

"It was madness," she finally said. "Some of women there in line started fighting over the shoes. I tried to stop them. Our own women... Jewish women... stooping to fight for shoes when our children are starving. They would not listen to my pleadings... but, I knew they would come. And they did."

"They beat you?"

"I... I don't know what happened. One moment they were fighting... the next, a club smashed across my head and I crumpled to the ground. When I woke, they all lay at my feet... three... four... maybe, five... I don't know. All gone... all gone..." she trailed off.

I threw my arms around her and rocked her back and forth, my tears adding to hers.

"But you survived, Mutter. You survived."

"Yes," she whispered in my ear, "but survived for what? What kind of life is this, zeeskeit?"

13

Rhen

November 9, 1940

Today is my wedding anniversary and today I stared at another new group of prisoners forming the same long line outside the gates of Auschwitz with the same stark fear draining the color from their faces. By now, a year since Hitler invaded Poland, with the thousands passing through the gate, the sharp pain and guilt in my heart dulled to assembly line donkey work.

Sensitivity faded, voices muffled, and the faces blurred into nothingness. Enemies of the State, Polish political prisoners, and German criminals morphed into nameless numbers, and the camp descended into a daily routine of sadistic beatings, tortures, and executions for the most trivial reasons. Every time I woke up in the morning, washed my face and looked into the mirror, I saw the real enemy staring back even though I never held the gun myself. Yet, even in that, I felt glued to my place.

Don't I have a choice? To live or die? To kill or be killed? "To be or not to be," I chuckled to myself. "Wrong play, Julia would say. Julia... Julia... Julia," I whispered into the chilled night air.

In truth, since my assignment to Auschwitz a year ago after failing to meet Eiche's standards for a higher echelon SS officer, I scanned the faces praying to see... and then, again, thankful *not* to see her for fear she might slip by and end up in the gas. Those fearful thoughts regulated themselves remembering Bernie's words that he saw her get on the train to Zurich. *Soon,* I kept repeating to myself, *soon I will be there. Somehow... but I fear she has forgotten me.*

My father made sure, after my disappointing failure, to ship me somewhere I would learn my lesson and grovel at his feet in appreciation for him not sending me to the front in Russia. I was thankful for that, at least, but the horrors feeding my brain on a daily basis in this hell hole was transforming me into something unrecognizable. *Even if I made it to Switzerland and back into Julia's arms, would she even want the man I've become?*

Survival was the key, and if it meant me obeying the orders of my superiors to bring about my happy future, then I would bury my feelings as deep as they would go. After spending the first year away from Julia at Dachau, training at the SS camp for advanced military and ideological indoctrination, Eiche assigned me to meaningless record-keeping in an office on the third floor of the Kommandant's headquarters with the red-slated roof. My office sat across the hallway from Eiche's own which had a direct panoramic view of the prisoner camp. Sometimes as I sat behind my desk sorting through endless prisoner names, I'd watch him surveying the camp with his hands behind his back like some powerful emperor wielding fate. To be sure, he held mine, and after too many disciplinary actions against me for daydreaming out my own window or touting my feelings about Hans's brutal actions towards the prisoners, he wrote to my father and reassigned me.

I knew very little about Auschwitz, except that it was another camp for political prisoners to the west of Krakow, Poland, set up to house political detainees and prisoners-of-war. Fortunately for me, my menial record-keeping skills kept me in an office in the Economic Administration building and out of dealing directly with the prisoners. From what my father said with his disappointing snarl, "You are too weak to deal with them. I had hopes for you after the incident in Tiergarten, but I feel that rare occurrence tainted the fuel you need for the more weightier matters coming to Germany."

When I asked about the weightier matters, he just smiled, handed me my reassignment papers and dismissed me. After being here in the camp for a little more than a year, I must admit there were times I stood at the platform and watched the guards unload the prisoners in sheer disbelief that the world I lived in turned into such a mad nightmare. Like standing on the edge of a precipice as you watch lemmings rush to their deaths and from the sheer momentum, as well as your own insignificance, you are unable to change the outcome. To stand in the way might send you tumbling right off the cliff with them, so I chose to stand to the side.

Not only that, but liquor did wonders to hide any guilt gnawing at my gut, and with the overwhelming numbers of Russian prisoners of war, along with the Poles, Auschwitz had a stock load of vodka and rum. Enough to dull my conscience every night, which I did more and more as the years passed and the realization that the chance to flee to Switzerland stretched further and further from my reach. Yet, in the meantime, I sent letter after letter to her at our meeting place... but never received a response.

My dreams always started with Julia in my arms and ended with her drifting away from me into the clouds, morphing into a nightmare as I drowned in blood, and jarring me awake as a bullet pierced Julia's heart.

As Germany stomped across Poland, and then into Norway, Denmark, and France, more and more prisoners arrived at the camp and I found myself sometimes buried in paperwork, all worthless grunt work for, in the end, most of the papers ended up in a fire.

I wrote again and again to the address in Switzerland, the one Bernie slipped into Julia's pocket, but after not hearing anything from her after six months, my hopes morphed into resignation. She was safe, but could not forgive me. So, I stopped writing and collapsed into the day-to-day drudgery of registering the endless stream of prisoners during the day, and the mindless numbing effects of alcohol at the canteen and entertainment at the cinema in the evening.

As the weary winter transformed into a stagnant spring of death and decay all around me, I awoke to the sun streaming through the window in the SS barracks and I sat up to greet the blue sky peeking through the wispy clouds. I wondered if Julia even remembered me or if in her new life as a Swiss citizen she had moved on and married another tall blonde Aryan. The thought nauseated my stomach so I dressed in my uniform and headed to the mess hall to eat. The aromas of eggs and sausages filled the air, and the soft hum of affable conversation and spurts of laughter greeted me. Since my demotion to a Rottёnfuhrer, two other fellows of the same rank sought to include me in their small clique, and they waved to me to join them at a table in the far right corner, away from some of the upper SS officers whose cigarette smoke formed a cloud above their heads.

Within minutes of sitting down, a young SS auxiliary woman served me a plate of eggs, blood sausage, fresh bread, and churned butter, along with a cup of coffee.

I leaned over and breathed the aroma of the coffee before taking a large gulp. As she eased away, I shouted over my shoulder for her to bring the whole pot.

"Ya," added Gunther, who leaned back in his chair with a wink, "Rhen needs it after finishing off two bottles of Schnapps last night; isn't that right, Rhen?"

Both Gunther and Rolf slapped their knees and guffawed, drawing the attention of the officers at the other table.

I wrinkled my brow and motioned for their silence. "No need to tell everyone in the room, guys. After all, I think you both matched me bottle for bottle. Besides, it's not like the old days when you could get a a good dose of caffeine to jolt you awake. I'm sure all they are serving is the state-approved decaf, which will do nothing for this headache throbbing in my brain."

They quieted and leaned in close, and Rolf slapped me on the back. "It is the nature of the beast, is it not, Rhen?"

The nature of the beast. I thought about his words as I finished the food and the pot of coffee, which ended up being a watered down version of roasted chicory and grain. Of all the ideologies pumped into our brains from this 'beast', the evils of caffeine and cigarettes seemed downright silly next to the evils of the Jewish problem, yet most of the Aryan soldiers I knew were more keen to tackle the harder problem over the simple evils of tobacco and coffee. And I knew, for a fact, that despite the declaration of purity pushed by Hitler, our supreme leader, a lot of the officers I knew still polluted their bodies on a regular basis with all three – cigarettes, caffeine, and Jewish girls; not to mention a healthy dose of Panzerschoklade, a drug-infused chocolate which was ideal for knocking out a hangover and for overnight bombing raids.

"I wouldn't mind some chocolate right now," I said, winking back at Gunther, "if the beast would oblige."

Rolf leaned in close, again. "I can get you some, for the right price," he said, rubbing his thumb and forefinger together.

I set down my fork and narrowed my eyes. "What price?"

"Anything good from the last load of Russians?"

"Just more vodka," I replied.

"That will do... two bottles for two bars of chocolate."

"Done," I said with a handshake, and we made plans to meet up later that evening to soothe our consciences while the 'beast' raged around us.

As I stood to leave, Kommandant Höss strode in through the doors and caught my eye, as well as my arm as I attempted to slip past him.

"You, Rottënfuhrer Montabauer, I was looking for you. I have a message from your father."

Standing straight before him, I waited for fate to send me in another direction. He reached in the pocket of his trousers and retrieved a small envelope, holding it out to me. He saluted a small 'Heil Hitler', to which I returned, and he dismissed me. With a dash back to the barracks, I propped up the pillows on my bunk and tore open the envelope. Two pictures fell onto the blanket in front of me, the words and images filling me with rage.

"To Rottënfuhrer Montabauer: This is a brief note to let you know that your mother is in the hospital in Berlin and as of now, I have no hopes of her surviving. She left a note this time and I found her at the bottom of the stairs. You can see from her injuries that she sustained severe head injuries from the fall and the doctors found high levels of Pervitin in her bloodstream. I will keep you updated and there is no need for your return from Auschwitz. Your duties there are more important than the selfish actions of your mentally unstable mother. Your father, Standartenführer Montabauer."

One at a time, I picked up the photos. The black and blue bruises on her face were a familiar reminder of growing up in a household where fear and intimidation, along with the threat of a backhanded blow, were the order of the day, especially when Herr Montabauer had too much to drink. And mother's tender and dreamy nature put her in the crosshairs every time as she pleaded with her husband to calm down from his tirades. She became my father's punching bag, an easy target to take out his frustrations. For years, I begged her to leave; and for years, she would kiss me on the cheek and say, "you are so much like me, Rhen. Never lose that. Don't let him beat it out of you. And don't change who you are just to please your father... or this Nazi Party."

And I tried to thwart father's efforts at every turn, at least for a while, even feeling the back of his hand when I went to my first Jazz club in Frankfurt at sixteen. I wanted to be a 'swing kid', a schlurf, but after a few more kicks to the gut from father's boot I acquiesced and put on the black uniform. Mother, however, continued to feel the blows after I left, and I knew these marks were not from a fall down the stairs. And if she died...

My gut roiled and I crumpled the pictures in my trembling fist. He taunted me with the photos, I knew that was his intention... to keep me in line after my dismal showing before Eiche. Now, under Höss's watchful eye, he would make sure I remained in Auschwitz until I became the soldier and son my father required. The electrified barbed wire encircling the camp was a swift reminder that I, too, was a prisoner of the regime I despised more and more with each passing day. And yet, I cursed myself for my cowardice. Wiping the stream of tears from my cheek, I stood up and marched back to face Kommandant Höss, who was now back in his office at the headquarters.

His secretary showed me in and I clicked my heels with a hearty 'Heil Hitler' as he looked up from the paperwork on his desk. He arched an eyebrow.

"Ah, Montabauer... you read the letter? Good news, I hope."

I sucked in a sniffle and fixed my jaw. "No, sir. My mother is in the hospital. I'm not sure she will make it."

The Kommandant nodded and leaned back in his chair, his face appearing unfazed by the news. "Hmmm... I am not surprised," he said. "Your mother was a delicate thing. Like a butterfly drawn to fire."

"You know my mother?"

He pointed to a chair across from him, and I sat. "Oh, dear boy, your father and I are close friends. When we served in Berlin before my assignment here in Auschwitz, your mother and father spent much time with me and my wife. You were just a boy, then, but we've watched you grow into a fine young man. No matter what happens to her, I am sure she is proud of you."

I took a breath and steeled my heart. "My father beats her. This is his handiwork."

Höss rubbed his chin with his fingers, still unresponsive to my revelation. He shrugged and narrowed his eyes. "Much has been said about your father, but we all know your mother has a problem with drugs. She is tainting her pure Aryan blood with such things. Your father told me when he gave me the letter to give to you that she possessed a high level of Pervitin in her blood stream."

My hands trembled as the anger flushed my cheeks. "It is a lie. She never had a problem. This is my father's doings." I stood up and leaned across his desk. "I demand you give me leave to go to Berlin to settle this matter."

The Kommandant smiled, a thin disingenuous grin as he, too, stood and faced me, eye to eye.

"You demand?" He chuckled. "Demand? Your passion for your mother is commendable, Rottënfuhrer Montabauer, but your father is in a much better position to handle this terrible affair. What can you do for her there that you cannot do for her here? No. Putting your mind on your work is better than pining away at her bedside."

I knew he and my father planned this from the beginning, so I played my cards. Standing back straight, I took another breath. "Then, Herr Kommandant, I wish to put in a request for immediate transfer."

He chuckled, again. "Transfer? And to where?"

"The front, sir."

The Kommandant looked about the room, waving his arms as if to encompass the whole camp. "And leave all that we provide here? You would trade a full belly and a desk job to life in a muddy trench?"

My insides seethed and I bit my lip. "At least I would know clearly who my enemy really is. Here, all I see is extreme abuses of power against defenseless prisoners of war."

He walked over to me, turning me around and eased me to the

window with an arm draped over my shoulders. "Hmm, Eiche reported to me of your former concerns." He pointed out towards a group of prisoners standing in a row, shivering from the cold blasts of wind as two guards barked orders at them while their dogs barked and snapped at their trembling legs.

"You see this all wrong, Rhen, as you look at the world much as your mother did. You know what we are fighting for here and you vowed an oath of loyalty to this cause. There is your enemy, and every soul that passes between the gates of this camp from now until our victory is your enemy. You think your enemy is only someone who rushes at you with a gun, or brandishes their fists at you? No, the real enemies are those who oppose us, no matter who they are. These prisoners you see here are only the firstfruits of what is coming to this camp, and I need men like you to help for the enormous task approaching."

He slapped me on the back and smiled. "Come now," he said, "I know what it is you need. Do you know of Solahütte?"

I shook my head, still watching the shivering prisoners. "No, sir, I do not."

"Ah," he replied, turning me back towards his desk as he reached inside the top drawer and took out a set of keys. "Solahütte is our retreat south of here on the Sola River. I have a lovely little cabin there, a quiet spot where you can rejuvenate yourself and come back refreshed to begin the task ahead of us. I am sure once you clear your head, you will recall your vow and be the man your father recommended to me." He held up one of the keys in between his forefinger and thumb. "And as a personal gift to you, to ensure your return, take my car."

"No," I said, "I cannot, sir... what if you want..."

"Nonsense," he said, gazing about the room with his arms outstretched. "I have plenty of projects to entertain me here at Auschwitz... believe me."

He, again, draped his arm over my shoulders and squeezed, directing me to the door.

"I am told," he whispered, "that the Heiferinnen, our female SS volunteers, show up to the resort by the bus loads. Perhaps after a week of good companionship and laughter, all this sadness over your mother will dissipate. Now, go, Rhen, and pack your bags. You will leave first thing in the morning."

Walking across the compound, past the line of prisoners and the chaos of the two dogs tearing one of them to pieces, I sensed the Kommandant's intense stare burning into my back as he watched me from his window. I gripped the keys in my palm with the sudden exhilarating feeling that I just unexpectedly arranged the ideal situation to escape to Switzerland. The thoughts in my brain ticked the imaginary boxes – check into the resort, spend a couple of days to ensure my visibility, drive to Switzerland... and yes, pack my SS uniform to ensure no one will question my movements... and last, find Julia. After that, well, who knows... all that matters now is to find her and escape this madness.

14

Julia
November 9, 1940

When sorrows come, they come not as single spies, but in battalions.
Rhen would say, '*wrong play, Julia.*'

Today is my two year wedding anniversary, yet instead of thoughts
of Rhen, my tears poured down my cheeks onto the pillow. Closing my
eyes, I reached across and palmed the empty space where my mother
lay next to me each night. Now, nothing. Now, she lay cold and alone in
the Jewish cemetery at Wiessensee. I couldn't even attend as the
restrictions prevented any of us leaving our assigned area, so Moshe
said a private Kaddish for her after dinner before we all retreated to
our rooms.

Just yesterday morning I rocked her in my arms as she told me
what happened in the rationing line. For an hour she cried, and then I
left her sleeping while I grabbed up the coupon book and headed to
the center myself. All she wanted was a better pair of shoes; what she
got was more horrific memories.

When I left the apartment, everyone gathered in the living room ,
arranging their own affairs for the day. Hannah and Elena bundled up
the girls to take them to another friend's apartment two streets over

where they did school lessons in private. Reuben kissed his wife and headed out to the Jewish community center to help support in any way he could, and Moshe sat in his rocking chair with a blanket over his knees, writing out Hebrew verses on scraps of paper. After everyone dispersed, he looked up at me and held out a single page for me to take.

"Here," he said, his voice just above a whisper.

"What is it?" I held the page in front of my face, frowning at the Hebrew characters written right to left. "I'm sorry, Moshe, my Hebrew is so faulty. Can you translate?"

He clicked his tongue and shook his head, his quiet reprimand and disappointment, but he acquiesced and read the verse aloud.

"*Ha`mishpakha sheli hi ha`koakh sheli veha`khulsha sheli.* Now, what did I say?"

I smiled. "You said, my family is my strength and my weakness."

He folded the paper and tucked it back into my hand, and I leaned over and kissed him on the cheek.

'My mother is sleeping, Moshe. I won't be but an hour, but while I am out maybe I will run by the center and see if anyone brought any tasty eintopf to share."

He raised his eyes, his wrinkled brow relaxing with a hopeful grin. "And maybe some fresh challah?"

I nodded, knowing that was an impossibility... but said nothing as I wrapped up in my coat and headed out the door, determined to get mother's shoes and maybe a few more potatoes to add to dinner. That was about all I could hope for, nowadays.

By the time I selected a pair of serviceable brown leather loafers and spent time chatting with a few of the women at the center, three hours passed and I hurried home with three more potatoes hidden in my coat pockets.

Opening the front door, the unnerving silence greeted me. No one was back home yet, so I headed to the kitchen and placed the potatoes in the sink for later. I placed mother's shoes on the table and tiptoed down the hallway, peeking in on Moshe who snored away in his bed, then turned back to check on my mother. Cracking the door, she faced away from me, still resting from her ordeal.

I let them sleep and returned to the kitchen to dice up the potatoes for another boring meal of broth, potatoes... and potatoes. Our ration allowance dwindled and the selection of nutritional foods evaporated before our very eyes. For myself, I wasn't worried... I would survive somehow... but my mother, and Hannah... as well as the two energetic youngsters in the house, well, their hollow cheeks and vacant eyes worried me.

Within the hour, everyone arrived back home, chatting away and relaying the rumors passed along of some of the atrocities against fellow Jews by forcing them into ghettos in the occupied countries.

"No," Elena said, as I heard the tale end of the rumor. "That cannot be true. And where is that? I've never heard of such a town."

"In Poland, I think... Grodno is what Lisle said. 15,000 Jews herded into one city block."

My eyes widenend. "How is that possible? Surely these are just rumors... and why would the Nazis even do such a thing?"

Hannah huffed. "Why do the Nazis do anything that they do? I am just saying what I heard... that is all."

Elena shivered, watching her girls play 'Ein, Zwei, Drei, Halt' in the living room. "Surely that won't happen here; do you think?"

"No, of course not. We are Germans, are we not? And on top of that, we are Berliners. Don't worry yourself, Elena."

I wanted to add to their story, saying 'nein' but my heart spoke something different. The night of broken glass still rang in my mind... and after all, *didn't we all think something like that would never happen in our fair city?* Plus, I remember Rhen's warnings and now wondered how much more he knew that he withheld from me. I set the pot to boil and wiped my hands in my apron, leaving them to continue their chat while I checked again on mother.

Creaking the door open, a sudden chill sped up my neck, tingling the hairs along my hairline. The moonlight filtering across her body rested in a hazy aura and the realization that she still lay prone in the exact position I left her this morning filled my brain. I pushed the door open a little more, my whisper catching in my throat.

"Mutter?" No response.

"Mutter, dinner is almost ready. Guess what we are having?" I feigned a small giggle, trying to awaken her. Still, she never moved.

Easing across the floor, half wanting to wake her and half hoping she rested in such a sound sleep that I prayed *not* to wake her, I leaned over her and brushed my fingers along her forehead, my fingers pushing away the strands of hair falling over her eyes. Even in the pale moonlight, I knew the bluish tinge of death. For a startling moment, I reared back, hands to my mouth and my eyes drifted down her body and rested on the empty bottle of pills in her splayed hand.

Fear seized hold of me and my mind blanked as to what to do. *Do I try to wake her? Do I call the others? How do I get her to the hospital?* Most of the ambulances, even here in the city, were commandeered for the war effort, and even if there were any, none of them would come for a Jew. With all of these thoughts flooding my mind, the pain surged downward and gripped my heart. The scream erupting from my throat sounded far away... someone else's body... someone else's life.

Within moments, Hannah, Elena and Reuben burst through the door as I crumpled to the floor, the words gurgling through my tears as I pointed to her.

"Mutter! Help her! Help me! Please..." I begged, clinging to Elena's skirt. Moshe scurried the girls from the room, their tiny voices chiming in unison questions of 'what is happening' and 'what's wrong with Julia's ma-ma'?

What was wrong with my ma-ma? I knew what was wrong. The same wrongness infecting all of us. Like a poisoned boil blasting open, the disease spreading until many could no longer take the pain. We heard the other rumors spilling across Berlin, across Germany... that of the rise in suicides among our people since the night of broken glass.

With the beating from this morning, the loss of Thomas and Kitty, the humiliating discarding by her husband, the collapsing world around her, proved too much to bear... even with me by her side. She left me. The words echoed through my body and I heaved. Elena pulled me to my feet and rushed me to the bathroom just as the little bit of food I consumed today poured into the toilet. Hannah held a glass to my lips as I crouched against the bathroom wall, her empathetic eyes pleading with me to drink.

"Come," she said, as the two of them lifted me by the arms, and helped me to Hannah's room, which did not help since gazing about at the room that was my mother's former bedroom made the tears flood even more.

"Where is she?" I asked, closing my eyes and pulling the covers to my chin.

"Don't you worry, zeeskeit. Reuben will handle everything," Elena replied.

"You just rest," Hannah added, her words snagging on her own tears. As the two women walked to the door, I sat up.

"Wait."

Hannah looked over her shoulder as Elena eased the door open.

"Did she leave a note?"

They looked at each other, hesitant, but Elena nodded, reached in her pocket and pulled out a folded piece of paper.

Reaching out my trembling hand, I motioned for it. "Give it to me."

"Perhaps you should wait, zeeskeit," Hannah said.

I wiggled my fingers. "Give it to me."

And so, she was buried alone. Two nights passed and I had no wish to move from my bed. From time to time I tilted my head to breath in the spot where Mutter's head lay on the pillow, desperate to hang on to the familiar scent of her hair. On the third day, I dressed in one of her dresses, sliding my feet into the loafers I got the morning of the incident, wrapped myself in my coat, and slid past Elena as she washed dishes in the kitchen sink.

My intent was clear, and I fixed my mind that my request would be met, even if I had to 'Heil Hitler' to do it. As I approached the checkpoint, knowing I had no papers to allow me to leave the area, I lifted my chin and marched up to one of the guards. He nudged the young man next to him and they both adjusted the rifles strapped over their shoulders.

The guard held out his hand.

"Papers."

I placed a single folded piece of paper in the palm of his hand, to which he unfolded and read. Showing the other guard, they chuckled and shook their head.

He put his hand on my shoulder and pushed me away.

"Go on, you worthless pig. We're not letting you through."

"I want to speak to Unterscharfuhrer Montabauer at the SS headquarters."

The guard chuckled, again, and shrugged his shoulders. "Sorry, we do not know an Unterscharfuhrer Montabauer."

The other soldier took the gun off his shoulder and pointed it at me. I took a deep breath and dropped to my knees.

"Please, sirs, I beg of you. I know Herr Montabauer. His father is Oberstrumfuhrer Montabauer, an assistant to Herr Höss. If you would just please pass the note to him and tell him that Julia is waiting for his call at her home."

The soldier pulled back the barrel with a click as the other one crumpled the note in his hand and tossed it into the bushes.

"What do you think, Heinrich, or is it too easy?"

I closed my eyes, ready to die. A loud smack of clapping hands startled me and I jumped, and the two men guffawed as they continued clapping as if witnessing the best show in the world. Scrambling to my feet, I ran all the way back to the Judenhaus.

15

Rhen

April 1941

After wasting away an entire day at the Solahütte, lounging by the Sola and uncluttering my thoughts, my mind fixed upon a plan and all the necessary tools for my getaway fell into place. I had a whole week to myself, to do as I pleased, with Höss car, and money in my pocket. The steps organized in my mind as I gazed across the sparkling waters – get up early, drive to Krakow, leave the car somewhere in the city, and book an overnight sleeper to Zurich. Simple enough... as long as nothing put a kink in the plan.

Höss was right about the Heiferinnen gathering at Solahütte to entertain the soldiers. That night, the first of my stay, at least 40 of us gathered in the main hall to celebrate the Tripartite alliance between Germany, Italy, and Japan, even though over a month had passed since the signing, the men looked for any excuse to throw a victory party. The women volunteers arrived on the transport bus just in time, all dressed to the nines in silks and furs, and more than a few already soused.

The only thing unexpected was the face I saw through the crowd once the lights dimmed and the music flowed. Rosamund Thoss oozed through the crowd in a coral silk gown with matching lipstick and perfect finger waves in her perfect Aryan blonde hair. The corner of her mouth turned up in a slight grin and she glided towards me with a glass of champagne held out for me to take.

"Well, well, if it isn't Rhen Montabauer." She sipped from her own glass, leaving an impression of her full bottom lip on the rim. Narrowing her eyes, she leaned forward and whispered in my ear. "I think the last time I saw you I left you quite breathless."

She stroked her thin fingers across the eagle buttons of my uniform. "My, my, who would have thought you'd ever become an officer, but the black suits you." She giggled, taking another sip of the champagne.

"What are you doing here, Rosamund?"

She raised her glass towards the other girls in the room, all cavorting and flirting with the officers and soldiers.

"Well, its what we do, isn't it? We, Heifferinnen. We can't have our boys lack for a little relaxation and entertainment, now can we?"

"So, you are all planning on being here all week?"

Biting her lip, she smiled a mischievous grin. "Of course... and now we have plenty of time to frolic; don't we?" She pinched my chin with her forefinger and thumb. "Come on now, Rhen; give me a smile... or are you still that romantic brooder I once knew?"

I jerked my chin away. "Leave me alone, Rosamund; those days are long gone."

Easing her hand down my side, she curled her arm around my waist and tried reaching under my jacket. "Come on, I always knew how to coax a smile."

I grabbed hold of her arm and pushed her away. Her thin eyebrow arched and her eyes sparked with a sudden understanding.

"Ah, I see... Rhen has himself a Fraulein now. Surprising, but I suppose all you SS boys must fall in line and find you a good Aryan wife to punch out good Aryan babies for the Führer. It's a shame... I might have made you a good Reich wife." She took another sip and set the glass on the table behind us. "So, who is she? Do I know her?"

"She's from Switzerland. You wouldn't know her."

"Switzerland? Ah, yes, your mother was from there, wasn't she? Hmmm, I guess you must keep the tradition going..." she leaned near my ear again. "But what she doesn't know won't hurt her, will it? After all, you came to Solahütte to enjoy yourself. I never expected to see you here, Rhen, and now we can rekindle some old memories."

I huffed. "Old memories? You mean the ones where you teased and never followed through?"

She giggled and threw back the rest of her champagne. "Well, you might be surprised how I've changed. This war has changed us all, hasn't it?"

Easing up close to me, the smell of her perfume wafted into my nose, and the champagne lightened my defenses. *How did I even know Julia waited for me in Switzerland? I've never heard from her, even though she knows how... from my own letters and through Bernie, who promised to be our go-between.* And now, here, a long-lost love swayed with me to Evelyn Künneke's *Sing, Nachtigall Sing.* She tilted her head up and brushed her mouth on mine, the champagne still lingering on lips.

"Perhaps you are right, Rosamund. After all, we used to have our fair share of fun, didn't we?"

She threw her head back and giggled, her hand squeezing my upper thigh. "Yes, we did; *yes*, we did. What do you have in mind?"

I nodded my head to the door. "See how many bottles of that champagne you can procure and I'll take you to a little spot where the moon glows over the Sola."

Her cheeks flushed with excitement and a rush of passion. "Ah, there's that romantic boy I once knew. I'll meet you outside in fifteen minutes."

We drove along the dirt rode parallel to the Sola river, the moon peeking out from behind full snow clouds ready to burst at any moment. Rosamund scooted closer to me, sliding her left hand in my pants pocket and shivering. And as we drove, I settled on my next plan of action... that is, what to do with Rosamund now that she intended on staying the week at the retreat. If I remembered right, her clingy nature meant she'd probably shadow me the entire time, so I knew I needed to handle this so as to slip away without her notice. There was only one way, and I knew her weakness – a lot of booze always knocked her out, so after we parked and kissed for a bit, I popped the cork on both bottles and urged her to drink.

"Come on," I said. "You are a lot more fun when you've had too much to drink. Remember when we went to Frankfurt to that dance club? Remember that little back nook in the dark?"

She giggled, pulling up my shirt and running her cold fingers across my chest while I poured champagne down her throat.

"Say some of that pretty poetry you used to say while I guzzle this bottle..." she said, slurring and giggling at the same time.

"Ah, my Rosamunde, my only Rose, that pleasest best mine eye, the fairest flower in all the worlde to feed my fantasye..."

She scooted her skirt up and pushed me over on the seat, but I pushed her back up and clicked my tongue.

"No, no... not yet. More drink, I think."

She laid back on the leather seat and chugged one bottle, then clicked the door handle and slid out into the tall grass which shimmered dewy wet droplets in the moonbeams, carrying both bottles in her flailing arms.

I peered through the window, watching her as she danced to the river while still pouring the bubbles down her throat. I chuckled, remembering this familiar path of hers. Drink, kiss, tease, drink, giggle, drink, drift away in oblivion. By the time I caught up with her, she stumbled on the rocks near the riverbank and plopped down in the water with a splash and a laugh. I shook my head and held my hand out to her.

"Come on, Rosamund, it's freezing out here."

She placed her hand in mine and winked. "You have somewhere warmer in mind?"

I leaned forward to help her to her feet, but she caught me off guard and pulled so I lost my balance and fell to the ground. In a breathless tumble, she rolled over on top of me, her wet body soaking through my clothes as she kissed my neck and ears. Those old familiar feelings warmed us both and I kissed her hard, enveloping her in my arms, then spun her onto her back in the wet grass. She giggled and wrapped her legs around me, pulling me tighter and ripping her dress in the process.

"Come on," she whispered. "I'm no longer teasing."

My body responded to her words and I ran my hands down her thighs, closing my eyes. Behind the darkness of my eyelids, images of Julia flashed in my mind, of her soft skin and sighs... of the innocence of our honorable union on the rooftop in Berlin. Nothing about this encounter was honorable or innocent, and with a sudden realization of the possibility that tomorrow my wife waited for me in Switzerland, I pushed away and sat up.

Rosamund laughed aloud, again, and finished off the first bottle. "Now who's the tease," she said, scooting up behind me and skimming her hands across my back beneath my shirt.

I took a sip from the second bottle, then handed her the rest. "Things are too different now, Rosamund. Once upon a time, I'd have died for you to come to me... just once. Perhaps that might have changed everything for us both."

Her hot breath blew into my ear. "It's not too late, Rhen; things are not done that cannot be undone," she purred as she unzipped the back of her gown, letting her capped sleeves shimmy off her shoulders.

I smiled as she tilted the bottle back to her mouth, my eyes drifting down to her white skin glowing beneath the moon. Yes, Rosamund always knew how to tease with incredible skill, and my mind and body struggled in a vacillating fight. *What about Julia, my wife? Or is she my wife? Is she alive? Is she dead? Who would know?*

No one knew of my marriage to Julia except for the Rabbi and Bernie, one of which probably lies dead in a concentration camp at this point, and the other who would cheer me on if I finally bedded this Aryan goddess and gave up on the Jewish beauty.

My father's beaming face alighted in my mind – his approving slap on my back if I brought Rosamund home as my wife. My indoctrination would be complete and we'd morph into a copy of my parents as I immersed myself into the party while she drank herself to death from loneliness.

Yet, my love for Julia reached deep into my soul... like breathing... a necessity... and my body struggled from the lack of her. I knew why I responded to Rosamund's soft touch, for I craved my wife after being apart for so long. And I wondered if during all this time if another man turned her head... if she struggled to give in to a different future.

Rosamund held the bottle above her mouth and the last drops drip onto her tongue. With another laugh, she fell backwards into the grass. The booze worked its magic on her once again and she drifted off to sleep.

Standing up, I walked down to the edge of the water and cooled my heated face with a splash of water, waiting a moment until I calmed myself; then I covered her with my jacket, gathered her up in my arms, and laid her in the backseat of the car.

We headed to Höss's cottage which sat a mile away from the main retreat, and within the hour, I slid off her gown, tucked her beneath the covers, and took a cold shower. Rosamund snored away the rest of the night, and I packed up my suitcase, loaded up the car, and headed down the road, leaving a note which simply said "I've gone back to Berlin; thanks for the night. I'll call soon". She'd never remember if we slept together or not, but at least the possibility of a future together would keep her appeased and silent. The road stretched out before me, as did my future. If no one waited for me in Switzerland, if Julia moved on, then my future with Rosamund was now secure; if Julia met me at the door with a smile, at least my conscience was clear.

By the time Rosamund awoke, I'd be miles away when she read the note. Eventually, I knew someone would find Höss's car parked at the station in Krakow, they might even trace me to Switzerland, but Julia and I would keep running as far as it took to make a new life for ourselves, away from all this madness, and all these people would disappear into our past.

However, I must admit, trepidation hovered like lingering notes on my sighs as I drove. After the first six months of not receiving any note from Julia, I made the decision to conclude one of two things: either she decided to move on with her life without me or something prevented her from writing. If the former, I was determined to have absolution and closure; if the latter, well, I'd move heaven and earth to overcome any obstacle in our way. Now, after over two years of no word, my mind wrestled again with the reasons for her silence. *What if she is dead?* my mind whispered, followed with a resolute 'nein' from my heart. No matter the reasons, closure was a necessary action, especially if I needed to move on with Rosamund.

After leaving the car along the curb at the train station and paying the ticket attendant to keep an eye on Kommandant Höss's car for a week or so until my return, I secured my ticket for Switzerland. The train chugged out of the station just before six o'clock in the morning with one train-change in Vienna, traveling the southern route beneath the burgeoning lines of the Northern front against the Czechs and Poles. The clack of the train wheels along the track lulled me into a peaceful trance. The Austrian countryside west to Munich stretched before my eyes, fields of quaint houses untouched by the ravages of war. Hatred and death fell away, and the shades of spring rustled through the trees. The countryside plunged down into a valley, rising in gentle hills all the way to the horizon, the foothills of the Alps. A winding stream coursed like a slithering snake following the path of the train tracks until veering away and disappearing into the thick evergreens. There, at the edge of the forest, a solitary house stood forlorn and forgotten with shuttered windows and overgrown vines climbing up the stone chimney. The cold emptiness made me wonder about all of our lives... about the people who used to live there. *Where were they now? Ripped from their home by the Waffen, or shoved into a dank, cramped ghetto... or worse, perhaps their bodies now lay beneath that cold, frozen ground with their own house to mourn over them?* Even these seemingly peaceful havens could not escape the creeping infection stretching from Germany. *How far will Julia and I have to run to escape the poison? Or is there even such a world any more?*

So many questions etched in my mind, desperate for answers, desperate to understand how the country I loved emerged after the Great War into a dazzling beacon full of cabarets, only to slip back into darkness at a rapid speed. *Was it truly the Jews fault for Germany's defeat, and the economic difficulties?*

But as was the case, and as my father often reminded me, questions were for unbelievers, those who had faith in our cause had no need for questions since common sense ruled the actions. And perhaps that was the reason for my own deep sense of doubt, *for how could one man deem a Jew an enemy of the State without answering all the questions? Or did Hitler's 'Mein Kampf' water the seeds already implanted in German hearts?*

Still, I couldn't help conjure up the days as a young Boy Scout, the days before Hitler banned the group and required our enrollment into the Jugend. He shattered our innocence, pummeling into our brains that one must obey or suffer the consequences. And he used all those themes of acceptance and brotherhood against us as we switched from one group to the next without hesitation. He groomed us for his ultimate goal, and the realization gnawed at my gut.

As the last of the sunlight glinted through the darkening clouds above, I willed myself to think of Julia and not of the sorrows filling my memories. The thought of seeing her overwhelmed me, and a long-forgotten refrain from *Where and When* popped into my mind – Benny Goodman's soothing horn and Penny Lee's silky voice reflecting my own feelings and the moment I imagined seeing her as she opened the door.

The forbidden words of "some things that happened for the first time seem to be happening again. And so it seems that we have met before and laughed before, and loved before... but who knows when or where" frosted across my lips and onto the window as I leaned my head against the the frame.

"We were different people then," I added as a note of caution to myself. *Who knows if we can begin again?*

The houses, and fields, and cows rushed by in a flash, tatting by like a moving picture at the cinema... and even, from time to time, a group of gray-clad uniformed soldiers huddled together on a train platform zoomed by. Here today, gone tomorrow, in more ways than one.

Looking down at the watch on my wrist, the standard issued one I acquired during the Jugend days - an elegant Primus with a black leather band and SS insignia on the face – the hour hand clicked midnight. By now, someone would miss the car I stole from the compound, and perhaps discovered my absence.

No matter, I thought. *If all goes as planned, Julia and I will carve out our own life away from all of this chaos. I wonder what she would think of America?*

As I closed by eyes, I could hear Max's words echoing in my soul. You are *such a dreamer, Rhen... Dreamers don't last long in the Devil's hands.*

But my whole outlook changed as I made a quick train hop in Zurich to the small town of St. Gallen. My mother, whose family were Swiss embroiderers stretching as far back as the 16th century, acquired a small cottage tucked beneath the heaven-reaching expanse of the Appenzell Alps as her inheritance, after her father died in the first world war with her mother following fifteen years later. She moved to the exciting city of Berlin as a young twenty-year-old, fell in love, married, and gave birth to me, yet never forgot the house beneath the mountains. She recounted story after story when tucking me in bed at night as a child, of her idyllic days breathing in the luscious crisp air and watching her mother's fingers work an exquisite embroidery of poppies and edelweiss. Not once did we ever visit the now abandoned cottage, but her vivid remembrances helped me know that this was the paradise to begin life anew with Julia. I prayed with Julia's fortitude and the money I gave her, that by now she'd transformed the house into a home.

Before the train pulled up to the station, I slipped into the water closet and exchanged my SS officer's uniform to plain clothes, and shoved the uniform into a duffel bag I brought along the trip. I knew the cloth would be great for starting a blazing fire in the fireplace as Julia and I planned our future.

The small hamlet of St. Gallen hummed with people, all moving about their daily lives – neighbors chatting at garden gates, a dog barking at a group of children kicking a ball in an open field, horse-drawn wagons filled with hay bumping along the cobbled streets, an occasional car horn honking to avoid the bicyclists ambling down the roadway, and the rich deep greens of well-watered grasses fed from the white snow capping the surrounding mountains. Pure elysium.

The sight shocked my senses for a moment and I wondered how such a place was left untouched by the Nazis, or was this picture-perfect heaven a facade hiding the rotting bones underneath. Most everyone knew of Switzerland's neutrality to the war, Hitler calling the little nation a medieval remnant and the people 'renegade Germans', but even with his threats and inner campaigns from the Swiss Nazi Party, Switzerland remained autonomous and untouched.

Looking at the oblivious community, I spat a huff, feeling very skeptical of the whole scene before me. My stomach growled, reminding me I had not eaten since dinner on the train the previous evening, so I adjusted the bag over my shoulder and headed to the city center to find something to eat.

At a quaint cafe, I filled my belly with an exorbitant amount of coffee and a helping of Rosti, a familiar favorite dish my mother used to fix with potatoes and fried eggs. The food did wonders for my frame of mind and I leaned back against the banquette, sipping more coffee, and watching the people walk by.

One glance at my watch, and then, up again... and I saw her. Clear as day, and appearing like an angel in a blue dress, she hurried past the cafe with a bundle of food in a basket hanging from her arm and her long dark hair covering her face. But I knew her, even after all this time.

Tossing some Reichmarks on the table top, I rushed out to the street, thinking to call out to her... but something stopped me as I watched her grab a bicycle and hurry down the street. Once she turned the corner, a sudden fear and anger crept into my heart, melding together to create something unexpected in my feelings towards her.

I never heard from her. And now, here she was, perfectly fine. Maybe she truly does not want to see me. Maybe she is married to someone else. Maybe she couldn't forgive me after all...

Since I knew where she was going, back to the cottage, MY mother's cottage, I went back into the cafe and inquired if anyone had a bicycle for hire to allow me to tour the surrounding area. In quick haste the woman at the till, a gray-haired busybody, narrowed her eyes at me when I handed her a Reichsmark and questioned me.

"Visiting from Germany, I see," she said.

I nodded, as she gave me change in Swiss francs.

"Family, here?"

I shook my head. She leaned forward with a whisper.

"Are you a Nazi? You've got the look of one of them."

"I am German, Fraulein." Squaring my jaw and returning the narrow-eyed stare silenced her for the moment, and before she reloaded, I headed out the door to the waiting bicycle leaning against the outside window frame.

Before long and with a few inquisitions of my own, I found the path leading out of the city, a substantial climb to the cottage. Pausing for a moment to look across Lake Constance, I took a breath and gathered my thoughts as to what I would say to her... or what she might say to me.

I sucked in another breath and headed for a cluster of fir trees to hide the bicycle and my bag with the intention of assessing if she was alone after all these years.

Easing round the back of the cottage, she appeared through the kitchen window, yet I still could not see her face. I climbed over the X-laced log fence to get closer to the window, when my pants leg snagged, sending me toppling to the ground and the loose fencing creating a cacophony of cascading thuds. I scrambled to my feet as she opened the door, and I hid around the corner, out of her sight.

As I waited, trying to still my breath, minutes passed and I decided to take a chance to look around the corner. The minute I peered, the unmistakable click of a gun hammer sounded in my ear and the barrel touched the back of my head.

I threw up my hands. "Wait, don't shoot."

"Who are you?" she asked.

"Please, let me turn around. You can see my hands, I have nothing on me. I mean you no harm."

"Turn around," she demanded.

Still with my hands in the air, I eased round. Our eyes met, and she lowered the gun. What seemed like eternity passed between us, still we stood with our mouths gaping open, both of us unable to find the words. Finally, she spoke.

"Rhen Montabauer... what are you doing here?"

I creased my brow. "What am I doing here? What are you doing here... Kitty Cappell?"

I took a step to the side, and she raised the gun again just as three small children rushed out behind her. The tallest girl, wearing a tattered tweed coat emblazoned with the white Juden arm band on her right arm, called out to Kitty.

"Kitty, what's wrong?"

"Get back inside, Lydia... I will handle this."

"I know what you are doing," I said. "You are smuggling children across the border, aren't you? You are a passeur for the resistance."

"Who wants to know?" she asked with a snarl. "I didn't think it would be you scouting out resistance fighters for Hitler, but if you think our former association will keep me from putting a bullet in your brain in order to protect these children, you are wrong. I will get particular pleasure in killing the Nazi who killed my brother."

I held up my hands in front of me. "Kitty... you mistake me. That is not why I am here. I'm looking for someone else... not you."

Like electricity firing a blinking bulb, her eyes lit up as the sudden realization occurred to her.

"Julia," she responded, lowering her gun, once again.

"Yes," I replied, determined to finally confess all and attempt to win her to my side, if even only to spare my life for a few more minutes so another soul on this earth would know of my love for Julia.

"Please," I continued. "I will tell you everything. I swear not to report what you are doing here, but you've got to tell me where Julia is right now."

She looked to the side, as if still recalling a memory. "The red suitcase..." she whispered.

"...was our signal for my cousin, Bernie, to give her the package which would bring her here," I added to her whisper.

Her eyes flashed up. "I thought he was a resistance fighter. I thought this was my assignment." She pointed the gun again and flagged me inside. "Go inside. Schnell, you stinking Nazi!"

And I did as she said, sitting on one of the creaking ladder-backed dining chairs while the tall girl, Lydia, tied my hands behind my back.

Kitty walked to the hallway with Lydia, ushering her back into one of the back rooms, her muffled Polish words lilting through the air like the dust particles swirling through the rays of sunlight streaming across the floor.

"*Powiedz innym, żeby spakowali swoje rzeczy. Wyjeżdżamy dziś wieczorem.*"

"*Tej nocy?*"

"*Tak. Nadchodzą naziści.*" The girl gasped and ran down the hallway. Kitty turned back, pulling another chair in front of me, and laid the gun in her lap.

"There is no one else coming," I said.

She chuckled. "Ah, so your Polish is good. Did they teach you that at the training camp at Dachau?"

I did not answer her sarcastic remark. "Kitty, where is your sister and mother?"

"Why should I tell you anything? I think, since I hold the gun, that you should speak first. Then, I will decide whether or not to answer your question or just shoot you."

She was right. Now was the time to play my hand, and prayed I held winning cards.

"You are right, Kitty. I will tell you all, but you must promise me to listen to everything I say before passing judgment. Are you sure you want to hear my confession?"

She fiddled with the gun. "Speak," she said, crossing her arms.

Taking a breath, I began. "Do you remember when you saw Julia at the Moka the night of her sixteenth birthday?" Her eyes widened and she nodded. "Well..." and I told her every last detail, including my undying love for her sister, as well as my abhorrence for the goosestepping path my father forced me to take. The cuckoo clock above the mantel peeped out a melody – an hour passed from the beginning of my story until I said the last words of "...she was suppose to be here, waiting for me. We were planning a new life... and I was to use my connections to help you and your mother escape, as well."

Her former fiery cheeks paled in the sunlight and a solitary tear ran down her cheek. "But I wrote to my cousins, Samuel and Gregory, telling them where I was, for them to bring them here... they were to help Mutter and Julia escape through the underground networks. I thought my little sister had joined the resistance, and when I saw her papers and the suitcase... I knew it would kill mother if anything happened to her. I couldn't let Julia do anything to jeopardize her life, so I took the fake documents and went to my contact in Berlin. When I showed him, he smiled and said it was a perfect plan to help smuggle Jews across the border to freedom, and not only that, but to help my own family. And then, like I said, when the man approached me from behind at the train station... I thought he was from my contact, especially when I discovered a packet with an address and money in my pocket. This haven here in St. Gallen has worked flawlessly for over two years now... like a God-send."

"And you never wondered why your mother and sister never arrived here?"

"I did have an answer," she snapped. "Samuel said that Aaron arranged Julia and my mother's passage on a ship to America, and that after I completed my assignment with the resistance, he'd give me information on where to find them. I never heard anything more so I assumed they were safe, so I immersed myself in helping Jews across the border." She paused and wiped her hand across her cheek. "And now, you tell me this... And how am I to respond to your declarations of infatuation?"

I shifted in my seat to set the final blow. "Not just infatuation, Kitty. Julia is my wife."

Her eyes vacillated between hatred and fear. "But, you are a Nazi! She is a Jew! Your laws forbid such alliances... our laws, though broken by many, warn against marriage with those not of our faith. I thought Julia would have learned from our own parent's failure."

"We love each other, Kitty."

She shook her head, standing up with a quick swish, almost toppling her chair, and gripped the gun in her hands. She stood at the window, the sunbeams piercing the slits in the shutters streaking across her face in uniform, slanted lines, then glanced over at me, her lip trembling.

"You stupid, rash, naive fools, playing at love like nothing else matters and putting my sister's life in the gravest of danger."

"It was not my intention to bring her harm," I growled. "I wanted to save her. You were the one who destroyed our chances."

She shook her head, again. "No, I don't believe any of this. How could my sister forgive what you did to Thomas? She would never marry the man who murdered him... unless..." she charged at me, placing the gun barrel between my legs. "What did you do to her? If you dared take away her honor, I will take away any semblance of manhood you have and leave you here to bleed to death."

"No," I replied, "please, listen. Julia understood what happened, more so than even I did. The chaos of the moment, my friend, Max, lying dead on the sidewalk... all of it... the anger... the songs in my head... it was all just too much to take. I begged her for forgiveness...

the same as I beg of you now."

She clicked the hammer, her stare locking with mine and the intensity burning into my brain.

"Please," I whispered. "I want to help. We've got to find your sister and mother."

"I don't need you," she blasted. "I have my own resources."

"You mean Samuel and Gregory?"

"Yes."

Swallowing hard, the saliva grated down my hoarse throat. "Kitty... both of your cousins are dead, as well as Aaron. They were arrested and sent to Sachsenhausen... and they never returned."

She gasped, falling backward onto the chair. "But... they were suppose to help them out. Are my mother and sister still in Berlin?"

My heart thudded against my ribs. "You mean you don't know?"

"I just thought... I imagined them safe on American shores. And now... all is lost."

"No," I retorted, squeezing my hands into fists. "You have to help me, Kitty, and I will help you. Listen to me. We both want Julia and your mother alive and safe. If you release me, I swear to the moon that I will find them and bring them here. As an officer, I have access to many more avenues that you as a hiding criminal do not have."

"How am I suppose to trust you? And isn't it ironic that you would swear by the moon, when I know Julia would say that no one should swear by something so inconsistent, nightly changing in her heavenly orb."

Her reference to *Romeo and Juliet* brought a smile to my face, and most surprising, Kitty's face alighted with a slight grin.

"Yes," she added, "I may have chided my little sister about her romantic notions, but I knew her well; however, not as much as I thought." She paused, walked around and untied my hands, placing the gun against my temple. "I'm not saying I trust you, yet, and definitely not saying that I forgive you, but I will pray that the love you say you have for her will be the saving grace in all of this. Go, find my sister and mother, but remember, I have eyes and ears in Berlin who will have no problem blowing your brains out in a dark alleyway."

I stood up, rubbing the rope burns around my wrists. "Thank you, Kitty. I promise to bring them to you, safe and sound."

She walked over to a side table next to the sofa, opened a drawer and took out a stack of letters and the paperwork she stole from Julia. I recognized the handwriting right away as my own, addressed to my grandmother, Amelie Keller, without a return post, and all of them still sealed.

"Here, you might need these."

I clutched the letters in my grip, realizing Julia never read my words of love and my desperation to come to her. My heart told me by now she forgot me, thinking I'd abandoned her, and instead of resigning myself to a life with Rosamund, a fiery need to tell Julia the truth, to find her and save her from Berlin, to hand her the letters in person, raged in my soul. I squelched the pain rising in my throat and looked up at Kitty.

"You never read any of them," I stated instead of questioning her.

She shook her head and pointed out the window to two headstones a few yards away from the house.

"Josef and Amelie Keller lie in the ground, and out of respect for her and whoever still wrote to her, I never read them. Who was she?"

"My grandmother," I whispered. "I told Julia I'd write to her using her name so as to keep our secret."

One of the children peeked out of the doorway down the hall, catching my eye.

"What about them," I asked. "Won't you need the identity papers to help more of them across the border?"

She smiled and winked. "No worries, Rhen. I can get more."

I left St. Gallen with a tenuous understanding between us. We did not shake hands on the agreement, but the goal of saving someone we both loved sealed the pact in symbolic blood.

I feared Julia and her mother were still in Berlin, and the nausea roiled anew in my gut thinking about the intense pressure mounting inside the city against the Jews. *I never imagined I would have to turn right back around and head back into the mouth of the volcano... but what choice did I have to save the woman I loved?*

As the train sped back to Krakow, another night of haunting dreams surged through my head as I tried to rest. With my Nazi uniform back on, I headed straight back to the one place I vowed never to see again. Auschwitz.

16

Julia

September 1941

Five months ago, a letter came in the mail with no return address and three lines scrawled across the page.

> *Please forgive me, Julia, I did not know. A visitor came to see you and he knows you are still in Berlin. I fear discovery, so my continued silence is necessary, but tell mother I am safe and hope to see you both soon. He promised to bring you both to me.*

The words brought a mixture of hope and despair beating on each heartbeat, and yet, still no sign of him. Either Kitty scared him away, or he gave up on our future, or perhaps, upon his return... his father sent him to the front. At any rate, here I remained with no Rhen to save me... and with no way to return a reply, Kitty remained in the dark about our mother or about my own fate. I assumed she had her reasons for the continued silence, perhaps her own fear of death, or the importance of the resistance work over the fate of her own family, so much like Thomas, but her lack of fight for us hurt my heart. Of course, she was not the only one who fled Germany and left their friends and families behind to fend for themselves as Hannah told me again and again of the tearful pleas of other families to their loved ones across the world to save them. The silent response echoed, not only from their loved ones, but from many political leaders who refused to believe the horrors wrought upon the Jews.

All of us walked about our lives in a vague semblance of life. The pressure from Hitler against the Jews here in Berlin swelled to such an excess that all of us felt at any moment the bubble would burst, especially as more and more news trickled in about the Jews in Poland. Not only that, just ago we were all ordered to wear a yellow star of David on our clothing, ALL of our clothing – labeled so that everyone might know who we are and how to treat us. Now that Hitler extended the war into Russia, all hopes for a quick resolution to what was happening to Europe faded with every new dawn.

For myself? I knew the dangerous thoughts living in my soul. *What is the point in going on? I've lost everyone in my life... and my own hope is no more than a filmy shadow.*

And yet, even with all the sorrow and madness thickening the air in Berlin, a tiny ember burned in my heart for Rhen. *Did I have reason for the hope?* No, not even the shred that he showed up in Switzerland... but the innocent connection we shared, even if only bound by Shakespeare's words, was enough to open my eyes each morning.

Innocent? Foolish? Naive, even? Probably, but in the midst of all this madness, the heart soaks up even the smallest sunbeam streaming through the dark clouds.

The others in the house moved on with a semblance of normality, at least the normality the Nazis allowed, and even that was getting less and less. For me, normality died when I found my mother's still body. Like a rash creeping up my skin, the idea of death haunted and intrigued me.

Every day we heard more and more reports of neighbors, friends, and family opting for taking their own lives out of a desperation to end their plague-filled days. There was a time I thought the idea abhorrent... but now... well, the thought of the brightness of a white peace versus the darkness of black hate appealed to me. Vacillating feelings were the order of the day.

The side of my face stuck to my pillow from the dried tears as I raised my head to note the time on my wristwatch. Even this small token, a dainty narrow-faced Kasper, a gift from my mother on my sixteenth birthday, burned my eyes with more tears. Seven o'clock in the morning. A knock on the door startled me and I looked up to see Elena's face peeking through the opened door.

"How are you, zeeskeit?"

I shrugged, and she blew me a kiss. "Are you sure you will be all right today? I have to take Moshe to the clinic today for his back pains, and I'm dropping the girls by Elyse's house for their studies. My mother is going with us to help out and Reuben won't be back until after work. I hate to leave you here alone with all that you've been through."

"No, you go," I answered back, almost relieved to have the quietness of the house. "I will be fine."

She nodded. "I left you some porridge on the stove. Please, Julia, eat something. You're wasting away before my eyes. Promise me."

I feigned a smile, a gesture more for her benefit than mine. "I promise," I replied, knowing I did not mean it. As Elena closed the door, she stopped and looked back over her shoulder. "Oh, I forgot to tell you. We all received our notice to report to Grunewald Station the first day in October... something about relocation. Did you get your notice?"

A chill raced up my spine and I sat up. "Relocation? What do you mean relocation?"

She shrugged. "None of us know, zeeskeit, but they told us to dress warm and we could bring a hundred pounds of our personal items. If you ask me, Hitler wants all the Jews out of Berlin, and I, for one, will be thankful to get away from him. So, we go."

She blew another kiss and closed the door. Once the shuffling feet headed to the front door... the final click and lock, my mind swirled with sudden possibilities. *Relocation?* I knew I could not leave Berlin, for if there was even the slightest hope that Rhen might come back to find me, then I must stay here... plus, I pondered the possibility of me finding him first. I had no doubt that if the others in my household received the summons, that one would follow for me in haste. The defiance my mother always warned me about, the chin-jerking, teeth-gritting rebellion returned and I set my plans to work.

Sitting up and fluffing the pillows behind my back, I took my book of *Romeo and Juliet* out and opened the pages to the spot my mind fixed upon. With everyone gone, I read loud and determined.

"Farewell. God knows when we shall meet again. I have a faint cold fear thrills through my veins that almost freezes up the heat of life. I'll call them back again to comfort me... no, wait, this dismal scene I needs must act alone."

My eyes flitted over the words spoken by Juliet, of her own fears and doubts, of waking inside a tomb before Romeo's rescue. For me, I already lay inside that tomb here in Berlin, awake with death all around me... and no Rhen to rescue me. My gaze rested upon the spot on my bed where I saw the empty bottle of pills in my mother's hand. *Shall I continue on this path... that of my mother and Juliet's? And yet, Juliet's death was fake... an act to help her on her way to Romeo.*

My plan formed and I removed a single sheet of paper from the side table, scrawling out the words to enact this scene. I wasn't the first Jew to pretend their suicide in order to slip into the dark night and to the underground. I knew of others, and for most, the plan worked. But for others... no, my mind reprimanded, *don't think that way. This small flicker of love still burning in my heart for my husband will light my way to him. I will find him, somehow... and even if he has moved on with his life, I will have closure.*

After reading my letter once more, the simple confession that 'I can no longer awake another day without my family, nor will I follow the demands of Hitler by relocating to another home. I follow my mother in her example and go to make a hole in the Rhine. God forgive me and I pray for all of you to find peace. Please, if Kitty ever returns, tell her that I love her and forgive her.'

With that, I dressed in my comfortable woolen skirt and cotton blouse, my mother's loafers, and wrapped myself in a heavy coat and scarf, and left the note on the bed. With my my book tucked into the back of my skirt, I eased out my window. Pausing and looking upwards to the rusted ladder still clinging to the side of the building, I recalled Rhen's pale face gazing down at me. *How was I to know that would be the last time I saw him?*

And so, my descent down the vine-covered lattice into the courtyard began my further descent into the underground as a uboater, a nickname given to those diving deep into the murky underworld beneath Berlin – an invisible ghost coming alive only at night and sleeping in garden sheds and drainage tunnels during the day. For six more starving months I hid and scrounged for food in garbage cans, fighting the rats and other hiding Jews... or digging in the soft earth beneath the trees in Berlin's parks just to find a grub or an edible root to stave off the incessant hunger pains.

One night, at great risk to myself, since most knew the Gestapo took great pains to search the parks of Berlin to rout out the Juden rats, I crept into Tiergarten near midnight. Far in the distance, a train whistle whirred into the chilled night air and I wondered if it took another load of Jews to wherever Hitler wanted them. The day Elena, Hannah, Moshe, Reuben, and the girls went to the collection point and onward to Grunewald Station, I hid in the shadows to watch the astounding scene. The platform swarmed with Gestapo, shoving people into cattle cars as fast as they could. My heart leapt to my throat to hear Elena and the girl's screams as they were separated from Reuben and Moshe - women in one car, men in another. The scene did not bode well in my mind... an eerie premonition of death... like sheep to the slaughter.

Now, beneath a cloudy sky, the falling mist formed droplets on my lashes, adding to the tears puddling in the corner of my eyes. I huddled into a bank of yew bushes near a small pond to settle down for the night. My stomach growled and I dug my fingers down into the loamy soil, searching for some acorns to cut the edge of my hunger. Nothing. I laid back against the hard ground as the rain pelted through the leaves and onto my face, watching as a searchlight scanned the clouds above me.

The clouds cried over Berlin and my own tears poured, resigning myself to dying right here in the beautiful heart of the city I once loved so much. Fog crept across the surface of the pond, hovering over me like my final shroud.

My skin prickled as a voice whispered through the dank air.

"Pssst."

I froze like a statue, praying the darkness blanketed over me to hide my hiding place under the bush.

"Pssst," it said, again.

Still, I did not move. Within a few moments of silence, my heartbeat escalated as the sound of footsteps tiptoeing through the fallen leaves greeted my ears. I turned my head to the side to see if I could make out the dark shadows creeping along the water's edge. Electricity surged through my veins as a hand reached out and touched me on the shoulder.

"Hush," the voice said. "I'm not Gestapo. Do you want something to eat?"

"Who are you?" I asked, unable to make out the features of the person, this boy from the sound of his voice.

He grabbed my fingers, shoving a handful of bread into them, and his face lit up as the moonlight peeked through a hole in the clouds. He was not a boy. A young man, perhaps my own age, sat near me, his face hidden by coal smudges and his blue eyes reminding me of Rhen's.

"Eat," he urged. "I can't stay long, and you shouldn't be here either."

"Who are you," I asked, again, in between mouthfuls of the stale bread.

His smile radiated across his face. "Jacob," he answered. "I'm with the Rote Cappell... do you know it?"

I shook my head. "The Red Orchestra? Are you Russian?"

"No, we are a resistance group here in Berlin. I sometimes wander the parks to see if I can find U-boaters hiding in the trees. How long have you been in hiding? When did you first dive?"

"I'm not sure... I think since last winter," I replied.

"Whew, six months" he whistled, quietly. He put one of his fingers to my lips to silence me, and he looked around, waiting for a few minutes more to see if anyone came through the trees. Finally, he removed his finger, and broke off another chunk of bread for me, to which I gobbled up like the starving child I was.

"Slow down," he said. "If you eat that fast after going for long periods of time without eating, it will all come right back up."

I nodded and started nibbling instead. "How long have you been with the resistance?"

"A year, more or less," he replied. "I'm originally from Munich, where my sister is part of the White Rose Network. We are all connected in some way or another with one goal in our minds – to bring down Hitler's Party."

I huffed in my throat and he must have sensed my skepticism over the enormity of the task ahead of them..

"Yes, you are right in how you feel," he replied. "But in all this we must find the crack in the system. There is always a fault line and we are determined to find it, no matter the cost. But look at you, you are shivering. Do you want some help? I can get you somewhere safe and dry."

As appealing as the offer sounded, I also knew there were many Jews seizing the opportunity to turn in fellow Jews to save their own necks.

"No, I have somewhere to stay."

His nod affirmed his understanding my hesitancy. "Look, I know you are scared, and you have every right to fear me. You don't know me, but I assure you that I am here to help. My friend, Mimi, is a secretary in a factory and she and her husband are active in the group and in hiding Jews. I'm sure she could find you a place to stay."

Still, I could not accept his help if I was to find Rhen. None of them in such a resistance group would understand my love for an SS officer, to be sure. So, I thanked him and declined, once again.

"Very well. I'm sure you have your reasons. Instead, then, let me give you some advice. Do you know the Jewish cemetery at Wiessensee?"

"Yes," I answered, knowing my mother was buried there.

"Go there and seek Hans Radski. You can find him sometimes hiding in Herr Schwarz's mausoleum. He can give you a better place to sleep and some food."

His eyes sparkled in the moonlight and I leaned across and squeezed his hand. To find kindness in the midst of hate was a blessing.

"Thank you," I said, and he disappeared as quick as the fog in morning sunlight.

I laid back in the wet leaves, my stomach still growling despite the bit of bread gifted to me from the stranger. Closing my eyes, the humid night air soaked deep into my bones, into my very soul, and I thought of my comfortable bed, snuggling beneath the quilt my grandmother hand-stitched that was to eventually cover my wedding bed after marrying Aaron. So much change and all due to that insane man governing all of Germany.

What is his agenda? I wondered. *His ultimate goal?* I knew very little about him, in truth, only what I had heard through listening to the rumors and whispers from other Jews. And from what little bit I heard from my father before he left, and from flipping through his treasured scrapbook one day while he was at work. Even then I shuddered at the pictures of my father standing side by side with the little man with the odd mustache, smiling with their dark eyes full of Aryan purpose. The scrapbook was full of newspaper clippings about Hitler's rise to power, even clippings from mother's Jewish newspapers such as the C.V.-Zeitung of the "Central Association of German Citizens of the Jewish Faith" which ran a reprinted review of Hitler's *Mein Kampfe* in the autumn of 1925. Most Jews dismissed the book as mere superficial and repulsive rantings from a pompous fool. How time teaches us all that more credence should have been given to the anti-Jewish attitude of the author. Instead of ignoring the rising fervor, or thinking the problem would just go away, perhaps more could have been done early on. *But what? What could any of us done?* Again, images of sheep being led to slaughter surfaced in my mind as the remembrance of other clippings bubbled up – so many reporting of attacks on Jews, or the desecration of many of the Jewish cemeteries.

Cemeteries, my mind whispered. Perhaps Jacob's suggestion of finding a hiding place would be better than hiding at Wiessensee.

I sat up and pulled my jacket close, gazing in the direction of Jacob's departure. My heart pounded in my ears, afraid of whispering out, but I knew I had to take the chance if I was going to survive another night.

"Pssst," I whispered, the sound echoing through the drifting fog. "Are you still there?"

The silence roared back to me and my heart sank; still, I tried once again.

"Jacob," my voice eked out.

I startled as a hand reached out and grasped my shoulder from behind. He pulled me further into the bushes, again putting his finger over my lips and shaking his head, his eyes wide with fear.

A scuffle of footsteps sped down the sidewalk near us and Jacob wrapped his arms around me, pulling me close in the darkness and my head rested against his chest, his rapid heartbeat thundering in my ear. From the corner of my eye, through the mottled dark leaves, the shiny boots of two Gestapo soldiers appeared as the soldiers raced towards the fleeing footsteps, stopping withing a few feet of where we hid. We both jumped as the unmistakable pop of gunfire singed the night air, the rat-a-tat-tat of the machine guns illuminating the darkness, and I gripped my hands over my mouth to muffle the cries surging from my gut. When the gunfire ended, the two soldiers scurried to inspect their casualties, and we remained silent as we heard them chuckling over the moans from their victims. Three more blasts, and silence followed.

Jacob and I kept quiet for what seemed like an eternity, clutching until our shivering melded into one another. We both were so afraid to speak until, at last, Jacob leaned his head forward and whispered in my ear.

"We have to move. We cannot stay here until the morning, else the sunlight will expose us."

"I thought you were gone," I replied, the tears finally rolling down my cheeks.

He shook his head. "No," he answered back. "I was afraid for you. After I left you, I saw the Gestapo coming into the park, so I doubled back to find you."

I closed my eyes and hugged him. "Thank God."

He smiled and hugged me back, placing a small kiss on my lips; and then, released me, his eyes widening. "Oh, I'm so sorry... I'm not sure why I did that..."

I shook my head. "No need to apologize, Jacob. It is the emotion of the moment."

He nodded and peered through the leaves. "Come on, I think we are safe if we head in the opposite direction along the edges of the pond. If I can get you to Mimi's basement, we can find you a hiding place on the outskirts of Berlin."

17

Two days I hid in the basement at Jacob's cousin's house while some other members of the Red Orchestra found me a hiding place with a family near Muggelheim. After a week of easing our way down the Spree to the Dahme, securing hiding spots along the way, Jacob and I tucked inside a barn in a field behind the family's farmhouse. We slept curled next to each other in the hay and awoke to the kindest blue eyes as Herr Dannauer, the owner of the farm, brought us a meal of fried eggs, sausage, and bread, along with fresh milk to drink.

For the first time in months, no... years, I laughed as both Jacob and I chatted about those long ago lost days before the war, of dancing at the Moka Efti. I told him about my one night there... my only night there... of sneaking out on my sixteenth birthday, yet I kept the encounter with Rhen safely stowed away in my heart.

Jacob revealed his own stories of the place, and of his arranged engagement to the dullest of Rabbi Aumann's daughters. When I asked if they were still engaged, his eyes lowered and the smile fled from his lips. He didn't need to tell me, the darkness returning to his face told me all, and the lighthearted moment was gone as quick as it came.

He shoved away his empty plate and stood at the open loft door, gazing out across the swaying grasses of the pasture land.

"You know I have to leave," he said, not looking my way.

"I know," I replied, finishing off the last of my bread.

"It's just, there is the resistance. I feel I have to do more, you see."

"Of course you must. I understand."

He gazed over his shoulder at me, crooking a half grin.

"But I will come back and check on you; I promise. I"m sure the Dannauer's will take good care of you. They are German, but are very against the things Hitler is doing to their country. Both of their boys were sent to the front, and both of them killed within a fortnight of each other."

He knelt down next to me and took one of my hands in his. And, curiously, I let him.

"We live in odd times, Julia," he said, his eyes now gazing deep into mine. "I think providence brought us together, and when all of this is over, when this war is over... perhaps we might build a life together far away from all of these bad memories."

I said nothing, turning my gaze out the doorway. Rhen's smiling face filled my mind along with Jacob's words.

"I know this is sudden," he added. "But, again, we live in strange times when we do not know from one day to the next if we are to survive. If I might have hope..." he said, as he lifted my fingers to his lips. In truth, as his warm lips touched the back of my hand, I closed my eyes and imagined my husband's; still, this brave young man saved my life. *Where was Rhen?* Jacob fought against the Nazis, Rhen was one of them... one who might at this very moment be killing some of my own neighbors... one who killed my own brother.

Leaning forward, I kissed Jacob on the lips, my body and soul longing for the intimacy, and he pulled me close, our mouths hungering for softness, for love, for acceptance. After a few moments of breathlessness and desire, he left me there in the barn, his eyes and heart full of hope for the fight ahead.

Love is a strange thing, indeed; taking hold in the midst of chaos, when every reason informs against it, especially in the case of mine and Rhen's love. And now, here I am presented with two opposing futures, the same as when I faced marrying Rhen or marrying Aaron. In that matter, there was no choice. I would have moved heaven and earth to choose Rhen over the oppressive and demanding husband Aaron would have been. *But now? What do I have before me?*

For all I know Rhen is dead on the front lines; or perhaps, the ideologies of his Nazi upbringing forced him to realize his stupidity in marrying a Jewish girl; after all, *didn't my own father love my mother once upon a time until his racist leanings got the better of him?*

Laying back in the hay, the sunbeams, filtering through the cracks in between the barn's wallboards, warmed my face. The milk cow right below me, safely stowed in her stall, lowed a quiet warning letting me know Herr Dannauer approached just in time to relieve her swollen utters... the same as every day since I came. *What is it now? A week... two? Three?* I barely budged from my dark corner behind the hay, walking each morning back and forth in the loft to keep active, and speaking through the floor slats when Fraulein Dannauer begged me to come inside. She was so kind, gifting me quilt upon quilt for my bed, and two new dresses plus a winter coat to replace my threadbare ones, always with another invitation to sit by her fire in the house. I never accepted, so afraid they might be discovered, so I remained in the barn, afraid to venture very far except to the river behind the house to wash early in the morning and to dump my night pot. Even in this remote location the Gestapo swarmed like ants, exploding out from their mounds if the slightest indention disturbed their ground... meaning, if any Jew stirred, they were sure to be there to devour the carcass.

Jacob visited four more times over the next three months, still embedded in this stupid war, and I almost resigned to the notion of a future with him. We connected on more of a spiritual plane, our faith binding us, rather than the emotional and intellectual bond between me and Rhen. In Jacob's world, beliefs and ideologies revolved around faith, thus spurring his fight against Hitler. With Rhen, they revolved around the heart which connected us since, as my mother so often reminded me, my heart ruled my head instead of the other way around. After endless conversations with Jacob, lying in the hay and gazing up at the clouds, I realized his personality grounded me whereas Rhen's personality helped me soar. In truth, I did not know which was the better one for me, but at this point, I had little choice in the matter.

Reaching in my pocket, I slid out my copy of *Romeo and Juliet*, flipping through the pages until the very lines I thought of flashed before my eyes. Reading them aloud, I chuckled, but whether from understanding the nurse's point of view or from Juliet's, I could not tell as of yet.

"O, he's a lovely gentleman! Romeo's a dishclout to him: an eagle, madam, hath not so green, so quick, so fair an eye as Paris hath. Beshrew my very heart, I think you are happy in this second match, for it excels your first: or if it did not, your first is dead; or 'twere as good he were, as living here and you no use to him."

I held the book to my heart and gazed out across the fields.

"Speakest thou from thy heart?" I asked the air. The cow lowed back and a tear rolled down my cheek.

"Amen," I replied back. "Thou hast comforted me marvelous much."

The farmer, Herr Dannauer peeked up at the top of the ladder to the loft, sliding a small basket of bread and cheese towards me.

"From my wife, Fraulein, and she bids you again to come inside where we have a nice warm bed for you."

I cocked my head and smiled at him, this kind gray-haired man with the crinkles at the side of his eyes when he smiled. I was sure he had seen much with those sky blue eyes during his time on this earth... too much pain, too much suffering... and to lose two children, their entire future wiped away in a split second... *and all for what?*

I palmed a piece of bread and took a bite, nodding to him. "Thank you; you and your wife are so very kind. I know the sacrifice you are making by hiding me... the dangers..."

"Bah," he baulked. "No danger for us, danger for you only. What does it matter for us? If we go because of extending a kindness, if the Führer shoots us in the back for saving another soul, what does it matter anymore? At least we go where we will be with our boys once again."

"And you *believe* that? Truly?"

"Da," he replied. "It is all we have left, and Hitler cannot ever take that from us." He pointed at me, shaking his finger. "And he cannot ever take that from you, remember that. You and Jacob... will have bright future, I see it."

The entire time I hid in the barn, I had never met his wife face-to-face for fear of stepping outside, and for three months Herr Dannauer entreated me to come inside. Jacob trusted them, the Red Orchestra trusted them... *what did I have to fear after all of this time?* After all, they had plenty of time to report my whereabouts, even if I doubted the Gestapo caring about one measly Jew hiding in Muggelheim. Standing up, I brushed the stray straws clinging to my wool skirt and took his hand as his helped me step onto the ladder.

We walked arm in arm to the quaint two-storied farmhouse, the smoke drifting lazily from the chimney into the dreary clouds, and the aroma of kartoffelpuffer, potatoes and onions, sizzling in an iron skillet on the stove filled my nostrils as we reached the porch. Safety and love emanated from every detail, from the squeaky screen door to the overabundance of crochet throws draping over every chair back in the living room. Herr Dannauer's wife peeked around the corner, her eyes widening and her pudgy cheeks pinked with excitement as she bounded into the room and smothered me to her voluminous chest. I didn't mind, though. It had been some times since I felt the warmth of a motherly touch, and I choked back the remembrances of the last time Mutter hugged me.

She ushered me to a chair in front of the fireplace, wrapping me with one of the crochet blankets, all the while ordering her husband to fix me a plate of the kartoffelpuffer and a warm glass of milk. She stood back, examining me, tapping her fingers to her lips and shaking her head.

"Dear me, look at you... nothing but skin and bones. But we shall fix this problem. No more sleeping in that barn, it is to bed upstairs for you."

I watched over over the rim of the glass, the milk forming a mustache along my upper lip as I guzzled the fresh creamy delight. I wanted to protest, to warn them again of the danger, but seeing the happiness my presence brought them filled me with a joy I had not felt for such a long time. *What harm could one night do?*

One night stretched into three and before I knew it, I was melding into their routine and helping with the chores around the house. All of us discovered laughter again, and I wondered sometimes by the look in both of their eyes if they were remembering, or perhaps imagining, the laughter they once shared with their own children. I knew they must, for my own mind crept back to happy times with my family... even the days when Papa was still around.

After dinner one evening, the sunset fired the horizon in orange and yellow as I sat on the porch with Fraulein Dannauer, with Helga, as I now called her. She showed me the simple skill of creating a chain with a crochet hook and some wool yarn, and we laughed at my obvious awkward fingers and the varying sizes of the links in my sad chain. But she was as patient as anyone I had ever seen, taking out the links and showing me how to begin again with a smile and a wink.

"Like this... see? It is nothing once you get the feel of it. Like love... you know?" She said with another wink.

I shrugged, not wanting to reveal too much to her about my situation, but her kind and curious face unloosened my tongue, especially when she nudged my side with her elbow.

"With Jacob? Nein? Da? I had note from him, he coming again tomorrow with two more for us to hide. He a good looking young man. Nein?"

I giggled, the embarrassing warmth flushing my face.

"Da," I replied back, still holding my tongue to anything further.

"He make a fine husband for you... and he did much to save you from the Gestapo."

"Yes, he did, Helga... but... well, what if I told you..." and about the time the words were about to spill, Herr Dannauer pushed through the squeaky screen door and pointed to the barn.

"Can't you hear Mollie's lowing? I can hear her clear across the house."

I jumped up. "Oh no, I'm so sorry, Herr Dannauer, I meant to go milk her earlier. We just got carried away with our crocheting."

He chuckled but crossed his arms, just like a father would do with an only daughter. I picked up the pail at the end of the porch and darted across the field to the barn, skipping part of the way and swinging the bucket without a care in the world.

Mollie snorted at me when I pushed open the barn door, and I sauntered over to the side of her stall, mesmerized by the intense glow of the sky. For a moment I wondered if the soldiers on the front lines could see this sky, for to me, nothing bad could happen with such a sky as this... almost like a gift from God. No bombs falling, no machine gun fire, no children crying, just peace stretching from horizon to horizon.

I smiled and patted Mollie on the rump, setting the pail on the ground beneath her udders and knelt beside her, rubbing my hands together to warm them up, then gripping the teats just as Herr Dannauer showed me. After four tries, and with Mollie shifting from foot to foot, a shiver crept up my spine. Something was wrong, and her agitated animal senses triggered the goosebumps tingling up my arms to my hairline. Very slowly I stood, backing to the back wall with my eyes fixed on the front barn door which swung slightly ajar.

A blood-curdling scream jolted through my body and the unmistakable pop of machine gun fire vibrated through the air. I didn't wait for the soldiers to barrel through the door, but turned and bolted across the field in the opposite direction, the barn hiding me from their sight as I made it to the thick forest of fir trees. From the distance, I watched them inspect the barn, leading Mollie away with a rope, and carrying some of the chickens under their arms as they smiled and laughed.

And in the distance, two other soldiers dragged the Dannauer's limp bodies from their house. The captain motioned towards the woods, sending out his group in twos to search for... for me; and I knew then that somehow they learned of my host and hostess's betrayal to the Reich. They always found a way, those ants... and I closed my eyes and took a breath, wondering how to get word to Jacob so he wouldn't come and bring more into the trap, for I knew they would wait in hiding for anymore to show up. For all I knew, Jacob already lay dead somewhere... or he revealed us to save his own life as so many did. At any rate, someone told.

No, I shook my head. *I can't think that way.* With the questions swirling in my mind, all I could do was run for my life, edging back along the Dahme, back towards Berlin. I had to find Jacob... or find Rhen... or die. So little options in this vast world.

"If all fails... I know how to die." I whispered Juliet's words as the tree branches left tiny scratch marks, slapping my face and arms as I ran with every ounce of energy left inside me, running until my throat burned from the gasping heaves, and my joints screamed for mercy. The last of the sunset shrank to darkness, leaving me alone deep in the pitch darkness of the forest. Once I could run no more, I tumbled down an embankment, my silent cries seizing me as I curled into a ball beneath a yew bush and passed out.

Three days later, after dining on grubs and grass, and drinking water straight from the Dahme, I trembled into Wiessensee Cemetery, a walking corpse in search of a final resting place. In full daylight, with the star on my lapel in full view, uncaring who saw me or if the Gestapo shot me down right then and there, I stood at the end of the path, watching a frail old man pulling weeds from around a marble tombstone. He looked up, confusion filling his eyes and I wondered if he imagined he gazed upon a ghost, but when I collapsed from sheer starvation and exhaustion, he rushed to me and helped me inside a small caretaker's shed tucked in the trees.

"Dear me," he said, helping me to a chair. "You took great risk to walk around in the daylight."

I looked up into his kind dark gray eyes. "And yet, are you not Jewish? Aren't you the Rabbi who tends this cemetery?"

He smiled and glanced over his shoulder, then placed a finger on his own lips to silence me.

"Come now, we will get you a warm blanket and a place to hide. After you are settled, I will bring you something to eat."

He wrapped a threadbare blanket around my shoulders, but I didn't care. His kindness in the face of his own tenuous situation warmed my heart and I followed him down the path as the sun sank to the horizon.

"Are you afraid of the dead?" he whispered, and I shook my head, already feeling well acquainted with those whose bones lay within. As we passed through the narrow paths weaving through the tombstones, he paused, gazing around the edge of one of the mausoleums. Wiggling his finger, he urged me forward, then we scurried across to another ornate mausoleum overgrown with vines and bushes. He pointed towards the bent iron gate shielding the front doorway and nudged me through the narrow opening. On the other side, I pressed my shoulder into the door and pushed, once, then on the second time, the door creaked open. Before closing the door back, the Rabbi whispered.

"Keep quiet and only come out at night if you need to, otherwise we will toss you bags of food through the window there," he pointed to a small barred window to the side of the door. "There are many others hiding here in the cemetery, but so far the Gestapo have not discovered us."

I nodded and he turned to leave.

"Wait, Rabbi," I whispered louder. "Do you know Jacob? He is with the Rote Cappell? He told me to come here."

He nodded and his eyes drooped in sadness, telling me all I needed to know.

One by one, all those I loved left this earth, and still every day I woke up, my eyes greeting another pain-stricken sun. After the Rabbi left and I nibbled on the bread he gave me, the muted glow of moonlight through the trees and the vines lit the inside of the crypt in a cold stark grayness. The marrow in my bones chilled and I gazed over the marble sarcophagus in the center of the small room. From the writing, the remains of some ancient Jew from the 1800s lay within, his bones and body safely stowed away from all the horrors inflicted today.

Climbing up on the platform, I lay prone with the blanket over me like a final shroud, and the slivers of moonbeams breaking through the ivy-covered columns and iron bars mottled over my body.

Without volition, Juliet's words erupted across my lips like some otherworldly oracle bespeaking my future.

"How if, when I am laid into the tomb, I wake before the time that Romeo come to redeem me? There's a fearful point! Shall I not, then, be stifled in the vault, to whose foul mouth no healthsome air breathes in, and there die strangled ere my Romeo comes? Or, if I live, is it not very like, the horrible conceit of death and night, together with the terror of the place, as in a vault, an ancient receptacle, where, for these many hundred years, the bones of all my buried ancestors are packed: where bloody Tybalt, yet but green in earth, lies festering in his shroud; where, as they say, at some hours in the night spirits resort; Alack, alack, is it not like that I, so early waking, what with loathsome smells, and shrieks like mandrakes' torn out of the earth, that living mortals, hearing them, run mad.

"O, if I wake, shall I not be distraught, environed with all these hideous fears? And madly play with my forefather's joints? And pluck the mangled Tybalt from his shroud? And, in this rage, with some great kinsman's bone, as with a club, dash out my desperate brains?"

I curled to my side, pulling my knees to my chest, letting the tears flow down onto the cold slab.

"Oh, that I had a sweet vial to take away this pain. O, Rhen, Rhen, wherefore art thou, my Rhen?"

And still, like every day before, my soul refused to die, and each morning as the sun rose, a twinkling of hope flickered deep inside me, praying that when I opened my eyes I might see my husband's face. Yet, day after day passed, and I etched into the marble tomb as if I belonged among the carved angels. Sometimes an entire day or two passed before the Rabbi dropped a small bag of stale bread and half-eaten fruit, probably scavenged from a pure Aryan's kitchen garbage left on the curb for Goring's piggeries. The irony. Judenschwein rifling though Nazischwein's food to survive.

For the most part, due to my own fears, I barely stepped outside the mausoleum after the Rabbi brought me here, only slipping out to take care of necessary functions in the nearby bushes, and I spoke to no one after witnessing the murders of the Dannauers. My body absorbed the water he left in a jug hidden behind the iron gate, but thankfully, all my normal bodily functions diminished close to nil as every cell inside craved nourishment, the same as my heart craved anything resembling love. Perhaps the same reason I clung to the naive hope that somewhere out there Rhen searched for me.

Would it be possible to stay hidden in this grave until he found me? Until the war ended and we could emerge arm in arm? What would Berlin even look like then? What about the world?

18

Rhen
Warsaw Ghetto, Poland
January 1942

Leaning against the wall of the guard tower, I sucked hard at the nub of my glowing cigarette, then flicked it over the barbed wire. After overseeing the endless lines of Jews filing through the gates, the population bulged to over 400,000. But with every person that passed through the gate, my eyes fixed on the women's faces, wondering if one day I might find Julia among the throng.

I knew finding her was hopeless at this point, especially thinking she might appear in Poland, but still the body and mind seeks hope even when nothing else is left. And I saw the same desperation in the eyes of every person passing by me, or wandering around the ghetto streets like frail ghosts in search of a sliver of food. And here I stood, my stomach full and satisfied with meals served to us in the SS commissary, stocked well with sausages from Goring's piggeries, breads baked fresh each morning, and French wines imported after the occupation. *But what could I do?*

My father made it clear to me after my next failure at Auschwitz that he would not tolerate his only son making a laughingstock of him before the Führer. He even threatened to send me to the front, but like a good goosestepping puppet, I threw my arm up in a perfect 'Heil, Hitler' and groveled to him... all with the purpose to continue my search for Julia and her mother. *How was I to know that he'd send me to Warsaw to help oversee the corralling of thousands into an area less than one and a half square miles?*

Now, nine months have past since since I arrived back from my trip to Switzerland, and my ruse with Rosamund continued as I lured her on with sweet notes to keep up my Nazi appearance. I intended on returning to Berlin after picking up Höss's car at the train station, but with only one day left in my "holiday" retreat, I knew if I did not arrive back at Auschwitz before the end of the week, his suspicions against me would mount. Even if I used Rosamund as an excuse for my absence, she'd reveal the note saying I returned to Berlin, leaving me with a lot of questions to answer from both of them. All of it set the perfect stage for suspicion, and with the Nazi echelon, suspicion translated into treason, and a swift kick into Spandau Prison whether guilty or not.

Upon my return to the camp, Höss inundated me with paperwork as the population of Auschwitz grew. Every time I mentioned anything about a small trip to Berlin to see my family, he reminded me of his gift to the retreat and that, in times like these, family life mattered little. "Work sets one free", he said to me on more than one occasion, with a laugh as he pointed to the sign arching over the gate to Auschwitz.

Still, with all of that, he shipped me back to my father with a letter of recommendation to "send him somewhere he can truly learn the meaning of what we are trying to accomplish here." Father knew keeping me in an office with my nose in a bunch of files was no way for me to get the full impact of Hitler's purpose for all of Europe.

"You are going to have to go somewhere you can get a sense of what kind of trash these Jews are. I don't need you in an office, I need you in the thick of things to roughen up those smooth edges of yours."

"But why, father, if you don't mind me asking?"

He pointed at a chair in front of his desk and ordered me to sit. Then, walking to the window, he crossed his arms with his back to me.

"Do you know what the Reich means to Germany? To your own future, Rhen?"

I rolled my eyes. I had heard this same speech from him countless times over the years, and it always began the same way, and I learned in rote the right things to say.

"Of course, father, it means the return to a pure way of life for us all, to the purification of the Aryan, and the eradication of impurities in any shape or form."

"Eradication... hmmm, interesting that you use that word. Do you know where I was three days ago before you arrived back in Berlin this morning?"

He glanced over his shoulder and I shook my head. Turning back to the window, he continued.

"I went with the Führer to a villa in Wannsee. Some of his top officials met with him to discuss the Jewish problem and a possible solution."

"Solution? What do you mean?"

"They are a blight on the world, Rhen, and in order to fulfill our Aryan purpose, we must be willing to eradicate the trash from the world."

"Hhmph," I spat. "But that is already happening. I see those in the Wehrmacht already killing Jews whenever they wish, not to mention what was done in '39."

Father pounded his fist on the wall and the glass in the windows shivered. "It is not enough; and this is the reason for the conference in Wannsee." He turned, facing me, and crossed his arms once again, his eyes resolute and black.

"Our Führer has tasked Heydrich to implement a final solution to the Jew problem. All Jews are now subject to deployment to labor camps, separated by gender, with the stronger to build roads, and the weaker to be weeded out by natural reduction. Those surviving will be dealt with appropriately, by whatever means necessary; and a new camp called Theresienstadt will be established as a camp for elderly or disabled Jews, with an eventual solution for Jews married to non-Jews or mixed descent."

His words of 'Jews married to non-Jews' singed my heart. "What do you mean, dealt with appropriately?"

A low grumbling chuckle rumbled in my father's throat. "What do you think it means?" He slid his hand across his throat in a slice, mouthing the word, "Eradication."

My heartbeat sped up, thinking of Julia caught up in this evacuation plan devised by Hitler and his horde.

"So, what does this have to do with me?" I asked, afraid of what his answer might be.

He walked over and opened up the top drawer to his desk and slid out a manila folder, dropping it on the desk in front of me.

"You are reassigned, once again; but I promise you this time, Rhen, that if you get sent back from this assignment, I am sending you to the front."

My eyes rested on the letters inked in black marker at the top of the sealed envelope. Just three words – Montabauer and Warsaw Ghetto – and he delivered me in person to the train station with no chance for me to get away to Julia's apartment.

And now, here I am, just another flunky herding cattle, and occasionally pointing my useless gun. The last time I shot a Jew it was Julia's brother, and that was the very last time. The endless and mindless games against these people ripped out the last clinging hope in my heart, dissolving my soul like paper in acid, and any thought of seeing Julia's beautiful face again disappeared with each body dropping to the ground from starvation; which is a daily occurrence, at least three or four times a day. And now, something else rises on the horizon and I'm afraid that the implementation of that 'final solution' is picking up speed.

Theresienstadt is complete, Auschwitz and Chelmno are pumping out ash to the sky, and the whispers among the guards late at night is that soon all the ghettos will be emptied of their inhabitants. I tossed and turned, shuffling in my bed, attempting to grab hold of elusive sleep, and wondering what to do if I'm ordered to squeeze the trigger of my machine gun and eliminate them all. *What if I saw Julia standing in the crowd?*

I squeezed my eyes shut, feeling imprisoned within the same confines housing the Jews, my mind echoing over and over again, "coward", "dreamer", "fool", and yet, if fate gave me one minute, no, one second for me to see my wife's face again, I'd take it without hesitation. I prayed she still felt the same.

19

Rolling over in my bunk at the requisitioned house across from the Ghetto, one especially purposed for SS officers overseeing the Judenrat beyond the gates, my eyes pried open, still tired after another night of insomnia. Hanging on a bent nail, my pressed SS uniform came into view, the silver buttons flashing in the morning sunlight.

Another day of wishing to escape from the dull blackness of this endless Nazi night into something worthy of humanity, perhaps even a good sound sleep with a clear conscience, or the sheer release of a pure wailing saxophone, or an innocent Shakespearean passage uttered across my wife's lips rendering me speechless.

No such luck. A knock brought me momentarily from my musing and the door creaked open. Standartenführer Breckelhoff stepped into the room with his hat under his arm and saluted the perfect 'Heil, Hitler'. Gazing up, my eyes addressed him up and down, noting his shiny clear blue eyes and blonde hair, the utter manifestation of the Reich – perfect, exact, handsome, his features in succinct proportion, his flawless salute, together with his tall stature, mirror-polished boots, and natural ease in his uniform. It was obvious he was a newly appointed stool-pigeon fresh from the Dachau school where he learned the gift of imitation instead of originality. Perfect little cut-out fools, all to resemble the Führer's ideal. I wanted to jump up and mess up his hair, or spit on his boots, but instead I did what I always did; I stood and returned a meager salute.

"You are on duty today, sir, along with me. We are making an inspection of the streets with Judenrat Grosman in about half an hour."

I nodded and yawned. "Yes, yes; I know. Is there coffee in the commissary?"

The boy smiled, his straight pearly teeth gleaming and his pasty white skin pinking. "Da," he replied, "they have some good Kaffee HAG all ready for you, sir. Shall I meet you at the gates to the ghetto?"

I nodded and waved him away, then turned to the window, still dressed in only my boxer underwear and t-shirt.

"Dress warmly," he said as he closed the door. "The snow swept though last night and Grosman assured me that all the frozen bodies would be removed before we arrived."

I shook my head as the door closed shut as my thoughts swirled in sarcasm. *Yes, make sure we don't see any corpses lying on the street... make sure to bury the dead.*

Outside, good Polish Aryans strolled along the streets, some awaiting the trolley which clacked along the track, its bell clanging as it approached the stop. Women and men entered and exited, some pulling their coats tighter to their chests, some smiling and nodding to each other in a friendly way, and all hiding the very sad reality which stood only a few feet from their semblance of normality. My eyes drifted from window to window, catching brief glimpses of people's lives just beyond the lace curtains, all living a mock existence in this dank, starving Warsaw. Most of the shops along the avenue were empty, leaving behind a void whispering 'forgotten' that I was sure would never be remembered again.

My mind drifted back to seeing Bernie in Berlin the same day I caught the train to Warsaw. On leave for a week from his assignment in France, a somewhat cushioned job of guarding the sequestration of the Louvre as thousands of pieces of artwork taken from French Jews were cataloged and shipped to Germany. Much to Hitler's chagrin, most of the masterpieces housed there before the occupation remained hidden from his reach. With Bernie's stint on the front lines as the troops barreled into France, and then with this travesty of watching stolen paintings cross his path, I saw my best friend morph into someone I did not recognize anymore. The Wehrmacht gave him a new personality, one transformed from the carefree wise-cracking Wagner-lover into a sullen robotic drone with a shaky trigger finger.

He was always the one to turn my brooding mind into thoughts of dancing and girl-watching, leaning heavier on those than Max who balanced us both by standing resolutely in the middle of us in personality and wit.

"Ah, Max," I whispered, my breath fogging on the window as I leaned my head against my forearm, the cold glass stinging my skin. "You are so fortunate not to see what is becoming of all of us."

Or of what is becoming of Berlin. Just a year ago, the railway terminus Potsdamer Bahnhof burned after an air raid, which was becoming a more and more frequent occurrence. Hitler thought he'd bomb everyone else, with no one being able to reach Berlin. He was quite wrong on that score. Now, the crumbled buildings and scorched limestone pocked throughout the city center, adding to the scorching we already did to the Jewish properties.

I dressed without haste, uncaring about the stroll through the Ghetto to ensure whether the Judenrat were upholding the safety and security of the people. In truth, I despised them, for they turned their backs on their fellow Jews for a few more slices of bread in their bellies, and the small amount of power it gave them. Some of them even acted chummy with us, as if the smiles and handshakes might ensure their life. For the most part, it did not. For me, I would rather see them stand shoulder to shoulder with their friends and family, braving the starvation and the cold, than try to assimilate or befriend the Nazis. And even in that, my mind reprimanded me, accusing me daily for my own part in not standing up to my father, or to anyone, for that matter, and renouncing the creed I swore to. And as always, I excused my reasoning, saying that I had a purpose behind what I did, that each goosestep brought me closer to finding Julia. If I made a stand, I'd find myself with my neck in a noose at Spandau.

What use would I be to Julia then? Another year in this exile from the life I might have known. How long did Romeo wait in Mantua before the priest sent the letter? And did I miss the note, the same as he did? Does Julia now lie in some cold mausoleum awaiting my rescue?

I balled my fists, willing myself forward, and headed straight for the Ghetto, passing on the rot-gut they called coffee, and met the eager shiny Breckelhoff at the entrance, both of us attired in our thick grey wool coats and leather gloves. Judenrat Grosman waved to us from the other side of the gate, and we entered.

People billowed out of the entrances to the buildings and onto the streets as we passed, desperate for the fresh air after a night of being packed in like sardines, seven to each and every room available, and my bones ached seeing most of them shivering in their threadbare clothes. A sorrowful silence followed me, broken only by the crunching of my boots in the icy wheel tracks along the road. A few of the men stopped as we passed, taking off their hats and bowing their heads, propped up like scarecrows against their shovels.

Grosman yelled at them to 'get to work', and I watched as the shovel blades plunged into the blinding white snow with a crispness and purity in stark contrast to the darkness of this hell hole on earth. Glancing up, I caught the eye of a little girl standing in a doorway, a volume of stories in her vacant eyes and hollow cheeks. Her innocent future gone in an instant, overnight. She probably slept sound in her bed the night the Gestapo broke through her door and ordered her family onto the trains that brought them here. She held a dirty ragged teddy bear clutched in the crook of her arm, probably the last remaining possession of her old life.

"Somewhere life is still moving forward," I said out loud, without thinking.

Breckelhoff nudged me with his elbow. "For us, at least," he said with a chuckle.

I thought of my inner turmoil; the slicing sounds of the spades, the frozen tears on the girl's cheeks, the fake camaraderie between Grosman and Breckelhoff as they stood there taunting the men to shovel faster. A bubbling anger rose to the surface.

"And yet, it is all a lie," I said, the words slipping from my tongue, blasting like vapor into the frigid air. Breckelhoff narrowed his eyes and pulled me to the side.

"Sir, are you well?"

"Very well," I replied back, my mind clearing for the first time in quite a while. I pointed at the other people walking up and down the street like corpses seeking their grave, the children with open palms and cracked lips, the solitary woman collapsed in a heap in the dark corner of another doorway, the snow drift covering over her bluish-gray rigid body, and the fractured market stalls where old men sold arm bands just to make enough to feed their family.

"Look at this travesty," I said, and Breckelhoff straightened, throwing his shoulders back.

"Da, sir, I will see that all of this is taken care of."

I shook my head and glared at him. "Are you happy?" I asked. His eyes widened, surprised at such an awkward question from one SS officer to another.

"Da, sir," he retorted back. "I am happy in serving the Fatherland. Everything is justified, and soon all of this will be a distant memory."

"A distant memory? That's not true, and somewhere inside all of us, we all know that these sights will never leave. The world has changed, and no matter where you go, the Fuhrer's struggles will have an effect for generations to come." I nodded to the little girl, directing his eyes to her. "Our reality is only Hitler's reality, not our own. He never consulted the common people, so we have to just acquiesce to whatever happens. Reality is hiding behind the swatiska, afraid to peek from the doorway, afraid of death. Once upon a time, she knew a different world, and probably imagined a future for herself. Sometimes, the future we imagine is only exchanged for someone else's and we are put under the yoke of furrowing out the dreams of those over us."

He chuckled, but I could tell from the blank expression on his face that the indoctrination had sucked every once of soul from his cells. He hadn't a clue what I was trying to say.

"Our future is bright; and the Jew furrows out that dream for us. See," Breckelhoff said, the sunlight glinting in his eyes as he urged me back towards Grosman who stood with this hands on his hips, barking orders at the men. The scraping of the blades hitting the pavement underneath grated my nerves, and I turned and hurried in the other direction, with both Grosman and Breckelhoff rushing to catch up to me.

I had had enough. Turning, I pointed at them both and ordered them to go around the eastern side of the ghetto and meet me at the north end, making sure to get a report from every Judenrat over each building as to food supply, sanitation, and housing. Both of them saluted and darted away, determined to fulfill their assignment.

Alone, I wandered through the streets, the crowds backing away from me, standing against walls with their eyes lowered and hands folded in front of them. From time to time, I'd stop at a group of women, all emaciated and afraid, and ask if they knew the Cappell family from Berlin. I knew such a question fell on deaf ears, since none of them spoke German, and none of the Jews from Berlin were sent to this ghetto. Still, I asked, and hope flickered in my heart with every step.

Eventually, my wandering led to Leshno Street, the "Broadway" of the ghetto, and my old musical leanings perked when I noticed a tattered sign blowing in the wind announcing "the Nightingale" at the Femina Theatre. Entertainment was tolerated by the SS as a way to normalize life for the Jews inside the ghetto, thus many cafes and concert venues popped up during the years.

My skin prickled as Julia's voice whispered in my ear, "… wilt thou be gone? It is not yet near day. It was the nightingale, and not the lark, that pierced the fearful hollow of thine ear. Nightly she sings on yon pom'granate tree. Believe me, love, it was the nightingale."

I spun around, greeted by only the tinkling sound of snowflakes papering the sky. Taking a deep breath, I entered the Femina, following a corridor to the cellar of the building, which opened up to a spacious room large enough to seat least 800 to 900 people, more of a cabaret-style arrangement than cinema. When my eyes adjusted to the darkness, a solitary young woman stood on the stage before me, her voice lilting out a sad melodious song. In the shadows and smoke cast by the dim carbide lights, the silhouette of a man sat on the front row haloed in cigarette smoke.

The young woman saw me and stopped, jolting the silhouetted man to his feet as he rushed around the seats, taking off his felt fedora to stand stick-straight before me.

"Please," I said, "go on."

"We are only rehearsing, sir." The man's brow wrinkled, and he shifted from foot to foot, fear gathering in his eyes.

I pointed to the nearest seat next to me and sat down, motioning for him to sit on the other side, to which he obliged. From our dark vantage point, he called out to the woman to start again.

Closing my eyes, I imagined that night at the Moka, dancing close with Julia, our bodies pressed together, swirling beneath the Turkish columns, red velvet drapes, and shimmering chandeliers. A lifetime ago... lost in a flash... overnight.

The woman's voice flowed like silk, and though I did not understand her Polish words, the meaning behind the mournful tone wrenched my heart. When she finished, tears burned the edges of my eyes, and we sat in silence to absorb the last notes lingering on the air.

Noticing her her teeth chattering, I thanked her and told her she could leave. The man next to me rested against the back of the wood theater seat and sighed.

"She will perform this evening, if you would like for me to secure you a table for you and some of the officers."

I laughed, knowing not a one of the officers would venture into the ghetto to a Jewish cabaret.

"Cigarette?" I asked, to which he removed a single hand-rolled one from his front coat pocket, probably his last one, and handed it to me, his hands shaking from either the cold or from fear of what I might do next.

I gripped it between my teeth, lighting the end and taking a long draw.

"Once, a long time ago," I fnally said, "I spent a great deal of time at the cabarets in Berlin."

He nodded, and waited for me to continue.

"What is your name?" I asked.

He fumbled inside his coat pocket for his papers, but I held up my hand.

"Nein," I added, "just tell me your name."

"Jurandot... Jerzy Jurandot. This is my theater, the Femina."

I pointed to the now empty stage. "And the girl?"

"Marysia Ayznshtat... our nightingale of the ghetto."

"Indeed," I replied back. "Very talented voice, I must say."

"Yes, she might be a star once we leave the ghetto."

I chuckled in my throat, thinking back to my tirade with Breckelhoff about all of our stilted dreams.

"Tell me about the theater, Jurandot. As a personal request only, not one for a report to my superiors, you understand? I wish to remember those days before the war... can you help me do that?"

Jurandot chuckled, as well, and opened his arms wide to

encompass the entire room. "That is what I do, Herr Kommandant. I offer a surrogate normalcy, an immersion in a pleasant past or a parallel universe. I do whatever I can to keep this place open even when people are starving, anxious, repelled by the growing piles of waste outside the windows, longing for breathing space among the hordes of shoving strangers, afraid of you officers coming in to round us up, or escaping the typhus-infected louse crawling from one stranger's coat onto yours."

"And you feel no shame in creating this fake world?"

He huffed. "Shame? I feel no shame. There is nothing different in this than reading, or gardening, or hiking in the mountains. It is all for our self-preservation; a physical and psychological escape. You enter the theater and leave behind the Judenrat, the walls of the ghetto, the typhus, and the hunger, even if it is only for two hours. Is that not what you used to do at the cabarets before the war?"

I nodded and closed my eyes, the fleeting images cascading through my mind like the falling snow outside.

"Seems almost cruel, though, when there is no hope of returning to that former life."

He huffed, again. "Cruel? Forgive me, Herr Kommandant, but this sort of cruelty is one we can bear when faced with the harsher cruelties we face as Jews."

I cut my eyes at him, and I knew he skirted dangerously close to what might be considered crossing the line. Any other officer would simply put a bullet in his head for speaking out... but he did not know that I was no ordinary punched-out paper doll dressed up in an SS uniform.

"So," I asked, "you are telling me that the illusion is worth it, even if only for a moment?"

His bottom lip trembled. "Of course, Herr Kommandant, for we are only given today. None of us know what tomorrow brings, so tonight we sing. Tonight, many will brave the hunger, the snow, and the dark streets just to live a moment in the bright warm sun. You must know that music does that... or why else would you have gone to the cabarets?"

I did not answer him. Crushing out the cigarette beneath the toe of my boot, I stood and gazed out across the stage one last time, wondering what will happen with these two Jews, the same as I wondered about Julia.

In one last hopeful moment, I walked to the door, paused and looked over my shoulder.

"Where are you from, Jurandot?"

"From here... from Warsaw. Why?"

I shrugged. "Do you know the Cappell family from Berlin?"

He shrugged in answer. "No. Jews?"

I nodded, and he chuckled.

"You know, not all Jews know each other, contrary to popular belief."

His retort brought a smile to my face, and I left him, returning to the blizzard winds slicing the snow across the streets. By the time I reached the entrance to the ghetto, I counted five more bodies frozen in the drifts... and I paused, my gut heaving as I recognized the dainty flower print dress peeking out from beneath a stack of bodies layered on a wagon as that worn by the little girl who just an hour ago stood in the doorway. Now, her small fingers splayed in a permanent frozen blossom like a lily breaking through the layer of glistening snow blanketing over her.

Swallowing the bile in my throat and rushing away from the calls of Breckelhoff, I hurried back across the street to my room and slammed the door shut, burying my muffled cries in my pillow as I crushed my officer's hat in my grip.

Will this never end? How far is Hitler willing to go to see his dream fulfilled?

20

After much pleading and promises to my father, I had enough of camps and ghettos. I swore to him to throw myself into any office work he could find for me at the headquarters in Berlin. Of course, I had my own reasons for wanting to be back there, but with a little fake peacocking about my love for the Fatherland and my desire to be closer to the heartbeat of the Reich, he acquiesced and allowed me to come back.

Just one month later from leaving Warsaw, he handed me a folder marked "Grossacktion Warsaw" and told me to file it in the top secret drawer.

As was my habit, I opened the cover and read. "Grossacktion Warsaw", code name for mass deportation and resettlement at Treblinka concentration camp. The ghetto was to be emptied beginning June of 1942 – this very month. My heart sank, thinking about the theater owner, Jurandot, and the young singer. No resettlement, for all who "resettled" in Treblinka never came out, being one of the Reich's top four extermination camps.

Walking back down to my father's office, I knocked on the door and waited for his approval to enter.

"Come," he barked.

Attempting to show genuine interest in the contents of the folder, I set it on his desk and tapped the cover with my index finger.

"Can you tell me about this? What is happening?"

A low sinister laughed rumbled out of his throat. "Isn't it obvious?"

"I just want to hear it from your mouth."

He leaned back in his squeaky chair and smiled. "Remember when I told you about the final solution to the Jew problem? Well, the time has come to implement Hitler's vision for a Jew-free Europe. We are sending them all to the extermination camps, clearing out all the ghettos. By this time next year, the vermin will be eradicated."

I arched my eyebrow, stilling my rapid heartbeat.

"Very interesting," I acknowledged. "So, my assignment to Warsaw would have been over anyway. Good thing I asked to come back here."

"Yes," he added, "a good thing. And I'm very proud of the intensity and focus you've shown since coming back."

I picked up the folder and headed back to the door. With my trembling hand on the doorknob, a thought struck me and I glanced back over to him.

"Father, what about the Jews here in Berlin?"

"All of them," he replied back. "They've all been shipped first to Lodz, then from there to Auschwitz."

"Good," I answered with a nod and a smile. "Soon, all of this will be justified."

I closed the door behind me, and leaned up against the wall, my stomach knotting to think all the while that Julia might have been at the Lodz Ghetto, just a two hour train ride from Warsaw.

Rushing back to my office, I picked up the phone and had the switchboard operator put me through to the office in charge of the transports leaving from the various stations in Berlin, and within the hour, I sat a desk in a back room pouring over name after name of those shoved into cattle cars on their way to Lodz. Page after page... the clock on the wall ticked by, each second clicking as my eyes scanned over the Jewish names.

And then, my heart leapt. A name popped out from list of those leaving from Grunewald Station.

Hannah Schwartz. Aaron's mother.

My finger sped down the names below hers, and I whispered them out loud.

Reuben Kaufman... Elena Kaufman... Danka Kaufman... Gerta Kaufman... Moshe Schwartz... on and on, still no sign of Julia's name anywhere.

The registry showed the train's destination as Lodz, but the date as October 1941. I knew any hope of finding any of them alive, especially since thousands were already taken from that ghetto and sent to Chelmno. And yet, Julia's name was absent from the list.

Another thought sprung into my mind and I rushed out of the office, racing up the stairs back to my father's office and barreled inside without a formal invitation. Both he and Hess leaned over his desk, assessing a map marked with red squares indicating various ghettos and camps across Europe.

With a perfect 'Heil, Hitler' I avoided a reprimand from my father as the two men stood up and returned the greeting.

"Father," I said, breathlessly, "send me to Lodz to oversee the final resettlement of the Jews. I'd like to do my part in pushing forward this agenda and I feel I cannot do that sitting behind a desk."

Father's eyes narrowed and Hess smiled.

"Well, well, Montabauer, seems your boy came around after all."

"But you just arrived back," my father questioned. "I was under the impression that you felt you could do more here in the heart of the Reich."

"Forgive me, sir, but I was wrong. Please, send me to Lodz."

Hess threw his arm over my shoulders, his dark eyes gleaming at me. "Go on, Montabauer, let's see what this eager young officer can do with this sort of passion."

And with that, by midday, I was granted the request and I rode the train to my family house to see my mother, who I had not seen since the pictures of her near death experience. All the memories of my childhood passed through my mind like some strange story I read a lifetime ago, a vague romantic fairy tale conjured by a fool full of birthday cake, hugs, and laughter. Of course, my mother was the only one flitting though those memories. Father remained the dragon in the black forest belting fire from his mouth whenever one of us attempted to break free of our fortress.

Walking up the steps to the house, I stopped for a moment and remembered Max lounging on the top step, awaiting me after the night we spent at the Moka. His last words echoed in my mind... "a curse on both your houses," and I shivered. I hurried past the steps and the memory to the front window, amazed at how everything looked the same as the last time I saw it. Father's leather chair still sat at an angle, facing the fireplace. A small vase of artificial edelweiss sat on the coffee table. A fire burned in the fireplace and the familiar scent of cinnamon mingled in my nose, and I remembered all the times mother sprinkled a palm full of the spice over the logs, the aroma filling the room... just another small illusion to create the perfect Reich household.

I pushed open the door and leaned in, breathing in the smell.

"Mother? Mother, are you here?"

After I eased the door shut and turned, she appeared at the top of the stairs still dressed in her white cotton gown and robe, rubbing her eyes awake from sleep.

"Rhen? Is that you?"

I hurried to the stairs, and she threw herself into my arms, kissing my cheeks and squeezing me with her frail arms. She reared back, cupping my face with her hands, smiling. But the tell-tale signs of her unhappiness shadowed over her face, the lines deeper across her brow, the shadows darker under her eyes, and the scars from her "fall" jagged across her jaw. Leading her over to the couch, I held her to me, my arms around her shoulders, noticing the unmistakable sharpness of her shoulder bones.

Finally, I looked into her face and sighed. "Mother, are you well?"

She sighed back. "Well? Of course, dearest, especially with you here. It's been too long.." she said, her eyes filling with tears as she tugged on the red armband around my upper arm.

"But look at you in your fine uniform. Papa would be so proud of you."

"He is," I answered back, lowering my eyes. "He is sending me to Poland to oversee a matter there."

She gasped. "Not the front, I pray."

"No, not the front. Just some other matters."

She laughed through her nose and rolled her eyes. "Other matters? Yes, I know of the other matters... Even though your father tries to keep me cloistered in this house, I am not blind to what is going on." She leaned back against the cushions, her long blonde hair streaked with silver puddling on sofa back, the firelight flickering in her empty eyes.

"So, what of you, Rhen? Tell me of your life."

I leaned back, as well, staring into the fire as the embers crumbled into ash. *Do I spill my guts about Julia, or placate her with imaginary notions about Rosamund?* "My life? What is there to tell? If you know about what is going on here in Germany, then you know what my life has been. None of us have our own life anymore, do we?"

She pressed her finger to her lips and whispered a hush. "Quiet, my son, we must not talk with such a tone in this house... not against our promised future."

"Ha," I barked. "Promised future? I'm not sure any of us have a future anymore."

She reached over and patted my hand. "Oh, you will, Rhen... long after your father and I are gone. You will find the love of your life, raise good blonde-haired babies, and the sun will rise for you each morning."

I shook my head. "And you believe that?"

Her bony shoulders lifted and a shadow fell across her face. "It is a nice thing to hear, is it not? That is what I used to tell you, remember?"

"Dreamers, mother; that is what we are. Forever looking to the disappearing horizon, forever with our head in the clouds instead of facing the realities around us. Why did we do that to ourselves?"

"For survival, Rhen... for survival. No matter who we are, we cling to hope for a better tomorrow, and in the meantime, we use clever devices to obscure the realities around us."

"And what is your device?"

She giggled, walked across the room, opened up a small burled walnut credenza and held up a small bottle of wine.

"Shall we?" she asked, and poured two glasses. "Your father keeps a regular supply in the basement, snitched from some Jew's house in France after the occupation, I suppose."

She sat back down, handing me the glass, and clinked the side, the ping echoing through the emptiness in the room.

"Let's drink to our Führer, shall we?" she said, throwing her head back with a sarcastic laugh.

I drank, but not to the Führer; I drank instead to the hope of finding my wife. After two long gulps, I palmed the glass between my hands and leaned forward with my elbows on my knees.

"Why did you never leave him, mother? What made you stay?"

From the corner of my eye, I saw her flinch and she threw back the last of the wine in her glass before she answered.

"Love. What else would make me stay?"

"Don't lie to me, mother."

"I'm not lying to you, my son. Despite all the hardships in this house, despite your father's harsh words at times..."

"Harsh words?" I belted. "It is more than harsh words, and it always has been. The last time you almost died..."

"No," she retorted. "It has not always been that way. When we were first married, a few years after he returned from the front lines during the Great War, we were happy. He was a different person then, Rhen, more like you than you'd like to believe. He won my heart with a poem; can you believe that? He is still there, somewhere inside, and all of my hope lies on him returning to me after this war is over."

I shook my head. "Hope. Ha! Isn't it amazing what a small four letter word does to us all? Even Hitler has his own variation of hope, doesn't he? And yet, we cannot return to the past, mother, no matter how hard we try. I think father is lost to you. Hitler and the Reich are his new mistresses, and I foresee doom for anyone close to our Führer."

She poured another glass of wine. "But he has assured me..."

"Of what, mother? Of a glorious return to Germany ruling all of Europe? Do you know what they are doing to people to gain this power?"

"The Jews must be eliminated, Rhen. They are..."

"What?" I seethed. "What are they? Judenschwein? Animals? Disposable trash? Tell that to the little girl I saw who froze to death in the ghetto in Warsaw, or to the ones filing into the gas chambers at Chelmno, their ashes pumping into the clouds."

"Lies," she said, taking another gulp from her glass. "Your father said it is propaganda started by them."

I grabbed her hands, the red wine splashing out and dotting her white night gown, and made her look at me in the eyes.

"Mother, you know me, better than anyone else, and I thought I knew you. Don't let father blind you with hopes of you recreating what you had with him in the past. I've seen it with my own eyes. The Reich is slaughtering people by the thousands and all of us are responsible for the atrocities. Each day we say nothing, or do nothing, we are accomplices and our silence gives approval to such actions."

She shook her head, her eyes filling with sudden understanding. The mother I knew, the dreamer who used to point out the constellations in the night sky and read me quotes from Shakespeare returned and she fell forward with her face buried against my chest, the tears spilling like a waterfall. I kissed the top of her head.

"I do understand, mother, believe me. We would all do mad things for love, especially in this world in which we live. Sometimes in our desperate attempt for normality, we build a world of illusion around us... just as you said, to survive. I actually heard the same from a Jewish man I met in the Warsaw Ghetto." I kissed her again and pulled her tight. "But we all deserve better. You taught me that those nights you showed me the stars, mother, and I swear to you and to my own heart that I will fight until my last breath to bring that about. This... this Reich is not the answer; this is Hitler's answer, not mine." I raised her face, cupping her jaw with my hands. "And not yours, either."

She nodded, her lips trembling and the streaks of her tears leaving salty trails down her pale cheeks. As I stood to go, an eerie premonition crept into my mind that this would be the last time I'd ever see her.

"No," she begged, clinging to my jacket. "Stay with me. I'm afraid."

I squeezed her hands. "I promise to come back and get you, mother, but first I have to set something right. And when that is done, I will come back for you and we will go far away from here. Perhaps back to your family home in Switzerland."

"Switzerland?" she repeated, her eyes sparkling upon the word. She gnawed on her bottom lip, and two tear drops dripped from her jaw, then she let me go.

I looked over my shoulder, one last time before closing the door, watching her slow ascent back up the staircase, her fragile body shaking as she gripped the handrail, pulling herself to the top floor.

As I stopped at the end of the sidewalk, sliding my hands back into my leather gloves, a light drizzling rain drifted from the clouds, a quiet grey whisper blanketing over Berlin. I took one step forward and the sound of a single gun shot echoing from the upper bedroom window broke through the soft silence.

21

Julia

July 1942

They discovered my hiding place just a month after I arrived. In quick speed, the Gestapo raided Weissensee cemetery, shooting some of the runners and hanging a few of the men from the oak trees. As for me and a few of the other women pulled alive from the graves of our ancestors, they beat us, then marched us to Gruneweld and packed us inside a cattle car bound for Lodz Ghetto.

Death breathed around me, whispering on my neck, crawling on my skin, tangling its fingers in my hair like an amorous lover. The stifling air inside the wooden box suffocated us all, and in the midst of summer, the heated air did little to hide the smell. And yet, we couldn't move. Forced to stand shoulder to shoulder, back to back, our sweating skin sticking to each other as we strained our necks upwards like little desperate birds in search of a single drop of water from heaven... or a vaporous inkling of kindness. Those who had helped me along the way faded to the horizon, crushed beneath Hitler's thumb, and the search for kindness evaporated with each passing day.

The train stopped at one of the other stops along the way, unloading some of the cargo at Lodz and leaving us all sweltering in the hot box. Two hours passed and ten among the one hundred stuffed inside the car dropped like flies, and some of the women tried to roll them to the walls to give us more space. From my place in the car, my eye was level with a small rotted out hole in the side facing the platform, and I watched the SS officers strolling, sipping their cups of water, and dabbing their sweating foreheads with wet cloths while taking shelter in the shade. Words of pure hatred floated on the slight breeze which from time to time drifted through the hole, the words searing my ear even as the wind cooled my eye as I scanned the faces in search of my husband. I felt sure if I saw him, if I called his name, he'd rescue me from this nightmare.

"Why are they not letting us off?" One of the women asked.

"Yes, are we not supposed to go to Lodz?" added another.

The woman next to me, a tall beauty with powerful brown eyes and elegant jawline held out her hands in front of her, strands of her own limp black hair in clumps in her palms. A single tear rolled down her cheek, catching in the corner of her mouth which she quickly inhaled before the water dissolved in the heat. I reached across and brushed the hair away, gripping her hand in mine.

"I am here," I said.

She looked up and feigned a smile, answering back, "My husband died in Auschwitz. I go to join him."

An older woman next to her, hearing her words, added. "We are all going to join him... they are gassing all of us at the camps. This is not a relocation to Lodz; this is genocide."

"Hush," another replied, along with a symphony of 'shhh's' and for the woman to 'stop frightening the children with your nonsense.'

Still, I squeezed the woman's hand tighter. "My name is Julia," I said.

She squeezed back. "Rebecca," she replied, along with 'don't leave me."

I shook my head. "No, I promise I won't."

By the time the train jolted forward, the moon rose clear in the night sky, and the women arranged shifts for groups of us to lie down and sleep. When it was my turn, the clickety-clack of the wheels kept me awake, sounding in my brain the reality that with each mile that passed, I traveled far away from my former life and closer to my death. *No matter, I am ready. Everyone I love is gone, so why should I care to wake another morning?*

Opening my eyes, Rebecca lay next to me, staring up at the forest of legs surrounding us. For a moment, with her vacant gaze, I thought she was dead, so I reached out to her. Her lashes fluttered and we pulled each other close.

"Are you married?" she whispered.

"Yes," I answered back, and the one-word confession opened the floodgates of my heart and I sobbed against her shoulder.

"What happened to him?"

"I don't... know... He promised... he promised... to... come for me."

Rebecca nodded. "Yes, they all promised, but how are we to fight against this hurricane?"

We said nothing more, and for fifteen minutes we dozed in each other's arms, preparing to once again stand and face the opening of the cattle car doors.

After another day passed, another group crumpled to the ground in death, yet even though their deaths gave us more space, the heat cooking the decaying bodies mingled with the putrefying odor of human waste and vomit. When the train whistle wailed into the night sky, announcing the arrival at our destination, all of us held our breath anticipating the blast of fresh air hitting our faces when the doors opened. Yet, with instant relief, the sight of the barbed wire fencing surrounding Auschwitz, the snarling dogs at the end of leases held by the guards, and the stern-faced matrons ordering everyone off the train gripped us in terror.

"Why are we here?" I whispered to Rebecca. "We were supposed to stay at Lodz."

One of the matrons, the one nearest to me as I held on to Rebecca's arm, laughed and pointed her baton at me.

"What does it matter? Lodz, Auschwitz, Dachau... they all have the same fate. Now, shut your mouth and keep moving."

She shoved me and I tumbled down the gangplank, landing in the dirt with my eyes fixed on the pair of shiny black boots before me. Some of the grains of sand scattered across them, and I held my breath, afraid to look up into the face of the boot's owner. He reached down and seized my arm, bringing me to my feet, and our eyes met.

I caught my breath, and he did the same. Behind his tightly buttoned collar, I saw him swallow hard.

"Julia," he whispered.

Bernie, I mouthed, unable to speak his name.

The matron approached and he shoved me to the fence, motioning for her to stop.

"I will handle this," he said, and she backed away.

Over my shoulder, Rebecca waved for me, her face disappearing into the crowds as they filed through the gate. Looking back at Bernie, my eyes drifted over him, noting the uniform of a Gestapo guard.

He shouldered the machine gun in his grip and stepped towards me, grabbing my wrist. I flinched and he whispered through his gritted teeth.

"Play along; I can take you somewhere safe."

Unsure of whether to believe him or not, I asked the one question only he could answer. "Is he alive?"

He gave a slight nod, and I added. "Does he love me?"

Another nod and I collapsed to my knees, burying my face in my tattered dress as hope coursed through my veins like a resurrection from the dead.

"Get up," he growled, wrapping his fingers around my upper arm and pulling me back to the train. Another of the matrons stepped in his path, and he ordered her aside.

"I am taking this prisoner into custody according to the Nacht und Nebel decree; she is now in my protective custody as a political prisoner and I will see that she is returned to Berlin."

"Stay here," he ordered me, and I leaned against the side of the train as he hurried down the gangplank and spoke with the Kommandant. A few minutes later, and without another word, he pushed me in front of him with the machine gun shoved in my back, ushering me to the front of the train.

Once inside the officer's car, now empty of its passengers, he pointed to one of the seats and sat across from me, both of us silent as the rest of the train cars emptied, the doors shut, and the whistle blared again to signal departure. My heart raced inside me.

A few miles down the track, Bernie removed his hat and laid his gun on the seat next to him.

"Well," he finally said, "this is unexpected."

I nodded. "Unexpected that you would save me."

His eyebrow arched. "Save you? No, I cannot do that; but I can delay until Rhen finds you. He is the only one in a position to save you now."

"What is *Nacht und Nebel*?"

"It was the only way to keep them from taking you inside the camp. The Gestapo, of which I am, have the power to seize a political prisoner under the decree without a trial, and, for the most part, they simply disappear."

"So, you are saying I can disappear? And wait for Rhen?"

"Again, unfortunately, no. The Kommandant and the other officers saw us getting on this train which is headed to Therienstadt to load up more Jews for Auschwitz; plus, we have about fifty from Berlin still in the back cars headed to the camp."

"So, then, what does it matter that you did what you did if I am going to end up in a camp anyway?"

He chuckled. "Do you still have your book?"

My eyes widened. "My book?"

"Yes," he said. "Rhen told me all about your fascination with Romeo and Juliet. He's always been that way, ever since we were boys, and I always told him that dreamers like him would never last in the midst of this war. Now, I am beginning to believe it is the dreamers who will survive and the lemmings who will die."

I said nothing back to his comment, too full of the possibility of seeing Rhen soon.

"So, Julia Montabauer, I will forthwith be your good Friar John and take the priest's message to Romeo telling him that Juliet will awaken in Therienstadt. And when we get to the camp, I will secure you a safe place to wait until he is able to come to you. Now, sleep; we have an hour till we reach Therienstadt."

22

Rhen

June 1943

"He's dead."

My voice trembled the words as I held the paper my father gave to me. I awoke this morning to a stunning sunrise, even feeling optimistic about the future, when he strode into my office and tossed a letter from his sister onto my desktop.

"I thought you might want to know," he said, all emotion void from his words.

"No, not Bernie," I replied as I slumped down in my chair. Now, this damnable war swallowed both my friends.

He took the paper from my shivering fingers and read over the note. "Yes, your Aunt Liesel says he died honorably, though, killed by an attack of Jewish partisans along the route from Thereinstadt to Auschwitz of last year. He fought bravely, I am sure, to rout out those rats."

"Last year? Why is she just now writing to us about this?"

My father shrugged. "Well, there could be many reasons, most likely that the partisans dragged his body off into the woods and he was not identified as dead until the troops found his body. With so much time going by, they probably only found his identification tags."

Which was probably the case, and made the imagery flashing in my mind all the worse. Poor Bernie, whose only thoughts at one time were dancing and having a good time, surrounding himself with beautiful girls with a martini in his hand; his body now corrupting into the dirt, alone, in some dark forest in Poland. The last time I saw him was outside the headquarters here in Berlin where he apologized about the note intended for Julia, and our missed chance to escape this madhouse. I heard the bravado he once had for the Reich fading in the tone of his voice, as he, too, witnessed far too much blood and gore for a young twenty-year-old to bear. The shock and awe of seeing fellow bunk mates blown apart, their bodies scattering across the fields of France like shredded confetti, transformed him. *How could it not?* I had not been to the front lines, but the sights of what I witnessed within the ghettos morphed my romanticism into sheer skepticism about any of us climbing out of this pit. Yet, still, my soul sought closure about my wife.

Father backtracked on his releasing me to go to Lodz, pumping me full of preparation work for what he described as the last implementation of the final solution. With the war dragging on for almost four years, a sense of either impending victory or ultimate doom hung in the air in Berlin. The officers, especially those closest to Hitler, buzzed around him and the offices like mad ants trying to repair the boot imprint of the Allied forces in their Reich anthill. Some, like my father, still foresaw success, while others scurried in quiet desperation, planning for their own escape to somewhere far away like South America. My only thought was still finding Julia.

The months passed by and the only information I obtained was information on the trains which left Grunewald for Lodz in October of

1941. From September of '42 till now, most of the inhabitants were part of the labor workers, with no deportations occurring, so I knew when I had the chance... when father allowed me a little time to myself, there was every hope I might find Julia's neighbors in the camp. And from there, they might be able to tell me what happened to her and her mother.

And then, unexpectedly, in one brief window of opportunity, my father marched into my office and gave me specific orders to assist Oberstrumführer Max Horn on an inspection of the ghetto's work force, since most his factory workers came from Lodz. Of course, I jumped at the chance, even if the short time we were there meant I had to expedite trying to locate the Schwartz family. My concern was that they already suffered the fate of the thousands shuttled to Chelmno the previous year.

We arrived by car, in luxury, since Max Horn was the director of Ostindustrie, which operated confiscated Jewish and Polish prewar industrial enterprises, such as foundries, textile plants, and glassworks, all used in support of the Reich. Needless to say, Horn was loaded with money, and to drive up to the gates of Lodz in his black 1936 Mercedes Benz convertible raised a great deal of shame in my heart... still, I followed him through the checkpoint, my mind fixed on a single purpose.

Chairman Rumkowski of the Judenrat met us and offered to escort us around the facilities, but Horn had only one thing on his mind, which lent well to my own detective work. He wanted to see the lists.

Rumkowski led us to the office building and on a large oak table, he hoisted book after book of names, along with the numbers of men, women, and children, those still living and those already sent to Chelmno. After about thirty minutes of page flipping and running my finger along the names, frustration settled in and I told Horn I needed a break. Standing outside the offices, Jews wandered the maze of streets in the ghetto, the same as I remembered from Warsaw, and my hope diminished with each passing face.

How in hell was I going to find five people in the midst of the almost 80,000 still living there, according to the list census?

Still, I knew I had to try, so I gripped my hands behind my back and wandered along the streets, stopping every once in a while and asking if anyone knew of a family by the name of Schwartz. Most denied knowing them, and I knew right away that some might be protecting them. After all, anytime anyone saw an SS officer come into the camp requesting names, the outcome was never good. Still, I pressed on.

After another hour and no results, I leaned against the wooden framework of the pedestrian bridge which spanned over Zgierska street and lit a cigarette. The gaze of passersby fixed straight to the ground, no one looking me in the face, until one young girl tightened her coat and stood at a distance from me, her sallow eyes darkened from days without food. I flicked my cigarette butt and motioned for her to approach.

"What is it, girl?" I asked.

"You are looking for Danka and Gerta Schwartz?" she whispered.

"Yes, I am."

She hesitated, looking from side to side. "I know where they are," she replied, "and I will take you there... for some extra bread, sir."

I chuckled. "You are bold to try to negotiate with an SS officer."

Her eyes widened and her skin paled even more, but I nodded and pointed her to walk and take me there. After a few minutes of shortcuts through alleyways, and walking up stairwells past crowded rooms, we came to a door at the end of a hallway. The girl knocked and an elderly woman opened the door. Without a doubt, I recognized her from years ago, even though her brown hair was now fully white, and the pain in her eyes overshadowed the former youthfulness. Aaron's mother, Hannah, caught herself on the door frame when she saw me and the girl reached out and grabbed her by the arm.

"Do you remember me?" I asked.

She nodded, then lowered her eyes and motioned for me to come inside. Once the door closed, the other family members stood from their rank, louse-infested pallets. They were all there, the women, at least.

"Herr Montabauer, sir," she said, trembling, "what may we do for you?"

I held up my hands, offering a gesture of peace.

"I only want some information from you," I replied. My heart rate sped up, wondering what her answer would be and if it would lead me closer to my wife... but then, I hesitated, knowing that they had no knowledge of our marriage and they, too, might seek to hide Julia from me if they thought she was in danger. No one said a word.

"I have information that you and your family spent the last days in Berlin before coming here to Lodz at the apartment of Oberstrumfuhrer Cappell, did you not?"

Hannah glanced over to her daughter, Elena, who clutched her daughter's hands.

"Yes," she replied. "Yes, we did, since you know that already."

"My superior, the Oberstrumfuhrer, is seeking information on his daughters... I believe their names were Katherine and Julia." I caught my breath, my voice stumbling over Julia's name as I swallowed the lump in my throat.

Still, no one said a word. Knowing I'd never use the Luger in my holster to loosen their tongues, yet not wanting to give any indication of my true feelings for Julia, I reached for the pistol. My finger wrapped around the handle, and Elena gasped.

"Wait," she blurted. "We haven't seen Julia since we left Berlin. She left a note, saying she was going to leave a hole in the Rhine."

My heart slammed against my chest.

"She's dead?" I replied, the sudden tears burning the corner of my eyes as I reached over and grabbed the back of the solitary chair in the room.

"No," Hannah replied. "But we noticed some food missing from the pantry, so we've prayed this whole time that she just went underground. We heard rumors from other Berliners here in the Ghetto that the Gestapo raided the Wiessensee cemetary and routed out the u-boaters hiding there and sent them either here or to Theresienstadt. Since she is not here, we assume she must be there."

I took several deep breaths, daring one single tear to fall, and once I steeled my nerves, I questioned her more.

"Your son, Aaron, he was with the resistance in Berlin?"

Hannah lifted her chin, gazing directly at me, her deep amber eyes slicing through me with such pride and courage. She did not answer, but I knew she feared me. How much I wanted to tell her she had nothing to fear, but any information I gave her would only speed her death if she was forced to reveal my whereabouts when I disappeared with my wife. A dozen or more people saw me enter their cramped room; it would not take much for someone to extract information if I told her the truth. So, I lied, and continued the ruse about Julia's father needing to find her.

"You believe she is in Theresienstadt... and you know she is still alive?"

Hannah shrugged. "Forgive me, sir, but that I do not know. All we can do is hope... is it not?"

I nodded, looking away from her. The young girl who brought me to them caught my eye, and I remembered my promise to provide more bread. Reaching into my pocket, I removed five Reichmarks and held the coins out to Hannah.

"I will be sure to let Herr Cappell know. Here, for you all. Don't use it all at once, else it might raise suspicion. Get some food and more blankets."

After leaving the room, trailing back through the damp, cold, urine-rank corridors, I shuddered to think what was next for Hannah and her family. And here I was, helpless to do anything for them. The meager amount of coins wouldn't do anything to put meat back on their bones, much less keep them from the fate awaiting them at Auschwitz. I couldn't save them all, but I could save one... if she was still breathing.

"Well, Juliet," I whispered, my warm breath mingling into the humid night air, "I will lie with thee tonight. Let's see for means: O mischief, thou art swift to enter in the thoughts of desperate men!"

And oh, I am fortune's fool, indeed, for when happiness is just at a fingertip's reach, fate comes to snatch it away and replace hope with despair. Here I was at Lodz, three hours away from Theresienstadt, only two hours by train, when Horn decided we needed to travel north to the area of Lublin where already upwards of 16,000 Jews worked for his company in a network of labor and concentration camps. While I tuned out most of what he said, he used the trip to expound the excellent use of the Jew as cheap forced labor which helped with the war effort, not to mention continued lining the pockets of all the officials on the board of directors.

Horn sped along the roadway through the forest just outside of Lublin, spouting his ideologies and punching the gas. As we rounded a curve, a blinding blast from the nearby treeline rocked the car, and Max swerved to the side to avoid the rain of rocks and tree limbs, smashing his fine car into a small ravine at the side of the road.

In the haze of the dirt-filled air, and the smoke from the bomb blast, my head pounded and arms lifted me, one on each side, clenching my upper arms and dragging my heels through the rocks with my head flopping backwards as the coppery taste of blood tinged my tongue. The shadowy figures let me go, throwing me against a tree, and as I raised my head I saw the vague outline of Max's car spinning its wheels through the gravel and speeding away with a few men in the streets firing their guns in his retreating direction. He saved his own skin and left me there without a word.

Once the blur of the blast eased away, and my mind cleared, although the pain pierced like a dagger through my skull, I blinked and made out three more strangers to the left of me, all with military-issued rifles strapped over their shoulders.

Polish resistance.

They laughed and shook hands, all delighted with their latest catch. Me. An Unterstrumfuhrer would suit their needs for a trade, or for just the sheer pleasure of blowing out my brains in retribution for the thousands lost to them.

The tallest one of the five-man group, a meaty Pole with stark blue eyes and grizzled beard, stood over me, pointing the gun at my head and ordering me to my feet.

"Get up; hands in the air and go there," he ordered in broken German.

He shoved the gun in my back and I followed the others into the darkness of the woods outside Lublin... but how far we were from the city, I had no idea. My only hope was that Max arrived to the camp and brought back enough soldiers to rescue me. Then, again, what did *this* Max care if I rotted away as a prisoner to the resistance movement, his sole interest in anything having to do with the war was strictly based on money, not on any loyalty to his fellow Reich brothers. His rank was merely a show to ensure the Reichmarks kept flowing to his pockets.

And now, they had me. We marched up to a small hillock clearing and my captor, the commander, tied my hands behind me to a tree, where I remained for the rest of the day without a word from anyone. After three hours of watching them huddle in groups, eat their bowls of porridge, and throw back a few bottles of vodka, I slumped over to the side, my face resting on a pile of leaves and pine needles.

As the sun set, the towering pines darkened and muted summer heat cooled with a passing shower, leaving the odor of damp leaves and humidity steaming from the ground beneath my cheek. I closed my eyes, training my ears on the distant murmur of voices, most likely planning their next attack, along with the incessant hum of mosquito wings buzzing around my head. With my hands still tied behind me, I succumbed to the stinging bites as they settled on my sweating brow and neck, and I wondered how much longer before the partisans put a bullet in the back of my head. Yet, even in this, with my eyelids squeezed shut, my thoughts drifted to Julia's face while somewhere deep in the dark verdant woods, a nightingale unleashed an aria which seared my heart.

Somehow, with Julia's face burning in my thoughts and the nightingale's sweet tune lilting on the air, the brief reprieve lulled me to sleep even as the faint nagging of my guardian's snores near me reminded me that the first twinkling of dawn might mean my end.

In my dreams, I ran to Julia across a field of red poppies as she stood on the edge of a cliff gazing across a vast wide world stretching out to the horizon. The wind caught her white linen dress and curled black hair in a tempest, and as she turned, the strands webbed across her face, revealing only her sparkling amber eyes and welcoming smile. With one hand she pushed back her hair, and with the other she reached for me... and yet, my legs slowed and the more I reached out my own hand, the wider the space grew between us. Both of us called out, our voices silent, and with one burst of sudden lightning from the clouds, she fell backwards from the cliff and the scream erupting from my throat seized me awake and I sat up, the sweat pouring from my face.

Before me, the guard sat leaning against another tree, shoving a chunk of bread in his mouth as he laughed at me, spraying bread crumbs across his grizzled beard. He lifted the pistol in his hand and pointed it at me, saying 'pow, pow' with a jerk of his wrist, and ending with 'soon, you Nazi scum... soon.'

It was right then and there I made a decision. "Every man for himself... survival of the fittest..." ran through my thoughts. I would do whatever was necessary to stay alive to save Julia from falling from the cliff, even if it meant helping these partisans achieve their goals. And perhaps by doing so, they might help me get to Theresienstadt. Still, I knew I needed to wait until the right moment.

After another day of silence from my captors, along with starvation, my guardian rounded the tree and untied my hands. Shoving the barrel of the rifle into my ribs, he directed me into the deeper woods. This was it, my mind whispered. It is now or never... but before I had the chance to speak, the rushing sound of water filled my ears and we emerged along the back of a babbling brook. He pointed to the water and I knelt down, my lips and tongue lapping up the cool refreshing liquid, the sensation chilling deep inside my empty stomach. After guzzling a fair amount, I sat back and splashed the water on my face and neck. When I opened my eyes, the entire camp of partisans, at least fifty men trailed down the sides of the river away from me, and the guard gripped my upper arm and pushed me in front of him to follow the retreating troupe.

"Where are we going?" I asked, but the man just glared at me without giving me any answer.

So we walked for almost the entire day. Even with the momentary sustenance of water, after two days without food took a toll on my energy. My mind drifted back to the little girl standing in the doorway at the Warsaw ghetto, her sallow starved eyes and hollow cheeks, and wondered how long she survived without food. Perhaps this was the partisans intent, to starve me, to make me feel the same effects of what the Nazis were doing to the Jews... and they would be completely justified in their doing so, even if I did finally get the chance to spill my guts and try to help their cause.

Walking along the path, and with death wagging a finger in my direction, taunting me with its nearness, the vividness of the woods around me flooded my eyes. Like the poetry which once brightened my romantic wanderings through Tiergarten, another of Shakespeare's lines haunted my brain.

"One touch of nature makes the whole world kin," I whispered to myself, the quote releasing a avalanche of wonder about me, an SS officer, a man sworn to the Nazi creed, a blonde-haired blue-eyed Aryan, following along behind this group of Polish Jewish partisans. Nature made us just mere men. Our own "weeds" borne on our backs merely costumes for this game we played upon each other. Trees and rivers and chirping birds cared not what party or race we belonged, thus nature did indeed make us all kin, all of us blessed in the golden shafts of light piercing the canopy of flitting emerald leaves, and the dragonflies darting past us like diving Luftwaffe planes dropping peace instead of bombs. A smile wafted across my face, recalling Bernie and Max's words about what the war would do to souls like me, that my romantic brain would be drowned in the Nazi propaganda. And yet, here it was, still in tact and ready to soar once again once Julia was again in my arms.

Without thinking, I paused along the path and closed my eyes, allowing a single beam of sunlight to fall across my face, and I absorbed the warmth, and Julia's face formed behind my closed eyelids.

"Julia, Julia, Julia," I said out loud, acknowledging her name to the forest and to anyone listening, almost as a mantra to the heavens... perhaps even as a prayer. For a brief moment, I felt lifted, hopeful, and wished when I opened my eyes that all of this was just a bad dream.

But the guard behind me growled and shoved the butt of the gun into my shoulder blades, bringing me to my senses. When I opened my eyes, reality met them. Germany still stomped across Europe with no end in sight, and I was still at the mercy of these partisans.

The days stretched into weeks and into months. After declaring my willingness to help the partisan commander, Michal, and surrendering my SS uniform to help sneak in one of the members to steal food and ammunition from a nearby Wehrmacht outpost, the commander eased his first thoughts of just murdering me and leaving me in the woods. So much so, that after six months of constant movement throughout the forests of Northern Poland, this captivity allowed a metamorphosis to take place as I released my Nazi persona and tried to find myself again. Still, even with the easing in restrictions, I was still a prisoner of war, and each evening acquiesced as one of the guards tied me back up and guarded me overnight.

I was alone in the camp of my supposed enemies, and while I watched them, from time to time, line up in battle-ready formation, rushing into the woods to fight, or defending a small village from tanks and soldiers goose-stepping through the town, always in their stealthy way, my meager help did nothing to ingratiate them to me. In their eyes, once a Nazi, always a Nazi, even when I begged the camp commander to take me to Theresienstadt and that I could help release the prisoners.

His answer was always the same. "Why Theresienstadt? We are closer to Lublin, or to Lodz, or Chelmno... what is so special about Theresienstadt?"

Finally, after the months passed from my capture and realizing they had no intention of trading me or killing me in one shot, and imagining something far worse down the line, I confessed the one secret I bore in my heart to the commander.

His reaction? The natural one. Sheer disbelief and utter disgust that I'd make up such a story to try to win my release. No decent Jewish girl would bind herself to a Nazi pig, and since I had no proof, just my insistence that she might be in Theresienstadt, of how much I loved her, and my desire to save her, he punched me squarely in the jaw and demanded I never speak of the Jewish girl again out of respect for the entire population of exterminated Jewish women.

Thus, during the six months, and more now, silence became my friend and ally, and my own accusing thoughts daily informed against me.

What could I have done differently? Why am I not trying to escape? Hope, again, slipped from my fingers, and I fell into a sort of zombie-like trance of rising each morning, eating my ration of thin fish soup and bread, and watching the camp buzz about with their daily activities and plans to kill another day's quota of soldiers or rushing into deeper woods in retreat. Time and again, I had the opportunity to escape, but for fear of a bullet in my back thus ending any chance of seeing Julia again, I remained with the group, trudging through the forests of Poland and watching as fellow soldiers for the Reich fell.

One such occurrence lasted for nearly two days when one of the runners announced that ten Wehrmacht soldiers stood just over the hill, backed against the river and guarding the rail bridge which likely meant either a transport of prisoners were on the way to one of the camps or a shipment of supplies was imminent.

Michal and his group worked like a well-oiled machine, planning out their strategy to take out the soldiers, as well as plans to blow up the bridge. It was the first time I asked Michal if I might help. At first, he grimaced and the hesitancy in his eyes bespoke his doubts about my sudden "turn", but with the added impetus that he'd execute me on the spot if I tried to warn the soldiers, and my nod of understanding, he relented and untied my hands. Under no circumstances was I to have a weapon... I had to prove myself using my bare hands.

For years now since killing Thomas, I swore never again to take another life. I vowed this to Julia that night on the roof, and so far in all this time, my conscience remained spotless on that account. I knew if I was to win the trust of the commander, thus provoking his willingness to help me get to Theresienstadt, then I needed to do something to catch his eye and approval.

Dressed in regular gray-green army-issued fatigues, my own uniform requisitioned by the group for other covert plans, I scurried along behind the men, falling to our stomachs as we topped the hill. In the distance, I counted ten men and one tank guarding each side of the bridge.

We stay in our positions until dark, hoping the cover of night might hide our approach, but the full moon shined a spotlight across the icy fields. Michal and the partisans waited in anxiousness, their fervor for the rightness of their actions thick in their words and teeming in their eyes, so much so that the electricity reverberated through me. I knew those soldiers near the bridge were my fellow Reich brothers, and at this moment it was either kill or be killed.

Here we were, fighting for one small bridge in the vast theater of occupied Europe. The immensity of the task ahead for groups as this one overwhelmed my senses, yet their passion transformed them from ordinary men into fighters whose only thought was to save their country... to save this one small bridge. War, indeed, transforms the meekest man into cornered animals. *And for what?*

My old self emerged, the doubts of the reasons behind this war, behind my own support of Hitler's dream, and the anger roiled in my stomach. *When did he get to decide who lived and died? When did God give him the right to shatter innocent lives?* In our indoctrination, we were told our cause was righteous and just, but at this moment all I saw was boys playing games, the same as Max, Bernie, and I used to do as youngsters as we played with our tin soldiers in the dirt.

I closed my eyes and my mind drifted back to those innocent days. Like the cool breeze kissing my cheek, the memories brushed by, and the images of the three of us lounging on our bellies near the pond in Tiergarten rippled in my mind – the hint of blue reflected in the murky green water from the sky above, the verdant smell of the leaves rustling in the crisp Spring air, and the pleasant nothingness of boyish peace – all punctuated by the theatrics of sounding out what we imagined as bullets whistling through the air, of soldier's bodies ripping open and writhing on the battlefield. How foolish we were; how naive. The reality we now face as grown-up boys is far grimmer that we could have ever imagined or enacted.

And as far as the righteous cause, the washing of our brains with endless propaganda, laying on this hill in the dirt and cold made me realize that that method was the only way Hitler knew to ensure complete control. Like taking a fist and pounding someone's face until they cry 'mercy', so the words were pounded into our minds until we all relented. We gave up our dreams in favor of a supposed brighter dream, and the realization that Hitler was able to do this with an entire nation and army astounded me with sudden clarity. Like waking up from a nightmare and shaking your head to clear your thoughts. I knew it was always there, the doubts about my own actions lingering and accusing me in the back of my mind, but I justified my actions... for all these years. And yet, how much more could I have done if I had deserted, if I had left with Julia that night instead of acquiescing to my father's demands to report to him and to Dachau that next morning. *Was the food shoved down my throat somewhat appealing to me, even if I tried to refuse the pleasing taste? Is that truly why I shot Thomas all those years ago, to feel the sensation of killing a Jew, to show my initiation into the Reich was of my own choosing and not something I just followed like a herded goat?*

Shame warmed my cheeks and a single tear rolled down my face. I truly believed at that moment, that these partisans knew more of love and the fight for protecting their families than anything the Reich ever taught me; and yet, still, in order to fulfill their own dreams for the future, blood had to be spilled.

I wanted no more of it... no more killing, no more propaganda, no more war and political agendas; I wanted to sit by a still pond with my lover's head in my lap as she read me Shakespeare, smiling up at me with the brightest smile. I wanted peace. I had to believe there were others like me in the Wehrmacht... *or was there?* Even Max and Bernie, as good as gold as both of them were, leaned more towards belief in the Reich than I'd like to admit, but still, there has to be others... or did Hitler succeed in routing out all personal convictions and transforming the entire country into a nation of zombified robots waving their Nazi flags and thirsting for blood?

Was I the only one in Germany who questioned the rightness of this seeming folly? I knew if I got out of this night alive, I was going to bring up this inner questioning to Michal.

The moon eased behind the gathering storm clouds, blanketing us all in muted darkness. Michal tapped me on the shoulder and gestured for all of us to head out, keeping out heads low as we scurried through the tall grass towards the unsuspecting men. Within firing range, we all crouched down, and one by one, the rifles popped in the darkness, the flashes sparking like firecrackers... and one by one, the men dropped like flies.

When the men on the other side of the bridge saw what was happening, they scrambled across, and the tank, like some otherworldly beast moved forward, its long barrel circling around until its one eye pointed in our direction.

With a boom, the monster's voice echoed across the waters and the earth near us blasted to the sky. Some of Michal's men howled in pain, but we kept moving forward through the thick smoke and raining debris. Another explosion followed, and more gun fire pierced my eardrums, and before I knew it, we rushed like madmen across the bridge in a wild symphony of bullets, screaming, and bodies falling to the water below.

Me and another fellow Reich brother met face to face, and I tackled him before he raised the Luger in his grip. We rolled down the embankment towards the water, and he pounded my face with his fist. Kicking up with my feet, I knocked him backwards, and lunged at him, returning the blows as I straddled over him. Wrapping my fingers around his throat as he twitched and struggled, time stilled and I peered deep into his fearful blue eyes. He was me. Another stooge of the cause. I was killing myself, all dressed out in his Nazi uniform. I promised Julia I would never kill again, but in that moment all I saw was a life for life for Thomas Cappell. A Nazi for a Jew. Yes, Thomas killed Max, and I killed Thomas, but justice called for my own murder, thus in one last act, as the young soldier took his last gasp, I killed all attachment to the officer I once was... Now, the only hope to rescue Julia remained on me, and help from the other side of this coin... something I should have done long ago.

After that day, and many more to follow, one by one rail bridges and lines were left blown apart and mangled leaving supply lines to the Wehrmacht fractured. The seasons rushed by, and the whispers and glances from some of the men in the camp informed me of their approval of my actions, yet even in that, stories surfaced that Hitler's end approached fast.

The resistance commander relayed to me the astounding news, "The Allies are winning, with more and more cities liberated across the European theater every day." The victories for the resistance movement blossomed as members within the Warsaw Ghetto and at Auschwitz revolted against the SS.

Michal made these facts clear to me one evening as I sat at one of the only fires lit as the chilly wind of October sliced through the air. He slumped down across from me with a look of victory in his eyes.

"Well," he finally said, scuffing his hand across his day-old beard, "You've made quite the name for yourself with the men. Your passion for helping us is quite noteworthy, I must say. I suppose you've heard the news that Paris is now liberated."

I shrugged, gazing deep into the tiny embers popping in the ash pit.

"You know what this means," he continued.

Still, I said nothing as I waited for either my death sentence or my release. "We've kept you for a year, and you've proved somewhat useful, but, in truth, I kept you alive out of amusement, to watch you squirm, to watch the meat fall from your bones, and to watch you fight with your conscience. Of course, you understand why, don't you? I could have done so much more to torture you or to use you as ransom or bait to take out a few more of your kind, but... you've intrigued me. I've always sensed something different in you. Not many officers would so willingly submit to helping us in our efforts. And now, it seems we are at the end of our association together... and I am wondering what to do with you. So many options. I could just kill you as I should have done at the start; or I could leave you in the woods to die, tied up with a note to whoever finds you that you are a traitor to the Reich, and let them kill you instead, which they will do in quick haste. Or..."

"Or, you could let me go find my wife," I said, lifting my chin and catching his gaze with mine.

His eyebrow arched and he huffed. "Still, after all this time, you would have me believe this?"

I shrugged, uncaring if he believed me or not; after all, my heart told me it was too late.

He pulled out two cigarettes from his pocket and lit them, holding one out for me. I took it and sucked in a long draw, releasing the smoke in a cloud. A few minute passed with us in silence, watching the flickering flames before us. Finally, Michal sighed.

"Why did you help us?" he questioned.

All my former personal doubts flooded in my brain, and with this new camaraderie between us, I lifted my chin and answered his question.

"In all this time you've kept me hostage, we've never known each other as simply men forced into this war. If not for my capture and your holding death over my head, you might have killed me and never known of my deep disbelief in this cause. Just as you said before that we do not know each other's story, you might have never known how killing goes against every nerve ending in my body. I joined up in some imaginary belief that I might win my father's approval, that my romantic notions of my own dreams were, indeed, too soft for this world, as my friends so often expounded to me. I killed a Jewish boy years ago out of sheer cruelty, blinded in a moment of passion and pain and power, three things which have been utterly stripped from me at this point. You've given me the opportunity to see things from the other side, yes, your passion and pain, but not from power, from sheer determination to survive. I admire you for that... I admire all of you for that. Your passion comes from the heart, and is something which inspires poets to write. You've given me back a little of myself, I think, for before the war, I used to believe in such things."

"Hmmm," Michal said with a nod. "In another world, I think we would be friends."

I held out my hand to him, and after a moment's hesitancy, he looked away and sucked again on his cigarette.

"I hope that we can be," I replied, still he did not accept the offer, and I lowered my hand. Instead, he glanced around us, his eyes scanning the treeline, and he gestured for my eyes to follow his.

"Do you know where we are?"

I shook my head, and he leaned forward, lowering his voice.

"We are only ten miles from Theresienstadt."

My skin prickled with goosebumps as he continued. "Just this past spring, four months ago, there was an uprising in the Warsaw Ghetto, and then, another just a week ago in Treblinka. The tide of the war is changing, Herr Montabauer, and the Nazis will face a reckoning as you've never imagined. God hears the cry of blood from the ground from all the Jews murdered. Tell me, though, with all this hope of friendship and your confession of what is in your heart, what is your responsibility in what has happened to Europe?"

I lowered my gaze, my thoughts resting on the image of Thomas Cappell's bleeding body sprawled across the stone path in Tiergarten... and then, to Julia's beautiful face awaking the last time I held her in my arms.

"I've only killed two Jews since this war began. I hope that my actions have shown my remorse and aided in my repayment of those sins."

He narrowed his eyes. "Wrong," he answered back, "for your loyalty to the Reich and your silence in not speaking out, even if it meant your death, means you are guilty of them all."

I shook my head as the weight of his words bore down on my shoulders.

"No," I retorted, "you are wrong. I tried to tell you... about my wife... about our separation and my desperate need to use my position to find her in the chaos of this war. Like finding a needle in a haystack... but, again, all you see is the Nazi before you instead of wanting to believe my story."

Michal huffed, again. "And do you wish to hear my story, as well, to know what Germany has done to my family? Even during this entire time, even with your help, I've watched you keep to yourself with your arrogant Aryan manner, and never once asking me or anyone about our lives and losses. Still, if what you say is true about your Jewish wife, you've learned nothing about what it means to sacrifice everything to save the one you love. You think choking a Wehrmacht soldier absolves you of your part in this war? You think you deserve to find your wife when you continued to oil the machine which took her from you?

"Ten times I tried to save my wife and children from the ghetto in Lodz, even suffering a gunshot wound which nearly took my life. And when I saw my wife mowed down by machine guns and my two daughters loaded onto the trains, I fled into the forest determined to do whatever I could to bring justice and plan their escape. What have you done? Flipped through pages in a book? Used your Nazi uniform to strut around a ghetto looking for a familiar face? Dreamed away your life while your wife rotted away in some concentration camp?"

"Shut up," I shouted as anger and embarrassment warmed my face. All of my own accusatory guilt burst from my heart, of my own cowardice... *was it cowardice?* Michal shoved all of my justifications back in my face, and yet, all my living had not done anything to bring me closer to finding her... after four years.

"I could have done more," I replied, burying my face in my hands, the shame blubbering out from my eyes and heart. "I could have done more... to save her... I know... I know. I may be too late... she may be dead. Please, forgive me."

In an unexpected move, a hand rested on my shoulder and I looked up through my tears to see Michal leaning over me.

"I finally believe you," he said. "In all of my years of fighting, I never saw a Nazi shed tears."

He reached out his hand and lifted me to my feet.

"Now," he said, "if you know you could have done more, what will you do to save her from Theresienstadt?"

I wiped away the tears from my cheeks with my fingers, my heart still burning with shame and remorse.

"She's dead. There is no way after all of this time..."

"You are wrong," he replied. "And I might not have told you if not for your sincere repentance. I might have saved her on my own with this next plan we are enacting. I assure you, she is alive... or at least, as of last week, she was."

My eyes widened. "What do you mean? How do you know?"

He smiled. "We always have people on the inside of the camps who regularly help us on the outside, and vice versa. Sometimes our plans work, sometimes they don't... but every success is a victory. When we arrived closer to Theresienstadt, I sent a message to see if there was a Julia Cappell in the camp. Turns out, she has been working in the lending library for over a year now. Unfortunately, we also received word that the camp is being evacuated, with most of the prisoners being sent to Auschwitz. We think it is because Hitler knows the end is approaching."

My heart thudded against my chest. "The final days of the final solution." I grabbed his arm. "Please, help me."

He narrowed his eyes. "Only if you continue to help us. We have a plan."

"Yes," I blurted. "Of course, whatever you wish."

23

Julia

July 1943

I felt oddly hopeful after Bernie left me at Therienstadt... a year ago. After a long talk with the Kommandant, espousing my literary skills along with Goebbel's overwhelming interest in Shakespeare, I was placed in the lending library at the camp. Now, after still no word from Rhen, hope faded again with each sunset, and any promise Bernie made me of telling his friend of my whereabouts was a vapid as the the dissolving morning mist.

The Nazis touted Thereinstadt as the 'spa town' where the elderly Jews could relocate and retire. The report spread throughout the camp for the next six months after my arrival in July of 1942 that RSHA chief Heydrich purposed using the camp as a propaganda machine, not to mention to lull Denmark's King Christian into a false sense of security since he mounted pressure against Germany to ensure the Danish Jews received proper treatment. If not for the fact that Hitler relied on the Danes to continue supplying ball bearings for the war effort, Thereinstadt might not have received the beautification endowed upon it. But, as everything else across Europe, the icing hid the rank and rotting reality hidden beneath the surface. As long as the Danish Red Cross and the International Red Cross believed the ruse, Hitler was in the clear to continue with his final solution.

On a daily basis, the aged and infirm disappeared on the trains heading east, and groups of young, healthy Jews conscripted into forced labor, along with over a thousand bright-eyed Jewish children selected from other camps created an atmosphere of fun and relaxation.

For the most part, I ignored what was going on around me, and lived my life in a monotonous routine: awaken, receive my food ration, go to the library, tend to the needs of those wishing to 'escape' in the pages of a book, return to the barracks, sleep.

If not for the formidable presence of the head librarian, Emil Utitz, whose daily doses of intellectual stimulation brighten the days, I might have relapsed into the former misery of despair. But Emil, with his round face and serious dark blue eyes, kept me active cataloging new book arrivals, checking out books to the prisoners who could afford the small fee, and each morning requested a new line from Shakespeare before I began my duties.

In truth, my heart began to finally let go of Rhen during those months at Thereinstadt, especially after receiving no word from him; after all, what better chance had we than the two opportunities gifted to us by fate. First, years ago when we planned to meet at the train station, and months ago when Bernie saved me from Auschwitz. Both times fate snatched away any chance for us to be together, just like Romeo missing the note sent to him by Friar Lawrence.

And so, I melded into the facade of the life I lived at the camp, sucking the marrow of Emil's words as he told me stories of his days meeting Kafka at the Cafe Louvre in Prague. During the quiet times, when most of the prisoners were out working, Emil, his wife, Ottilie, and a couple of the other assistants, sat in a circle reading or reciting passages from various books. Goebbels banned Kafka's books, but Emil filled our ears with quotes and quips, along with his own psychology about what living inside the camp was doing to all of us.

Each night, instead of reading lines from my copy of *Romeo and Juliet*, I'd take out the small nub pencil from my shoe and scrawl Kafka's words on the back pages... those which resonated with the life we now lived.

"It's only because of their stupidity that they're able to be so sure of themselves"... that one made me snicker.

"From a certain point onward there is no longer any turning back. That is the point that must be reached" ... this one stuck to me like glue sense it spoke of every decision I had made to this point.

And "Logic may indeed be unshakable, but it cannot withstand a man who is determined to live"... this one made me think.

Did I still want to live? And if so, why? Why after seeing so much death and destruction, shedding so many tears, accepting loneliness, loss, and unrequited love, did I not simply stop breathing?

One day, months before the visit of the Danish and International Red Cross to the camp, I asked Emil what he thought of my questions of life and death. I even dared telling him, the second person ever in my life, that I was a widow and my husband abandoned me to this life. Still, I never uttered the fact that he was a Nazi SS officer who, once upon a time, vowed to save me from this fate.

Emil leaned against the library ladder and gazed out through the solitary window.

"You see," he began, "we attach ourselves to these words which help us escape the travails of our lives because they speak to our core. Kafka's words reflect my own beliefs, that of truth and law binding an individual as a prisoner for the rest of his life... and sometimes circumstances do that to us, as well, oftentimes without our consent, as we can well attest to, can we not?"

I nodded and he continued. "Pessimism, negativity, and uncomfortable reality. He used to say, 'man is a fragile entity of insignificant possibilities, thus we accept the conditions presented.' What else is left when we are faced with nothing? We wake up, we breathe, we live, with the grayness of life given to us. Sometimes the sun breaks through the fog, but most times, it does not. Still, we breathe... on and on and on, until the powers over us, whether God or man, subjugates us under his command and against our will. For he has 'put eternity inside us' and set us in a world where eternity can never be achieved."

I needed to hear his explanation, even with the utter bleakness and utter lack of hope. Perhaps, this is all that we have, this nothingness, or perhaps this subjugation by the vile mustached man herds us into a world against our will. And he is winning as he breaks the last shred of hope in our hearts.

Being a dreamer in such a dark world is painful, and from that day forth, I tucked my copy of *Romeo and Juliet* beneath my pillow and never read another single line.

And yet, again, hope dangled in front of me like the tiny 'fly' on the end of an angler fish's lure. Another small group of prisoner's arrived from Lodz ghetto, Berliners, from what I heard, all brought in to propagate the lie of Therienstadt, and my heart perked up wondering if I might know any of them. From the single window of the library, a narrow lane stretched north to south, leading to some of the barracks. Oftentimes, new prisoners marched from the trains past the window, but more often than not, I kept to myself, dusting the shelves or straightening the books. This day, my skin prickled when the train whistle blared out its arrival early that morning, and when the new arrivals followed the guards down the dirt path in front of the library, my gaze fixed on the passing faces. Almost two years had passed since I saw Elena and her girl's faces, but I knew their eyes. My heart leapt into my throat, and before I knew it, I darted to the door and stood at the stoop while they passed. The guard raised his gun and pointed at me, but I stood still and kept my eyes fixed to Elena's worn shoes.

"Get back inside," the guard yelled, and as I backed up, I raised my eyes to her. A small tear trickled down her cheek, and she reached for her mother, Hannah's hand.

Circumstance or governments imprison us, but even in that cage, hope continued to gasp for air.

After we all reunited in the barracks that night, our tears overflowed as I scooted close to Hannah on her narrow cot, both of us sobbing onto each other's neck and falling asleep, our arms clinging to each other.

Later in the week, I managed to convince Emil to get at least one of the girls, Danka, to help in the library, although he warned us on several occasions to stop our endless chattering. Still, Danka filled in so much about where they had been and what happened to them over the past two and a half years since I last saw them.

After seeing them loaded up into the cattle car at Grunewald station, they ended up at Lodz Ghetto where they remained up until their selection to help with the propaganda film at Thereinstadt. Danka and Gerta were pretty girls with healthy cheeks and wide eyes, so they were an easy pick, and after showing resiliency in their work assignments at Lodz, both Hannah and Elena were picked since they needed good German speaking Jews to add to the 'ambiance' of a well-functioning work camp. My heart drummed in my chest when Danka relayed the news of an SS officer, Untersturmführer Montabauer, confronting them in Lodz, saying my father was looking for me and my sister... and later, Elena assured me that they told him nothing since, in truth, they had no idea where I might be... or even if I was still alive.

Still, with all the questions swarming through my head, and the constant missed chances, I could say nothing to no one. The secret weighed down my heart and I spent days crying myself to sleep.

When the Red Cross delegation arrived that summer, the camp hummed like a thriving bee hive, and the atmosphere relaxed as Kommandant Röhm escorted the two men around, pointing out different picturesque spots enhanced during the 'beautification project'. After my duties at the library, most of us spent hours whitewashing the housing complexes, planting gardens, and Emil oversaw the entertainment portion of the visit, arranging for an orchestral arrangement to greet the visitors. The illusion worked, even with Paul Epstein, the 'supposed' mayor of Thereinstadt, following close behind them with his knees knocking and a fresh purple bruise under his left eye. Still, no one questioned his injury, and even if they had, Paul knew better than to reveal the truth.

When they stopped in the library, Emil, Danka, and I, along with the other assistants stood in a row with our heads bowed.

The international representative stepped forward, shaking Emil's hand and stopped in front of me.

"What is your name?"

I stayed silent, until the Kommandant spoke up.

"Go ahead; tell us your name."

"Julia, sir."

He smiled. "Just Julia?"

"Julia Mu... Cappell, sir."

"And do you enjoy your work here at Thereinstadt library?" he delved.

"Yes, sir," I replied. "Very much."

The four of them walked around the library, nodding and laughing, cocking their heads sideways to read some of the spines, and then, left. Afterwards, everyone was 'ordered' to a field near the camp to enjoy watching a soccer game, then Emil hurried to the newly built community hall as the delegates enjoyed a performance of Brundibár sang by the angelic voices of the camp's most beautiful children.

A fantasy created solely for the purpose to enhance lies. And it worked, and the SS added to the lie by producing a film of us all in this fake world to show to the world the benevolence of the Fuhrer. He gifted the Jews with their own town, and the images spoke for themselves. All the rumors floating around about gas chambers and mass executions had to be false after such a film as this one. And I, for one, felt ashamed at my part in the play. But, true to form, the facade crumbled after the two delegates disappeared to the horizon, and the news about what an enjoyable time they experienced in Terezin dissipated.

Just a week later, after a night of sweltering heat and very little sleep, a scream jolted us awake, along with the pop of gunfire. Hannah reached across her cot and grabbed my hand, and the girls scurried to their mother's side. We recognized the sound, which escalated along with the piercing wail of the train engine arriving to the gates.

Two armed SS guards blasted into the barracks, shoving women from their beds, and kicking them with their boots.

"Schnell, get up! Now!" they barked, along with their fierce dogs who snapped at us as we hurried to the center courtyard. Hundreds crowded in makeshift rows, attempting to arrange an order to the chaos, and we all pinched our cheeks to appear healthy and worthy of keeping as viable workers.

We recognized the routine, even though it had been months since a transport had left the camp. Many had fallen into complacency. I was not among those, since my romantic notions vanished after Bernie left.

Kommandant Röhm strode up and down the line, looking at his clipboard, and pointing at various ones in the crowd; the first to go was the ones particularly selected for featured roles in the propaganda film. I was sure they needed to get rid of any evidence that might eventually speak to the contrary about the facade created here... and then, with my thought, I realized they had to eliminate all of us to keep this secret.

The steady stream of packed cattle cars flowed back and forth again on a daily basis and the population dwindled at Theresienstadt. Each morning at roll call and selection, I steeled my heart, waiting for the guard to call out my number, and each evening, more whispering gossip spread from mouth to mouth – excitement building hearing the news that the Allies took Normandy, pushed the Wehrmacht back across France, and approached Paris. No wonder the sudden rush to rid himself of the rest of the Jews. Hitler and his henchmen were like guilty children caught with their hands in the cookie jar, devouring the rest in one big gulp to hide the evidence, even though the crumbs scattered across their lips and shirt fronts.

And so, when the time came for our selection that August, the five of us – me, Hannah, Elena, Gerta, and Danka linked our arms and lifted our chins as we walked up the gangplank into the cattle car.

Right before the doors slid shut, I looked up and saw Emil standing in the distance. He held up his hand, waving a small piece of paper in his fingers... a token of what he taught me, and of what words did for me while working for him at the library. *No, they did not help me escape, they helped me face reality.*

"We are far from everything,
that we once liked so much.
You can only lead us back,
through appropriate reading,
that a ray of the earlier world,
illuminates the darkness here."*

* actual poem by anonymous Therienstadt prisoner

24

Julia

October 1944

I am still an essential worker, even with my frail bones poking through my paper-thin skin. Yet, when I waved goodbye to Emil as the cattle car doors shut and the engine jerked forward to Auschwitz, I leaned my head against the wooden slats and resigned myself to death. So many times during the past four years I faced such a fate, so now felt like a peaceful acceptance. The last train ride before death. We all knew what Auschwitz meant, and while some cried in silence, most of us, all one hundred packed in the small car, stood in somber reflection of what lay before us. Hannah gripped my hand, and Elena whispered scriptures into her girl's ears.

And when the train squealed to a stop, whistle blaring, and the doors clanged open, chaos roared in our ears. Dogs barked and snapped, and matrons in dark uniforms with severe brows and stern lips ordered us down the platform, herding everyone into a line funneling into a gate below a rusted arched sign.

Albeit Mache Frie.

Time stilled and all the memories from the past, from the day I fell in love with a SS officer named Rhen Montabauer till now, flickered through my mind as if I sat in a comfortable cushioned seat at the cinema with the images reflected in my intent gaze. I knew the words, having already seen them painted on the wall at the gate to Theresienstadt, and considered, for a moment, the meaning behind the facade.

"Work sets one free," I whispered, to which the nearest matron to me, chuckled, pointing her baton at me, and adding,

"Work sets one free, through crematorium number three."

My skin prickled, noting the sheer hatred and delight mingling in the woman's smile and eyes.

"Schnell," she shouted, shoving some of the women in front of me.

Fear and cold saturated my bones, and as I continued gazing up at the sign, soft angelic snowflakes drifted from the clouds mingling with gray ash billowing from the tall chimney stacks silhouetted against the sky. All of us heard the rumors of the crematoriums, but never in my wild imagination could I imagine that they were true.

Gerta, who was wedged in front of me next to her mother, opened her mouth and leaned her head back to welcome the flakes on her tongue.

"No," I whispered, firmly, and she, thankfully, closed her mouth. I understood her innocence. I was there, once upon a time. Now, my lips clenched tight, afraid of the ashy snow raining down on our faces.

As the line in which we stood streamed into Auschwitz, the doors to the boxcars slammed shut behind us, and the pulsating steam from the train engine added to the hazy atmosphere surrounding us. We walked in this otherworldly dream... no, nightmare... and my mind reeled back to all those innocent days of long ago, back when my only worries was if I might find a man to love me like Romeo loved Juliet. Still gripping the book hidden in the lining of my coat, more out of homage to those carefree days than any remaining belief that Rhen fit that dream, I paused beneath the sign and recalled my cousins, Samuel and Gregory, standing outside my window at the apartment in Berlin, touting their promises to crush the Nazis beneath their shoes, or the day father announced his departure from our family and his loyalty to the party, as well as the day Rhen killed my brother, Thomas. All led up to this day, and all the promises he made me the day he stood before the Rabbi and crushed the glass with his foot, vanished in a heartbeat.

Yes, once upon a time, a handsome German prince saved me, a Jewish princess, in more ways than he could have ever imagined. He transformed me, and set my soul on fire, leading me into womanhood, and promising me forever. He said things like this would never happen. Perhaps he fooled himself, as well... and perhaps, the shame of knowing who he is, and who I am, is the reason for our ultimate separation.

What seemed like an eternity passed through my thoughts, until the forceful jab in my back from the matron's stick and the sound of Hannah's voice echoing my name released me from the trance. Before I realized it, I fell to my knees. Aaron's mother and the guard struggled with each of my arms like two children fighting for a rag doll.

"Get up," the matron screamed. "Schnell; get up, you stupid Jew."

"Please," Hannah pleaded. "I will take her. She is just in shock. Come, Julia, come along with me..."

In the chaos, my book tumbled to the ground, caught beneath the shuffling feet of the women herded through the barbed wire fencing. I darted for it, oblivious to the barking dogs pulling against their leashes at my sudden bolt. By the time I slid onto my knees, bruising and bloodying them against the frigid ground, and snatched the book from destruction, they were on me, snarling and biting, whilst the guards pulled me to my feet. The matron eyed me up and down, her icy blue eyes sending shivers more harrowing than the cold winter air burning my skin. With one swift blow, she struck me across the cheek. My head jerked to the side, my curls cascading across my face and hiding the disgust in my eyes; yet I could see her, as well as the two Strumtruppen clutching Hannah by the arms in between them.

"Please, Julia, hold your tongue..." she cried out. She did well to advise me to silence, for I had long given her grief with my sass and defiance, starting with my opposition to not marry her son, Aaron; although my reasons remained hidden from her, even to this day.

The matron eased close to me, snatching the book from my grip, and gritting her teeth until her pale lips narrowed into a thin line.

"She speaks well, you filthy Jew. You had best not say anything back to me else I will let the dogs finish with you." She held the book up, brushing the dirt from the cover and revealing the title.

"Ah," she continued, "we have a romantic pig here. Romeo and Juliet?" She narrowed her eyes. "You know the Gaulieter of Berlin, Herr Goebbels, is an avid Shakespearean. He would be pleased to see you reading this instead of that rancid Torah. Perhaps, I will take this little treasure for my own, a nice little decoration to my desk to remind me of the first pig I killed with my baton."

"No," Hannah shouted, but I remained stoic, my eyes never wavering from the matron's face. Her stern lips curved into a sadistic smile and she raised the club high into the air. Still, even with my lips trembling and legs weakening, I did not look away. I wanted her to remember my face, my conviction, my unflinching bravery in the face of death... I wanted her to remember me in her dreams. Swallowing hard as the baton came down in a sudden swirl, the woman turned, finding the target for her full-on assault. The crack of the baton meeting bone struck like a bolt of lightning, and a spray of blood showered my face. I blinked, waiting for the pain to flood my body. Once my eyelashes stopped fluttering, I focused and pushed back the hair from my face. The blood droplets on my lips tasted coppery and familiar.

As the realization of the images in front of me took shape, a wail from deep in my gut erupted. Hannah lay in a crumpled heap at the feet of the Strumtruppen, a bloody pool radiating from her head and eating away the mud-stained snow beneath her.

"Take her," the woman yelled, motioning for the guards to shove me back into the line. My hands reached for Aaron's mother, and my cries pleaded... to no avail. Some of the other women in the line streaming towards a long building near the chimney stacks, grabbed hold of me, enveloping me into their arms and hushing me with their scared voices. A strong arm wrap around me, hustling me away from the sight of Hannah's prone body. Looking up, Elena kissed me on the cheek and pulled me closer as her two girls clung to their mother's skirt, their innocence shattered to see their grandmother bludgeoned before their eyes.

"Stay close to me," she whispered, fighting back her own tears to stay strong for her girls. "Say nothing else. That woman, she is the Rapportführerin, the head woman commander here at Auschwitz. Some of the women have heard rumors about her, calling her *die hayne von Auschwitz*, the hyena. You know what hyenas do? They feed on dead flesh and laugh while they eat."

Past the shivering shoulders and gray faces, I saw the building ahead of us – long and ominous, the doors gaping open like some human-devouring monster as the women in front of us disappeared into the dark void. I breathed deep, swallowing my tears, readying myself to join my mother in heaven; then, whispered back to Elena.

"Are we about to die? Is this the chamber we heard of when we were in the Ghetto?"

Elena shivered. "I don't know," she squeaked out like a mouse cornered by a cat.

I raised my chin and wiped the blood and tears from my cheeks with the back of my frozen fingers.

"Let me be taken, let me be put to death; I am content, so thou wilt have it so. I'll say yon grey is not the morning's eye, 'tis but the pale reflex of Cynthia's brow; nor that is not the lark, whose notes do beat the vaulty heaven so high above our heads; I have more care to stay now, than will to go. Come, death, and welcome! Julia wills it so."

As the shadow of the doorway came over our head, Elena whispered back.

"Leave it to you, Julia, to spout poetry in the midst of darkness."

And just as the doors closed behind us, the Rapportführerin grabbed hold of my arm and jerked me back up the stairs to the side of the descending crowd. Elena and the girls screamed, reaching for me, then disappeared down the descending staircase. Without saying a word, the matron stood there chuckling as my eyes scanned the passing faces, the fear-stricken children clinging to their mothers, the solemn resignation in the men's faces, the tears flooding down the women's cheeks. *Surely, this is not real? Surely, the rumors are not true?*

My eyes followed them as the last of the group disappeared through the doorway, and spontaneously, words erupted from my mouth.

"Thou detestable maw, thou womb of death, gorged with the dearest morsel of the earth."

The Rapportführerin laughed again. "Quite appropriate, I must say. And is this a line from *Romeo and Juliet*?"

"Yes," I replied as the tears eked from the corners of my eyes.

"Well, good. This is good. I will read it this evening while you stand here and count your blessings."

She strolled away, flipping through the pages of my book, but not before divesting me of my coat and leaving me shivering in just my thin striped prison clothes as the evening clouds burst out with snow.

"Is it a blessing that I am still alive?" I whispered.

She glanced over her shoulder and with a sickening laugh, pointed to the smoke stacks, and said, "Keep an eye out for your friends."

For no reason at all, except meanness and cruelty, the Rapportführerin left me out there for nearly a day and a half in only my prison uniform and no shoes. By the time she marched back up to me, tiny crystals hung from my eyelashes, and my teeth chattered so violently I wondered if they might ever stop.

She sidled up next to me, her foul breath blasting onto my face.

"I see you are still alive. Well, seems you are determined to live, so we must find a place for you. Let's see how long you last working in the Kanada." She pointed to a large mound of personal belongings at the end of the ramp nearest the train tracks.

"Schnell," she ordered, without giving me a moment to warm up, "get to work. Join the group and make sure all of this is sorted and sent to the Kanada before the end of tomorrow."

One of the other women pulling out clothing from some of the bundles motioned to me and I walked near to her, noticing her blue and white Star of David armband. She directed me to follow her example, and before long we had a pile of clothing before us to sort through, and she pulled out a long woolen coat from the stack, and opened it up for me to put on.

I shook my head, my eyes darting from side to side, looking for the matron.

"Go ahead," the woman urged. "It is an advantage working in the Kanada, for we can sometimes procure pieces to wear and for trade."

I slid the coat on and pulled it tight to my body, desperate to extract any amount of warmth I could.

She reached in her pocket and pulled out a small silver flask, unscrewed the top and offered me a swig. "Here," she said, "this will give you some more warmth. One of my selected trades from last week. By the way, my name is Marta."

I took the flask from her and gulped down the liquid.

"Julia," I replied back, coughing.

The liquor burned down my throat and I recognized the smell as brandy, a favorite indulgence of my father. Within a few minutes, the shivering lessened and I continued with the sorting and toting armfuls to the different carts which led away to a long warehouse near the crematoriums.

"What is all this stuff?" I asked. "And why is this called the Kanada?"

The woman's eyebrow arched upwards and she looked towards the steps leading down into the cellar of the building where Elena and the girls descended.

"It is their belongings... all of the Jews who come here have to leave their items here before going there to the showers. Kanada is the nickname given to the warehouses that hold their items; you know, a land of plenty."

"But how will they know whose is whose when they need them back?"

Marta shook her head and the wrinkle between her dark eyebrows creased. "You've heard the stories, right? How do you not know what happens to those who descend?"

Her words iced my veins, and the sudden realization struck me that I'd never see Elena and the girls again. The Rapportführerin's words of 'keep an eye out for your friends' burned in my brain when I realized what she meant... the ashes from the smoke stacks. I fell to my knees, sobbing into the mounds of clothes beneath me as I lifted one of the dresses, recognizing it as the one Danka wore.

"Get up," Marta whispered, pulling me to my feet. "Straighten up or they will change their minds about sending you here. You are fortunate to have this job. Why did she send you here anyway, as most pray to get this assignment? It is the best job here in Auschwitz."

Honestly, I did not know, but almost felt it might have something to do with my book, which she took as a souvenir of her execution of Hannah. When I said this to Marta, she nodded, and added that this particular Rapportführerin had a particular fondness for anything that she had in common with Herr Goebbels, so perhaps my own affinity for Shakespeare was the reason I found myself with such a lucky break.

But, in truth, I did not see how any of this was lucky. With every dress, pair of shoes, eyeglasses, diamond ring, baby blanket, yarmulke, or prayer shawl piled into a heap in the warehouse, a whole history of people's lives vanished before my eyes. Erased as unimportant; silenced. And the burden of sorting gripped my soul, knowing that bodies once filled out the clothing. Never again; their ashy remains drifting upwards into the clouds. I prayed that God himself gathered the ashes into his arms and set a time limit for the destruction of these Nazi bastards.

25

Rhen

October 1944

Theresienstadt Concentration Camp

Michal gave me a list of names and my old uniform, and two other resistance fighters, also adorned with stolen SS uniforms, and sent us on an assignment to procure a truck and load up as many of those on the list as possible, most of whom were family members of those in the group. Our goal? To drive them out of the camp with the pretense of shipping them to Auschwitz. Michal counted on my expertise in all things having to do with the SS and I assured him of everything going smoothly. My sole purpose, outside of helping the resistance group, was finding Julia at the lending library.

As the covered truck sped down the roadway leading to Theresienstadt, my pulse quickened and when the gates to the camp came into view, I ordered them to stop so I could collect myself before approaching the checkpoint.

We drove up slow, and I rolled down the window.

"I am Unterstrumführer Montabauer from headquarters in Berlin. I have orders for a selection and I need you to open the gates."

The Gestapo guards clicked their heels and pushed open the gate for us to enter, where we were greeted by none other than the camp commander, himself, Karl Rahm. I knew of him, as he served under Eichmann in Vienna, and had visited the headquarters in Berlin on more than one occasion. I knew the key was to appeal to his cynical side, appealing to his torturous nature which he brandished with rashness.

With a quick 'Heil, Hitler', Rahm shook my hand, as well as the two "SS officers" with me.

"Well, well... to what do I owe this visit, Herr Montabauer."

My eyebrow raised, shocked that he remembered me.

"Ah," I replied, "you remember me from Berlin?"

"And your father, as well. How is he?"

"He is well; thank you for asking. And as far as this visit goes, well, we all know the speed with which these deportations are progressing, but we've had a special request which might appeal to your sense of swift elimination."

He laughed. "Swift? Where did you hear that? I much prefer things slow and drawn-out." He slapped me on the back. "You know, to see the fear in their eyes."

I followed along with his laughter, but my gut wrenched, and my two companion's knuckles whitened as they balled their fists. Unfurling the piece of paper out of my coat pocket, I held the official-looking letter out to him, which he scanned and with a quick snap of his fingers, he gave to two of his guards and sent them on their way.

"I'm not sure you'll find any of them on this list, Herr Montabauer, but here's hoping. If they are family members of the resistance scum, then I hope you choke every one of their scrawny necks. I wish I could participate." He nudged me in the side with his elbow. "What do you say... let me take a couple of them to my office?"

I fixed my mouth in a straight line and glared at him. "Unfortunately, Herr Kommandant, we require all of the names on the list; but I am sure you do not lack for sufficient bodies to select from the Appell each morning."

He nodded. "Quite right; quite right. Shall you join me in my office, then, for a drink? I have some of the finest brandy, a bottle sent to me by Herr Eichmann just last month."

I held up my hands in protest. "Nein, I do not drink, but while we wait, perhaps you might take me on a brief tour of the camp. I hear you did some outstanding work during the visit of the Red Cross last year. And I hear you have an excellent lending library."

"Ah," he said with a prideful twinkle in his eye. "Of course... come, follow me this way."

We walked up and across, through the maze of parallel streets until arriving at a unassuming building along a narrow path. After stepping inside, a frail gray-haired man looked up from his desk, then rose, casting his eyes down to the ground.

"This is Emil Utitz, the librarian here."

I glanced around the dusty room, the sunlight shooting beams of light across the rows of books from the single window. The air smelled of leather, ink, and sorrow.

I pointed to a back row of books.

"You... Utitz... show me some of your books on good German poets."

Utitz scurried past me, and I followed, while my two companions distracted Rohm with warnings about possible uprisings such as happened at Warsaw and Sobibor.

Emil slid a handsome leather-bound book from the top shelf and turned to me, his eyes still unable to meet my face... that is, until I said her name.

"Julia Cappell, where is she?"

His frightened eyes met mine and a shadow fell across him.

"Julia? She is not here."

"Fetch her for me."

"I cannot, sir."

"Why not?"

He nodded towards the Kommandant. "Herr Röhm has had transports leaving daily to Auschwitz. For a long time, Julia and her family were viewed as essential workers as they did much to help with the beautification project here, and Julia worked tirelessly here at the library, but we heard new orders to start evacuating the camp and so she and her family were on the transport which left two weeks ago."

Again, so close. My heart sank and I took the book from his trembling hands.

"Ah, Hans Johst," I replied, "a good choice. 'When I hear the word culture, I release the safety on my Browning' - such a clever line and aligned him with the Nazi ideals; do you not agree?"

"Yes, sir."

I wanted to say more, to ask about Julia, how she looked, what she said, did she speak of her husband, did she smile, did she still carry her copy of *Romeo and Juliet*... but Röhm interrupted and announced that the chill was aching his hands and he wanted to get back to the yard to see if my list was filled.

Handing the book back to Utitz, I paused before turning, managing one simple question before leaving.

"Did she take her book with her?"

Utitz's eyes widened and he nodded. "Yes, sir, she never went anywhere without it."

And with that, we headed back to the main yard, where only ten of the fifty on the list waited for us inside the truck. Röhm shrugged when the guards told him that most on the list had already left for Auschwitz.

"No matter" I said, shaking his hand. "I appreciate your cooperation, and perhaps my father will send you a case of French wine in thanks."

Röhm's smile stretched from ear to ear. We saluted our obligatory 'heil' and my two companions and I simply drove out of the camp with ten resistance family members beaming as the truck sped down the road. Among them, Michal's youngest daughter.

+++++

Julia

October 1944

Auschwitz Concentration Camp

My day and a half in the cold upon arrival to Auschwitz seized hold of my lungs and refused to release. A chill deeper than the winter wind tightened its fingers around my soul. Everyone was gone... everyone who I loved in my life. My father, lured by a greater and purer family within the Reich; my mother, gone by her own hand out of sheer hopelessness; Thomas, from his own Jewish bravado and belief that one man can stand up to a pride of hyenas; Kitty, perhaps dead, perhaps living my life in some small town in Switzerland, at any rate, gone from my life; Aaron, perhaps dead or imprisoned as a resistance fighter; Hannah, his mother; Elena, the girls, Reuben, Moshe... all dead. *And Rhen, what of him? If not dead, my heart has erased him from my soul. If I saw him now, would those old feelings burst to life from the cooling embers? After all I had seen, and from the years of nothingness, of terror, of blood, of fear and cold, how can anything spring to life from emptiness, from abandonment?*

I laid on my cot, the fleas jumping across my face in search of warmth from the frigid air. With a nudge in my back, Zofia Kowalska, a recent Polish arrival, awakened me and my eyes eased open to see her kneeling next to me, her head cocked and her blue eyes full of worry. She touched her fingertips to my forehead.

"*Jesteś chory*," she whispered in Polish. We never understood each other, but I knew what she said without understanding the words.

"Yes," I mumbled, the words catching in my dry throat. "I am sick."

She pointed to the doorway, the outside floodlights pouring over the main front yard.

"I know," I said. "It is time for roll call, the appell."

Every ounce of energy left in my body resisted but I forced myself to stand as she pricked her finger with a shard of stone and rubbed the blood into my pale cheeks. She was right to worry, and I sensed today was my turn for selection. I could not hide the coughs, nor the weakness in my eyes. After months, no, years of reprieve as fate pushed me to my limits as I waited for my husband to rescue me from the crypt, I knew, just as Juliet knew, the time for death approached. Something went horribly wrong all those years ago, perhaps the day Kitty stole my red suitcase. Or perhaps the day Rhen kissed me at the dance hall.

Zofia linked her arm with mine, easing through the door of the barracks behind the line of other women, and hurried us to the back of the group. She made sure I steadied myself on my own, then stepped an arm's length apart, awaiting our numbers announced and for the Kommandant to inspect the last remaining skeletons standing before him.

"200160," a voice called out, and I answered, my own voice rattling over my crusty lips and my hand flew over my mouth to suppress the coughs which followed.

Just to answer one word, to say 'present', sapped the last of my strength, and I collapsed in a heap, my eyes fixed on the shiny leather boot of the Kommandant as he stood over me. Just a little while longer, and my suffering will be over.

+++++

Rhen

October 1944

Auschwitz Concentration Camp

The train ride from Theresienstadt to Auschwitz was a trip to hell. After Michal reunited with his daughter and I fulfilled my part of the deal, his utter joy spilled out and he granted me release with the assurance of helping me get to Auschwitz. As much as I appreciated his willingness to help, I knew this next trip was one I had to do on my own, so we shook hands and shared a glass of vodka in a toast to the end of this war. His last words, an invitation to his home after all of this was over was a nice conclusion to what could have ended tragically, but even in that, I knew I'd never see him again. When word got back to my father of my visit to Theresienstadt under the guise of releasing prisoners associated with the resistance... well, my father was a clever man, and after previously getting word of my capture by the group outside of Lublin, no doubt he knew of my treason. Either way, if captured by the Allies, or captured by the Nazis, I was a dead man. *What did I have to lose at this point?*

So, I donned my Nazi persona once again, and boarded the latest transport to Auschwitz; an hour's ride full of wretched smells and wailing cries from the caged prisoners – like bleating helpless sheep sensing their imminent slaughter.

When the train pulled into Auschwitz, the flurries falling from the clouds drifted in a mesmerizing innocence, dotting the hair and shoulders of the prisoners filing out of the cattle cars. I pulled my coat tight and strode straight up to Kommandant Höss who stood nearby overseeing the new arrivals from Theresienstadt.

"Heil Hitler, Herr Höss," I said, throwing out my arm. He raised his from the elbow, without looking me in the eye.

"Herr Montabauer, I am surprised to see you here."

"Why is that, sir?" I asked, as I stood next to him.

"Your father is looking for you. He called here, asking if I had seen you and added some nonsense about you showing up at Theresienstadt with a group of Polish resistance fighters. And now, here you are arriving with the train from that very camp."

I huffed, my warm breath frosting in the chilled night air. "It is amazing the stories these Jews come up with to disparage us, is it not, Herr Kommandant? Do you think they would let an SS officer go if they had their hands on me?"

Höss narrowed his eyes. "I suppose it might depend on what that

SS officer might do for them."

I knew the lure he was using and decided to broach the subject first. "You, of course, are referring to the group of prisoners I escorted out of the camp? The ones now lying in a ditch in the woods, along with their partisan associates?"

His eyes widened. "Indeed?"

"Jawohl," I said with a smile. "And I am reporting to my father immediately after my visit here to Auschwitz. You can even escort me there in one of your vehicles, if you doubt my story."

He rocked back and forth from heel to toe with his hands behind his back for a moment, considering.

"And, Herr Montabauer, to what do I owe this visit?"

"The same as I did in Thereseinstadt. There is a particular prisoner, a known resistance fighter whose brother I killed in Berlin, who I wish to escort personally to headquarters."

Höss's jaw flinched and I wondered if there was any way my act would break his steely resolve. His unbreakable and fierce manner was one of the reasons he was assigned as Kommandant of the most efficient of the killing camps across occupied Europe. Still, I had a card to play, and knew just how to ensure his help with finding this particular prisoner. After a few more minutes of silence, of us staring at the endless stream of Jews flooding down the gangplanks, I cleared my voice and lowered it to a whisper.

"And just so you know, sir, I never believed the rumors."

He jerked his head and glared at me. "Rumors?"

I smiled. "You know, of the girl... the Auschwitz girl, Eleanore."

Höss shifted on his feet again, and lowered his voice, as well. "Where did you hear such talk?"

I had him, and I knew it. "Your wife, Hedwig, was friends with my mother, remember? I think they shared a lot of things between them. I'm sure she knew of my mother's depression which caused her to take her own life two years ago."

My admission of my mother's demise cinched it, and Höss ushered me to his awaiting car. As we drove, he spilled his guts about his relationship with Eleanore, confessing his infatuation with the young blonde-haired Austrian who came to Auschwitz as a political prisoner, a member of the resistance group near Vienna; even disclosing the possibility of a child which she aborted a few months ago.

"Where is she now?" I asked, acting concerned for her welfare and playing on his sympathies for their affair.

He shrugged as the car pulled up to his office building inside the compound.

"In some hospital in Munich from last I heard. After the abortion, I left her to die in the bunkers. How could she do such a thing? She was granted the label of Reichsdeutsche, so she might have been released after a time. But now? I hope she rots in hell."

"And your wife, how is she?"

Again, he shrugged. "Well, you know, with all that is going on, who has time for a wife and after Fritz Bracht filled her with the stories of what was happening in Auschwitz, of which I tried to shield her, along with her own suspicions about Eleanore, she moved north of Flensburg with our eldest son. I haven't seen her in quite a while."

I looked away, feeling more disgust at his sad tone than empathy, still I replied with the obligatory 'I'm so sorry' which aided in his trust of me.

He turned the car off and leaned back against the seat. "So, tell me of this political prisoner you are so anxious to locate. A girl?"

I nodded.

"Ah," he said, his eyes cutting towards me in a knowing understanding.

"No," I replied with a stern brow. "You are mistaken. This girl is a Jew. There is nothing between us. Your mistress was Austrian, not a Jew."

He held up his hands. "All right, all right, Herr Montabauer; no need to get incensed. Early tomorrow morning, you come to the appell and we will see if we can find this woman. Unfortunately, I have to tell you, we've been running the crematoria non-stop for months now, with more than 10,000 being gassed a day. The likelihood that she is still alive is very slim, but no worries, for if she is dead you won't have to worry about taking her back to Berlin for her execution, right?"

My heart skipped a beat, but I smiled anyway.

"Jawohl, Herr Kommandant."

He slapped me on the shoulder. "Good; now, let's go eat. I have a new cook at my villa a few miles from here, and you can get a good night's sleep before roll call at 5:30."

And with that, the car roared back to life and we sped through the gates to his villa where a young Jewish girl named Beth served us spaetzle and sausages. Höss talked endlessly about Hitler's politics and the situation with the war, still living in that Nazi dream world that victory was in sight. After a few glasses of wine, and my head full of propaganda along with his dissertation of pride as he spouted about having to dig enormous trenches to bury the vast numbers of dead Jews conveying through the camp, I excused myself and collapsed into a deep sleep in Höss's cushy guest bedroom.

26

November 9, 1944

Julia collapsed at my feet. In just those few moments before, when she answered 'present' to my voice calling out her assigned number, when her hand flew to her mouth and our eyes locked, the past four years vanished and all the love I held on to so desperately flooded out of her eyes and into mine. I prayed I did not mistake her look, for when I saw the flutter of her lashes, her eyes widening, and the twinkle of the morning stars in her dark irises, knowing that she lived... that our love survived this damnable war... I rushed to her as she collapsed to the ground.

"Schnell," I shouted at the matron. "Get her to the infirmary."

Höss laughed at me as I ordered the two women on either side of her to carry her to the medical rooms.

"Ah," he said with a wink, "and she is nothing to you. What do you care if she dies?"

I clicked my heels together and walked away from him as he continued with the appell and selection. Over my shoulder, a line of prisoners deemed not worthy to live another day filed into the buildings to take their "shower" and leave this mortal coil.

+++++

Am I dreaming? Am I dead? Did my eyes deceive me, or did I just lock eyes with my beloved Rhen? I heard my number called, and somewhere in my mind, his voice beckoned my soul, and when I saw the starlight twinkling in his blue eyes, the past four years vanished and hope rushed back through my veins with such force, I fell to the ground, overwhelmed with joy and fear in the same breath. Joy to see the same love still lingering in his eyes, and fear of discovery as we stood in the midst of the one place that might, in truth, separate us forever.

By the time I awoke from my collapse, the moon glowed over the camp, hazy behind the ashes still pumping into the sky. I rubbed my eyes and sat up, gazing from side to side and wondering if what I imagined was indeed a dream.

Reaching out to the woman next to me, I touched the back of her hand and jerked away, recognizing the cold stiffness of death emanating from her lifeless skin. On the other side, another skeletal frame peeked out from beneath a shroud-like thin blanket, the moonlight alighting her hollow fixed eyes. I was surrounded by death, and yet, a shimmer of hope awoke in my heart as I prayed that I did indeed see Rhen in the compound yard. *And yet, where is he, if I did?*

+++++

Damn this war... damn my Nazi oath... damn anyone who keeps me from getting to Julia tonight. Even if we die together on the same cot in the infirmary, shot through our heads or hearts, at least I will hold her again in my arms.

After a brief visit to the Kanada, and procuring a couple of bottles of brandy, as well as stealing one of the matron's coats, I marched to the infirmary and held out the bottles to the two guards on duty. I only had until the morning to enact this plan, if you can call it a plan, for my mind raced with the pros and cons of what I should do. After they accepted the bribe, and my encouragement to look the other way, they wandered off with a wink and a nod to acknowledge whatever salacious ideas I had in my head for a rendezvous with either a willing nurse or a prisoner against her will.

I pulled the lapel of my coat over my nose as the aroma of death, disease, vermin, urine, and excrement saturated the air. Stepping over bodies laid in rows on the floor, some already dead, some on the verge, and others laying in stark horror as they fought to live. Like something out of Dante's Inferno, I walked from level to level, witnessing the demonic horrors of decay. And then, I saw her... her fragile body resting on a blood-stained cot. Pausing to watch her in the moonlight, I waited till I saw her chest rise and fall to assure myself that she was still alive, then kneeling next to her, I took her hand in mine and kissed the back of her fingers as gently as I could... so afraid that even a brush of my lips might break her frail bones.

She opened her eyes and her smile lit up my soul.

"Rhen," she whispered, "you found me."

A single tear trailed down my cheek.

"Please, forgive me... I should have tried harder."

She reached up and touched my cheek, gathering the tear on her fingertips and bringing the salty liquid to her lips.

"Your one tear is enough to flood my soul... and today is our anniversary."

"Yes, my love... it is... and I have more tears to follow which will quench your thirst until you can take no more."

Leaning forward, I urged her to wrap her arms around my neck, and I lifted her. My heart shattered feeling the feathery weight of her body, the bones poking into my own flesh. I carried her into a private examination room, one of Mengele's sanctuaries, and helped her stand while wrapping her in the coat.

Even in her weak state, she clung to me, and I held her against me. No words, just a delicate kiss as soft as a snowflake coming to rest on the lips.

After a few minutes of us both absorbing each other, I leaned her head back and whispered to her.

"Julia, we've got to leave... right now. I know there is much to say, but we will have plenty of time once we are out of Auschwitz. I have everything arranged. Höss believes you are my prisoner and has lent me a car for me to take you to Berlin. He thinks we are leaving in the morning, but we have to leave tonight else he might track us to ensure my story holds true. I have food and blankets in the car, and all we have to do... all you have to do, is walk out of here with me like a German Rapportführerin; do you think you can do that?"

Her eyes fluttered and I feared she might faint again, so I held her against me, desperate for my strength to pour from my pores into her body.

"Please, Julia, you can do this. I know you are weak, but this is our chance... perhaps our last chance."

She opened her eyes and raised her chin. "Yes, I can do this... I will do this. Every breath I have taken, every time I defied death led me back to you. Go; I will follow you."

And she did, with all the strength left in her, she pulled up her pant's legs to hide the stripes, pulled the coat tight, and walked to the car, past several SS guards, pushing through the snowdrifts with her head held high. No one noticed the dark circles beneath her eyes, or her thin hair, all they saw was the SS coat which gave assurance to all onlookers that she belonged... and as she slid onto the leather front seat beside me, I reached across, grabbed her hand, put the car into gear. After a brief conversation with the gate guard about a secret late-night rendezvous with the Kommandant and this beautiful Rapportführerin, he opened the gate and we drove right through.

A few miles down the road, Julia laid down across the seat with her head resting against my thigh. My heart raced, from her nearness and from the desperate need to get as far away as possible before the morning's light. Straining my eyes in the darkness, I peered at my watch. 12:45. We had almost five hours before twilight, so I hit the gas and headed south, thinking that the Kommandant might assume I left early to head west to Berlin.

After five and a half hours of driving, we eased along a roadway running alongside the Danube, and I turned down a dirt road leading away from any main villages. I knew I took a chance heading into Austria, but I knew, somehow, I had to get us to Switzerland. But first, I had to ensure Julia's health, so after driving down endless mazes of back roads, I parked near what looked like a small farmer's cottage. In the bright moonlight, the vacant windows and crooked door revealed the absence of life, as well as the climbing vines trailing over half of the front facade.

I reached over and felt Julia's forehead, sensing my damp pant leg as sweat poured from her brow. As much as I wanted to get as far away from Auschwitz as possible, I knew she needed to rest. Easing the car around the back of the house, out of sight of the road, I waited a few minutes more to ensure no one rushed out with a gun in their hands, which would not be unexpected as most of the villages and town across occupied Europe had felt the effects of the Nazi's crushing blows.

Leaning over to Julia, I lifted her head and bundled the blanket beneath her, then kissed her brow as I slipped out of the car.

"I will be back, my love. I'm just going to check on this place... perhaps a good spot for us to rest for a bit."

Walking though the cottage, which remarkably still smelled of ground flour and fresh hay, most of the furniture still stood in fair condition in the two room cottage – two ladder-back chairs, a long oak table near a dry sink with a pump, and the other room held a bed covered in quilts and leaves which had blown in from the window. The shutters banged back and forth against the side of the house, and a few mice scurried into the dark corners.

With one sweep, I flipped the top quilt and sent the leaves to the floor, then pulled in the shutters and locked them.

"Yes," I whispered. "This will do."

I went back out and took Julia in my arms, cradling her like a small child, and tucked her beneath the quilts in the bedroom. Still, her cheeks burned red from the fever and I wrapped my arms around her.

"Julia, please, stay with me. Don't leave me... not now... not that we have every chance to be happy." I kissed the top of her head and picked up a basket full of wood left near the fireplace, and stacked the remaining logs inside the hearth. With a few sparks of a flint, the fire blazed and after a few minutes, the room warmed.

Julia thrashed back and forth for the next few hours, and my eyes filled with tears watching her fight for life.

"Thirsty... so thirsty," she cried, so I rushed out and gathered the items from the car – the bread, cheese, wine, dried beef, and a basket of dried fruit. It took me at least twenty pumps at the sink before fresh water flowed, so then I filled a wooden cup and took it to her.

Half the water spilled as I lifted her with an arm around her shoulders and with shaking hands she tried to bring the cup to her lips. But my heart relieved to see two gulps going down her throat, and she sighed and laid back.

While she slept, I watched her in the moonlight piercing through the tiny slats in the shutters and my mind drifted back to the play... our play... and how Romeo must have felt coming upon his dear wife lying in the crypt with death lingering on her angelic face.

Sitting next to Julia, I entwined my fingers with hers and kissed each fingertip.

"Thou art not conquered, my love."

I took off my coat, hat, and shoes, and slid beneath the quilts near her, our bodies warming one another as I pulled her close, her head resting against my chest.

And peace fell across us as the drizzling sound of the snow drifted down over the house, and we fell asleep – happy and unafraid of what the morning held.

My mind flooded with dreams during the night – running into the deep forest chased by a madman who wore a Nazi flag draped across his breast. When I woke in a sweat, my heart pounding, I glanced over to Julia who still slept peacefully beside me.

In the early morning light, with the fire now a crumbling pile of ash, the din of scurrying mice rattling in the other room met my ears and I rushed into the room as they scattered across the dining table. There, before me, crumbs trailed behind them from the bread I left out. Still, even with their tiny indentions, we had enough to last us until we reached Switzerland.

Taking another stack of logs from the kitchen hearth, I carried them into the bedroom, rearranged them in the fireplace and lit another fire. Once the logs crackled into a blaze, I sat for a moment and considered our next plan of action. Julia coughed out, stirring her but did not awaken her, and I knew the hacking resided deep in her lungs... settled in... sucking her breath and the life from her body. I had heard coughs like this before; some of the men in the resistance camp had such coughs, ones that later took them to their death. Once she settled, and the raspy breathing took on a steady rhythm, my thoughts returned to our situation.

We could keep going... or we could stay here. Looking around the room with a sudden new understanding, at these furnishings which, at one time, belonged to a family... a family driven from their home by war, or famine, or perhaps they were Jews and sent to the gas chambers. Still dressed in my uniform, I suddenly felt uncomfortable, unwelcome, in this house which possibly held the memories of a family whose life clicked along in peace until the ideals of the party stripped them of it all.

How can I stay here? How can I hope to find any sort of peace in any place I go? Won't the memories of the past haunt us forever?

The silence and blanketed peace had a way of allowing the horrors of war to bubble up from the depths, whereas the chaos and fight for survival kept them tucked down inside, filed away and sorted while more important things battened them down.

We are fools to think we can escape everything... but we used to believe that. Now, how will we push through this? How will either of us survive this fever, the one in my brain and the one in her chest?

And the most nagging question wracking my thoughts... *how can we recapture what we had? Where can we go? Is Switzerland our future? America?*

Not here in Austria, and certainly not ever again in Germany, whose personality changed into a harsh, cynical, blood-thirsty, violent, and greedy succubus... far from the resplendent land full of towering fir trees and majestic castles along with a history of courage, bravery, art, and music.

But even with all the questions looming, looking over at her sleeping near me, my heart filled with a love for life, and a desperate need to get us both to the other side of this Everest. In Julia's face, all the hope in the world lay there in her smile and the twinkle in her eyes. She encompassed all my days of hope and hopelessness since even at my weakest moments, those days when I almost surrendered, her face pushed me forward, and her whispers a mantra to my heart.

When she opened her eyes, tears flooded my own, and when she reached out her hand to me, my heart burst.

"Rhen?"

"Yes," I replied, scooting close to her and wrapping my hand over hers.

"I was afraid you left me," she said, her voice soft and grainy.

"No, never again. Are you hungry? I have some food."

"A little, I think. It is hard for me to tell these days since so many passed when I had nothing. I got used to the feeling of hunger."

I squeezed my eyes shut and pulled her close, the tears burning my lower lashes.

"No one should get used to that feeling. And I swear, you'll never feel that ever again once you are better."

I reached over to the plate of food I set on the side table, and gave her a slice of bread. She nibbled like the mice, but at least she could eat in the midst of this fever.

"You are still feverish. I will get you some more water."

"No," she said, grabbing my hand. "Stay with me."

And I did.

We cuddled for much of the day, nibbling on the dried fruits, drinking the water, sleeping when tired, which was a lot, as if our bodies tried to make up for all the restless nights over the past four years, and enjoying sweet tender kisses in between Julia's moments of feverish delirium.

And the snow kept falling, packing us in tight, burying us in this haven away from the world. A few days later, awakening in the morning, a soft golden glow from the morning dawn filtered through the snowdrifts which reached halfway above the window, pressing against the shutters and pushing snowflakes through the slats which melted in the warm room.

I continued to nurse Julia, and she continued to suffer from the incessant hacking cough, brought on, as she told me, from nearly two days of standing almost naked in the compound yard when she first arrived at Auschwitz.

But this morning, with the sunlight sparkling across the snow, her fever broke and she lifted herself to a sitting position next to me. Her gaze fell on the shards of sunbeams stretching across the bed covers.

"Well, we've spent so much time in bed," she said. Her cheek blushed and she glanced over to me. "And yet, not as a husband and wife."

I brushed my fingers through her hair. "Not for lack of not wanting to, but you've been so ill, my love."

Even though the weakness still lingered in her eyes, she reached across and unbuttoned the top button of my shirt, then caught my eyes with a smile.

"I feel much better today, my husband. Perhaps we shall defeat death after all."

For days, perhaps weeks, time and the outside world no longer mattered. We folded up my uniform, her prison clothes, the matron's coat, shedding the past and entwined our naked bodies and souls around each other. Even when the fire in the hearth and the food on our plate dwindled away to nothing, the fire and hunger of our passion fueled us, satiated us, and refueled us again; and just as the needed sleep strengthened us, so did the endless hours of love.

In the subdued moments in between sating our passion, in the early morning twilight, our words echoed the years we "grew up" apart from each other, of our common struggles, as well as our unique place separated from the rest of the madness just a few miles from us. We had no idea after these months what the world or war looked like, and while we remained in our hidden ice castle, we connected on a deeper level than we might have if we had lived an ordinary life. We talked for hours on every subject imaginable, politics, faith, poetry, life, love, of how many children we wanted, and of growing old together in a house overlooking the ocean; and she softly cried into the pillow as she read and reread the letters I wrote her, ones that gushed my undying love for her. I told her about the different things I witnessed in the ghettos and the impact it had on me, and she spoke of those who helped her along her journey as she wandered from hiding place to hiding place. She remained quite silent when I told her about Kitty, and about Bernie's death, and I suppose she reflected on all the missed chances, all the "notes" which never reached Mantua. Yet, in these reflections, like rain falling on a spring day, nourishing the new growth, our romantic dreams emerged and we found a semblance of our former selves, giggling and reciting Byron and Shakespeare once again as we planned for our future.

She snuggled against me after eating a bowl of watery muesli and sighed.

"The Rapportführein at Auschwitz took my book."

"I wish I had known," I said. "I would have gotten it for you before we left."

She shrugged. "No matter. I suppose things like that don't matter anymore. Shakespeare's poetry is only for times like this, quiet memories shared between you and I, when once upon a time they were for dreaming about the future and the hope rising from the horizon."

"We still have hope, my love," I whispered, as I wrapped one of the quilts around me, stacked our last bundle of logs in the hearth and lit another fire. Julia's cough sputtered out in raspy barks, and she pressed her hand to her chest with a grimace.

"How long have we been here?" she asked.

"I'm not quite sure, a few months, I suppose. We are down to our last rations and I took enough for at least three months," I replied.

"Where are we?"

"Somewhere west of Vienna, along the Danube."

"What are we going to do, Rhen?"

Leaning against the mantel with my eyes fixed on the flickering flames, I had no answer to give her.

"We could just stay here," she eked out in between another round of coughs.

"I promised you Switzerland."

"Switzerland was for another life taken from us, my love. At least Kitty has that life now and she is alive. I suppose I should be thankful for that. As for us, we must live the life we have now and not mourn for the past. If we dwell on everything taken from us, we will never live."

I smiled at her, marveling at her wise words and angelic face, but her smile faded away and her eyes filled with resignation.

"The snow is melting, our food is nearly gone, and we have no more wood. We must live with what little we have left."

I looked away from her, back into the flames, not wanting to face anymore of this life's realities, so I quoted Shakespeare to take us back to a few moments ago when all that mattered was a beautiful poem.

"Not a whit," I feigned a fake chuckle. "I defy augury."

"Wrong play, once again, my love. You did that once before when we stood on the roof of the apartment building in Berlin. And yet, even as we jump from play to play in profound lines, we cannot escape the providence in the fall of a sparrow, or that life is a passing shadow, or... that death will amorously keep me as his paramour. From hour to hour, we ripe and ripe. And then, from hour to hour, we rot and rot; and thereby hangs a tale."

A tear rolled down my cheek and spotted on the dusty floorboards beneath my bare feet. I glanced over my shoulder at her, and her brow and eyes shadowed over with a truth I did not want to hear. Still, she spoke.

"I'm dying, Rhen."

+++++

Rhen worked like a mad man after I spoke those words as if he dared death take away our chance at happiness. When the snow melted away, he went in search of food and managed to beg a couple of loaves of bread from an elderly woman as he passed through one of the small villages to the north of our hidden farmhouse.

When he finally came through the door, my heart leapt, for, in truth, I feared fate might separate us again before we had the chance to live these last few months... or however long I had left.

I told him I was dying, and truly believed it, for I suppose a body knows when it is happening. This endless cough in my chest, the pain behind the hacking increases day to day... and there are times when he is outside chopping wood or setting traps for hares, that I can barely breath. But Rhen is determined that I live, and little by little, his efforts are resurrecting this little abandoned farmhouse.

In transforming the place into our safe haven, he discovered a stack of old dingy Victorian clothes from the former residents, which we donned, and a wireless hidden beneath the floorboards, and we determined the house must have been used early on in the war as a hideout for partisans who hid the radio before their own capture or death. After finagling with the knobs, the familiar notes of Wagner lilted through the air.

For one evening, the music transported us back in time... to the night we kissed at the Moka Efti and once again, in my imagination, I stood before him in my white silk gown, and Rhen adorned in an elegant tuxedo.

He spun me around the room as the chandeliers sparkled above our heads. No war, no Nazis, no Jews, no hatred, no broken glass windows, no ghettos or camps, no blood, no years of separation... just me and my husband, a 1945 version of Romeo and Juliet, waltzing in a small farmhouse somewhere in the Austrian countryside.

We listened to the radio almost every night as he moved it around the room, trying to find a signal. When we found a channel coming out of the now Allied-occupied Western Austria, the news that the Russian Red Army liberated Auschwitz three months ago, and the Americans liberated Dachau just yesterday, sparked his hope even more. When we heard the number of survivors, only 7,000 as reported by the Reds, and 30,000 from Dachau, I wept into my pillow... and my weeping prompted a violent coughing fit... this time with blood.

He held me against him, rocking me back and forth, willing me to hang on with his words.

"Please, Julia, don't leave me behind. They say the Allies are now near Munich... only two hours from us. We have to stay alive so they can hear our story, else I am sure they will arrest me when they discover who I am. And they will take you from me... we will be parted once again."

"Yes," I said, my voice just above a whisper. "I promise I will try, my love."

+++++

Julia died in my arms that night, just after midnight. Once I knew the date of the liberation of Auschwitz, I calculated the date of her death, determining over the course of our short marriage... the six years from the day we took our vows in the basement of the hospital in Berlin till now, we spent only 6 months together in total. Six months of utter love and happiness.

I know I should be grateful. I know I should continue living my life for her, filled with the love she showed me. After all, she said, "if we dwell on everything taken from us, we will never live"... but what did I care anymore. My very reason for living lay beneath the quilts, her once rosy cheeks paling more and more with each passing minute.

I have no more tears to shed. Hitler has taken everything that both of us held dear and I will not pay for his crimes as one of his SS officers. I know what I must do.

I took out one of the sheets of paper I discovered in one of the kitchen drawers, along with the ink bottle and pen, dipped the tip and finished our story. When the ink dried, I laid the page on the table next to the bed.

As I dressed us both in our former costumes, a Jewish prisoner and a SS officer, the ground beneath my feet trembled and the roar of tanks filing across the pasture outside the window came into view as I pushed open the shutters. In the blinding sunlight, three silhouetted soldiers marched towards the farmhouse.

I crawled beneath the quilts, took Julia into my arms, and held the Luger against my temple, speaking the lines of the play which echoed our life and our love...

"I still will stay with thee;

And never from this palace of dim night

Depart again: here, here will I remain

With worms that are thy chamber-maids;

O, here will I set up my everlasting rest,

And shake the yoke of inauspicious stars

From this world-wearied flesh. Eyes, look your last!

Arms, take your last embrace! and, lips,

O you the doors of breath, seal with a righteous kiss

A dateless bargain to engrossing death!

Come, bitter conduct, come, unsavoury guide!

Thou desperate pilot, now at once run on

The dashing rocks thy sea-sick weary bark!

Here's to my love!"

+++++

The pop of gunfire reverberated across the field, and Major Frank Conners of the 42nd Infantry division sprinted towards the house, along with Private Collins and O'Neal. They burst through the doors, guns raised.

The scent of burning firewood, baked bread, and gunpowder wafted through the air, and the three men tiptoed across the creaking floor boards.

Just a few more steps, and the Major peeked into the bedroom, then motioned for the others to follow him. He stood near the bed, gazing at the scene before him – a young woman dressed in a striped prison uniform like the ones he saw from the concentration camp, a faded yellow star over her heart, and next to her, a young man attired in the black uniform of a SS officer with one bullet hole through his temple. The Luger rested on the floor beside the bed and the spray of blood splattered across the girl and the wall.

Private Collins whistled and shook his head. "Do you suppose she killed him?"

Conners shook his head. "No, look, he is holding her in his arms."

"Major? You need to see this," replied O'Neal.

The Major turned around and took the paper trembling in O'Neal's fingers. He cleared his voice and read the words out loud.

"Rhen and Julia Montabauer forevermore... married November 9, 1938 in Berlin Germany – star-crossed lovers."

Collins pointed to the two stars linked together on the page, a swastika and a star of David, as the Major continued.

"A glooming peace this morning with it brings;

The sun, for sorrow, will not show his head:

Go hence, to have more talk of these sad things;

Some shall be pardon'd, and some punished:

For never was a story of more woe

Than this of Juliet and her Romeo."

THE END

AUTHOR NOTES

Thank you for reading, *Star Crossed*, and for the continued support from the love of my life, my darling husband, who would sacrifice anything for me, and throughout own perilous struggles over the past years has taught me the value of life over possessions or anything else in this world.

I, also, want to thank my fans and the readers whose continued encouragement, not only with my writing, but for the support of The Historical Fiction Company, gives me the impetus to push harder and reach deeper in my writing. Even after 25 years of writing, I am still learning with each novel written, and hope one day to write the literary masterpiece still waiting to emerge in the back of my brain.

As far as the notes for this novel, while I tried to stay true to the events depicted in WW2, especially in relation to the events which happened to the Jews, most of the events mentioned throughout are actual or based on actual events, such as the Jews who hid in the Wiessensee Cemetery in Berlin. The timeline was the trickiest part, since I wanted to cover the entire four to five years from Kristalnacht to the liberation of Auschwitz, so as to show the development of the plotline as well as the development and change of the characters involved, thus the reason for the spans of time and setting Rhen and Julia in a selection of events than one long saga... else my book, I assure you, would have been as large as "Les Miserables". As it is, I hope the timeline main events made sense.

Also, I've included a link to my personal website where you can find the research links and books I used to develop this story, some of which I found incredibly fascinating (such as Höss's affair with the Austrian political prisoner, or the beautification of Theresienstadt concentration camp, the Femina theater in the Warsaw Ghetto where 'the nightingale of Warsaw" actually performed, the woman who became a Rabbi during that time, and Emil Utitz, the librarian of Theresienstadt who actually hung out with Kafka at the Cafe Paris) - so many stories!!

The character of Rhen's father, Herr Montabauer, was a fictional character from my own imagination, but his association with Goebbels is loosely based on Werner Naumann who was Goebbel's personal aide.

For a long time, during the years after the Great War, Berlin boomed as an electric city full of cabarets and night life, and the Resi and Moka Efti night clubs were the go-to places for dancing, drinking, and carousing. Some (but not all) of the Jews in the city considered themselves 'Berliners' and some attempted to assimilate into the normal life outside of their Jewish heritage. When the violence started rising in the city, a lot of the Jews ignored or even dismissed the danger, thinking their assimilation as German Berliners would protect them from any outright threats. A lot of Jews married outside of their faith, having children known as "Mischlings" when the Nuremberg laws were passed... and when enforced, a lot of the SS officers who had

Jewish wives were given free passes to divorce their wives on the grounds of keeping the Aryan race pure. But, in the end, even being a Mischling, in a lot of cases, did not keep them from the horrors of the Ghettos or from the gas chambers.

As always, in keeping with theme of this series - "The Fractured Shakepeare Series", I could think of no better setting to modernize the exquisite tragic tale of Romeo and Juliet. To have told a story still set in medieval Verona, to me, would have been just another endless adaptation. I wanted the story of their tragic love to echo through time... to show the connection throughout generations and how love, above all, breaks through boundaries, even in the most difficult of circumstances.

More about these points and other research can be found here:
www.dk-marley.com
Or you can follow me on Facebook at:
www.facebook.com/therealdkmarley.author

REVIEWS ARE APPRECIATED

HISTORIUM PRESS

www.historiumpress.com

COVER DESIGN by

White Rabbit Arts at

THE HISTORICAL FICTION COMPANY

www.thehistoricalfictioncompany

Lightning Source UK Ltd.
Milton Keynes UK
UKHW011008030323
417983UK00015B/701

9 798986 256436